Gray Riders

By Ernest Francis Schanilec

Also by Ernest Francis Schanilec

Blue Darkness
The Towers
Danger in the Keys
Purgatory Curve

GRAY RIDERS

Author - Ernest Francis Schanilec
Publisher - McCleery & Sons Publishing

International Standard Book Number: 1-931916-38-1

Printed in the United States of America

DEDICATIONS

Gray Riders is dedicated to the people of western Missouri, whose ancestors were victims of the conflict between the states during the years 1861 through 1863.

It is also dedicated to my former editor, Joe Dashner of Vergas, Minnesota, who passed away in June of 2004..

ACKNOWLEDGEMENTS

I THANK THE FOLLOWING for their assistance in editing, critique-reading, and proofing: Vern Schanilec and Faye Schanilec of Camas, Washington; Ardith Hoehn of Fargo, North Dakota; Joanne Leinen of Vergas, Minnesota; Patty Schumacher of Bradenton, Florida; Rob Schanilec of Northfield, Minnesota; Clayton Schanilec of St. Paul, Minnesota; and Nancy Brekke of Perham, Minnesota.

Thanks to Joe Dashner and Nancy Dashner for their editing assistance, contributing to my previous novel, *Purgatory Curve*.

Additional thanks to the following institutions in Missouri: Lone Jack Museum; Cass County Historical Society; Frontier Military Museum in Drexel; The Jesse James Farm; Missouri Department of Natural Resources; Battle of Lexington Historical Site; Pleasant Hill Museum; The Museum in Lee's Summit; and the Butler Museum. Some of my information was referenced from the writings of Romulus L. Travis in *The Story of Lone Jack*, and Edward E. Leslie in *The Devil Knows How to Ride*.

The photograph for the cover was made possible by Skip Demann, Trip Demann and Dan Voight. The three men ride with the Jesse James gang during the Northfield, Minnesota Bank Robbery reenactment. Assisting with the photography for the cover was Rob Schanilec of Northfield, Minnesota.

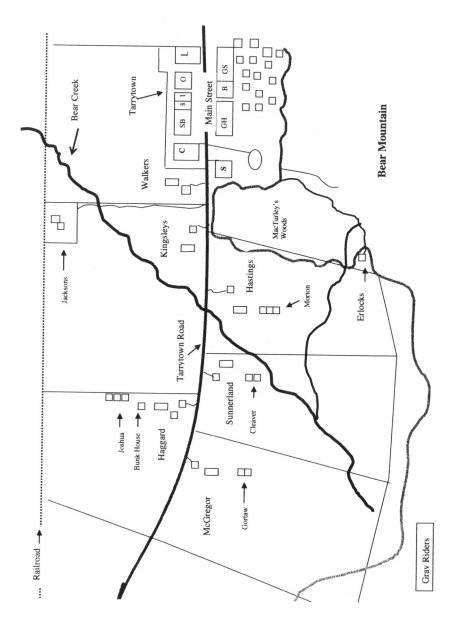

THE FAMILIES

WALKERS:
George and Angie
Sons:
  Will, age 21
  Carr, age 14
Daughters:
  Helen, age 18
  Jessica, age 15
Their land encompassed Tarrytown to the north and the west.

KINGSLEYS:
Martin and Beth
  Son Abel, age 18
  Daughter Sarah, age 13
Their land bordered the Walker's to the west.

JACKSONS:
Priam and Virgilia
Sons:
  Jordon, age 19
  Elkanah, age 18
  Baskhall, age 16
Daughters:
  Elisha, age 15
  Brittany, age 13
They lived on a forty acre plot in the northeast corner of the Kingsley land.

HAGGARDS:
Ben and Anna
Sons:
  Justin, age 20
  Jubal, age 15
Daughter Clarissa, age 24
Their land bordered the Kingsley's.

HASTINGS:
Henry and Emma
Sons:
   Grady, age 19
   Thomas, age 13
Daughter, Genevieve, age 18
Their land was on the south side of Tarrytown Road and bordered
MacTurley's Woods.

MORTONS:
Samuel and Tullaby
Son Sammy, age 19

SUNNERLANDS:
John and Mary
Sons
   Lafe, age 22
   Jesse, age 19
Their land adjoined the Hastings's and was traversed by Bear
Creek.

McGREGORS:
Orly, a widower
Sons
   Mitchell, age 20
   Paul, age 19
   James, age 16
Daughter
   Jennifer, age 18
Their land bordered the Sunnerland's.

1

THE RYTHMIC SOUNDS OF HOOVES beating on the damp roadway reached the ears of the three horsemen hiding in a small clearing in the nearby woods. It was spring in western Missouri in the year 1861, and rainfall had been abundant.

The horsemen watched as a couple perched on the bench of a wagon came up the roadway. "Who that comin'?" asked one horseman.

"Look like a farmer...wagon full."

"Jest what 'er lookin' fer. Whoa!" The horseman pulled on the reins, holding his frisky horse back. "Not yet," he whispered to his horse, patting it gently on its mane.

When the swishing sound of wagon wheels reached them, the leader yelled, "Let's go! Hee-yah!" The riders galloped toward the wagon.

The pair of black horses pulling the wagon were no match for the yelling, oncoming riders. The horses, already partially blinded by the setting sun, became terrified and careened off the road, galloping out of control. The farmer braced and desperately pulled on the reins.

A ball fired from a revolver caused the farmer to stand momentarily before plunging off the wagon, falling brutally to the ground.

The woman screamed, but to no avail, as the horses attempted to jerk away from one of the intruding horsemen. One of the front wagon wheels struck a rock and broke into fragments—sending the wagon tumbling. Sacks of flour and sugar went flying through the air, breaking, open and strewing their contents as they landed.

The lady, propelled from her seat, fell to the ground. She rolled twice and then lay still as the two horses pulled the crumbling wagon in a circle.

———

JOHN SUNNERLAND SMILED WHEN HE PASSED by a healthy field of green. His wife, Mary, sitting next to him, was looking straight ahead, anxious to get back home.

She had spent the day visiting friends and relatives in the nearby town of Tarrytown. She and John had stopped at the general store before leaving. The owner, Seth Miller, had said, "That should do 'er," as he tossed the final sack of flower into the wagon.

"See you after the crop's in, Seth," said John as he flicked the reins and the horses moved forward.

As they passed by the white, wood-framed church, Mary looked up and admired the stately, silver bell that hung in the belfry. We can almost hear that stately bell at home, she thought.

Her eyes wandered south of the road, to the single-room schoolhouse, the last building on the west of town. The playground was empty and the children and schoolmaster had gone home for the day. She felt sad that the school had not been there for her sons. It had been built a few years too late.

Shadows from the sun had stretched well beyond the school building. The cemetery, higher up, was also blanketed with the shadow. Beyond and above, the eastern slope of the mountain was blanched with spectacular light. The dips and western slope had turned dark. They look like black holes in the mountain, she thought.

Her husband flicked the reins and the two black horses responded with a trot, pulling the wagon past the beginning of MacTurley's Woods. She watched the grassy area that buffered the timber from the road.

"John, look at those pretty crocuses," Mary said.

"Ah've always appreciated how you have liked plants and flowers," John responded. "It's one of the reasons ah look forward to spring." He couldn't see the plants because he was focusing on the team, but he felt that that's what she wanted to hear.

Mary thought about the birthday present she had bought for her son, Jesse. He was going to be twenty years old next week. Her husband had nodded when she showed him the brown leather vest.

When Mary heard the yell, she assumed her two sons were riding out to meet them. She looked up and saw three horsemen emerge from the woods, galloping towards them.

"John, they don't look like our boys," she said.

———

GRADY HASTINGS AND WILL WALKER WERE RIDING their horses on the Walker property, down near the creek, when they heard a gunshot.

They had been talking about the possibility of Missouri seceding and a war between the North and South. Will, tall and straight in the saddle, had told Grady that his father didn't favor secession. "We don't need free help," Will said to Grady, repeating what his father had said.

Will's long, blond hair settled down on the back of his neck as his blue-gray eyes looked up toward Tarrytown Road. After hearing the loud snapping noise bounce off the hills and dissipate into the valley, he pulled on the brim of his white hat.

"Where did that come from?" Will asked, his long blond hair sweeping his neck as he looked around.

"Over toward MacTurley's Woods," Grady answered. "Let's ride over and have a look."

Grady's mother had cut his dark brown hair short and trimmed the bulk of it only two days earlier. Grady didn't like his hair to look scraggly like many others. His high-crowned, peaked, black hat was pulled slightly low on his forehead.

Grady Hastings spurred his horse, and the two young men rode up the slope and onto the road. His horse broke into a gallop, and Grady's dark blue eyes gleamed with excitement as he yelled, "There's a run-a-way pair of blacks over there!"

"Hey, what's that?" yelled Will. "Looks like someone on the ground."

The two riders chose to ignore the two black horses and galloped toward what they thought might be a person. Grady leaped off his horse and rushed to the side of the mangled body lying on the ground. "Sweet love o' Jaysus, it's Mrs. Sunnerland!" Grady exclaimed.

He felt her neck. "She's dead, Will....Where...Oh God, look over there," Grady said anxiously. He brought his teeth together and extended his lips, slightly puffing his narrow sideburns. He could see the crumpled hulk of what could be another victim. After dropping the reins, his boots made imprints in a sea of flour while rushing to it. "Will, he's dead, too...."

Will rushed over to Grady, who was kneeling by the second body. Grady turned the man over. "Look at that, Will. He's been shot in the back." Grady stood—feelings of fear radiating through his body. His dark blue eyes scanned up and down the road, seeing no one.

Grady Hastings and Will Walker had been close friends since they were children. They often went riding during lulls in the farm work. When it became apparent that Grady was showing a romantic interest in his sister, Helen, Will had been delighted.

The two young men were in shock after finding two of their neighbors dead—murdered. Grady gazed toward his home and thought about his parents. He couldn't see their house because of the woods. He looked toward Will and saw him facing anxiously toward his home. Will turned back toward Grady, his narrow face showing strain. Will's sideburns and mustache were sparsely populated with hair.

"What should we do?" asked Will, brushing away tears.

"Ah'd better ride home and get Pa," said Grady. "You better do the same."

Grady put the whip to his horse and headed west. After galloping by MacTurley's Woods, he gained sight of the Hastings's farmhouse, still over a mile to go. Instead of following the Tarrytown Road to where it intersected with their farm roadway, he galloped his horse across the fields.

2

WHILE APROACHING HIS HOME, Grady panicked, not knowing how his parents were going to accept the bad news. He pulled on the reins. He was hoping to find his father on the porch alone, temporarily sparing his mother.

Flashing back, he thought about his grandfather who had died when he was five years old. It was he, Adam Hastings, who had purchased the three thousand acres of land from the government during the same year Missouri became a state—land that stretched for approximately two miles in any direction.

Grady, at age nineteen, was the eldest of three children born to Henry and Emma Hastings. His sister, Genevieve, one year younger, and his brother, Thomas, had celebrated his thirteenth birthday.

His father wasn't sitting on the porch. He dreaded the thought of going through the door and announcing the tragedy. Pausing, he turned his head and gazed at MacTurley's Woods which lined the entire eastern border of their farmland. The trees were visible all the way to the top of the high hills to the south—Bear Mountain.

———

THOMAS HASTINGS HAD REACHED AGE THIRTEEN the previous month on the second of April, in the year of 1861. Exhausted after helping with field work all day, he decided to lie down in the loft even though it was still daylight. His brother, Grady, and sister, Genevieve, also slept up there.

Climbing the narrow, wooden steps that accessed the loft, he paused and looked down. His mother and father, sitting at the kitchen table, were talking in low voices. His mother would not have to remind him to go to bed that evening because he was so beat.

The rocker in the far corner moved slowly. His sister, Genevieve, was meticulously working a ball of yarn with a long needle. The long, dark braids that started at eye-level were dancing on her shoulders. She had her mother's hair and her father's dark brown eyes. Missing from her appearance was her mother's square chin.

Thomas lay on his bed and gazed at the far wall. The multitude of knots in the pine logs comforted him. Smiling, he focused on Gabriel, a knot, which he had named during his childhood days. He had fantasized each knot to be an angel or a star in the heavens. The rocks in the fireplace were earthly mountains rising above water masses. The earth narrowed and extended to the very top of the roof, totally surrounded by stars.

Thomas was tall for his age, his toes projecting just beyond the end of his bed. His long, strong arms were nestled on his chest. Two large pillows supported his head—necessary because of his wide shoulders. His dark, straight hair spread out on the pillow.

He opened one of his clear blue eyes and looked at the screen at the far end of the loft—the screen that gave his sister, Genevieve, privacy. He looked at the other side—His brother's bunk was empty. Closing his eyes, he listened.

The voices of his parents, Henry and Emma, became louder—their discussion intensified. Thomas heard the words *Lincoln*, *secession*, *North Carolina*, *slaves*, *Quantrill*, *jayhawkers*, *redlegs*, and *war*.

Thomas gathered from his parents that jayhawkers and redlegs were names used for people who pillaged and burned homes in Missouri. Most of them came from Kansas, and they represented a violent type of abolitionists—those against slavery.

He heard a horse galloping, approaching from the direction of Tarrytown. My brother rarely returns at a gallop, he thought. Usually, he sneaks in quietly—a lot later, too.

Thomas heard the sound of boots on the porch—hurried footsteps. He heard his father rush to the door. His gut feeling told him something was wrong. Slipping out of bed and pulling on his trousers, Thomas tip-toed down the narrow stairway.

He saw his father stop short of the door, and he heard Grady talking, rapidly. "They're both dead, Pa. Somebody shot 'em...Mr. Sunnerland, that is. Mrs. Sunnerland got thrown from the wagon and killed....Her neck got broken."

Thomas felt pain. He thought about Mrs. Sunnerland....Her warm smile and hand always greeted me when I knocked on their door. She always led me to the table and patted me on the head, before rounding up some sweets. I cannot imagine her being hurt like that. He felt terrified.

"Son, get the horses hitched to the buckboard. Ah want you to take your mother to Sunnerlands. Have your mother help you tell the boys what happened....Do the best you can....Then, hustle back. Be sure to take along a pair of Colts and your musket. Ah'll saddle up and ride to John and Mary's remains, pronto," he heard his father say anxiously.

The pain in the pit of Thomas's stomach was growing more intense by the minute.

Henry came out of the barn with his horse. He then ran back in the house. Reaching above the door, he removed his gun belt from a rack. There was a Colt revolver in each holster.

Genevieve was standing next to Thomas, near the door. Her face was pale, and moisture was building in her narrowed, dark brown eyes. She wore her long, white nightgown, and her dark hair was covered with a white night bonnet.

"What are you doin' up Thomas? Ah thought you were asleep," his father said, his voice crackling with anxiety.

"Pa, I heard what happened. I want to go along and help."

"Nonsense, you stay with Genevieve."

"But, Pa, you're gonna need some help! Please let me go along. Genevieve will be all right."

Henry hesitated, his dark brown eyes shining, and looked at his son, whose face was contorted with fear. "You're right, lad. Put on your coat and let's go. You can ride behind my saddle. Genevieve, get your coat on and go with your mother."

———

HENRY HASTINGS, FEELING THE ARMS OF HIS SON around his waist, halted his horse when he saw the crumpled body of Mary Sunnerland lying in a heap. Her neck appeared twisted grotesquely, and was not aligned with her shoulders. "Don't look, son," he said abruptly.

He flipped the reins and directed his horse to the second body lying farther up on the road. Dismounting, he checked out the back of John Sunnerland, looking for the bullet hole. His son had it right— a red smudge on his shirt right in the middle, he thought disgustingly.

Henry noticed the empty holster slung to John's gun belt. The horses that had been pulling the wagon were feeding in Walker's field. The pathetic remains of the buckboard dragged along the ground as the horses continued to feed. Following the trail of gouges in the ground, he searched for a musket or Colt revolver. Henry didn't see either.

Minutes later, he looked west and saw two riders approaching. By the intensity of the gallop, he knew that Lafe and Jesse Sunnerland were arriving. Henry wished that he could somehow remove the bodies—to prevent the Sunnerland boys from seeing what he and Thomas had.

Henry watched the shorter and stockier brother Lafe leap off his horse and run to his mother. Feelings of despair overwhelmed Henry while watching Lafe cradle Mrs. Sunnerland. Tears filled Henry's eyes as Lafe held his mother close with his large, brawny arms. Lafe's hat came off while pressing his face against his mother's chest, exposing a thick head of blond hair falling down to his shoulders.

Standing on the road halfway between the two bodies, Henry felt intense anger as he watched the leaner and taller Jesse bend over his father—his dark, large eyes filling with tears.

His son, Thomas, as instructed, had run into the field where the two blacks grazed. He watched Thomas unhitch the horses and steer them to the road.

Two horsemen were galloping over from the east. That's got to be George and Will Walker, he said to himself.

Grady and Emma arrived with the wagon minutes later. Henry watched his wife, her blue eyes concerned and shining, hasten over to Lafe. Henry lowered his chin when Emma put her hand on Lafe's head and then put her arms around his shoulders, resting on his barrel-shaped chest.

Grady had gotten off the wagon and helped Thomas with the horses. Henry saw him bend over and pick up something from the ground.

Henry watched as Jesse approached his brother, Lafe. "They got it, Lafe."

"Got what?" Lafe asked angrily, his voice squeaking.

"Our father's money pouch—dirty heathens....Killin' our parents wasn't enuf for 'em."

Lafe lowered his chin to his chest and put his hand up on Jesse's shoulder. He wrapped his large arms around his skinny brother. Henry looked away from the two boys who were silhouetted against the darkening western horizon. It was too much for him to bear.

"What ya got there, Grady?" asked Thomas.

"Hmm, looks like part of a spur...probably belongs to Mr. Sunnerland."

Grady steered the wagon to where Jesse remained on his knees.

"Let's load the bodies onto our wagon...John first, Grady," said Henry Hastings. "Sorry, Jesse, but we're going to have to take the remains of your parents into town."

Jesse looked at Henry with his large, dark eyes, and lowered his head. His long arms appeared to be dangling in space as he was desperately attempting to clear his mind.

Will and George Walker helped Henry and Grady Hastings load the dead body of John Sunnerland into the wagon.

"It ain't Mr. Sunnerland's," Grady said.

"What? What do you mean?" asked his father.

"Ah found a piece of a spur on the road."

"Oh yeah, better hold onto that, Grady," said his father.

"Hold onto what?" asked George Walker, his dark eyes glaring, his face serious.

"Grady found part of a spur on the road. Looks like a fresh break," said Henry while glancing down at George's boots.

Henry Hastings rode his horse behind Grady and the wagon as it headed for Tarrytown. Thomas sat on the seat with his brother. The two grim-faced Sunnerland boys flanked the wagon as it rumbled down the Tarrytown Road.

They remained in their saddles when the wagon stopped in front of the undertaker's parlor. The tears that streaked down their cheeks were noticed only by the Walkers and the Hastings—darkness protected their privacy.

3

THE ROAD THROUGH TARRYTOWN WAS DESERTED at dawn, except for a cat crossing the street, heading for the barbershop. The town's three hundred and six residents were still in their houses on this April morning in 1861. The plodding of hooves echoed across the valley as they trotted on hardened dirt in the middle of Main Street.

Henry Hastings glanced around as he rode through town. Two days had passed since the brutal slaying of the Sunnerlands. People don't move around much before sunrise, he thought. On other trips, he would see March, the town drunk, sleeping on the boardwalk. He must be spending the night in the livery—or in jail.

The town was built on a flat section of land at the northern base of Bear Mountain, a series of extraordinarily high hills running east and west, barely enclosed within the rising and setting of the sun in the spring of the year.

The valley below bottomed into a narrow, deep creek that drained Bear Mountain and the hills to the north. The creek, which originated several miles to the northeast, flowed into Bear Lake, twenty miles to the southwest.

The creek had more than one name—outsiders referred to it as

Devils Creek, while the local ranchers and farmers called it Bear Creek.

The bottom land of the creek plus the surrounding flat lands were mostly owned and occupied by farmers who raised horses, cattle, hemp, corn, and grain. A typical parcel of land spread out over at least three thousand acres.

Being mid-April, the farmers were busy planting the crops. Henry thought about his hemp and the money it could bring if rain remained plentiful. Last year ah hauled four wagonloads to Lexington. This year ah'm set to haul six, hopefully.

Most of the homes in Tarrytown were wood frame and located in clusters between the business district and the sloped terrain of Bear Mountain. Three two-story houses, which belonged to the mayor, hotel owner, and bank president, were set apart from the other homes. They perched on ridges of land that formed as a result of centuries of erosion caused by water running down from Bear Mountain.

The main street that ran east and west through the middle of the business district was dusty when dry, but it became a muddy bog during and after heavy rains. The deep ruts of wagon wheels were a never-ending hindrance for women attempting to cross the street.

To the chagrin of local businesses, railroad surveyors in the 1850's had bypassed Tarrytown. The tracks that originated in St. Louis angled toward the capital, Jefferson City, and continued on to Kansas City. The line of tracks missed the town by only a couple of miles—they paralleled the Walker's, Kingsley's, and the Haggard's northern property lines.

As a result, Tarrytown didn't have a post office. Once a week, depending on the weather, Lance Milburn, who worked for the General Store, would ride to Stillman Mills to fetch the mail. Henry Hastings had always mused and wondered how the residents, businesses, and the farmers in the area would sense when mail was comin'. For those who didn't have that sense—mail was stored for them in a special room provided by Seth Miller, owner of the store.

The beauty of the valley was stunning—the mountain to the south and the hills to the north. Hastings admired the land as he watched the sun rise over the tree line.

He had business to conduct in Stillman Mills, a town five miles to the east, beyond the slopes of Bear Mountain. The new sawmill in Stillman's Mill, next to the railroad tracks, besides manufacturing dimensional lumber, also produced grist with a grinding implement in a side room. My harvest will result in at least six wagon loads of corn, he thought.

Early afternoon, Henry Hastings mounted his rested horse and began the ride back home on the road toward Tarrytown. He stopped and watched the train chug its way out of Stillman Hills. The tracks angled away from the road as they extended toward Kansas City. He was fascinated with the column of white smoke that funneled straight up from the locomotive. Not a breath of wind, he noticed. He was experiencing intense sadness with the loss of his neighbors, John and Mary Sunnerland. Henry Hastings's dark brown eyes watched as the last of the train disappeared out of sight.

Setting his horse to a trot, his head, topped with a black Stetson hat, bobbed with the pace. His bulging mustache, which closely matched the color of his hat, covered his upper lip and spread to the beginning of his cheeks. Long, pepper colored sideburns widened as they stretched downward from a head of thick, dark brown hair. They were trimmed sharply at the jaw line. His square shaped jaw was neatly shaven.

Henry looked straight ahead as he thought about his wife. Hunching over a bit in the saddle, he smiled, visualizing her sky blue eyes. Sure a lot different than mine, he thought.

Looking to his right, he saw the beautiful valley that bottomed at Bear Creek. Clumps of brush and trees near the bottom are perfect hiding places for deer. That had to be the Walker herd grazing not too far from the road.

Approaching Tarrytown, the first building he saw was the livery stable. Toby Miller owned and operated the gray-boarded structure that resembled a stockade. The flat roof was not visible from the road. Henry smiled, remembering Toby and George Walker at the saloon, wheeling and dealing about five acres of land. Out back of the building he saw four horses grazing in a fenced area—the five acres. Toby got what he was after, he thought.

Ah wonder why Toby didn't go after the vacant space across the road? It was at least as wide, but probably not as deep. The owner of one of those three big houses part way up the hill may have plans, he thought. Banker Herron is a shrewd businessman.

Next to the vacant space, across from the livery, was the General Store. It was the first in line of three business buildings. Henry wasn't sure what the stone figures and mysterious designs meant. They were perched above the brick on the outside wall—architect came out all the way from Kansas City, he had heard.

Henry pulled up in front of the General Store and dismounted, tying his horse to the hitching rail. He stomped his boots on the boardwalk, disposing of a loose layer of dust before entering. Henry took off his black Stetson and shook the dust off. He ran his hand through his dark brown hair, and then put the hat back on.

"Howdy, Seth," Henry said and reached into the candy jar.

"What can ah do for ya today?" asked the owner of the store.

"Just checkin' to see when that new harness is comin' in."

"I'm expectin' a shipment later this week from St. Louie. Should be on it," Seth said.

"Any news about the Sunnerlands?" Henry asked.

"Damn able thing, ah say. Killin' them two makes no sense....They've never harmed a soul."

"Me 'en the boys are all packin' our guns every day...even to church," responded Henry. He walked out on the boardwalk and stood by his horse, looking across the street at the constable's office and jail. If we catch them heathens, they're not going to spend much time in jail, if any, he thought. But the hangman's noose will reach 'em soon, one way or the other. He was annoyed with his newly acquired habit of looking at everyone's spurs. Ah imagine others are doin' the same.

He saw Digger Phillips leave the bank and walk across the road. Musta' got paid by the Sunnerland boys, he thought. Henry watched the undertaker go into his building next to the constable's office.

Henry stomped a boot down on the boardwalk. He remembered helping with the project. It had taken eight wagonloads of lumber from Stillman Mills. Every top board was cut even, except for those in front of the barbershop. Shol Clarity had insisted on cutting his own—the independent cuss that he was. At least his hitching rail was straight. Smites, there must be space for a hundred horses up and down Main Street, Henry said to himself.

He got on his horse and looked at the bank building and the Grand Hotel just beyond. Henry gazed at the big sign, *Frontier Saloon.* It's six times as big as the hotel sign, he thought. It's the most popular business in town. Three horses were tied up at the rail in front, but more would join them later. As he remembered, the saloon took up about half the space on the ground floor of the hotel.

The last time that he had taken his wife out for dinner at Mama's Kitchen, she had remarked about the workmanship of the ornate stairway. It connected the saloon and hotel lobby to the upper level which boasted twenty-five guestrooms.

Ah, but she had been dressed in such splendor, he thought to himself. Her blue-green, silk, taffeta dress was something to behold. Henry smiled as he remembered putting his hand on the skin of her soft, white shoulder.

Across the road from the hotel, he saw Shol Clarity with scissors in hand looking out the window. Uneven planks out front of his shop stood out like a sore thumb. The barbershop is not my favorite place to go, Henry thought to himself. The same goes for the undertaker's next door. Ah'm in no hurry to do business with Digger Philips, he thought, chuckling.

Henry dismounted and walked his horse by the Smith Building. The entire ground floor consisted of rental apartments. A stairway inside the east wall accessed a doctor's office which filled the entire upper floor. Dr. Orville Wells had come into town a couple of years ago—odd lookin' wagon it 'twas, Henry thought. It looked like a black box with a curtained window.

The doctor was a small man who had a kind face with a mustache and bushy, gray hair. He always wore a bowler hat. Snippy little guy, Henry thought to himself. The doctor must have liked Tarrytown, because he set up his shop a couple of days later. Henry smiled and thought about the curious looks on the faces of his two sons as they had watched the doctor move his tools from the wagon to his office.

———

BEYOND THE SMITH BUILDING and a vacant space of land stood a white wood-frame church. It was the last town building on the north side of the Tarrytown Road.

Henry looked up at the ornate belfry and admired the silver bell. He remembered that the first attempt to raise the bell with ropes and pulleys had failed. After more failed attempts, the successful idea came from March, who was sitting on the ground, bottle of whiskey in hand.

"The pulleys was in the wrong place...should be closer together," March had told some of the men. He smiled widely while the bell was being fastened in the belfry. The workers had reluctantly taken his advice. Many of them patted the top of his head while on their way to the saloon to celebrate the successful mounting.

"Great ah-dea ya had, March," Henry heard one of the workers say. "Wouldn't be the same, without ya roun' 'ere, huh, March?"

The space surrounding the church provided more than adequate space for carriages and horses. Current pastor, Zack Wilson, was the church's original head. He does a strong job of preaching and pounding the pulpit on Sundays, Henry thought. Henry was glad that he and others resisted cutting down the oak trees that stood tall in various sections of the churchyard. He especially admired the three trees on the eastern edge. Pastor Zack had said, "There wouldn't be enough space for parking carriages." He was wrong.

Looking across the road from the church, Henry admired the cross which marked the center of the cemetery. It rose high above the tombstones that dotted the hillside. Wagon wheel tracks extended from the church to the cemetery. Soon a wagon would be used to transport the remains of the Sunnerland's. He cringed at the thought.

Henry's eyes focused on the one-room schoolhouse which rested on a flat piece of land west of the wheel tracks, halfway between the cemetery and the Tarrytown Road. The grounds around the school extended to the beginning of MacTurley's Woods. Henry was proud of that schoolhouse. It took nigh onto half a year to entice a teacher. Henry smiled when he saw a group of youngsters run out onto the grounds followed by Miss Nicole Stoner. She returned his wave as he spurred his horse into a trot, heading homeward.

Looking at MacTurley's Woods, he admired the beautiful trees. A grassy area about a hundred feet wide separated the Tarrytown Road from the woods. He could see the treetops on the steep slope that extended all the way to the top of Bear Mountain. Henry halted his horse about halfway along MacTurley's Woods and watched two eagles soaring.

Reining his horse into a walk, he scanned the ground carefully, looking for more clues from the Sunnerland disaster. No one has found John's musket or Colt revolver, he said to himself. Dismounting at the site, he searched the grassy area—still no sign of John's guns.

Henry looked toward the clearing in MacTurley's Woods. That's where the killers waited, he said to himself. The hoof prints that Grady and ah found didn't tell us anything. They could've been made by any of the horses around these parts.

Ah reckon the distance was too far away from the Kingsley house for anyone to see what happened, he thought. He got back on his horse and they trotted westward. He stopped at the last part of MacTurley's Woods. Here the landscape changed to brush and grassland, marking the beginning of his property. Again he looked at the Kingsley buildings and estimated the distance from there to the site—too far, for sure, he reasoned. No one could have seen what had happened from there.

4

PREACHER ZACK WILSON LED THE FUNERAL PROCESSION away from the church and up the slope toward the cemetery. He was dressed in a black robe and carried a large, black book. His long strides quickly closed the distance between him and the white cross. A gray rabbit that had flushed ahead of him didn't stop running until it successfully reached the shelter of the timber.

Directly behind him, a pair of white horses pulled the undertaker's wagon. Digger Phillips sat stoically on the bench, gently prodding the horses with his reins. Behind the wagon walked the survivors of the Sunnerland family: Lafe, age twenty-two and Jesse, age nineteen.

Most everyone walked in pairs, except for Thomas Hastings who walked alone behind his sister and brother. Grady and Genevieve followed their parents, Henry and Emma.

Thomas watched his father wrap his long arm around his mother's waist. He remembered how carefully she had slipped the black bonnet over her head of dark brown hair. It was parted in the middle and swept back, perfectly bunched. Her long, black dress was generating small puffs of dust as she walked.

He glanced behind and briefly met the blue eyes of Orly McGregor, the tall Scotsman, who was walking with his daughter, Jennifer. She avoided Thomas's glance—tears were streaming down her cheeks. The three rugged McGregor boys walked side by side behind their father.

Thomas remembered visiting the McGregor farm on more than one occasion. He liked all of the boys, even though they played jokes on him from time to time. The three of 'em doubled up with laughter when their pet ram chased me into the barn, Thomas remembered. Right now, he felt too sad to even smile.

Thomas's parents had allowed him to visit the McGregor's farm even though it was farther away than the others. The McGregor's farm roadway coming off the Tarrytown Road was well beyond the Sunnerland's and the Haggard's.

Thomas's feelings turned to sorrow when he looked ahead and saw the coffins in the wagon. The poor Sunnerlands, he thought, are inside those boxes.

After reaching the cemetery, the silent procession separated into clusters of family, friends, and neighbors surrounding the grave. Thomas looked up with his blue eyes at the huge, white cross that towered over the cemetery. It wasn't very far from where he stood. His rounded face and puffy, red cheeks were exaggerated by the rays of the sun.

The first sound that came from the preacher's mouth sounded like a hawk's screech, Thomas thought.

I wonder where Keeya is soaring today—probably near the woods where rabbits are plentiful. I've seen many a bunny wiggle helplessly in the hawk's claws after being plucked from the grass.

The lean-bodied preacher cleared his throat and began talking. His voice penetrated the stillness of the air, the words bouncing off the high trees next to the cemetery. It's not as if I needed to hear them twice, Thomas thought.

The preacher signaled the end of his prayers with a loud thump— the black book snapped shut. He looked up and nodded at the undertaker. The wheels of Digger Philip's wagon creaked as it slowly moved ahead and turned to follow the trail down the hill.

The gathering of the people around the gravesite began to break into small gatherings, most of them following the wagon. Only the two Sunnerland boys and some of their neighbors had remained.

Thomas turned his head westward toward MacTurley's Woods, his long, dark hair brushed back partially over his right ear. On a small grassy knoll, he saw two riders. He saw them remove their hats. They rode with their backs as straight as the tree trunks in MacTurley's Woods.

"Look, Pa, there's two men on horses over there," said Thomas softly as he swept his fingers across his eyes. He had a difficult time blinking away the tears—something he felt necessary to hide. The two Sunnerland boys didn't even flinch during the time they stood by the coffins, he had noticed.

"Who're they, Pa?" Thomas whispered to his father as he swept his fingers over his eyes again, his long, dark hair fluttering in the breeze.

"Why, that looks like Cole Younger. He's a friend of Lafe's and lives in the Lee's Summit area. That's his brother Jim on the other horse, ah reckon."

———

CONSTABLE FRANCIS MULDOON SAT on the edge of his desk. He scratched his right ear and watched as people filed into his office and settled onto wooden folding chairs borrowed from the church. The constable had nodded approval to Lance Milburn. Lance had spent part of the morning transferring the chairs with a wagon. Besides delivering mail, Lance did odd jobs for the constable and Seth Miller at the General Store.

The constable's trousers were neatly tucked into a pair of shiny, black boots. The trim, front edges of his black, suede vest were spread apart a couple of inches by his generous midriff. His thick neck supported a head with a firm and unshaven square jaw. The thick brown hair on the top of his head was parted in the middle and trimmed neatly just above the ears. His narrow mustache, with a narrow gap just under the middle of his nose, curved down and around the corners of his mouth.

The constable's office was often used for town meetings because of its convenience and adequate size. The constable's eyes surveyed the room and he estimated that all the people in the room had been at the Sunnerland's funeral the previous day. He was relieved that the Sunnerland boys had decided not to attend today. It would have made it a lot more difficult for people to talk, he thought.

The constable slid off the desk and raised his hand. Planting a fist on his right waist, he slowly worked a thumb and forefinger along the sides of his chin. "No mistake, boys. The wanton killin' of the Sunnerlands was the work of the marauding jayhawkers. Robert Packard over at the hotel saw some of 'em ride through town not more than an hour before the Sunnerlands left for home. Ah reckon they rode out ahead and had waited in ambush," the constable said with authority.

George Walker ran a hand over his hairless scalp. What little hair he had was dark brown and straight, swept back behind the ears. He had a clean-shaven face—no sideburns or mustache.

"Why did they pick on the Sunnerlands? They've never caused anyone any problems," George Walker asked.

His farm bordered Tarrytown to the north. He and his wife, Angie, had raised four offspring. Will was the eldest at twenty-one years of age, and he was at the meeting standing in the far corner. Next to the long, blond-haired Will, serious-faced Grady Hastings stood, his emerald green eyes narrowed.

Orly McGregor, who was sitting in the second row, stood up. He was the biggest man in the room, not quite as tall as Justin Haggard. The gray streaks in his reddish beard and mustache moved when he opened his hidden mouth. The McGregors owned the property next to and west of the Sunnerland's.

"This is the first killin' we've had near Tarrytown. Ah hear that a few miles from here, in other parts of Jackson County, there has been some. Does that mean that we have to change our way of life...carry guns...escorts to school and church?" Orly drawled in his Scottish brogue, looking around the room.

Henry Hastings, sitting next to McGregor felt the floor boards move when the big Scotchman sat down. Henry drew his fingers down one of his pepper-colored sideburns, leaned forward and said, "Dunno what to do, Orly, but ah reckon that a mere handful of radicals are causing all the problems. Ah'm talkin' about the jayhawkers, 'en as the constable put it, the reborn puritans....Ah 'eard the Quantrill band is fighten' 'em most every day. We're caught in the middle." There were a few nods and grunts of approval to Hastings's comments.

Ben Haggard stood. He owned and farmed land on the north side of the Tarrytown Road, bordering the Kingsley's to the east. He looked around the room with his hazel eyes. Running his fingers through his curly, black hair, he said, "The federal government has no call to tell us our business. The politicians are the main cause of the problem...reacting to radical pressure groups, who hang around Washington like flies." Ben's sideburns were mostly gray, and they became bushy at the chin line. His long, thin, black mustache matched the color of his eyebrows, which were shaggy and'tilted. "I talked to Joshua about being free. He told me that he's happy where he's at...doesn't want to be free. Always got plenty to eat and clothes to wear," he had said.

Haggard, along with the Hastings, Sunnerlands and the McGregors were the only landowners at the meeting who owned slaves. "Ah'm gonna bring him a load of lumber to fix the house before winta' sets in," he added, compressing his lower front teeth into his upper lip.

Martin Kingsley took his turn at talking. His farm was north across the road from the Hastings. His neighbors were the Walkers to the east and the Haggards to the west.

Martin had donated forty acres in the northeast corner of his property to his former slaves. They operated a chicken and goat farm and were paid for working on the Kingsley farm.

"Men, if the people supportin' Lincoln have their way, it's going to mean war...for shuh. If they would just have patience...the slavery issue will go away all by itself, ah reckon," Martin said, the top of his hairless head reflecting light from the windows. All his scraggly hair was gray except for the mustache. He had the longest beard in the room, trimmed at about four inches below his chin.

He looked up at the ceiling and added, "ah find that it cost me less after ah freed Priam and his family. They still help out and ah pay 'em. They make enough money off their chickens and goats to buy groceries and stay warm in the winta'."

George Walker looked at Martin and nodded. He stood and ran his fingers up and down his clean shaven chin. "Redlegs and jayhawkers, ah 'eard 'em called. They have no business out this way. Ah'm agin' slavery....Ya all know that. Ah sided with the legislature....They voted right. Men and women need to be free...to choose where they live and what they do for a livin'."

Constable Muldoon watched the stiff, lean farmer sit down. Now, there's a poker face if ah ever saw 'un, he thought....'Tis rare to ever get a smile on that man's face. The constable was concerned about George Walker and his political views. They were different from most others. He seems to be dead set on supporting the Federals.

———

EDITOR C. M. CHASE OF THE *TRUE REPUBLICAN AND SENTINEL* wrote: *A jayhawker is a Unionist who professes to rob, burn out and murder only rebels in arms against the government. A redleg is a jayhawker originally distinguished by the uniform of the red leggings. A redleg however is regarded as more purely an indiscriminate thief and murderer than the jayhawker.*

A bushwhacker is a rebel jayhawker, or a rebel who bands with others for the purpose of preying upon the lives and property of Union citizens.

William Clarke Quantrill was often thought of as a bushwhacker. He became the leader of a band of men, which at times included the historically famous Frank James, Jesse James and Cole Younger.

The contents of the first two paragraphs above were taken from a novel by Edward E. Leslie: *The Devil Knows How to Ride.*

5

MARTIN AND BETH KINGSLEY WERE SIPPING COFFEE in their kitchen the morning after the meeting at the constable's office. A drop of coffee fell from Martin's gray beard. He dried the bushy, gray hairs with his hand.

Looking out the window toward the bunkhouse, he saw Bert, his foreman, mount a horse. Martin was the only rancher in the neighborhood who raised black beef cattle.

Martin smiled, watching his son, Abel, trot his horse toward the bunkhouse. "That young man has what it takes," he told his wife while scratching the scraggly, gray hair above his right ear. He was proud of Abel. Never have to tell 'em what to do. He's usually one step ahead of the rest of 'em, Martin thought.

Beth joined her husband by the window, and he put his arm around her narrow waist and squeezed. She cringed and said, "Not now, Martin." He removed his hand and patted her behind.

"Look, Martin, there's Sarah. Did you notice how pretty Sarah looked in that new dress at church on Sunday? My, she's already thirteen. Before we know it, she'll be riding off with some lucky, handsome young man," said Beth, her short, light brown hair swinging when her head turned.

"Yup, Ah notice how she's lookin' at that young Hastings. Fine young man, but she's too young yet...got some growin' up to do," he responded.

"She could do a lot worse, Martin. Most o' them young men in Tarrytown are long on loiterin' and short on learnin'. That young Hastings...he likes the books....Gotta good future."

Her mouth opened slightly, exposing overlapped, narrow, front teeth under her thick, upper, red lip. "I shudder to think what's goin' to happen to our youngins' if war breaks out."

"We've been lucky so far. Most of the killin' and burning has spared us...except the Sunnerlands, of course. But then, we don't know who did that dastardly deed," said Martin.

She looked at her husband with her rounded, hazel eyes. "The loss of those two sweet people has broken my heart. I feel so sorry for those two boys."

"If war does break out between the north and south, I doubt it's going to involve us this far west. It's mainly an eastern problem: Virginia, Maryland, and the Lincoln people," added Martin.

Beth placed her hand over her narrow face, showing only her pointed chin. "God help us all."

———

PRIAM JACKSON GRASPED VIRGILIA'S WAIST with his brawny arm, his huge fingers resting on her stomach. He was sharing the pain of hearing about the brutal death of the Sunnerlands with his wife. Priam and Virgilia had married on the Kingsley property twenty years ago when they were slaves. The land that Martin Kingsley had deeded to them was the biggest joy in their lives, next to their five children.

The shiny, bald spot on top of his head was surrounded by short, partially-gray, kinky hair. Cleanly shaven, he stood aside and looked at his wife with his small, black eyes.

"Dunno why it happened, Virgilia....Ah hear some folks on the boardwalk at Tarrytown talkin'. They said something about Puritans.

Don't know what that means."

"If we mind our own business, we'll be just fine," responded Virgilia.

"Gotta tend to the chickens," said Priam and picked up a pail from a hook on the wall. "Jordon and the othe' boys are ovah at the Kingsleys as usual. Now Ah gotta do the work round heah," he added sadly.

"Ah hope our boys are learnin' somethin' at the Kingsleys. Massa' Martin's folks are tryin' to teach our kin—teachin' that will do 'em good," said Virgilia.

"Martin Kingsley has always been fair to us. Now we've got our own land. We are surely the luckiest people on this earth," responded Priam. "Ah hear Mr. Kingsley say that the reapin' will be early this yeah."

"Elkanah brought home some readin' last week….Say he got it from Abel. Wonder if we should try Brittany in that school?" asked Virgillia.

"Ah dunno if that's the right thing to do yet. There's still folks aroun' here that looks down at us colored folk," answered Priam.

"Next time I see the Massa', I'll speak to him about it…see what he say. Maybe we can send Elisha to schoolin', too."

"If the war come, we may be forced to jin' up with Lincoln and the north. Heaven help us all," Priam responded.

"Dunno, Priam…Elkanah seems to joy in being with the Hastings boys. I saw him out ridin' with the older one—Gradee, his name."

"Good people, all them across the road—mighty good people," responded Priam.

————

BEN HAGGARD'S MIND REFLECTED ON THE MEETING that he had attended in Tarrytown. He toured his grain fields on horseback. Ben rode to his northern property line which ended at the railroad tracks. My fields of wheat show great promise, he thought, smiling.

His facial expression turned serious when his thoughts shifted to slavery. Most of my neighbors are for secession, but one of them is not. Ben Walker is dead against it. Hastings, McGregor, and the Sunnerlands like things as they are. Kingsley has given his slaves some land and set them free. Ben clenched his lower front teeth into his upper lip.

He got off his horse, pulling on his hat brim. His bushy, gray sideburns exaggerated the width of his face. Ben examined the structure of the railroad bed. It ran in either direction for as far as he could see. Ah wonder how many wagons of rock and iron it took to build it. The trains sure make a lot of noise. Ah can hear 'em go by, all the way from my house, he thought. Ah wonder if some day those long, rattling boxes will haul my wheat.

While riding back toward his home, he estimated that his wheat would be ready to harvest in three to four weeks. He wondered if this was the last year he would be able to use slave labor. It's a mighty lot of work cuttin' all the stalks and threshing out the grain.

Joshua had said there would be at least fifteen good, strong pairs of hands to help with the reaping. Ben thought about his wife, Anna, and her words on slavery, "We've got to do what the Kingsleys have done. The country is turnin' against slavery."

Ben lifted up his round, light-colored Stetson and wiped his brow on a red bandana. His curly, black hair was a mangled mess. Rubbing a hand over his face, he smiled and thought about Anna. She insists that ah maintain a clean-shaven face, but does tolerate my trimmed, black mustache even if it curls around my lips. Anna has said that my mustache made up for my shaggy eyebrows.

He looked over toward the shacks where Joshua and his family lived. Those are a sorry state of buildings over there, he thought. Maybe ah should take a wagon into Stillman Mills and bring home that load of lumber which ah 'ave promised 'em.

He thought about his daughter, Clarissa, who had married a banker's son from Stillman Mills. She's 24 years old already. Man sakes, Anna and ah are gettin' old, ah reckon. His thoughts remained on his daughter's family. He smiled and said to himself, ah hope they bring their two boys out a lot this summer—skinny Matt and tubby Billie.

Justin, his eldest son, was four years younger than Clarissa. Last night in bed, Ben remembered saying to his wife, "ah'm proud of the way Justin manages the herd. He's going to run this place some day."

Jubal, on the other hand, likes the books, he thought to himself. By the time he's as old as Justin, he'll probably have moved on to the city to pursue learnin'. Ah don't like the idea that either of my sons wouldn't stay with the farm. My wife believes otherwise, and keeps bringing home books from Tarrytown for Jubal to read. The boy's stayin' up too late, burnin' down the candles.

"Jubal's got the looks," Anna had said. "He looks more like my father every day. He's got the same small, dark penetrating eyes and very thick black hair."

Anna was full of talk last night, Ben remembered. She had said, "Every time that I cut Jubal's hair, he reminds me even more of my father—hair combed straight back, never letting it get long enough to reach his collar.

"Not so with Justin. He likes his hair longer over the collar. Nothin' much I can do about that," Anna had said.

"He's old enough to make up his own mind," Ben had responded.

Anna had laughed. "Justin's attempt at growing a mustache has been a failure at best. Some day he'll have a bushy one. He sure has your silver-gray eyes and your black curly hair."

———

JUSTIN HAGGARD TOLD HIS FATHER that he was riding west to check on the fences. What he didn't tell him was that he planned on meeting Jennifer McGregor. They had a rendezvous place pre-arranged in a stand of timber near the western border of the Haggard property. Why did my father wink and ask me if ah was going to have a good time? he thought, laughing.

At six-foot five, Justin was the tallest person in and around Tarrytown. In church, Justin used the height to his advantage, constantly staring at the pretty Jennifer McGregor. Last Sunday, she was the prettiest girl in church. Ah sure hope that she didn't drop the slip of paper ah placed in her palm on the way out of church.

Justin's facial hair wasn't mature enough to sport a mustache. The fuzz of dark hairs above his lips were hardly noticeable, he noticed, frowning, as he looked in a mirror.

Riding along the southern split-rail fence line, he watched their herd of cattle inside the fence. They graze so peacefully. He sat on his horse and counted. Hmm, seems that one is missing, he thought. His father had suspected that someone in the area might be rustling livestock. The Hastings usually had one or two missing, but that happened because of the Erlocks. They wouldn't dare come across the road, he said to himself.

When he rode up to the grove of trees, he saw the yellow, plaid house dress that he knew Jennifer wore at her home. She was standing in a small clearing, her horse feeding in a grassy patch a short distance away. A white apron was draped across the saddle. She must have escaped from the kitchen, he thought. Doesn't matter…the love of my life, Jennifer McGregor, is waiting.

Dismounting, he took Jennifer by the hand and looked into her bright, blue eyes. Her full, red lips were centered in her rounded face. She was wearing a warm smile. The breeze flitted her dark, reddish hair as Justin put his arm around her and kissed her on the lips.

6

ANGIE WALKER HAD GOTTEN DRESSED after she and her daughters cleared the table following a big breakfast. Her husband and her son, Will, had thanked her and gone back outside. She had asked Will to get the carriage ready. She planned to ride into Tarrytown and buy material for a new dress for Jessica. Her daughter and other young ladies were part of a group selected to participate in a special church sponsored event in May.

Standing in front of a mirror, she put the finishing touches to her short, dark hair. It was parted in the middle, clung closely to the side of her head, and was tied into a bun in the back. She carefully placed a bonnet on her head.

Entering the drawing room, her crisp, crackling voice asked, "Are you ready, Helen?"

"Do I have to go, Mother?"

"Yes, you can help Jessica and me find just the right material."

Angie was pleased that her husband had instructed their son, Will, to provide escort. The decision came about because of what had happened to the Sunnerlands, she knew. After she took her position on the seat of the carriage, George handed her the reins. She watched as her husband assisted their daughters onto their seats. She looked back and saw Will, mounted and ready.

Angie Walker tightened her teeth together, her cheeks bulging in her square-shaped face, and directed the team up the dusty roadway toward the Tarrytown Road. She smiled while listening to Jessica's giggles. Her youngest daughter was dressed in blue, matching her blonde hair and sparkling, blue eyes.

Angie looked at her daughter Helen. She's gonna attract the best of 'em, she thought. Those dark brown eyes and long, dark hair, and a petite dimple make her a beautiful young woman. Helen wore a plain tan dress which was tightened at the waist with a white satin sash. Angie was proud of her daughters, and she felt secure knowing that Will was riding only a few strides behind the carriage.

After trotting the team up their roadway, she slowed them after turning onto the Tarrytown Road. She looked at the schoolhouse where her son, Carr, was doing his learning. We are so fortunate to have a school, she thought.

She set the horses to a walk as they came abreast of the church. Further up Main Street, she felt the stares of a group of men standing on the boardwalk in front of the saloon. Flicking the reins, she was rewarded by the horses as they began a fast trot that got the carriage to the livery quickly.

Pulling up in front she said, "Top of the day to you, Toby. Would you take care of the team? We've got shoppin' to do."

Angie's deep green, cotton seteen dress showed off her slim waist.

It lightened in color as it caught a ray of sun. She accepted Toby's assistance in stepping down.

"No rush," she heard Toby say while he moved quickly to assist Jessica and Helen from the wagon.

Angie stood and watched with amazement when realizing for the first time that Jessica was taller than Helen. She is one slim lady, Angie said to herself. Ben and I are gonna have to feed her more and put some meat on that frame.

The three women stepped onto the boardwalk and walked toward the constable's office located on the high ground of Main Street. They crossed carefully and stopped in front of the General Store. Short of the door, they studied the items in the display window. "Oh, look at that," Helen said with her warm, soft voice. "Isn't that pretty material?"

A blue bonnet caught Angie's attention when she heard someone yell. Turning, she looked up the road toward Stillman Mills. A dust cloud was created by a horse and rider. "Mother, we can get the mail today. Looks who's coming—Mr. Milburn," Helen said.

Angie stared at the rider and knew it wasn't just the mail coming— there would be special news. Lance Milburn was lashing at the rear end of his horse. Lance never rode that hard when he got close to town. Usually, he intentionally slowed his horse near Main Street to antagonize the people who were anxiously waiting.

"War...we're at war! Fort Sumter's been attacked!" she heard Lance Milburn yell as he jerked on the reins, bringing along a huge cloud of dust. His soft, felt, narrow-brimmed hat had fallen onto his shoulders. Lance removed the red bandana from around his neck and wiped his forehead where hunks of dirt had accumulated. He was a slim, short man with a full head of hair. Long, black, and gray whiskers covered most of his face.

People began to spill out onto the boardwalk on both sides of Main Street. A man wearing a barber's apron, his face covered with lather, emerged from the barbershop. The black clad undertaker had come out of his office and strode rapidly across the street. As Lance dismounted, two men came out of the general store and assisted him with his stuffed saddlebags. Angie noticed that one of them was her son, Will.

Three cowboys came running up the boardwalk from the direction of the Frontier Saloon. One of them screeched and whooped, and the other two fired their pistols into the air. Angie became irritated with their behavior. "Don't they know that many lives will be lost?" she asked herself angrily.

The constable came out of his office along with the two Sunnerland boys.

Lance had drawn a crowd, and they backed off as he brushed the dust from his clothes.

"It's happened!" he exclaimed grabbing a newspaper from his pouch. "South against the North. We're at war!"

"Are we South or are we North?" asked Jesse Sunnerland.

"Dunno," said his brother Lafe, his voice squeaking. "Doesn't matter. We're going to catch whoever murdered our parents. They're gonna pay."

Angie saw Mitchell McGregor grab a newspaper from one of the saddle bags. He looks like a scarecrow, she thought, with his long, blond hair sticking out in all directions from under his hat. His face, populated with brownish freckles, moved from side to side. As he read, his normally large, blue eyes appeared even larger.

Handing the newspaper to a man next to him, Mitchell said, "Gotta tell my pa." He ran over to the rail, mounted his horse, and galloped out of town.

"Come on girls, let's go into the store," Angie said, her voice crisp and crackling.

"Don't you think this pattern is beautiful, mother?" Helen asked softly, smiling.

"Yes, I like that. Come here, Jessica," Angie responded.

"Oh, Mrs. Walker, there's a letter for you here," said Seth Miller from behind the counter. He was wearing a black apron.

"Thank you, Seth," Angie responded and held the envelope up to the light coming from the window. "Helen, it's from my brother, William."

Seth handed her a knife blade, and Angie moved to a separate counter and opened the envelope.

She read:

Dearest Sister,

I've come to a crossroad in my life and have made a very difficult decision. By now you probably have heard that the war has begun. I have decided to join the Union cavalry in spite of knowledge that my decision is going to prove unpopular with many Missourans.

Part of my reason for joining the Union is because I was taken prisoner during the fight at Independence. I did have a choice. And I sincerely hope that you accept my decision. My wish is to visit you this summer.

William.

———

SUNDAY MORNING AT THE HASTINGS'S HOUSE brought with it the normal hurry and hustle to dress for church. Thomas, as usual, was the first in the family to be ready, except for Grady, who had the responsibility of hitching up the team to the carriage.

Thomas walked to the front door and turned around. He wore a tan, broadcloth summer suit, and a black, satin, striped, silk waistcoat.

When Thomas went out the front door, Grady was tending to the team. His horse, Spots, was waiting patiently behind the carriage.

Thomas stepped up into the carriage and sat down on the rear seat. His sister, Genevieve, dressed in her usual plaid, came out next and she took a seat next to him. He felt a wisp of wind and grabbed the wide-brimmed, flat, crowned hat with his fingers.

Finally, his parents came through the door. He watched his mother being guided toward the passenger side of the carriage. She wore a magenta trimmed blouse and skirt with three layers of ruffles. She's beautiful, he thought. He watched his father assist his mother onto the front seat.

"Good job, Grady," Henry said and untied the reins.

Thomas admired his father's black wool coat that matched his cutaway suit. Ditto suits they were called, he had heard—and a fancy, brocaded, double-breasted vest. On Sundays, Thomas's father would wear his bowler-shaped hat. No one else around here wears a hat like that—the top pushed down, forming a bowl, he thought.

Thomas watched Grady walk away from the team, his gray, wool trousers tucked in black boots. The tails of his black wool coat sailed as he mounted. He's wearin' his black Sunday hat today, Thomas said to himself, smiling.

He saw his father flick the reins and the horses moved ahead, drawing the carriage up their roadway. The sun blinded those temporarily sitting on the passenger side seats as the carriage turned onto the Tarrytown Road toward the church.

Hair rustling in the breeze, Thomas gave his sister a light shove after she attempted to straighten his tie. The road was dry and dusty, and he was glad that his father didn't get too close to the carriage ahead. Looks like the McGregors, he thought.

Grady was following behind on his paint. Thomas wasn't all too sure why his brother didn't ride in the carriage with him and his sister. There was room, but he suspected it had something to do with Helen Walker. Her name was brought up at the dinner table on Friday and he saw his brother's face change to a radiating red color.

As they approached the crossroad that led to the Walker's farm home, he noticed that the Walker's carriage halted at the intersection to allow them to pass. Thomas noticed the usual waves when he looked back, and saw that his brother had stopped and waited for the Walkers to turn onto the road. Thomas saw Grady remove his hat and bow. "Magnificent, did you see that?" Thomas asked his sister snidely.

"See what?" asked Genevieve.

"Our distinguished brother must like someone in the Walker carriage…at least enough to favor their arrival ahead of himself."

"When did you first figure that out? Ah…you're going to school, little brother—that's where you're getting all your smarts," Genevieve said sarcastically.

Thomas grimaced and slid to the rail at the far end of the seat, looking ahead and ignoring his sister for the balance of the ride. We won't be the first ones there, he thought while observing horses and carriages moving about the churchyard.

"Good mornin', Sir. Ah'll take dat," said Joshua after Thomas's father halted the horse in the church yard.

The Walker buggy pulled up alongside, and one of Joshua's offspring spurted over quickly to take the reins from Mr. Walker.

"What are you two googlin' at?" Grady asked his sister and Thomas as he assisted pretty Helen from the Walker carriage. He shot them a dirty look from his narrowed, green eyes.

Thomas jumped out of the carriage landing on his brown, high-topped shoes. He sprang to the other side, curtsied, and raised a hand up to his sister. His dark hair had recently been clipped by his mother, and it only covered half of his right ear. "Ma'am," he said loudly, sneaking a peek at his brother.

"Ah do declare, Thomas. Ah noticed you giving Sarah Kingsley the eye after church last Sunday," responded his brother laughingly. "Ah reckon you really like those full red lips, don't ya…huh…huh?" Grady added.

More carriages were streaming into the churchyard. As they came to a stop, each was taken care of by one of Joshua's family. Even though Joshua and his offspring were still slaves of the Haggard's, they accepted the coins placed in their open palms on Sundays.

Responding to the gong sound coming from the silver bell in the belfry, Henry Hastings placed his arm inside Emma's elbow and guided her toward the church door. The large, glittering brooch she wears is magnificent, he thought. She was wearing a weighty blue skirt which had two long satin ribbons hanging down from the waist.

They were followed in by the Walker parents who appeared irritated at the banter and flirting going on between their daughter and Grady Hastings.

Inside, Thomas's father had chosen the third pew from the front on the left side—good choice as any, Thomas thought. He waited for his father to guide his mother to the middle. He hesitated, hoping that Grady would enter the pew next. Feeling a shove, he knew that wasn't going to happen.

All talk had ceased when the preacher made his appearance. Zack Wilson was dressed completely in black except for a white shirt. He was a tall, skinny man with an unusually shaped face. The high cheekbones that narrowed sharply to form a cute little mini-chin disappeared into his neck.

The preacher signaled, and the organist and the congregation erupted in song. Thomas didn't sing, only moved his mouth. He could hear the booming voice of his father—embarrassing, he thought. When the singing ended, everyone sat.

The preacher walked totally around the pulpit in one direction, then reversed his direction to walk around again. Thomas perked up his chin—what's with the games today, he thought. Pastor Zack nodded at the organist and began his sermon. "Friends. There's evil surrounding us."

Thomas's laugh was thwarted by his father, who poked him with an elbow.

The pastor, irritated by the interruption, continued. "It is wrong to take up arms agin' each other. Almighty God will punish those— those that do not obey his word, his law."

Twenty minutes later, the sermon was still in progress. Thomas glanced at his father and smiled—the man with the booming voice was sound asleep. At last the sermon ended, and Thomas saw his mother nudge her husband. Henry came alert just in time to stand and participate in the final song.

On the way out, Thomas sneaked around his father and mother while they were exchanging pleasantries with the preacher. He watched his sister, who appeared to be looking for someone. Thomas nodded and grinned as Will Walker walked up and bowed to her. Uh-oh, another one, he thought.

7

Two MONTHS AND PART OF ANOTHER HAD PASSED since the Civil War had officially begun. Grady Hastings was riding into Tarrytown. He was happy that the harvest of grain and hemp was completed. Arriving in town, he had gotten the family mail and was about to mount his horse when he saw a large cloud of dust on the road coming from Stillman Mills.

"Must be thirty to forty riders," said a man sitting on a boardwalk bench in front of the saloon.

"Ah don't see any flags. Wonder who they are?" added Toby Miller who had come out of Mama's Kitchen.

Many of the citizenry and visitors were on the boardwalks of Tarrytown as the column of two reached the town limits at the livery stable. There wasn't a flag or any music, but there was something majestic about the posture of the riders, thought Grady Hastings.

The two lead riders pulled up in front of the constable's office. One of them dismounted and tied his steed to the hitching rail. The other rider's horse reared and snorted. He got his horse under control and also dismounted, his stirrup slapping against the leather girth.

Constable Francis Muldoon was standing on the boardwalk. Grady watched as one of the riders approached the constable and they shook hands. He gazed around and noticed expressions of relief among the onlookers.

Five of the six riders who led the column were dressed in gray uniforms—a color such as no one in this community has ever seen before, Grady thought. He was standing next to the General Store owner, Seth Miller. "Mr. Miller, are those real soldiers?" asked Grady.

"Ah reckon so they are, son," answered Seth. "See that tall one with the black hat on that gray mare? Not in uniform."

"Yeah, ah do. Who is it? Do you know him?"

"Naw, ah don't know him, but unless ah'm mistaken, that's Frank James."

"Who's Frank James?"

"He's a farmer from north of here...north of the big river. See that man behind him? That's Cole Younger from out Harrisonville way."

"The Gray Riders...that's what ah'm going to call 'em," said Grady.

"I suspect they're here to do some recruitin', so better watch out. They might be after you," Seth said, laughing.

———

SERGEANT YORK WAVED TO ONE OF HIS CORPORALS. "Have the men dismount and head over there—Mama's...have a real meal."

The sergeant followed the constable inside, looked out the window, and saw his men gather in front of the hotel. "They haven't had a good meal in a week, Constable. Belle Streeter's gonna take care of 'em. She runs a grand eatery, Mama's Kitchen."

"Sergeant, what's the deal? Ah hear the legislature has voted to stay in the union."

"True 'tis. The governor and most of the people want it the other way, though. That's why we're here. The story that ah heard east o' 'ere is that the reformers killed two of your citizens a couple of months ago. Is that true?"

"Yup, it's true....Been pretty quiet around here ever since, though. Never did catch the culprits....They'll hang sure, if we do."

"Constable, we're afraid that there's going to be a lot more of them redlegs comin' around. Don't underestimate 'em. They're a wicked lot. Twon't be a bit surprised if some Union cavalry shows up eventually, too. Ah heard Lincoln don't like what he's hearin' about Missoura, so far. He's already appointed a general to this territory—Lyons is his name."

"The people here and whereabouts don't want any part of the

war. They just want to do their farmin' and go about their business," said the constable.

"We wish the same. Meanwhile, where's a good spot to camp? Ah've got thirty-six men and forty-two horses. We'll need some feed and supply."

"Go check with Seth Miller. He'll give you a good enough deal on what you need for the horses—the men, too. There's a great spot for campin' on the creek out beyon' the Hastings's place. Check with Henry. His place is the first, past the school, beyond MacTurley's Woods. Ah, that's his kin right over there on that paint. Grady is his name."

The sergeant looked out the window. His men were all inside the café. "Thanks kindly, Muldoon. We'll do some talkin' agin'."

Sergeant York went outside and walked across the road where the slightly stooped young man with long, narrow, dark sideburns was about to mount his horse. That must be that young Hastings feller, the sergeant thought.

8

"PA, THIS IS SERGEANT YORK OF THE GRAY RIDERS," said Grady. "He and his men need a place to camp."

"Gray Riders...now who are they supposed to be?" Henry Hastings asked.

The sergeant laughed. "Mr. Hastings, your son made that one up. Ah'm with the Missouri State Guard. My troopers are Missouri citizens, just like you. They've volunteered to keep this part of the state free from the redlegs, jayhawkers, and the like.

"We're here under the command of General Price, officially of the Confederate Army and our State Guard. Hopefully, if needed, we'll pick up a few recruits from roun' 'ere. You've got some impressive looking, able young men in this area."

"Tell you what, Sergeant. Ah reckon ya could ride down the creek a mile or so where it widens. There's ample water and graze for yar horses. How long ya plan on stayin'?"

"Not sure, Hastings. A couple of days or so should do it."

———

THOMAS HASTINGS WAS ONE OF SIX STUDENTS in the seventh grade. He was paging through a book which his teacher, Miss Stoner, had brought that morning. It was filled with maps of all parts of the country. He was especially interested where Washington was and the relationship of its location to the battle of Manassas.

He had heard in town yesterday that the first big battle of the new war was fought at Manassas Junction, and a southern general by the name of Stonewall Jackson had won a big victory for the Confederacy. Thomas's sympathy and feelings lay with the South. He listened to the men and agreed that the federal government had no business telling Missourians how to raise cattle and grow grain.

Thomas was excited and looking forward to the next St. Louis newspaper that would be delivered to Stillman Mills. Stonewall Jackson—what a name, he thought. He's my first war hero. Grady had told him that the Gray Riders, who were camped down on the creek, were made up of some local boys—Youngers and James.

"The Youngers have a brother about your age," Grady had said. "The James boys are from up north of the big river."

Thomas wondered what that Younger's name was. He looked up when he heard the bell ring. Miss Stoner was signaling a recess break.

Twenty-two students rushed to the door, all anxious to get a breath of the outdoors. Miss Stoner smiled when Thomas handed her the book on his way out. After joining Carr Walker out on the grounds, they walked toward the woods, watching the skies for a sign of Keeya, his favorite hawk.

"What side is your family gonna join?" asked Carr, his blond hair flittering in the breeze.

"My Pa is against federal interference. He said we're goin' to stay out of it. If push comes to shove, we'll join the Confederacy," answered Thomas.

"It's a different view at my house. Pa says we're goin' with the law—the legislature. They voted to stay with the Union. We'll do the same. My older brother agrees."

"Carr, wouldn't that be somethin' if we ended up against each other in battle? Shootin' at each other, I mean. That'd be awful. I couldn't shoot at ya."

Carr Walker looked up at this friend with his light brown eyes. "We'll never do that. No one has to shoot at another. It's like playin' a game. We have our sides, but the war will be over soon. Ah hear it's going to be done with, after the next big battle," Carr said.

"There's that danged bell. We better get back in there or Miss Stoner will clip our ears," Thomas said.

"What's that dust over yonder?" Carr asked, his eyes narrowing.

"Probably more of the Gray Riders. You know about them, don't ya?"

"Yeah, Pa and Will were talkin' about 'em yesterday. They're camped on your land, ain't they?"

"Look, there's a flag—they finally got a flag," said Thomas.

The two boys watched as the riders were almost abreast of the school grounds.

"That's no Gray Riders. It's the Union cavalry!" exclaimed Carr.

"Well, I'll be hog-tied," answered Thomas.

For the first time since the war talk began, Thomas felt weakness in his stomach. *No one has to shoot at another.* Carr had just said that.

"Boys, you must come in…."

Miss Stoner's mouth gaped open when she saw Bluecoats riding by. "Come in this instant!" she exclaimed.

Thomas and Carr obeyed the teacher and took their seats.

———

GRADY AND TWO OF THE HASTINGS'S HIRED HANDS busied at rounding up a small herd of cows. A cloud of dust on the Tarrytown Road caught his eye. He pulled the reins of his horse to watch, his emerald green eyes widening. "Boys, forget the cows for now. Ah'm ridin' home, and quick. That's Union cavalry on that road over there."

Grady galloped westward, reaching the house well ahead of the cavalry. "Pa...Pa...there's Union out there...on the road!" he yelled while dismounting eagerly.

"What's that you say, son?"

"Cavalry—Union cavalry. See the dust."

Grady was excited, breathing in short gasps. He could only watch as his father appeared dumbfounded—just stood there not moving or speaking.

Suddenly, he stiffened. "Grady, ride hard...ride over to the Sergeant. He and his boys are down the creek a way. Tell him."

Grady heard no more. He leaped back on his gelding and applied a spur, galloping southeastward past the buildings toward the creek. He knew exactly where the Gray Riders were camped.

Grady Hastings kept looking back as his horse galloped along the length of the creek, leaping over small bushes. The dust cloud was moving slowly.

Rounding a stand of trees, Grady could no longer see the riders and the dust. Instead, he saw a tall, man dressed in gray watching him as he approached the camp. After Grady braked his horse, he almost got thrown over its' head.

"Whoa there, young feller."

"The Cavalry...the Union!" Grady exclaimed.

"Where...where and how many?" the sergeant asked, his eyes as blue as the sky.

"They're coming down the road by our house...a whole slew of 'em!"

"Which way they goin'?"

"Thata' way, ah reckon." Grady pointed west.

The sergeant turned and opened his mouth wide to yell, "To the saddles, boys!" Grady, on his horse, watched with amazement as the Gray Riders prepared quickly. Within minutes, they were mounted and formed a column of two, some of the hooves pawing the ground.

"Hooey!" yelled the Sergeant and the column began moving

rapidly down the creek toward the road.

Grady waited until the last of them had passed before he followed. He trottèd behind the Riders until the curve in the creek allowed him to see the road, then he stopped.

The Gray Riders spread out and galloped full tilt toward the Union cavalry. Grady felt excited. His insides were bubbling. He let out his own whoop when the cavalry halted and quickly reversed direction. He saw the big, back ends of many horses, bobbing up and down like giant balls. The distance between the cavalry and the Gray Riders began to widen—the attacking horses were tiring.

Grady stood and watched until all the riders had disappeared beyond the corner of woods. Grady galloped his horse back to the farm.

His father, dark eyes rounded and gleaming, was mounted on a horse. He had been watching the cavalry retreat.

"Pa, the Riders are whippin' 'em...see?"

"No shots fired yet," his father answered, his eyes narrowing.

The sound of galloping horses was suddenly drowned out by massive gunfire. Grady couldn't see beyond the timber, but visualized the Riders chasing the Bluecoats past MacTurley's Woods.

———

THOMAS HEARD THE SHOTS COMING FROM THE OUTSIDE while sitting at his desk in the school. The other students and teacher heard the shots, too. He watched Miss Stoner move quickly to the window. "Class, everyone gather over here by the wall. Do not be afraid," she said firmly.

Thomas and Carr disobeyed and edged over to the window. "Look Carr, the Unions are retreatin'."

"Retreatin', yes, but they're headin' over this way," Carr answered, his face expressing concern.

The terrified students crowded together as horses and riders thundered by. The thudding sounds of bullets hitting the building caused some of them to wince and duck. Some of the younger students began to cry. The teacher gathered the youngest students around her and sat down on her chair behind the desk.

"Don't anyone go outside. You are all to remain right here. This'll be over soon..." Miss Stoner said, her voice trailing off.

A window shattered, and shrill screams erupted from the students. Another glass window breaking resulted in more screams. Thomas heard a dull thud from across the room. A bullet struck a picture, knocking it to the floor. The horrifying neighing of a horse was heard as it slammed into the building.

Thomas glanced out the window. He saw a Bluecoat lying on the grass, next to a horse that was spewing blood—its eyes gleaming with terror.

Another horse and rider brushed up heavily against the outside of the building. The horse reared and the rider fell off. Thomas saw the rider get up and run around the far corner. He grabbed Carr's arm when heard the back door being kicked open.

Thomas peeked over the desk and saw two Bluecoats enter the room. "Look, Carr, the Unions are in 'ere," he said softly. He couldn't control his curiosity. Thomas looked in horror at one of the faces, as it was covered with blood. Some of the children continued to scream.

Several of the students began to cough as the smell of gunpowder infiltrated the room. A third window had been broken and more smoke filtered through. Some of the children rubbed their eyes as the coughing intensified.

"Stay back!" yelled one of the Bluecoats as he waved a pistol at the ceiling.

For the first time, Thomas saw a Gray Rider go by, then another, and another. He saw some of the Bluecoats disappear into the woods just beyond the cemetery.

At last, the gunfire near the school ended. The shots that Thomas could hear were off in the distance.

The two Bluecoats in the schoolhouse crouched down and were peeking out the windows. Another cluster of Gray Riders rode by, and Thomas heard some horses neigh as their riders halted near the back of the school.

Suddenly, the room seemed to explode, and Thomas fell to the floor. Three Gray Riders had entered and were exchanging gunfire with the two Bluecoats. Six...seven...eight shots in quick succession—the noise was excruciating. Suddenly all was quiet.

Thomas heard one of the Gray Riders say, "It's over." Thomas peeked over the desktop again. He saw the Rider lightly step toward the students huddled around Miss Stoner. "Better stay down—could be some more," the Rider added.

Thomas dropped back down. He got up on his knees and saw three of the Gray Riders dragging a Bluecoat through the door. He poked Carr. "It's all over. Let's go see."

Carr didn't move. Thomas shook him. Then he saw it—a small, red hole between his eyes.

9

THOMAS STOOD AND YELLED, "Miss Stoner, it's Carr...he's...."

Miss Stoner rushed to Thomas's side and looked down, "Heaven Almighty...have mercy...have mercy...."

She looked back at the students, who were all watching her intently from the back of her desk. "You all stay right there. We'll have help here soon."

She knelt down by Carr Walker and took hold of his hand. She looked at Thomas and tried to talk. Words would not come.

Thomas heard a noise at the door. He saw his brother, Grady, dash into the room. Thomas frantically waved, his throat too rough for words to come out.

Grady rushed over. "Are you all right, brother?"

Thomas's eyes filled with tears, and he pointed to the floor. Grady knelt down by Carr Walker, shaking his head and saying nothing.

Miss Stoner returned to her students, who were gathered around her desk. She gathered them as close to her as she could and began to cry. Her sobbing sounds were multiplied by some of the students, who also began to cry.

Minutes later, Belle Streeter from Mama's Kitchen, and Lady Constance from the Frontier Saloon, rushed into the room. They rushed to Miss Stoner. "Is everyone all right?" Belle asked, her round face expressing concern.

"No, we're not." Miss Stoner gestured toward where Grady and Thomas were standing.

Belle Streeter's generous body proportions dwarfed the students and Miss Stoner. Her skirt rustled as she hastened to where Carr was lying on the floor. Belle looked down, her eyes widened, and she gasped. Kneeling down by the fallen Carr Walker, she said calmly, "Grady, would you go outside and ride for the doctor?"

"Hurry!" Belle exclaimed, looking up and staring at Grady with her large, blue eyes.

"Yes, ma'am, ah best do it quick," Grady stuttered and rushed out of the room, his boots clattering on the wooden floor.

———

PASTOR ZACK WILSON, AS CUSTOMARY, was dressed in black as he led the procession up the hill toward the cemetery. George Walker was next in line. Alone on the buckboard wagon, his chin tilted down as he worked the reins of his team. Lying behind him on the wagon bed was the casket of his son, Carr.

Walking behind the wagon was George's wife, Angie, and his other son, Will. His wife had her hands clasped in front of her waist as Will guided her with his hand, grasping her left elbow. Helen and Jessica, the Walker daughters, followed closely behind—tears streaming down their cheeks.

The Hastings family followed behind the Walkers. Thomas walked next to his brother, behind their parents and Genevieve, his sister. His father walked stiffly and had his hand wrapped around Emma's waist. She wore a long, black dress and her head was covered with a black bonnet.

Except for the squeaks made by the wagon, the sound of wheels turning, and the plodding of the horses' hooves, the air was dead quiet.

Neighbors and townspeople following behind the Hastings were strung out in a long line.

After everyone had arrived at the gravesite, Pastor Wilson spoke. "We are gathered here to pay our last respects to an innocent young man...one who has been a victim of violence." He continued with words and prayers for about five minutes before closing his book.

Turning, he placed his long-fingered hand on the slumped shoulder of Angie Walker. "Peace be with you," he said, and began the long walk back down the hill.

Thomas watched four men slowly release the ropes to lower the casket to the bottom of the hole. Each member of the Walker family threw a clump of dirt on the slowly disappearing coffin.

He turned and looked down at the school. There's where it all happened, he said to himself.

After the Walker family turned away from the grave and began the walk back, the Hastings followed. Part way down the hill, George Walker's shoulder brushed against that of Henry Hastings. George said, "ah'm holding you accountable for the death of my son."

Hastings appeared shocked and taken aback. "George, what are you saying? Surely, you don't mean that."

George Walker's dark eyes glared at Hastings. His long, narrow face appeared dead serious. One corner of his mouth quivered.

"Henry Hastings, you encouraged and abetted the enemy. You and your son were the reason why the gray marauders attacked our government's cavalry. My son got shot because they entered the school....You could of just as well have pulled the trigger," George said bringing his lips tightly together.

Emma Hastings pulled on the arm of her husband. She whispered, "He'll feel differently later....Grieving does that. Henry, let's go home."

Thomas stumbled on in shock after hearing the strong words and accusations by Mr. Walker. Walking down the hill, he couldn't imagine how his father could possibly be blamed. Thomas needed to get back home and talk to his mother about the incident.

The carriage ride home for the Hastings was silent—not a word spoken. Thomas's father appeared to be extra heavy with the whip—the horses wasted no time pulling the carriage to its destination.

Thomas saw his father open a cabinet door and bring out a bottle of whiskey. He filled a glass and sat down by the table. His mother walked over to her husband. She put an arm around his shoulder. "Please don't let what George said get you down. I know it was unexpected and uncalled for, but...."

Henry brought the glass to his lips and drank until it was empty. "Ah think you're right, Emma. He'll see things differently in a day or so."

Grady came down the stairs dressed in his denim work clothes. "Ah'm goin' out to see how the boys are doin', Pa."

Thomas saw Genevieve climb the stairs, her braids bobbing with each step. He got up off the rocker and walked over to his father. "Pa, there's no way it was your fault. It could've been me instead of Carr. Then, what would Mr. Walker have said?"

The rest of the day went by very slowly for Thomas. He changed his clothes and was sitting out on the porch in his dark gray, duck trousers. I wonder how many more times the Union cavalry is gonna ride by here? he asked himself. Best they stay away.

That evening, at the dinner table, the Hastings family ate quietly. After dinner, Thomas helped Genevieve clean up the kitchen. He dreaded going to bed, knowing that he would be having disturbing thoughts.

He stayed up later than usual, attempting to read his geography lesson.

"Thomas, it's time for bed....You know that," his mother reprimanded.

"Yup, I know, Mother, but I'm tryin' to get as tired as possible so I can sleep."

Emma walked over to the rocker. She got on one knee and put her arms around Thomas's shoulder. "This will all pass....It will pass. You sleep as late as you wish tomorrow morning."

Later that night, Thomas woke up several times seeing the face of his former best friend, Carr Walker. Thomas could not rid his mind of the recurring sight of the red hole and wide-open eyes. He had been experiencing mental torture ever since it had happened. How could they possibly blame us? he asked himself.

10

THE POUNDING SOUNDS OF HAMMERS could be heard all the way to the constable's office. Two days after the funeral, workmen were repairing the damage to the schoolhouse.

The community searched for a replacement for Miss Stoner. She had resigned from her teaching position the day after Carr Walker's death.

Several of the concerned citizens gathered for a meeting in the constable's office. Mayor Owen Pritchard presided. "Folks, we've had a taste of the war. My sympathy goes out to the family of young Walker."

Grady Hastings was at the meeting, too. He noticed that his father was anxiously glancing toward the door. Grady suspected it was because the Walkers were missing from the meeting. Grady had hoped that Mr. Walker would apologize to his father for his accusations on the day of the funeral. The loss of Thomas's friend, Carr, had been bad enough, he thought. Blaming my father was too much.

Not only were the Walkers absent, but so were the Kingsleys.

Both Sunnerland boys were present. So were Orly McGregor and his three sons, Mitchell, Paul, and James. Ben Haggard was there with his son, Justin.

Tall, bearded McGregor raised his hand and stood. Next to Justin Haggard, he was the tallest man in the room. His red hair was streaked with white, as was his bushy mustache. His father had immigrated to America from Scotland in the year 1842. Orly carried on his father's ambition to raise horses and cattle.

A space opened between his mustache and the bulky hair on his chin, and his words came out, "ah'm not for slavery. Ah'm for freedom. The federal government sending troops here does not smell of freedom. We don't need their protection. You all know what happened to my neighbors. It's the lawless redlegs who we need protection from. The Union military has no business here. They only cause trouble. Ah would rather have the Gray Riders around....They protect our interests. If any of my sons join up, it will be with the Missouri Guard."

Ben Haggard remained seated and ran his fingers through his black, curly hair. He added, "McGregor, ah agree with you. Ah's for sendin' the governor a statement to keep the Union army out of here. Ah's hopin' that givin' up our sons to fight in this senseless war will never happen." Ben scrunched his lower front teeth into his upper lip and looked toward the front door.

The man dressed in a vested suit and sitting close to the door stood, and walked over to the constable's desk. Douglas Herron, owner of the bank, had a large stomach that threatened the black buttons of his striped waistcoat. He removed his rounded, black hat and set it on the desk. "Boys, ah know most of you are siding with the Confederacy, but ah would feel a lot safer if the Gray Riders went elsewhere. The Bluecoats are here to keep order."

He coughed twice, cleared his throat, and continued with a wheezing voice, louder than before. "With due respect, Henry, ah reckon making it easier for the Gray Riders to hang around may not be in our best interests. That's all ah've got to say, boys....Got to git back to the bank."

After the meeting disbanded, most of the participants hung around on the boardwalk. They watched as six riders rode into town from the west. They hitched their horses in front of the saloon and entered.

Lafe Sunnerland was standing next to Grady Hastings, his barrel-shaped chest rounding into his shoulders. "Ah'm goin' in there and talk to 'em. They're part of the Gray Riders. Wanna come?"

"No, not today, Lafe…maybe another time," answered Grady.

Lafe, followed by his brother Jesse, crossed Main Street. Jesse was four inches taller than his older brother, almost as tall as his father had been. His sideburns were dark with pointed tips, ending just above the jaw line. Jesse's eyes were large and dark, just like his mother's.

When Lafe walked, his wide, rounded shoulders swaggered to keep up with his bouncing legs. His hair was lighter colored than his brother's, and he maintained it shorter, trimmed up on the neck and at the top of the ears. The makings of a mustache formed under his nose.

The two Sunnerland brothers entered the saloon.

———

"YOU BOYS NEED SOMETHIN'?" Madeline asked.

Lafe's large, gray-green eyes looked up at the smartly dressed bar maid. "Yeah, couple of beers," his voice squeaked.

Madeline brushed away a long curl that had draped over an eye. "Anything else, boys?" she asked.

"How about a kiss, lass?" Lafe asked and stood, touching her arm.

Lady Constance, owner of Frontier Saloon, had been sitting at a table near the wall, close to the bar. She said loudly, "Now, boys, I'll have to ask ya to behave like gentlemen."

Rising from her chair, she walked over to Lafe, hands firmly placed on her hips. She towered over the startled cowboy.

"Yes, ma'am," Lafe responded meekly and tipped his hat.

Lady Constance smiled, her long eyelashes jutting out from her greenish eyelids. "Madeline will be happy to serve you boys, but ya gotta behave. Do ya understand, Mr. Sunnerland?"

She turned and walked away, her floor-length skirt rustling as she moved.

Lafe sat down and his face turned a crimson red. "There's yar first lesson on how not to treat the opposite sex, Jesse."

Jesse laughed and took a long swig of beer from the glass that
Madeline had set on the table.

Lafe's eyes followed the bar maid as she rambled to the bar. He
looked around the room and saw two groups in the room. The gray-
clad group was clustered at the bar. Four of them were sitting on
stools and the other two were standing. One of them had three stripes
on the sleeve of his coat. The other group consisted of five men sitting
at a table playing cards.

One of the men in gray standing next to the bar walked over to
Lafe and Jesse. "Howdy, boys. Ya all from roun' 'ere?"

"Yeah, just up the road a bit. How about you?" asked Jesse, his
dark eyes narrowing.

"Ah hail from a few miles out of Springfield."

"South of 'ere, ain't it?" asked Lafe.

"Yup, about a four-day ride...ah'm Corporal Smith, Missouri State
Guard."

"This is my brother, Jesse. Ah'm Lafe Sunnerland."

"Was it your parents that were killed here three months back?"

"Yup, ah reckon it 'twas," Lafe drawled.

"Terrible killin'. Ah understand it was the redlegs that done it,"
said the corporal, watching Lafe out of the corner of his eye.

"There were three of 'em. They rode off, up the mountain. Some
of us trailed 'em the next day, but we lost the tracks up in the rocky
area," said Lafe. He reached in his pocket and drew out a piece of
metal. "See this...that's come off one o' 'em. If ah find a match to
this, ah'm goin' to kill the man who is wearin' it."

The corporal put out the palm of his hand. He worked the broken
piece of spur around in his fingers. "You boys should join us...become
part of the guard."

"Ah'm thinkin' about it," answered Lafe. "One of us needs to
stay on the farm."

"Have you heard about what's happenin' in my area, Springfield?"

"No, can't say that ah 'ave," Lafe responded, his voice squeaking.

"There's this Union General by the name of Lyons. He's taken
over the town. The Guard's gatherin' down below near the creek—
Wilson's creek. Soon as enough fellas arrive, we're goin' ride up

there and drive 'em out. Sometime next month."

Jesse looked at the corporal with his large, wide-open, dark eyes. "A battle...a real battle?"

"Ah reckon. Ah'm expectin' they'll be at least three thousand. The Yankees got some big guns up there. We're goin' to surround 'em."

Lafe raised his mug. "Here's to good luck, Corporal."

"Thank ye. Did you hear about your neighbors north of town?"

"No, what happened?"

"Well, nothin' really happened except some of 'em jined up with the Yankees, ah reckon. They may be down there in Springfield now, as I speak."

"Do you have any names?" asked Jesse.

"Will Walker, for sure. There are others...dunno their names."

Lafe, confused and in shock, said, "Come on, Jesse, we better get goin'. Good talkin' to you, Corporal...best of fortunes."

The two Sunnerland boys shook hands with the Corporal and left the saloon.

———

THOMAS WAVED TO THE TWO SUNNERLANDS as he watched them trot by the school on their horses. He missed Carr. Lately, during recess, he had stood outside alone and thought about his missing friend. The Sunnerlands returned his wave and increased their gait to a slow gallop.

Thomas wasn't sure what to make of the new schoolmaster, Ebenezer Styles. He looked so thin that Thomas felt like sharing his food with him. The schoolmaster, dressed in black trousers and coat, appeared to be without a chin. The stiff collar topping his white shirt was fronted with a two-strand black tie.

Mr. Styles rarely smiled, the total opposite of Miss Stoner, Thomas thought. Learning from him was totally different. The new master spent most of the time teaching writing and reading. Thomas was more interested in geography and history. He smiled as he remembered what he had heard in town. "Walking together, the preacher and schoolmaster look like two black sticks coming down the boardwalk."

When school ended, Thomas walked down to the road and waited until his father showed up with a buckboard. He removed his bandana from around his neck and wiped his brow. It's about as sticky and hot in that school house and it can get, he said to himself—a bit better out here.

"How's the new schoolmaster treatin' ya, son?" his father, who was wearing his high-peaked, tan work hat, asked.

"Good, Pa. I liked Miss Stoner better, though."

Henry Hastings laughed. "Yeah, ah can see why."

Thomas's father turned the team around and laid the whip. The wagon rumbled west past the wooded area and turned onto the roadway that led to their house.

"Wash those dirty hands," Genevieve said when he entered the house. "Dinner will be ready soon."

"I'll do that when I'm good and ready, sis," Thomas responded sarcastically.

He mellowed and gave his mother a hug. "How's the new master, Thomas?" she asked.

"Well, he seems clever enough, but I would like learnin' more about geography and maps."

"Oh, he'll get to that soon enough."

Before anyone touched any food, Henry Hastings, his thick, brown hair pasted down on his head, put his head down and said with a deep voice, "Lord, bless this table. Bless this farm. Bless this land. Bring it peace."

Grady ate quietly for a few minutes. "Pa, ah hear that Will Walker joined the Union army."

"Yes. I've 'eard that, too," his mother said.

Genevieve lowered her chin and talking ceased for a few moments.

"A'm thinkin' about joinin' the Guard," Grady said, his face glowing.

Henry cleared his throat. "Son, why don't ya wait a spell? Ah reckon that this whole thing could blow over by the time snow comes."

Genevieve said, "Grady, that sounds excitin'...joinin' the Missouri State Guard, I mean. I hear that Abel Kingsley is considerin' joinin' the Union. He's been talkin' about riding over toward Springfield."

"What's goin' on at Springfield?" asked Emma.

"There's a battle about to brew, ah hear," Grady answered, his emerald green eyes widening. "After we whip those Yankees there, the war will be over. They'll never try us again."

Henry stared at Grady. "Not so sure, son. Ah heard in town yesterday that the Unions are massin' along the river, east of here, near St. Louie."

"No matter. We're goin' to whip 'em good," answered his son.

Dinner had ended. Thomas picked up a book and sat on a chair by the window. His mother and sister busied themselves with the dishes. Grady picked a musket from the rack and walked out toward the creek.

His father went out on the porch, took a seat on the swinger, and lit a cigar. Thomas visualized a puff of smoke from Grady's musket when he had heard the shot. That ain't what I see through the window, he thought. That's my Pa's cigar smoke.

Thomas walked outside and stepped up onto the porch. He heard another musket shot that he assumed came from Grady. "Pa, is Grady gonna join the guard?" he asked.

"Ah reckon that he already has, son....He already has," responded his father as he blew out a puff of smoke from his mouth.

11

EMMA HASTINGS LOOKED AT THE CALENDER. It was the first day of August, 1861. She heard the team pull up by the house. Looking out the window, she saw her husband get off the bench and say something to Thomas, who was astride his horse.

Emma stepped outside, and Henry helped her into the black-roofed carriage. She saw her husband snap the reins. The horses broke into a trot and headed for the road. She looked back and could see Thomas following closely behind on his gray. Glancing at her husband, she could see the lines in his face. He's worrying deep, and I'm not surprised, she thought. Emma didn't speak during the twenty minutes it took to get to Tarrytown.

After arriving, she looked back and saw Thomas guide his horse to a hitching rail and dismount. Henry directed the team to the livery.

"Here they come!" she heard someone yell.

Looking westward, she saw a huge cloud of dust. As the column approached the town, everybody was out on the boardwalk. Several of the bystanders removed their hats as the flag bearer approached. I don't remember seeing a flag like that, she thought. It's so blue.

In the middle of the flag, Emma saw two bears standing on their hind legs, grasping a decorative circle with their forelegs. Three curved rows of white stars above the circle stretched beyond the bears.

Two men in gray uniforms led the long column of riders. The larger one had three stripes on his coat—the other rider had two stripes.

Cheer after cheer emerged from the lips of the onlookers. "Go get us a Yankee, Justin!" Emma heard one of the Haggards yell— young Jubal, she thought.

Emma put her hand to her mouth. Tears filled her eyes as she watched her son ride by. He looks so tall and straight, she thought. His long, narrow sideburns spiked down from his dark, gray hat. She tuned into the rhythmic clop-clop and became mesmerized with emotion.

Feeling a tug on her shoulder, she turned. Her other son, Thomas, was smiling and waving.

"Look, Ma. Did you see Grady ride by?"

"Yes, son, I did," she answered, sniffling. "Saw Justin, too. He was ridin' right next to Grady."

"Look mother, Lafe and Jesse Sunnerland...the last two...oh, and...front of 'em must be Mitch McGregor. No one else roun' 'ere has a straw colored, bushy top like that," Thomas said.

By the time the column had passed the livery, the crowd had thinned, and most of the onlookers drifted back into the buildings.

The Hastings and Haggards remained on the boardwalk and watched until the last of the riders passed out of sight.

——

AT 4:00 THE NEXT MORNING, THUNDERCLAPS, loud and frequent, rumbled in the dark sky. Heavy rain splattered onto the roof, awakening Thomas from a deep sleep. He had dreamt he was at Wilson's Creek chasing Yankees. Feeling his damp body, he slipped out of bed.

The bed where his brother had slept every single day of Thomas's life was empty. Before going down the stairs to fetch a drink, he noticed a small wooden cross on the pillow of his brother's bed. Nodding, he thought of his mother.

Returning to his bed, Thomas lay awake the balance of the night. When daylight came, it continued to rain outside. He heard his father go out the door.

"Brew us some coffee, Genevieve. I'm goin' out to help your father with the calves," he heard his mother say.

Thomas burrowed deep under the blanket and put the pillow over his head. He heard his sister mutter something as she carefully stepped down the stairs.

The rainfall continued on through the day. Late that afternoon, Thomas saddled his horse and rode over to the creek. The water in the creek looked turbulent and was well out of its banks. Getting off his horse, he grabbed a stick and swished it through the water. He heard the sound of hoof beats and looked up. Three riders were approaching from the south. Their horses broke into a gallop.

Thomas mounted quickly and galloped his gray home. He had sensed danger when he saw the riders, fearing they were the Erlocks.

After arriving at the barn, he dismounted and walked to the edge of a clump of trees. He watched as the three horsemen angled toward the road and headed east toward Tarrytown.

——

THE ERLOCKS WERE A PROBLEM for Henry Hastings. The shack they lived in, near the top of Bear Mountain, was in dire need of repairs. Since MacTurley's Woods were not owned by anyone, they had free rein to do as they pleased. Other then causing trouble, they raised chickens and dogs, most of them in and around their shack. Henry could not prove his suspicion, but he was certain they also rustled his beef.

He didn't mind if they slaughtered one for their own use to satisfy hunger, but in early April, a good-sized steer had been found dead, partially slaughtered. The coyotes had been rummaging, but the knife cuts were obvious. Henry had talked with the constable, but he was the only law officer in the area, and he wasn't very interested in riding up the mountain to challenge the Erlocks.

Constable Muldoon had said, "ah shudder when them boys ride down 'ere. They fill their bellies with whiskey and pick a fight in the saloon with any stranger that comes by. There's nigh onto a whole slew of 'em up there. Ah'd just as soon stay out of their way."

The previous summer, Henry's son, Grady, had shot two of their dogs after riding pasture and catching the two trying to kill a calf. Later, Victor Erlock had ridden down and threatened Grady. "If you ever shoot another, ah'm goin' to kill one of your horses, or maybe you."

Henry remembered his son saying that old man Erlock was the meanest he'd ever seen. "Fire in those eyes...whiskers look like millions of spider legs. Henry had warned his boys and Genevieve not to ride anywhere close to the Erlock's. After the Sunnerlands were killed, he didn't allow his daughter or wife to ride without an escort of men with guns.

Henry rode over to the slave shacks that were a quarter-mile south of his barn. Samuel Morton was a good man. He and his family did a great job of bringing in the hemp this year, Henry thought. It was the most productive crop that ah have ever had. Eight wagonloads had been delivered to Lexington only a week ago.

Sammy, Samuel's eldest son, was Grady's age. Henry worried that Sammy would get involved in the war. Sammy is my most valuable property. Henry had seen that look in his eyes last week...the yearning for freedom. Actually, ah should consider giving the Mortons a piece of land just as Kingsley did, Henry mused. It seems to work out well over there.

That boy must be at least 6 feet 3 inches tall, Henry thought. He's all muscle. No way would anyone around here want to face up to him, one on one. Ah reckon that he could take on five or six of 'em Union boys. Henry remembered watching Sammy lift a large rock from a hole in the ground. Ah wouldn't even have tried.

Sammy's mother, Tullaby, is a strong woman, Henry thought. She's a perfect match for Samuel. Amazing how she keeps those shacks and her children so clean. Henry was trying to remember the name of their second born. He was a lad a couple years younger than Sammy.

Off in the distance toward the creek, he saw Samuel reining two horses that were pulling a plow. Henry spurred his horse and rode over.

"Whoa...whoa...whoa," spoke Samuel when he saw his master ride up.

"Good afternoon, Samuel. How's the plowin' goin?"

"Good, Massa' Hastings...good."

"Hittin' any rocks?"

"A couple...no problem...went roun' 'em just fine."

"You're doin' a good job, Samuel."

"Thank ye, Massa'. Ah shuh do try."

"You're family got enough to eat, Samuel?"

"Shuh do. Ah shuh happy with that beef you give us. The grain, too, Massa'."

"Well, keep up the good work, Samuel," Henry said, then hesitated. He thought about bringing up the idea of giving Samuel land and freeing him. Perhaps this is not the right time to bring it up, Henry thought, and rode off toward his barn.

After dismounting and unsaddling his horse, Henry headed to the house. He thought about Grady, who had gone away to the war. Henry sat on the porch and thought about the three riders that Thomas had seen—probably the Erlocks, he thought. I'm sure missin' Grady.

12

GRADY AND HIS COLUMN HAD RIDDEN ALL DAY. He had never spent a full day in the saddle before. His back ached and he couldn't stop coughing. The dust that he inhaled was beyond anything he had ever experienced.

After dismounting, the riders unsaddled and released their horses to graze. Their leaders had chosen to camp next to a creek that had ample water for the horses. Every rider had a leather pack that contained, among other supplies, a small tent.

A uniformed guardsman joined the group and instructed them on how to set up the tents. They also were given information on a time and place for eating. "See that big tent up yonder? That's where the eatin's are. Ah'll let you know when it's time."

When their turn came, Grady and his fellow riders stood in line and had their bowls filled. They gathered in small clusters and ate their meal outside the tent. A jug of homemade Missouri whiskey made its way along the outreached hands of most of the men. After running his tongue around his lips, Grady smiled.

There wasn't anyone not laughing, when a tent collapsed and engulfed Jesse Sunnerland, who was embarrassed to the hilt. The guardsman instructor turned upon hearing the laughter. "Sunnerland's got it right," he said. "He's showin' ya all the wrong way to set up a tent."

More laughter erupted. Justin Haggard's head bobbed up and down and he began choking from excessive laughter. He was forced to stand, towering over everyone, before bending over and clutching his stomach with his right arm. A tear had rolled down from one of his silver-gray eyes.

"How far is this place where we're headin' for?" Grady asked a corporal who had come by.

"Another four days ride, ah reckon," the corporal answered.

Sleep came quickly that first night, but there was a lot of shifting and stirring when rain fell in torrents about 4:30. Grady grimaced when he laid his palm down on the wet ground. He learned that the next time his tent would be pitched on higher ground. He shivered the rest of the morning because of wet bedding and clothes.

The next day, Grady joined up with Justin Haggard and they rode side by side. When riding had ended and saddles were removed, they built a small fire in front of their tents, which were placed properly on high ground. A big improvement from the first night, Grady thought.

The corporal came around and said, "ah see you boys are catchin' on…knew it wouldn't take ya long." He laughed and spat a tobacco wad clear across Justin's tent.

On the third day, they were long in the saddle when the sun appeared, about mid-morning. "First time I've been really dry since that first night," Grady told Justin.

During the middle part of that third day, the column halted at a large ranch spread out over a beautiful valley. Grady and the men watched the sergeant negotiating with someone from the ranch. Before moving on, the column had ten extra horses.

That night, Grady felt comfortable in the tent as a result of learnin' how to stay dry. His thoughts were on the day they rode through Tarrytown—that first day—feelings of glory while riding past his peers. Never would he forget the look on his mother's face as she reached out for his hand. It seems like months ago, he thought.

On the fourth day, their column joined up with another one that was at least twice as large. Not only were there riders, but teams of horses pulling wagons—must be a dozen, he thought. Grady estimated there were over a thousand Confederates massing for battle.

Tents strung out as far as Grady could see on that fourth evening. The smell of smoke and the sound of strings from a banjo and fiddle were comforting to him. He thought about his father who would be sitting on the porch with a brandy and a cigar at this time of the evening. His mother and Genevieve would be clearing the table, while his brother had his face stuck in a book.

Grady, alert and ready on the morning of the fifth day, emerged from his tent. The air was dry and warm. For the first time since leaving home, his system had digested food correctly. He noticed there was a spirit of enthusiasm among his fellow riders. Grady and Justin had befriended Jeb Wright, a rider from Stillman Mills.

Jeb, a member of the column that had attacked the Union cavalry at the schoolhouse, said they killed eight Yankees and had lost only two. Jeb had been critical of the two Yankees who took refuge in the school. "Cowards, that's what they were," he had said. "Hiding behind children and a defenseless teacher is what they were doin'."

By sundown of that day, the column, now over half-a-mile long, arrived at a base camp. A corporal gathered Grady, Justin, Jeb, Mitchell, the two Sunnerlands and others together. He told them that they were going to spend time learnin' strategies and how to shoot Yankees.

———

"ANYBODY KNOW WHAT DAY THIS IS?" Grady asked the men around him.

"It's the ninth of August," one of them answered.

The sun was lowering and approaching the horizon as Grady watched two riders approach. After they dismounted, Grady recognized the insignia of a colonel and a lieutenant. During the past few training sessions, Grady and his group were indoctrinated to recognizing the insignias of the officers. Each different region of the Missouri Guard had a different flag. Grady's group flag was blue with red trim with a large, white cross at one end.

Grady and the others responded to the Lieutenant's request for everyone to gather. "Ah'm Lieutenant Bigwood. This is Colonel Riseburg. He gonna to talk to ya. Listen up."

"Fellow Missourans, Tomorra' there's likely goin to be some shootin'. Sergeant York is your leader. You are all obligated to follow his instructions and directions. If yar in battle and get separated, 'tis ya responsibility to regroup roun' ya flag. Study ya flag….Watch for it….It could save ya life."

The Colonel talked for another twenty minutes. "Good luck, and God save Missoura."

Grady and Justin, short of words that evening, experienced sleep close to midnight.

———

IN THE MORNING, GRADY AWOKE to what he thought was the sound of horses. "Do you hear somethin'?" Grady asked Justin while watching the sky brighten in the southeast.

"Yeah…."

Jeb Wright already saddled, stood by his horse. No orders were necessary. Everyone knew that someone was approaching. Stopping to listen, Grady thought the sound was getting louder.

Wads of mud kicked up from the hooves as a corporal and two other uniformed riders brought their horses to a halt. After dismounting, the two non-striped riders who rode up with the corporal distributed two packets of jerky-like food to each man on the ground.

Grady and the Gray Riders had been camped by a stream called Wilson's Creek. Looking up toward the western slope of a large hill, he saw splashes of light emerge through the trees at the top.

Feelings of tension churned in his stomach when he noticed movement on a side hill to the northwest—not horses—men on foot, he thought.

Within ten minutes, all the tents were down and stored in saddlebags. Grady and Justin, munching on sticks of jerky, stood by their horses anxiously.

The upper rim of the sun was about to emerge when the sound of gunfire sent shivers up Grady's spine. Sergeant York rode up and yelled, "All mount and follow me!"

For the first time, the Riders had an opportunity to follow their flag. It was carried by a uniformed rider who had one stripe on his shoulder.

Puffs of white smoke drifted gracefully above the hill, where Grady had seen men moving earlier. Feelings of excitement were growing. The first rays of the sun had brightened up the colors of their flag, fluttering in a breeze above a horse's head.

His feelings turned to fear when he saw men running down the hill, some falling. Gunfire had intensified, coming from the direction of the hill. Our militia is in retreat, he thought fearfully.

Grady became confused when the sergeant raised his hand and directed his horse away from the action, down toward the creek. Grady was anxious to help those in retreat. Hearing massive gunfire coming from the hill, he saw an officer come riding up from the other direction. A flag bearer and bugle holder were right behind him.

The officer signaled and the sergeant yelled, "Ho! Follow me!"

The column formed and crossed a second creek. Grady heard someone say, "Skeggs—Skeggs Creek."

"Spread it out!" Sergeant York yelled.

Other columns had joined Grady's group and he experienced his first reaction to the sound of bullets blitzing past and overhead. Tension sprayed his stomach walls as he looked up and down the line. A rider appeared and trotted along the length of the riders. Grady was certain that it was an officer—a lieutenant, he thought.

Suddenly, the officer drew his saber. He raised it and screamed, "*Charge!*"

Clods of wet soil were flying through the air, one of which hit Grady in the cheek. He focused mostly on keeping his horse on a viable path, and staying in the saddle. He lifted his revolver from the holster. He clutched the gun, while holding the reins in his right fist.

His tension disappeared, and he joined the others, screaming and shouting, "*Yaaaah! Yaaaah!*"

Puffs of smoke, which had been dotting the landscape, drifted and melted together, filling the nostrils of the riders with an arid smell. Grady coughed, still holding his revolver in his right hand. He hadn't had occasion to shoot the Colt yet. He heard the blast of a musket and the scream of a ball as it flew close to his head. He saw a bluish figure on the ground off to his right. Pointing his Colt toward it, he pulled the trigger for the first time.

Suddenly, he saw three Bluecoats aiming their muskets at him. He ducked and continued to pull the trigger, the Colt barking with each pull. One of the Bluecoats had fallen. "Blam! Blam!" The third one fell, and Grady saw Justin, the barrel of his revolver smoking. Grady yelled, "Heee...Justin!"

The horse next to him lost its' legs, and the rider went flying over the top of its head. The Yankees ahead of him were in full retreat, some falling and getting dragged by their horses. Others that fell remained where they landed.

The intense screaming continued as Grady and his group rode well past the hill where he had seen ground militia earlier. He felt excited to see Union foot soldiers far ahead retreating, loping toward the spires in the distance.

"Flanking," was what the colonel had mentioned earlier. The Guard cavalry had flanked the Union infantry on the big hill to the northeast. Grady felt elated. It all happened so quickly, he said to himself. The noise and smoke were more than he could've ever imagined.

Sergeant York signaled a stop, and his horse immediately lowered its neck and began to nibble Missouri grass. The sergeant's troop gathered around him. While counting, Grady saw him smile—casualties were few.

Up and down the line, Grady saw Missouri Guard flags returning from the direction of Springfield. He felt relieved and hoped that the battle was over.

Walking their horses back, the column had broken into clusters of six and seven. They came upon an area where many dead and wounded were lying on the ground—mostly blue uniforms.

Grady noticed a Bluecoat sitting with his back against a tree. Grady stopped. The soldier appeared wounded and there was something familiar about his frame and head, he thought.

Grady dismounted and walked over to the Bluecoat. Glorious victory feelings of a few minutes ago bowed to a mind-set of *shock*. The Bluecoat's face, which was plastered with mud and blood, belonged to his close neighbor and friend, Will Walker.

Grady knelt down beside him. "Will, it's Grady...Grady Hastings!"

Will Walker looked up, his reddened eyes expressing sadness and disbelief.

"Can you ride? I'll take you back to our camp," Grady said anxiously. He got out his canteen. "Ah got water, Will."

Grady helped Will raise his head, and put the container to his lips.

After one sip, Will whispered roughly, his voice waning, "Grady, take my pouch. Ah've some writin' and other things in there. Would you see that my mother gets them?"

"Yes! But, hang on, Will. I'll get you back to our camp....We'll find a doctor."

Grady held his breath while watching Will's body quiver for a few moments, then it became still. Grady closed his eyes and thought of home. Will Walker had died in his arms. Minutes went by, and Grady just sat there, holding his friend, until his sergeant rode up.

"Come on, Hastings. Let's get back to camp. There'll be squads out soon to pick up the wounded...and the dead."

Grady laid down his friend's head. He reached across Will's body, picked up a hat, and placed it over his face. Grady Hastings was deeply saddened. He thought of the Walkers and how they had reacted to Carr's death in the schoolhouse.

Grady followed the sergeant and others toward their camp. He looked up at the sun. It seems like an eternity has passed since we left the camp just before sunup, he thought.

He was relieved when Justin and Jeb rode up, both unscathed from the battle. "Thank ya, Justin," Grady said and raised his hand. "Ya saved me."

Moment's later, Lafe Sunnerland and the two McGregors joined them. Lafe raised his hand and yelled, "ah-yeah!" He leaped out of his saddle, his light, gray eyes sparkling. The top three buttons of his shirt were missing, strands of threads remaining. Light brown chest hairs were sticking through the crevice.

"We whipped them Yanks!" Jeb yelled.

"Drove 'em all the way back to Springfield," added Justin. "They got a real taste of us Missourans."

A sergeant came by. "Good job, boys! That was the finest charge I've ever seen!"

Justin asked excitedly, "Why don't we go after 'em, Sergeant York? We've got 'em on the run."

"Our food and ammo is about gone. Horses are beat. We all need rest. This battle is over."

Grady tempered his celebration and looked back where his friend and neighbor, Will Walker, lay dead. Something is dramatically wrong here, he thought. My best friend lies dead up there by that big tree. He was killed by one of us. Why should that be? What did Will Walker ever do to hurt anyone? He closed his eyes and accepted the bottle, feeling the sharpness of the liquid as it churned in the bottom of his stomach.

THE CONFEDERACY SCORED A VICTORY at Wilson's Creek, even though they didn't break through the union line. Major Sturgis, who had replaced the slain General Lyons, had ordered a retreat back to Springfield about 11:00 a.m. because of lack of ammunition and fatigue.

Bloody Hill, above Wilson's Creek, was the focus of the severest fighting. Skegg's branch, which flowed into Wilson's Creek, was where the Gray Riders and other Confederate Cavalry routed the union forces. Disorganization and lack of proper equipment prevented the Confederates from pursuing the retreating union force.

The victory buoyed the hopes of General Price and the Missouri State Guard. They eventually carried the war all the way to Lexington on the Missouri River not far from Kansas City.

GRADY'S GRAY RIDERS SPENT THE AFTERNOON resting and tending to the wounded. One mile beyond their camp was a surgeon's tent where the wounded were treated.

The dead soldiers were buried next to a grove of trees above the creek. One of the lieutenants, who had ridden up to supervise the burying said, "The Yankees lost over a thousand. We didn't lose nearly that many."

Looking toward Springfield, Grady could see wagons in the distance. The Yankees were picking up their dead and wounded. Grady thought about Will Walker and home. The lifeless body of his friend may be on one of those wagons heading back toward Springfield. He stood and saluted, trying to deal with his feelings.

13

HENRY HASTINGS FLICKED THE REINS. He was transporting Thomas to school and Genevieve to her new position at the General Store. Emma had decided to come along—shopping in mind.

She sure takes care of herself, he thought, when he had helped her into the wagon. Her waistline hasn't changed a bit. He smiled when noticing the yellow, red, and tan plaid gingham house dress. Emma must have left her white apron in the house.

He looked into the field, the gouges and ruts still visible from the overturned Sunnerland wagon. The tension in his stomach had intensified on that day in mid-August. They hadn't received any word from or about the Gray Riders. Each trip that he made to Tarrytown filled his mind with anxiety, expecting to hear dreadful news.

Henry glanced at his wife. Her bonnet was well secured to survive the additional winds created by the speed of the horses. She looked straight ahead, and he wondered if she felt the same as he did.

"Look, a deer!" he heard Thomas exclaim. The animal was coming up from the creek below and veered sharply from the wagon. Henry looked back and saw the deer bound across the road, seeking shelter in the nearby woods. He noticed both Thomas and Genevieve watching the animal from their makeshift seats in the back of the wagon.

Two red-tail hawks landed on the surface of the road ahead. Their beaks were pecking at prey, and they waited until the last moment before fluttering upward and away. Henry saw them settle on a tree branch at the edge of MacTurley's Woods. The wheels of the wagon bumped slightly as they passed over the remains of the prey, a rabbit. Genevieve coughed from a wave of dust that had been sucked back into the wagon.

Henry turned the team into the schoolyard and saw Ebenezer Styles standing on the planked stoop in front of the door. After halting the team, he saw Thomas jump over the side of the wagon, carrying a leather bag.

"Good luck, Gen. Hope your first day goes well," Thomas said.

"Thank ye, Thomas. You behave, now...hear me?"

As Henry guided the horses and wagon back on the road, he noticed Schoolmaster Styles had placed a hand on his son's shoulder. Gotta do some growin' if he's gonna catch up to the schoolmaster's height, ah reckon. He saw Thomas waving to his sister as the schoolmaster guided him through the door.

"Hee-yah," Henry bayed and flipped the reins to send the team into a trot as they entered the town. Tugging on the reins when they pulled up to the General Store, Henry halted the horses. He stepped down to the ground and assisted his daughter off the wagon. Next, he walked around to the other side. "Here ya come, Emma...down safe and sound."

"Thank ye, Henry. I'll be in the store."

Henry got back up onto the wagon and drove the team to the livery.

"Good morning, ladies," said Seth Miller, the owner of the General Store.

"Mr. Miller, I hope that Genevieve works out for you. She's a hard worker and follows instructions well," Emma said firmly, while tapping down her hair on the sides of her head.

"I'm sure she'll do just fine, ah reckon so. Come on back here, Genevieve, and I'll get you started," Seth Miller answered.

"Is this mail day?" Emma asked.

"Yup, sure is. We're expecting Lance—not sure when. He could show up almost any time."

THOMAS HASTINGS stood with the others as the schoolmaster
led the class in their final prayer of the day. After the final "Amen,"
Thomas put on his roughed-up, gray bowler hat and beat all others to
the door. After exiting the school, he began the walk toward the road.
His instructions were to hang around the General Store until
Genevieve ended her work for the day. He expected his father to
come at that time.

Seeing three riders coming down from the mountain, he retraced
his steps and waited by the corner of the school. His father had warned
him about the Erlocks. No doubt, that's them, he thought.

After the riders passed, he ran to the road. Passing the church, he
saw the preacher standing in the yard, walking to-and-fro and reading
from a black book. My new teacher sure resembles the preacher,
Thomas thought while watching a small flock of pigeons fly into the
belfry. He continued walking until he reached the saloon.

The heads of three horses, tied up at the rail in front of the saloon,
turned to watch him as he approached. Thomas was glad that
Constable Muldoon was sitting on a bench across the street. Those
horses likely belong to the Erlocks, he thought. He waved to the
constable, who must have been asleep—hat pulled down over his
eyes and all. The constable didn't return his wave.

Before entering the General Store, he saw a wagon approaching
from the west. As it neared the buildings, Thomas's eyes saw the
high, brown, deeply-creased Stetson. That meant George Walker was
in the middle of all that dust. Since Carr's death, Mr. Walker had not
communicated with the Hastings. Thomas felt sorry for Mr. Walker.
He too was headed for the General Store as he guided the horses over
to the boardwalk.

GENEVIEVE WAS SMILING. She had just made her third sale of
the day when George Walker entered. Instead of her usual gingham
plaid, she wore a blue dress with vertical red lines.

"Hello, Mr. Walker."

"You work here, do ya?" he asked, his facial expression serious.

"Yes, I started just this mornin'."

"You'll do well, Miss. Is Seth here or abouts?"

"He's out back. Mr. Walker, ah...."

"Yes, Genevieve," George asked, his chin elevated a bit, his eyes glaring at her.

"Have ya heard anythin' from Will?"

"Nothin, except...except...."

"Except what, Mr. Walker?"

"He 'en others fought in the big battle at Wilson's Creek...up near Springfield. There were a lot of 'em killed, ah hear. We can only hope and pray that Will wasn't one of 'em. Yar brother, too, Miss."

"Oh, Mr. Walker. I hope and pray, too. Please let me know if you hear anythin', will ya?"

"Ah will, Genevieve....Ah will...." George paused, "ah'll go out back and see if Seth be there."

Genevieve saddened while watching the sorrowful expression deep inside the man's eyes. She became instantly concerned. He is a troubled man, she thought.

"Ma 'am...ma 'am. Ah need four of those corn syrups."

"Sure thing, Mister Walker."

While counting the money, Genevieve heard a yell outside.

"Must be the mail comin," the customer said.

Seth Miller and George Walker had come in from the back room. "Made another sale, Genevieve, ah reckon, huh?"

"Yes, Mr. Miller. Wonder what's all the yellin' for outside?"

"Ah, you go see. Ah'll watch here."

Genevieve darted outside onto the boardwalk. A group of people had gathered in front of the store. She recognized her brother, Thomas, leaning on a long stick.

"What's goin' on, Thomas?" she asked.

"Rider comin'...must be Lance and the mail."

The rider had slowed his horse to a walk as he came abreast of the livery. He had waved to Toby Miller—jerking on the reins to keep his horse from turning into the livery. Why is he so slow?

Genevieve asked herself.

She had been watching her brother, who along with others, anxiously waited for the mail rider to arrive. They had been loitering on the boardwalk in front of the constable's office for the past hour. Why doesn't he hurry up? All these people are anxious to read the news and get their mail.

Finally, Lance pulled up in front of the store. He appeared to be enjoying the power, she thought—should be ashamed of hisself, making us all wait like that. One of his saddlebags was stuffed with newspapers, the other mail. The men, who had been waiting, surrounded him after he dismounted.

"What's the news?" Owen Pritchard, the mayor asked.

Genevieve saw Lance struggle with his balance after attempting to stand—his legs wobbly and unsure. After steadying himself, he unfurled his bandana and wiped his eyes and brow. Genevieve reentered the store, followed by the crowd carrying the mailbags.

"It were at Wilson's Creek!" the dusty rider exclaimed.

"Wilson's Creek, where the sam hill is that?" asked one of the men.

"Says here...out by Springfield....Ne'er heard of that place."

"Ah hear of it," said an old man, stooped over, supported by a cane. "Ah useta pan gold on that creek."

Genevieve had seen that same elderly gentleman go into the Smith's Apartments several times. That must be where he lives, she thought.

The old man continued, "It's a peaceful place. Nary a soul roun', usually."

Her brother had an excited look on his face. He was scanning the front page. "Jaysus, it says here there were over a hundred of the State Guards killed," said Thomas contritely. He added, "Look 'ere, at least a thousand Yankees, including their general."

"Their general!" exclaimed Jubal Haggard. "Who might that be?"

"Says here, it's a man named Lyons," responded Thomas.

"Hear that? Justin has kilt himself a general," Jubal Haggard turned and said to Clarissa, his older sister. His beady, dark eyes were beaming with pride.

Genevieve saw George Walker throw the newspaper on the floor. He appeared disgusted as he stomped out of the General Store. She wanted to go out and talk to him. I don't dare, she thought.

14

JUBAL HAGGARD'S ENTHUSIASM WAS SHOWING. His brother, Justin, had been away for close to two weeks, fighting for the Missouri State Guard. Jubal's father, Ben, had returned from Tarrytown yesterday and brought home news...good news. I've never seen my mother so happy, Jubal thought.

"The State Guard has defeated the Yankees at a creek—somewhere far south," his father proclaimed. Justin's Gray Riders were a part of the guard.

"What do you think of that, Matt?" Jubal asked his five-year-old nephew. "Big, huh?" He patted the chubby, little boy on the head.

Matt and Billy had been visiting the farm since yesterday, when they had arrived by wagon. Ben Haggard had traveled to Stillman Mills and brought Clarissa and her two young sons back with him.

During the return trip, Ben had stopped in Tarrytown and bought a newspaper. Jubal saw the headline of the newspaper. *Guard Routs Yankees*, it blared in large letters. He laid it on the kitchen table and tried reading the story underneath.

Jubal had shared his mother's enthusiasm about Justin, who they hoped would come home safely. "Justin can take care of himself," she had said.

"Hey, Billy, watch it!" Jubal yelled. His nephew, Billy, had pulled the cat's tail again. "She's gonna bite ya if you don't watch out, Billy boy." Billy was three years old. Built like a ball, Jubal thought.

On the other hand, five-year old Matt was as slim as a fence rail. Jubal had agreed to watch the two boys that morning. His sister, Clarissa, had made him an offer that he couldn't refuse—ice cream at Mama's Kitchen.

Jubal's father was approaching, coming on foot from the barns. "Hey, you two rascals! Are ya behavin'?" Jubal heard his father ask jokingly.

He watched his father remove his hat and run his fingers through his curly, black hair. Pa's gonna let me ride Prince before winter sets in, Jubal thought. Next year, he may even let me join the Riders. Jubal's light gray breeches were neatly tucked into a new pair of dark brown boots.

Jubal had gone to school for only four years, but he had learned to read some—a spell of writing, too. But that newspaper print is too small and the words are too long, too, he thought.

Jubal admired his mother's looks. Anna was tall and slim. Her long, black hair splashed over her narrow shoulders. He wondered where she had gotten that olive-looking skin. Clarissa had told him it was because she was *Italian*. Jubal wasn't too sure what that meant. "Across the ocean," his sister had said. "That's where the Romans live...the *Italians*. You look just like 'em, Jube."

Anna Haggard was a sharp dresser too, Jubal thought. She had on a summer dress printed in a paisley pattern of blue and white. She wore a jacket over a three-tiered skirt.

Jubal wondered why his sister Clarissa was so short. Justin is the tallest, for sure, he thought. I'm getting up there, too. Pa and Ma are both tall, and I hope to be, too.

————

THOMAS HAD LEFT THE SCHOOL and was walking toward the General Store. He was expecting to get picked up by his father after school as usual along with his sister, too, when she finished with work. He moved to the side of the road to make way for a wagon coming from the west.

"Woah," he heard Mr. Haggard say. "Hop aboard, Thomas, always room for one more."

"Hello, Mr. Haggard. Hello, Jubal. I see you got the two rascals with ya today," Thomas said.

"Now, Thomas. My sons are not rascals. Not even close to what you and Jubal were at that age," responded Clarissa laughingly.

"Giddy-yap!" yelled Ben, grinning from ear to ear. His thin, black mustache got wider, and appeared to extend close to the gray sideburns, which mushroomed at the jaw line. He flicked the reins and the team continued on into Tarrytown. Ben brought the wagon to a stop next to the General Store and dropped off his passengers—all laughing.

"I'm gonna visit with Genevieve, first," Thomas said. Clarissa, her two boys, and Jubal followed him into the store. After Thomas talked to Genevieve for a few minutes, Clarissa said, "Here, Jube, take this and buy yourself and Thomas an ice cream at Mama's."

The two young men raced to the door. Outside, Thomas looked east. The dust cloud he saw on the road coming from Stillman Mills was larger than usual, he thought.

He ran inside the store. "Mr. Miller, there's a lot of somebody comin' down the road from Stillman Mills."

Seth Miller had been stacking boxes on the upper shelves. He came down the ladder and wiped his brow with his sleeve. "Can you see who 'tis, son?"

"Naw, I can't...too far away, yet."

"Let's go out and have a look," Seth Miller said. "Would you stay here, Genevieve, and take care of those people yonder?"

Thomas led the way out the door. "Do ya see any flag, Jube?"

"No flag," Jubal responded.

"That's good....Means they ain't Yankees," said Seth Miller.

As they approached the livery, Thomas exclaimed. "It's the Riders—the Gray Riders! They're back!"

"Well, ah'll be all," responded Seth. "The Riders come home, ah reckon so."

Thomas and Jubal were overwhelmed with excitement and ran up the boardwalk. They stopped and stared. Thomas noticed that some of the men were wearing uniforms. He let out a series of whoops, "Woo-we...woo-we!"

He recognized the sergeant on one of the two leading horses. Then he glowed with pride and excitement. His brother, Grady, was riding next to the sergeant and was wearing part of a Missouri Guard uniform—the jacket. Only about a dozen wearing 'em, Thomas noticed.

"There's Justin!" Jubal yelled.

Thomas looked at the tall rider. Is that a mustache? he asked himself, his eyes focusing on a semblance of black hairs above Justin's upper lip. Sideburns, too. They were curly, not like his brother's— straight and narrow.

The column pulled up in front of the constable's office after the sergeant had signaled a halt. Thomas and Jubal ran across the road. Justin was still mounted, his tall frame slightly bowed from the long ride. Jubal reached up and grabbed his hand.

Thomas stood on his tiptoes and held his brother tightly around the waist. "Hey there, little brother, why ain't you in school?" asked Grady, his green eyes sparkling.

"School's done for today. Genevieve's working over at the store. Look there! She's in the winder."

Grady waved to his sister, then gladly surrendered his horse to one of Toby Miller's hands. After the column totally dismounted, the horses were led over to the livery.

The sergeant headed into the constable's office, and the rest of them crossed the street in the direction of the saloon.

"Howdy, Thomas...ya, too, Jubal," Jesse Sunnerland said, smiling. He'd been riding near the rear of the column with one of the Youngers.

Jesse rushed to catch up with his brother, Lafe, who had been riding behind the sergeant, alongside Justin Haggard. When he caught up, he gave Lafe a pat on his rounded shoulder. Jesse towered over his brother whose short, wide frame was headed for the saloon door.

"Lafe, glad you made it back," Thomas said while watching Lafe's big boots stomp onto the boardwalk.

"Howdy, Thomas. Gonna jin us for a taste?" Lafe asked laughingly. His voice sounded like the cries of a blue jay.

"My Pa would whip me," Thomas answered, grinning.

Lafe Sunnerland appeared ten years older, Thomas thought. He watched the Riders use their hands to swat the dust off their clothes before entering the saloon.

Thomas looked westward and saw his father approaching with their team and wagon. He ran toward the team, catching up with it near the church. His scratchy bowler had fallen on his back, held around his neck with a rawhide. "Pa, Grady is back! So are all the others—Justin, Lafe, Mitchell, Jesse."

"That's great news, son. Hop aboard and we'll head over to the livery."

As Henry guided the team past the saloon, he said, "Looks like they're all in there."

Thomas was beaming with excitement while sitting next to his father on the buckboard seat.

After turning over the rig to Toby and his workers, they walked toward the saloon. The people remaining on the boardwalk were shaking hands and slapping each other on the back—a big day for Tarrytown.

The inside walls of the Frontier Saloon were bombarded with the sounds of loud voices when Thomas entered with his father. He saw Ben Haggard pass a bottle to Justin. The Rider took a drink and feigned handing it to his brother, Jubal. Thomas smiled when seeing Justin retract the bottle after Jubal anxiously reached for it. Justin's silver eyes glistened, and his mouth opened slightly as he smiled widely.

Thomas and his father pushed their way through the crowd and found Grady and Genevieve. Thomas noticed that his sister was beaming, but Grady's expression showed deep sadness, his emerald green eyes narrowed, his forehead furrowed.

Thomas wondered why his brother wasn't celebrating. Suddenly, he noticed Genevieve had collapsed onto Grady's chest, his brother's arms grasping her around the waist. Thomas looked at his father and saw a puzzled expression on his face. Thomas could hear his sister sobbing.

"What's wrong, Genevieve....Why are you crying?"

"Thomas, Will Walker was killed at Wilson's Creek, fightin' for the Union."

THE LONE RIDER SAT STRAIGHT IN THE SADDLE as he passed through Tarrytown. He nodded to three men, who were sitting on a bench across from the Frontier Saloon. Loud music coming from the saloon reached his ears. William Farnsworth was dressed in black trousers and a brown shirt. He had ridden over from Lexington to visit his sister, Angie Walker.

Because he was currently a member of the Union cavalry, he intended to make his visit as inconspicuous as possible. William did not participate in the Battle of Wilson's Creek. Word had gotten back to his command in Lexington that they had lost the battle. He was wondering if his nephew, Will, had returned home by this time.

He was saddened when passing by the school house. That's where my nephew was killed. William was glad that he wasn't with the cavalry unit that was attacked as it moved past Tarrytown, heading westward. The letter, which he had received from his sister, explained that his brother-in-law, George, blamed the death on the Hastings family.

After turning onto the Walker roadway, he set his steed to a fast trot. Dismounting by the house, William tied his horse to a railing and stepped up onto the porch. He was expecting that George would've heard him coming, and would be looking out the window with a Colt in his fist.

"It's William," George said loudly.

The door opened and his sister came running out to greet him. "Oh, William, you made it...I'm so glad," Angie said, her voice crisp and crackling.

"Sorry about Carr," William said softly and hugged his sister.

"We're tryin' to deal with it...so tragic. I'm worried about Will....He may be home any day. Have you heard how the battle near Springfield turned out?" Angie asked.

"Our side didn't do very good. I hope and pray that Will survived it," William said.

Angie and William stayed up late. They sat next to the wood fire and visited well into the night.

The next morning, shortly after sunrise, William said goodbye to his sister. He steered his horse northward to avoid going through

Tarrytown. After crossing the railroad tracks, he headed straight for Lexington. I'll be there by nightfall, he thought.

15

GRADY HAD RIDDEN UP THE WALKER'S ROADWAY many times in the past, but then to take part in shenanigans with Will. His insides were fluttering with feelings of hardship and dead ends. He realized that his efforts could be rejected. Ah will never forget the attack that Mr. Walker induced on my father at Carr's funeral, he said to himself.

Halfway up the roadway, while heading for the Walker's house, he stopped his horse and gazed out over the valley. The green of summer was gone—replaced by oranges, reds, and yellows. There was a stand of trees down by the creek which he and Will had played in when they were kids. But now play was over—this was war.

He noticed movement in the field next to the road ahead—a red fox scurried across the road and into the field on the other side. It stopped, with nose pointed backward down the length of its body. Sensing further danger, the fox commenced running at full speed, tail bobbing elegantly from side to side.

Grady turned over words and expressions in his mind, *Yar son died bravely....Will did not suffer....He gave me this to give to you.*

There wasn't anyone about when Grady walked his horse to the front porch of the house. Before dismounting, he deeply sucked in a volume of air. Ah gotta try to relax, he thought.

After tying his reins to the rail, he heard the front door open. His heart skipping a beat, he looked up and saw George Walker standing on the porch, the top of his head shining.

The two men stood and stared at each other for what Grady thought was an eternity. The silence was broken when Angie Walker came through the door. She walked over to her husband, grabbed his arm, and snuggled to his side.

"What do ya want, Hastings?" George Walker asked, his voice wavering, and his long, narrow face reddening.

"Ah just got back...back from near Springfield. There was this battle."

"Spit it out, boy....Did you see Will?"

"Yes, sir, ah did."

"Well?"

"Your son...Will...he was killed."

Angie Walker shrieked. She put her arms around her husband's waist, both her knees bent and she began to slip downward. George grabbed her and assisted her to a settee.

George remained standing and looked down at Grady. "Come on up 'ere, son, and tell us what happened."

Grady reached in his saddlebag and brought out a leather pouch. He walked up three steps and stepped onto the porch. "Ah was returning from the battle when ah found 'em. He was wounded, and asked me to give you this." Grady stepped to the settee and handed the pouch to George.

"Did he suffer much?" George asked.

"No, he died in my arms."

Angie laid her face against her husband's chest and began sobbing. "Oh no...." Her voice trailed off.

"Was it at Wilson's Creek?" George asked, one corner of his mouth twitching.

"Yes, sir...'twas there...where the battle was."

"Did he get a proper burial?"

"Yes...in the field...both sides buried their dead...markers were made."

"We appreciate you coming to tell us...to bring us Will's things. Now, would you please leave us alone? We need some time."

"Yes, sir." Grady saluted, turned and made for his horse. He mounted, feeling total remorse as he looked at the Walkers huddled together on the settee.

When he got back on the Tarrytown Road, he turned left. Arriving in town, he tied his horse to the rail in front of the saloon and entered.

GRADY SAW SOME UNFAMILIAR FACES in the Frontier Saloon. After his emotional visit to the Walker's, he was relieved to see Justin Haggard and Lafe Sunnerland sitting at the bar. He walked up behind them and placed an arm on each of their shoulders. "Howdy, boys, ah need a whiskey, bad."

"Grady, you look pale. Where ya been?" Lafe asked.

"Over to the Walker's...had to tell 'em about what happened to Will."

"He was ridin' for the wrong side," said Justin while lifting the bottle to his lips. After wiping his lips with the back of his hand, he handed the bottle to Grady.

"None matter...lot of ours got kilt too," responded Grady. "It could've been me, if that man standing right there hadn't come around, ah reckon." He raised the bottle to his lips.

Grady had noticed a group of ruffians at the other end of the bar. They talked with loud voices, especially the one with the red plaid shirt, suspenders holding up his trousers. A bunch of hillbillies, he thought. They all wore broad-brimmed, low-crowned, dirty hats.

"Who's that bunch over there?" Justin asked.

"Looks like some of 'em Erlocks," Grady answered.

The man with the red plaid shirt had noticed that he was being watched. He sauntered over. "Well...lookee...lookee...we got ourselves some soldier boys he-ah."

"Best you don't bother us, mister," said Justin, his mouth remaining partially open, while lowering a hand to his belt.

"Sorry, boys, glad to 'ere you're a doin' your duty," the man answered sarcastically.

Grady watched the man walk away. Returning his attention to his two friends, he saw that Lafe Sunnerland's face had paled considerably.

"Did you notice the spur? That hillbilly has a broken spur." Lafe reached in his pocket and pulled out a piece of metal. "See this? It came from one of the bullies that kilt my parents."

"How can you be sure?" Justin asked.

"Only one way to find out," answered Lafe in a squeaky voice, his pale, gray eyes glowing with excitement.

"Ah...hold it, would ya, Lafe?" Grady responded. "I'm not up to a fight at the moment. Instead, why don't you go across the street and tell the constable?"

"Ah need the man's boot...match it with this piece."

"Woah, Lafe. Grady is right. There're a whole slew of 'em. Another time would suit us better," Justin said anxiously.

"It's boiling my blood, and ah'll hold up for now, but before we ride out again, ah need to settle," Lafe said. They saw Lady Constance rise from her chair, near the wall by the bar.

"Tell you what. Why don't we get a few more of the boys together and take a look at that boot tomorra'?" Justin.responded, putting a hand on Lafe's shoulder.

Lafe watched Lady Constance walk to the bar and place her hands on the top. He nodded, and she returned to her seat.

16

TWO DAYS LATER, SEVEN OF THE GRAY RIDERS, including Grady, had gathered at the Hastings's farm. "What you all up ta?" Henry Hastings asked Lafe Sunnerland.

Lafe held up the metal piece. "Remember this, Mr. Hastings?...remember on the road?...my parents?"

"Yup, ah do remember....What ya plan to doin'?" '

"I found a match, ah reckon—one of the Erlocks."

"That's a heap a lot of suspectin'. Yar sure it's the one?" Henry asked.

"Gonna find out," Lafe responded, his face saddened.

"Can't stop ya, son....You do what you have ta."

LED BY LAFE SUNNERLAND, the seven riders trotted their horses eastward, toward MacTurley's Woods. Behind Lafe, next in the single column, was Grady. Jesse Sunnerland, Justin Haggard, Mitch, Paul, and James McGregor followed.

Grady noticed the change in the leaves on the first week of September—colors—all sorts of 'em. He was especially attracted to the orange oak leaves.

The column angled southeastward until coming abreast of the woods. Near the corner of the Hastings's property line, Lafe signaled a halt with his arm and dismounted.

The others remained on their horses and gathered around. "Boys, all I want is a look at that boot 'e had on. Ah have to take it off of 'em. Are you all with me? Could be some fightin'." Grady and the others nodded.

When they arrived at a clearing, Lafe signaled a halt. "Their shack is somewhere back there." He pointed. "Grady, what's the layout?"

Grady dismounted. "Lafe, around those cluster of trees, there are two shacks. He pointed. The larger one is where they live…well, sometimes. What I mean is that sometimes they share with the chickens…then, there are the dogs. Don't know how many. The smaller building is a shelter for the chickens."

"How many are there and what guns do they have?" asked Lafe, his light, gray eyes glowing.

"Dunno about the guns. Likes of ah shotgun or two…maybe a couple revolvers. Never 'ave seen any of 'em with a musket," answered Grady. "There're three of 'em boys and the old man. Now, he's one tough, mean character, ah reckon."

"Do ya know what name the red shirt guy has—the one with the broken spur?"

"Naw, Lafe. Ah dunno any of their names," answered Grady. "Goin right up to the door could mean getting' shot, though….Wouldn't advise that. Best we wait for some of 'em to come out."

Grady looked up at the sun. It was partially obstructed by patches of clouds with hazy splotches of cottony white, and was approaching the noon position. "Or, we could leave our horses here and barge in there with guns a ready. As ah remember, the house doesn't have many winders, and the ones that are there, are so dirty....Can't see out of 'em much, anyway."

"Let's find a place to keep the horses. Jesse, would you stay with 'em?"

"Ah, shoot, Lafe. Ah wanna be in on the revenge. It was my mother and father, too, you know," answered Jesse firmly.

"Well, all right. How about you, James McGregor? Would ya stay with the horses?"

"Yup, ah reckon that ah can do it," James responded, his back as straight as an arrow.

The rest of the men dismounted. Lafe took the lead and towed his horse forward. The others followed in single file.

Lafe put up his hand. "We'll leave the horses here with James. Follow me, boys," he said, his voice reducing to a whisper.

The six men led by Lafe stayed partially hidden in the trees until they were abreast of the house. He whispered, "Grady, would you and Justin break in the back door when you hear me, Jesse, and Mitch crash through the front?"

"Gottcha," Grady replied softly.

After Grady heard the crash and shouts, he put his shoulder to the door. It collapsed and dropped to the floor inside. The deafening barks and yelps from the dogs drowned out the screams of the two women. Grady was followed into the room by Justin.

He saw Lafe pointing his revolver at a dog. The roar of the gun firing was excruciating to his ears. Lafe fired three more times, and the dogs lay dead on the floor, smoke partially filling the room.

Grady looked around anxiously, afraid that other Erlocks might be lurking in the house.

"*You there*! Take off ya boots!" Lafe yelled while waving his pistol.

"Whad ya do that fer?" asked the man in the red shirt meekly.

The two women were huddled in the far corner. Jesse had spotted one of the Erlock boys sneaking over there. The women put their hands over faces when Jesse stomped over to them. He reached behind and lifted up a musket. "Look at this, Lafe, Pa's musket."

Lafe looked at his brother, his eyes lowering to the weapon. Poking the red-shirted Erlock in the stomach, he said, "ah want your boots. Take 'em off...right now, or you're dyin' right 'ere, on the floor, in front of your kin!"

Victor Erlock had been sitting on a bench. He stood, his dirty, white undershirt partially covered by suspenders that were holding up a baggy pair of black trousers. He yelled, "You all get the hell otta 'ere! What right ya got?"

Lafe walked over to Victor Erlock. "Ya best advise yar son to take 'em boots off, otherwise yar gonna die, too."

Lafe returned to the red-shirted man, who was still sitting on the floor. Lafe pressed the tip of the gun barrel against his neck and shouted, his voice ending in a high-toned scream, "The right boot! Take it off! Last time that ah'm gonna tell ya!"

The red-shirted Erlock looked up at Lafe, his eyes gleaming with fear. Slowly, between grunts, he pushed on the edges of his right boot until it dropped to the floor.

Lafe put his gun back in the holster and reached into his pocket. Bringing out the metal piece, he picked up the boot and matched the metal to the spur. "It fits...you devil. *You killed my parents!*" Lafe exclaimed.

The Erlock began to shake, globs of sweat breaking out on his forehead. "Naw...naw...'twernt me. My spur git broke years ago."

Lafe grabbed his father's musket out of Jesse's hands. "How about this, you devil? How did this git 'ere?"

"Get all the guns, boys....Toss 'em outside. I'm takin' Mr. Redshirt for a walk!" Lafe ordered, his face contorted with rage.

The four men found one shotgun and four revolvers. Taking the weapons outside, they threw them into a brushy wooded area. "Help me tie those hands," said Lafe as he prodded the red-shirted Erlock against a tree.

After binding the wrists behind Erlock's body, Lafe cupped his hands over his mouth and yelled, "Bring my horse 'ere, James!"

James McGregor came around the grove of trees leading Lafe's horse. Lafe opened a saddlebag and pulled out a rope—one end tied into a noose. He placed the noose around the Erlock's neck.

"Lafe, maybe we should leave this to the constable," said Grady, his voice trembling.

"Do no good," replied Lafe. "His law is weak….He never dare come up here."

The red-shirted man moaned and groaned as Lafe pulled on the rope, partially dragging the man. He threw the other end of the rope over a branch. "Over here, Paul."

Lafe tied the loose end of the rope to his saddle. He mounted and spurred the horse, pulling on the rope and raising the kicking Erlock off the ground. Grady watched as Erlock struggled and eventually stopped moving—his eyes bulged, and his tongue stuck out between two rows of stained teeth.

Lafe backed up his horse, and the body crumpled to the ground. He dismounted and reached into his breast pocket. Plucking out a piece of paper, he pinned it to the dead man's shirt. "Let's go boys," he said.

"What did ya tell 'em in the paper, Lafe?" Justin asked.

"Next time we come, it'll be you, too, Erlock, and your other boys, too."

Lafe rode over to his brother. He leaned over and put an arm around Jesse's shoulder. Grady watched as the two brothers quietly celebrated their revenge.

The seven riders rode silently back to the Hastings's farm. Grady dismounted and watched as the other six nodded their heads and rode off toward Tarrytown Road.

17

THOMAS WAS FINISHED WITH SCHOOL FOR THE DAY. He had been sitting on the bench in front of the General Store waiting for Genevieve to finish her job. He expected his father to show up with the team at any minute.

The horse coming down the road from the west was not his father's. A single horse was pulling a black carriage. Not the usual conveyance on a weekday, he thought. As it got closer, he saw a young man with a young lady beside him—Justin Haggard and Jennifer McGregor.

Thomas waved as they passed, but they ignored him, absorbed with each other obviously, he thought. My sister was devastated when she heard of Will Walker's death. Thomas had not been aware of the romance that had existed between Will and his sister.

She has changed, he thought. Her smiles are short-lived. She goes to bed much earlier than usual. Sometimes she joins father on the bench after supper. She's never done that before. She's hurtin' bad.

The happy, smiling couple's carriage pulled up at the livery. Minutes later, he saw them walking across the road and up the boardwalk.

"Thomas, my blue-eyed friend, is ya keepin' an eye on the road?" Justin asked jokingly.

"Sometimes, I think it needs an eye-on, 'specially today," Thomas answered, chuckling.

The couple walked past and entered the door to Mama's Kitchen.

The next horses that approached from the west belonged to his father. Thomas could tell by the size of the dust cloud. His father pushed the horses sparingly. When Ben Haggard or Orly McGregor's wagon approached, the dust cloud was much denser and higher than the wagon.

Thomas went inside to fetch his sister.

"All set, Genevieve…good job with the Sampson's. That Tully can be a bit of a nuisance," said her employer.

"Good day, Mr. Miller," said Genevieve as she exited with her brother, Thomas.

Genevieve's long braids flapped out of control as she and her brother climbed into the wagon. Henry turned the team, and they headed westward. While passing by the empty churchyard, Thomas noticed two wagons parked at the school. He could see the schoolmaster helping youngsters onto a wagon.

———

GRADY HASTINGS RODE WITH THE TWO SUNNERLANDS
toward Tarrytown and they met his father.

"Where ya headed?" asked Henry.

"Pa, the constable wants to see Lafe and Jesse. Ah'm goin' along.
Be home after a bit."

Grady feared this day would come—when the constable would
want some answers regarding the hanging death of the Erlock.

"We're gonna hafta lie," said Lafe as they pulled up in front of
the constable's office.

"Mebee not, but ah reckon the constable never did have any use
for the Erlocks. He'll probably want us to get rid the rest of 'em,"
Grady said.

The three young men stomped their boots on the planks and
slapped their clothes with their hands to rid the dust. Led by the short
and stocky Lafe, they entered the constable's office.

"Howdy fellers, have a seat," said the constable.

"The reason I asked you two over…that means ya two, Lafe and
Jesse…ah have a complaint 'ere. It seems one of the Erlock boys got
hisself hanged. Know anythin' about that, Lafe?"

"Yeah, that's what ah heard, too, constable. He probably stole a
horse from someone on the other side of the mountain—they killed
him for revenge."

"That's what ah was thinkin', too, Lafe. You folks weren't out
that way, recently, by any chance, were ya?" Constable Muldoon
asked firmly.

Lafe looked out the window. "Hey, looka' here fellers… Justin
and that McGregor lass…Jennifer, that's her name."

"Ah, yeah…they make ah handsome couple," said the constable.
"Lafe, ya didn't answer my question."

"Pa always told us to stay away from them Erlocks. Ain't that
what he said, Jesse?"

"Yup, 'e shuh did. We obeyed 'em him good, too," responded
Jesse, his slim face turning away from the constable.

"That's good advice. Your father had my respect. If ah ever catch up with them that did…ah'll hang 'em….You've got my word," said the constable.

"Thanks for comin' in, boys. Why don't you go across the street and have a whiskey? Ah'll jin ya in a bit."

———

TEN MINUTES LATER, CONSTABLE MULDOON crossed the street and entered Frontier Saloon. He sauntered over to the table where Grady and the Sunnerlands were sitting.

"Gotcha an extra glass," said Lafe as he pulled the plug out of the bottle.

"No thank ye, Lafe. There's a couple of riders just came in from out Stillman Mills way. They're over at the livery—gray uniforms, ah think.

"Have ya selves a good time, boys," said the constable as he exited the saloon.

Minutes later, two uniformed Missouri State Guardsmen entered.

"You Grady Hastings?" one of them asked.

"Yup, that's me. What can I do for ya, Sergeant?"

"Ah've been sent down here by Colonel Riseberg. He says we need you fellas again, for a swing up north. He says you all did such a fantastic job at Wilson's Creek. We'll need you to help us drive the Yankees out of Lexington."

"Uh-wee," responded Lafe Sunnerland.

"We're going to gather just east of Harrisburg. Bunch of us'll be there by weeks end," the Sergeant continued. "Can you pass the word around?"

"Sure can, Sergeant. It's been a little dull roun' 'ere anyhow, lately," responded Grady.

18

JORDON JACKSON CHOPPED THE HEAD OFF A ROOSTER.
He watched the feathered body creating multiple, red, circular
patterns, while sputtering and fluttering on the grass. The other two
chickens, which he had beheaded minutes ago, were lying still.
Digging a hole behind the gray-boarded shed, he buried the pale heads.

Mama's goin to feed us good tonight, he thought. Grabbing the
three remains by the legs, he strode to the house.

"Whatcha doin there, Brittany?" he asked his little sister. Jordon
smiled. He liked her long braids, which mama had spent a good hour
with last night.

"Ah's feedin' Pokey," Brittany responded.

"Pokey? Why call ya cat dat?" he asked.

"He's just dat….Pokey."

Jordon had heard all about the Gray Riders and how they beat up
on the Yankees in Springfield. He had no idea where Springfield
was, but according to what he heard in town, "it was five days of
ridin'."

"Here ya are, Mama," Jordon said as he handed his mother the
three chickens.

"Thank ye, son. Your pa says ya interested in jinin' the Gray
Riders."

"Yes-um, ah is. Pa says I can go talk to Justin Haggard about
jinin' 'em. Supposed to meet 'em in town today."

"I'm real proud of you, son. We're Missourin's, just like everyone
else. I hear Will Walker got himself kilt sidin' with the Yankees. We
want no part of 'em, them Yankees. That's for sure."

After supper, Jordon's father, Priam, helped him saddle the horse.
They owned only one. It, along with the saddle, was a gift from Martin

Kingsley. "Good luck to ye, Jordon," Priam said as Jordon mounted. He looked back toward the house and saw his mother, brothers, Elkanah and Baskhall, and sisters, Elisha and Brittany standing on the porch. He trotted the horse off a bit and stopped. Looking back, he saw the sun glinting on five pair of black hands, which were wavin' and wavin'. Jordon raised his right arm straight up. Saluting his family, he nudged the horse and headed for the road.

———

JUSTIN, GRADY, AND MITCHELL sat at the bar at the Frontier Saloon. They were enjoying a beer in anticipation that they would ride out tomorrow to join the State Guard.

The wide-shouldered Mitchell McGregor asked, "Where do ya suppose we're goin' this time?"

"Mitch, ah hear it's north this time, towards the big river," answered Justin. "Lexington...either of ya two heard of that place?"

"Yup, my brother Thomas has maps. Ah reckon it's not that far from 'ere," Grady said.

"Look who just came in," said Justin.

Grady and Mitchell turned. "Uh-oh, looks like them no-good Erlocks. Ah didn't think they'd ever show their faces roun' here again," Grady said, his eyes narrowing.

"Ah don't think we should do anythin' about that now. Good thing Lafe ain't here," Justin responded.

Justin watched as the two ruffians joined three others sitting at a table on the other side of the room. After turning and facing the bar, he said to the bartender, "Another beer, Brett. How about you boys?"

"Yup, ah'll have another," Grady responded.

"Me, too," said Mitchell as he lifted the brim of his hat and exposed a thick glob of straw-colored hair. His large, blue eyes, set close together, glistened between freckled cheeks.

They heard the door open while they continued to visit and enjoy beers. Hearing the sound of soft footsteps didn't cause them to turn their heads, but loud, boot thumps and a threatening voice did. "Nigra's ain't allowed in here!"

Justin saw one of the Erlocks holding up his palm against Jordon Jackson's chest. "Back otta' here, nigger," the Erlock said menacingly.

Justin looked up into Jordon's eyes. The degradation and embarrassment he observed overwhelmed him. Justin got off his stool, hastened over, and grabbed Erlock's arm. "Ah thought Lafe Sunnerland told you and your kind not to show ya faces roun' 'ere again," Justin said firmly.

"Mind your own business, ya nigga' lovah."

Lady Constance rose from her chair. She signaled her bartender. Brett reached underneath the bar and brought up a shotgun. He looked over at his boss and saw her raise a palm. He lowered the shotgun.

Justin gave Erlock a shove, sending him reeling, his backward momentum stopped by a chair. Erlock got up, his face red with anger, and waved to the others at the other end of the room. Four mean, tough-looking hillbillies rose from their table.

Justin saw what looked like the locomotive of a train coming at him as the three ruffians approached.

Justin landed a fist on the jaw of the first Erlock, again sending him backward onto the chair again. He then grabbed a chair to defend himself against the rest of them.

Grady and Mitchell leaped off their stools. They quickly got between Justin and the approaching Erlocks. Justin cracked the first Erlock for the third time, sending him flying against the wall.

"Whoa, stop right there," said Grady. "Let the boys have it out."

One of the Erlocks stepped forward with a knife in his hand. "Any ah ya wanna take me on?" he asked, his face smiling with a sneer.

Mitch moved quickly and kicked him in the groin with his oversized boot. The Erlock doubled up and was knocked backward by Mitch's massive fist. The hillbilly thudded to the wooden floor.

Grady was sparring with two of the ruffians when Justin grabbed one from behind and spun him around. Grady dodged a fist and landed one of his own into the belly. The attacker doubled up, and Grady licked his bleeding knuckles. Meanwhile, Justin landed a direct hit on the jaw, and the ruffian went down.

One of the Erlocks grabbed a bottle from a table, and smashed it on the edge, creating jagged edges. He lifted his arm and was about to strike Grady in the neck when Jordon's long, dark fingers grabbed the ruffian by the wrist. The Erlock shrieked in pain as Jordon twisted. The cracking sounds of bones breaking drew the eyes of everyone in the room.

Minutes later, both Erlocks and their hillbilly friends were down. One of them attempted to rise. Mitch kicked him in the jaw, sending him sprawling. Justin grabbed one of them under the shoulders. "Open the door, Mitch, ah'm draggin' 'em out."

Mitch's hat had slid off his head and onto his back, held there with a leather cord. He had a bleeding bruise just above his right cheek. Pushing his straw-colored hair away from his eyes, he opened the door.

Jordon Jackson was standing against the wall, watching the Erlocks being dragged away. "Come on over, Jordon. Have a beer with us," Justin said after they finished dumping the last of the Erlocks on the boardwalk. "They're not gonna botha' ya no more."

_____

LED BY MAJOR GENERAL STERLING PRICE, the Missouri State Guard had moved northwestward in early September. Their target was a Union Garrison in Lexington, adjacent to the Missouri River.

General Price had amassed a large number of troops, both cavalry and infantry, along with supply wagons and artillery. By the middle of the month, his cavalry had pushed the outlying Yankee skirmishers back into the town.

The Union garrison at Lexington was led by Col. James A. Mulligan, who had amassed 3,500 men. They had engaged General Price's men south of town on September 13, but were forced back into their fortifications.

Using the Missouri River as a background, Price had bottled up the Union forces in the town. The General decided to wait for supplies wagons and reinforcements before proceeding.

_____

THE BOARDWALK SWARMED WITH SPECTATORS as the cavalry column approached from the west. Thomas beamed with pride watching his brother. Grady rode in the front, his hat pulled low over his eyes. The hat was gray, not his usual hat, thought Thomas. It matched his uniform. Some of the others had uniforms, too. Thomas could plainly see the two stripes on the shoulder of his brother's jacket.

Genevieve joined Thomas on the boardwalk. They stood at the edge of the planks for the best view. Thomas waved with one hand, then with both hands. He knew his brother noticed them even though Grady's head remained stoic—staring straight ahead.

Jennifer McGregor walked over and stood next to Genevieve. Thomas noticed tears in her eyes. Waving frantically, she shouted, "Justin, God be with you!" Justin, who was riding next to Grady, turned and waved.

Thomas wondered what it would be like to have a girlfriend. He had noticed Sarah Kingsley smiling at him in school, her blue streaked, hazel eyes shining. I wonder what that meant. The small patch of reddish freckles on her cheeks, and her fully rounded, red lips made her as cute as anyone that he'd ever seen. He wasn't sure about his feelings for her. Did he dare talk to his mother about them? he wondered.

The sound of a drum across the street excited the crowd. Thomas noticed a person across the road, in front of the constable's office. He was drumming a beat to the sound of the horses' hooves striking the hard-packed road. "Tharoo-Umpta-Toom...Tharoo-Umpta-Toom."

The drumming seemed to straighten the backs of the riders as they rode on. Some day, I'll be doin' that...ridin' with the Gray Riders, Thomas thought. Thomas saw tears in the eyes of Jordon Jackson as he rode by—his back straight and looking tall in the saddle—riding next to Paul McGregor.

19

THE DRAMATIC FAREWELL IN TARRYTOWN hyped the mental state of Grady and the other Gray Riders. As Stillman Mills came into view, Grady could feel a letdown. He already missed his family, and he feared that he would never see Helen Walker again. Gray knew the ride to Harrisburg was going to be tedious.

Passing through Stillman Mills, their morale was reinforced by several people on Main Street. They clapped and cheered as the Riders trotted their horses through town.

"How far is Harrisburg?" Justin asked.

"Gonna take us the rest of the day," answered Grady.

He looked up at the sun and decided it was time to feed and water the horses. Leading the column to a creek, he signaled a halt. The men all dismounted and led their horses down to the creek.

Paul McGregor removed his dark brown hat and got down on his knees to taste the water. "It's good, Grady. Ah'm gonna fill the canteen."

Grady noticed Paul's neatly trimmed, dark brown hair matched his hat. He sure looks different than his brother, Mitch, he thought. The big one looks more like a gorilla

"What's gonna happen at Lexington, Grady?" Paul asked in his Scottish brogue, his blue eyes bulging out from his narrow nose and face.

"The Union has a strong force there—too many, General Price thinks. He wants to drive them out, away from the big river."

"Think we can do it?" Paul asked.

"Yup, we'll be jinin' up with over a thousand of the State Guards boys. We should be able to whip the Bluecoats in a day."

Paul picked up the reins of his horse and walked it back up the slope.

After the horses were fed, Grady signaled, and the column formed and headed north. They stopped for another hour, about mid-afternoon. Grady thought the ride was extraordinarily tedious, and was gladdened when he spotted a church spire towering above the trees in the distance.

When they passed through Harrisburg, Grady was surprised there weren't any people about. They've probably seen enough of the likes of us, he thought.

Outside of Harrisburg, in a farm field east of town, Grady saw a massive spread of white tents. He had never seen as many horses and men in one place before. A group of sentries greeted the Riders a short distance from the camp. The one with the stripes on his shirt pointed and said, "Hello, boys…would ya head toward that cluster o' trees? There's some space for ya over there. The Colonel will be with ya later this evenin'. He'll explain where we're goin' tomorra'."

Grady felt proud that all his riders carried tents and other provisions. They had learned what type of equipment was needed during the tedious ride to and from Wilson's Creek.

Grady signaled, and the Riders dismounted. He removed his pack from back of the saddle and dropped it on the ground. Justin Haggard and Mitch McGregor did the same. They removed their saddles and walked the horses to a grassy area next to the timber.

"Plenty of good grass here," Mitch said, twisting his wide torso back and forth to relieve the stiffness.

Walking back to their equipment, they busied themselves setting up their tents. Grady pushed his saddle to the rear of his tent and prepared his sleeping area.

"Here, have a swig," said Justin, handing Grady a bottle after they got a fire going.

"What would this army do without ya?" Grady asked laughingly.

"Come ova' 'ere, Lafe. Got some reinforcement," Justin said, his silver-gray eyes shining.

Grady noticed that Lafe Sunnerland had changed after hanging one of the Erlocks. He wondered if Lafe was feeling some guilt. But, the constable had said, "*If ah get my hands on them who kilt the*

Sunnerland's, ah'll hang 'em all."

Should be no different if the constable did the hangin' or we did, ah reckon. Grady made a mental note to remember to talk to Lafe when he had a more opportune situation. There will likely be plenty of time in the days ahead, he thought.

After the first bottle was empty, Mitch McGregor threw it back over his head. He reached in his saddlebag and fetched another. "There's more where that came from, boys," he drawled in his Scottish brogue. Twisting the cover off the new bottle, he lifted it to his lips and swallowed, his Adam's apple bobbing two times.

"Here ya go, Grady," Mitch said and giggled.

GRADY AWAKENED BEFORE SUNRISE AND could hear someone stirring. Closing his eyes, he rolled over and tightened the blanket around himself. His courage and adventurous attitude had abandoned him for the moment. Grady's thoughts were fearful of what could happen during the upcoming day. He visualized Will Walker sitting against the tree—so much blood.

He had tried to sleep, but couldn't—probably cuz of the headache, he thought. Later, he was jolted by a loud penetrating voice, "Everyone up...come on boys, we've got work to do!"

Grady struggled out of his tent. "Can't handle the whiskey, Hastings?" asked Paul McGregor jokingly.

THE COLUMN STRETCHED OUT OVER A MILE LONG with the Gray Riders approximately in the middle. They rode four abreast instead of the usual two. Mitch and Jordon had joined up with Grady and Justin. They had been in the saddle most of the morning when the Colonel ahead signaled a halt.

"Who's that?" asked Justin.

"Dunno, but it sure looks like a general," responded Lafe Sunnerland.

One of the Younger boys said, "That's General Price."
Grady had heard of General Price. "Jaysus, he sure looks fresh."
Grady watched with awe and amazement as General Price rode over toward them. The general edged his horse over to Jordon Jackson. "Welcome, Missourins," the general said to Jordon. His head turned toward the group. "I hear ya all one of my best fightin' units. We gotta big job ahead of us over there by the big river. I'm countin' on you boys to drive out the Yankees and save Missoura."

After the general had moved on, a colonel rode over. "Follow me," he said.

They rode for close to an hour with the Colonel leading their column to a small grove of trees. Grady could see buildings scattered on a hillside to the east. That has to be Lexington, he said to himself.

After the colonel halted the column, he rode back along its length. "See those buildings? That's the outskirts of Lexington. Beyond those buildings are union fortifications that command the high ground above the big river.

"Follow me…we're heading down to the bottom."

The column followed the colonel until they could see the water. Down below, Grady could see many men removing bales of hemp from a large building. They were dragging the bales down toward the water and pushing them in. Another group of workers were dragging the bales out of the river and rolling them partially up a grassy slope. The men spread the bales out along the entire width of the clearing.

"Have your men dismount here. Leave four with the horses. Take yar muskets and advance up the hill toward them bales," the colonel said.

Grady felt reluctant to leave his horse behind. He felt naked on foot, but he obeyed the command and led his Riders on foot up the hill toward the bales. The sound of distant gunfire shattered the stillness and sent waves of fear into the pit of Grady's stomach. When they reached the bales, Grady heard horses approaching. He looked back and saw the colonel again.

"Corporal, have all your men get behind them bales, four behind each. Stay behind them and push them upward toward the top of the hill. Those that are pushing, have the man behind you carry your musket. Be sure to keep the bales between you and the windows in that brick building up on the hill. They're Bluecoats with muskets in 'ere."

Grady watched as puffs of smoke partially obstructed their view of the brick building. He looked along his flanks and estimated about eighty men behind the bales. Grady had heard that the Missouri Guard had provided over ten thousand men for this engagement.

The intensity of musket fire had increased dramatically. Then he saw clusters of men coming down the hill from the direction of the building, some of them falling.

"Follow me!" the colonel yelled and began advancing up the hill on foot, all the while encouraging teams of men to push bales in front of them.

Grady teamed up with Justin and two other soldiers. They handed their muskets to the men behind them, and began pushing one of the wet bales up the hill. He heard a bullet whiz close overhead. Next, he felt one hit the bale. "Uh-wee!" he yelled and looked at Justin.

Lots of leverage there, Grady thought, while watching Justin's long body, boots anchored in the turf, right shoulder wedged against the hemp. Ah reckon that he could push that bale up that hill by himself. For heaven's sake, don't stand, Justin, you'll stick out like a giraffe.

They both ducked as artillery shells screamed over their heads. His body went numb as he felt the impact of a shell hit the hemp. "Hey, Justin, this is great! The bales work!"

His Riders were spread out in a row as they advanced against the Yankee line. Grady raised his arm. He could see the Bluecoats were close. They were kneeling in the brush and firing. After making sure the bales were in a line, he formed his troops into two rows and gave the order to fire. As the first row reloaded, the second row fired.

"Advance ten strides!" he yelled and they put their shoulders behind the hemp and pushed it up a little further. They went through the firing routine again. After repeating the manuever four more times, he saw some of the Bluecoats scurrying away. Looking back down the hill, he saw two of his Riders lying on the ground. One of them lie still, and the other attempted to crawl down the hill.

He saw Mitch McGregor break rank and run toward the crawling Rider. "Justin, hold here, would you? Ah'm going to see what Mitch is up to."

Grady heard the yell. He arrived to see Mitch down on his knees with his hands wrapped around his brother's leg.

"Grady, Paul's hit in the leg. We gotta stop the bleedin'," Mitch said in a panic.

"Mitch, soon as we can, we'll get a wagon."

Dashing over to the other Rider lying in the grass, he knelt. "My God, it's Jordon," he muttered. Turning him over, he saw an ugly, dark, red wound in the middle of Jordon's chest. He felt an instant, sharp pain in his stomach. Holding his breath, Grady retched and gasped to fill his lungs with air. Gently grabbing Jordon's hand, he feared the worst. "Oh no, he's dead! We've lost Jordon!" Grady exclaimed and looked around, feeling his heart falling into his stomach. Placing Jordon's hand on his bloody chest, Grady grieved.

He thought about Paul McGregor—nothing more ah can do for poor Jordon. Mitch and Paul need a wagon. He remembered the tented field hospital at base camp about two miles in the distance.

Grady yelled, "Mitch, if we can git him back down the hill and back to our horses, we'll find some rope...tie off his leg."

Mitch had picked up his brother in his arms and began trudging down the hill, bullets screaming overhead. Grady watched with amazement and admiration as Mitch reached the bottom safely and lay his brother down by a tree.

Looking up the hill, Grady noticed that the Riders had advanced a bit further, and were continuing to use the bales as a shield. A cannon ball hit a bale and exploded. Grady realized at that moment why the bales had been soaked in the river.

Grady ran up the hill to rejoin his Riders. While panting and gasping for air, the sound of galloping horses sent feelings of fear up Grady's spine. He felt immensely relieved when he turned his head and saw a number of Missouri Guard cavalry troops galloping up the hill toward him.

"*Charge! Charge!*" an officer screamed.

Grady fixed his bayonet and made sure his musket was loaded. He commanded the Riders to leave the bales and charge up the hill. To his delight, the Bluecoats had left their positions and were disappearing over the crest.

He and the other Riders neared the top of the hill when they heard the clashing of metal and pistol fire. The riders had caught up with the enemy. He hoped the battle had ended for the Gray Riders. No way could the Bluecoats survive that charge, he said to himself.

After reaching the summit of the hill, Grady watched the retreating Bluecoats scatter in all directions, many of them falling. He signaled his Riders to halt—they needed a rest. Most of them were gasping for air. After Grady and the others dropped to the ground, the colonel rode over.

"Hastings, it's all over up 'ere. Take your boys back down the hill and have a rest. You've done a great job. There's talk of the entire Union garrison surrenderin'," the colonel said, smiling.

On his way down the hill, Grady picked up Mitch's musket and hurried to the bottom. He saw Mitch kneeling by his brother.

Looking up, Grady could see some of the Riders who were on their way down stop to pick up the body of Jordon Jackson. Grady felt remorse for the fallen Rider, Jordon Jackson, and his family.

At the bottom, Mitch had his shirt off and was tearing it into strips. He got out his knife and cut away his brother's pant leg. Meticulously, he tied a tourniquet above the wound. Grady noticed the extraordinary look of dedication and determination in Mitch's blue eyes.

"Grady, would you watch 'em? Ah'm gonna find me a wagon," Mitch said, his freckles reddened.

Paul McGregor, barely conscious, emitted garbled groans. Grady picked up his hand—he felt no pulse. "Hang in there', Paul. You're gonna be fine. Mitch's bringin' up a wagon real soon."

Looking up, Grady was deeply saddened watching the boys vigilantly carrying Jordon's remains down the hill. They carried the body near to where Paul was lying, and set it down by a tree.

Grady thought about his visit to the Walker's. Who's goin' over to the Jackson's? Probably me, ah reckon.

Justin came over. He stared at Jordon's body, putting a hand to his own forehead. "Damn, how did that ball ever get through the bale?"

"Dunno...Jordon must 'ave stood or somethin'," answered Grady, his voice fading.

Justin asked, "How's Paul doin'?"

"He's alive...gotta get him to the field hospital. Mitch rode out to find a wagon. Watch 'em, would ya? Ah got the heaves....Jordon gettin' shot in the chest like that...shirt soaked with blood."

Grady heard Mitch's shout, "Hah! Yah!" as a galloping pair of horses pulling a wagon approached. Mitch applied a whip as the wagon rumbled toward where his brother lie. He braked the team next to a bale of hemp. Jumping off the wagon, he took a knife and cut the twines. Grabbing chunks of hemp, he tossed them onto the wagon bed.

Jumping back onto the seat, he yelled again, "Hah! Yah!" Sparing no time, he wheeled the wagon next his brother and jerked the reins taut.

"Steady now," Grady said as he and Justin lifted Paul onto the wagon. They jumped on and helped Mitch guide him onto the bed of hemp.

"Grady, ah'm takin' Paul to the field hospital that we saw yesterday."

"Just a second...ah'll put Jordon up there, too," Grady said.

"Hurry, Grady, hurry!"

"Hah! Yah!" Mitchell shouted, heavily flicking the reins.

"God speed, Mitch," Grady said, his face expressing deep concern.

20

THE WAGON ROCKED MENACINGLY FROM SIDE TO SIDE as the wheels engaged an endless array of pocket gopher mounds. Mitch applied the whip to the team constantly and glanced at his brother every chance he had. Finally, he directed the horses and wagon off the field onto a smoother roadway.

Grady felt the pain that he knew his neighbor, Paul McGregor, experienced while bouncing around in the middle of scattering hemp fibers. Grady's horse was maintaining a course, staying next to the wagon. He worried about the smoke coming from one of the rear wheels. As it intensified, Grady prayed that the wheel wouldn't burst into flames.

He knew that bringing the smoke to Mitch's attention would not change anything. Time was of essence, and the big tent came into sight less than a mile ahead.

Justin Haggard rode up alongside. "How's he doin', Grady?"

"No way o' knowin', Justin, but ah've seen his arms move more than once....He's still alive."

Grady's hope increased as the wagon rounded a curve and the tent loomed ahead. Mitch's wagon had only a short distance left, and he continued to apply the whip. Grady noticed the fearful and desperate look in the horse's eyes. The last time that he had witnessed a horse look like that, it had dropped dead within a minute.

Grady's serious concerns about the smoking wagon wheel and the horses disappeared as Mitch brought them to a stop in front of the entrance to the medical tent. Some of the Riders were already there to help remove Paul from the wagon, if needed.

The groaning sounds that he heard coming from Paul McGregor disturbed him, but were welcome as the boys gently removed him from the wagon. Paul had survived the rough ride.

Grady glanced back, and he could see the last of the sun dropping behind the hills to the west as Paul was gently lowered onto a gurney. Grady placed his hand on Paul's head....It felt warm. He helped Justin and Mitch carry Paul through the opening.

What he saw in the tent was grotesque, at the least, Grady thought. There were men lying all over the floor. The gowns that the doctors and assistants wore appeared splattered with blood. Groans coming from all over the floor were minor, compared to the screams, which came from patients on the table.

"We'll be outside, Mitch," Grady said contritely.

Grady followed Justin out where long, narrow, spectacularly-colored clouds hung just over the horizon. They stood outside the tent and watched the sky, patiently waiting for news from Mitch.

An hour went by, and Grady peeked into the tent. He saw Mitch cradling his brother. Then one of the aides had gone over and said loudly, "You...you're next." Grady watched the aide and Mitch place Paul on a blood-splattered table. Grady put his hand over his mouth and nose to shield them from the stench coming from the tent.

When the screaming started, he stepped out and accepted a bottle from Justin. "Thanks, Justin. Let's hang around until Paul is done. I'm afraid that he's gonna lose that leg."

"Oh, God, Grady, what are we gonna do with Jordon's body?"

"Ah dang, ah forgot all about 'em. He's still in the wagon. Soon as we find out what's gonna happen to Paul, we'll haul him down to where we're gonna camp, down by the creek. We'll get hold of a shovel and give him a decent burial there, ah reckon."

"Why don't you ride down there and get Lafe and Jesse? I'll stay here and wait....Oh yeah, bring some whiskey."

Justin mounted his horse and rode off toward the creek. Grady sat down against the outside wall of the tent and closed his eyes.

Minutes later, Justin returned with Lafe and Jesse. They dismounted and Lafe asked, "How's it goin' in there, Grady?"

"Dunno, Lafe. Paul's been on the table for a long..." Grady was interrupted by a long, terrifying scream—He gasped and held his breath.

"Here, Grady, better have some of this," said Jesse, his slim frame leaning lightly against the canvas.

Grady lifted the bottle to his lips. "Here's to you, Paul. Ah pray that you make it." He took a long swig from the bottle and sat down.

Passing the bottle to Lafe, Grady watched him sit down and take several swallows.

Jesse said, "Save some for me, Lafe."

The screaming stopped, and they all looked at each other, Lafe's light gray eyes narrowing.

"Suppose he died?" asked a stern-faced Justin.

The moon had cleared the tree line to the east and lit up the white tents down by the creek. The three Riders looked up anxiously as Mitch emerged from the tent. The big Scotsman filled the lighted opening for a moment before advancing. They silently watched as he walked toward them, his chin down.

Mitchell took off his hat and dropped it to the ground. His red sideburns merged with a bushy mustache and neatly trimmed beard. He crouched. "Give me a shot of that," he said.

Mitchell drew in a considerable volume of whiskey and sat. "I talked the doctor into removing only the lower part of the leg. The bloody butcher wanted to take all of it."

"Tomorra', ah'm takin' Paul home. 'Cordin' to what ah 'ear, the battle in Lexington is ovah. The Unions have surrendered. Let's all head for the creek and set up camp. Ah'm starved."

During the night, Grady heard Mitchell get up several times. He could hear the grating footsteps disappear in the direction of the medical tent. Mitch's vigilance continued until daylight. No one in the camp, except for Mitch, stirred that morning. The Riders were exhausted from the travel and battle.

As the sun's bright rim appeared at the top of the tree line, Grady heard horses' hooves approaching. Colonel Riseberg, accompanied by Lieutenant Bigwood, reined their horses to a halt. "Boys, you did a fine job yesterday. Ya gave the Yankees no choice but to surrender," Colonel Riseberg proudly said as he saluted.

Mitch stood and drawled in his Scottish brogue, "Colonel, my brother is in that tent over there. He's lost a leg. Ah wanna take him home today."

"Ya certainly can....All ya from Tarrytown way can go home for now. The fightin' is over for the time being—hopefully forever," responded Colonel Riseberg.

21

SARAH KINGSLEY STUBBORNLY ABSORBED the roughness of the carriage ride. She looked forward to Sunday—seeing Thomas Hastings in church had warmed her heart the previous Sunday—dressed so smartly, he was, she thought. She especially admired his white collar folded down over a red cravat tied into a bow—his dark gray schoolboy suit was a dream.

Her father, Martin, turned the horse onto the road. It was Sunday again, early October, and they were heading toward Tarrytown.

Sarah had heard her mother talking to her father as they were walking out to the carriage from the house. Sarah shared her mother's sad feelings that Abel was not attending church. She saw great sadness in his deep-set hazel eyes. I think his already narrow face has thinned even more since the Sunnerlands got killed, she said to herself.

Abel had chosen not to take sides. Because of a family decision, Abel seldom appeared in Tarrytown, and limited his outings only to the Kingsley property.

Sarah knew that Abel silently favored the Gray Riders. He had told her that. However, Sarah also respected her father and it was his wish—demand—that they remain neutral.

Sarah admired her father in other ways. He was decent to her mother, Beth, and he's also very supportive of me, she thought. I liked the way he took an interest in what I was learning in school. After a school day ends, I feel proud that my father is always there, waiting for me. He helps me up into the carriage, and tightens his hands on my waist on the way up.

The streaky gray markings in his beard and hair are very attractive, she thought. They were perhaps a little too shaggy, but she liked them that way. Somehow the dark eyebrows didn't belong—shaggy as they were, and almost black. The two vertical creases that occasionally formed on the sides of his mouth were certainly a sign that he was extra concerned. There had been more creases added after the Sunnerlands were killed.

The day that Carr Walker was shot and killed, she had been down on the floor behind the teacher's desk. The breaking of the windows had been terrifying. Her feelings for the two Union soldiers that took refuge in the school were disdainful. Imagine, she thought, a school full of children and the Bluecoats hid in the same room—cowards they were.

Her mother pointed toward the school as they passed, possibly at the bald eagle that soared over the grounds. Rabbits beware, she thought. On more than one occasion, Sarah had seen one of the furry little animals plucked from the ground by the huge predator.

She had always liked her mother's name, "Beth." It's a storybook name, she thought. I like the way she shows me how to dress. Hmm, our bonnets are both blue this morning. My mother's skin is much fairer than my father's leathery and wrinkled skin. Her speckled, blue, round eyes match her bonnet.

As her father slowed the horse, Sarah looked for signs of the Hastings's buggy in the churchyard—there it was. Thomas was walking toward the church with his sister, Genevieve. Oh, he looks handsome this morning, she thought. He's wearing that satin waist coat. I really like that. Except for the schoolmaster, he is the tallest in school.

Acorns crackled as the Kingsley carriage wheels approached a hitching rail tucked in between three trees. The leaves are much more orange than last Sunday, she thought.

Sarah waited until her father helped Mother down. "Watch that board, it's got a split in it," her father said as he helped Sarah to the ground.

The three were walking toward the door of the church when another carriage turned off the road. "Well, ah'll be dog-gone!" her father exclaimed. "That's George Walker. It's been a long time."

———

THOMAS WATCHED PANSY GOODEN SWAY her body and undulate her head as she worked the keys of the organ. He turned his head and smiled when he saw Sarah Kingsley wiggle and slide toward her parents, who had just sat down. He wasn't sure why he couldn't sing, but maybe it had something to do with what his previous teacher, Miss Stoner, had said. "Awful, Thomas, plain and simple."

Everyone is standing and singing *Nearer My God To Thee*...everyone except me, he thought. Even though he kept his head straight ahead (well, just a little over to one side), he was in a good position to watch Sarah Kingsley.

The singing ended, and he watched Pansy flip a page. That meant there's going to be more, and soon, he thought. Looking up, he saw the preacher approach the pulpit. Sure resembles schoolmaster Styles. Well, not exactly the looks, but the stance—and the black suit.

Thomas thought about his brother. The last news they had heard was that the Gray Riders were in a battle near Lexington. He knew where that was—north, by the big river. Missouri—same name as my state. Must be our river, he said to himself.

It wasn't official, but rumors had it that the Missouri Guard had won a big victory. "Drove 'em clean up agin' the big river," he heard a shaggy man say the other day while waiting on the boardwalk. The man had just come out of the saloon and walked with difficulty. Thomas wasn't sure his word was worth much. Better than bad news, he thought.

He felt his heart surge. He snuck a look at Sarah and caught her doing the same. Their eyes locked for a moment. It's a good thing she looked away, or my heart wouldn't have started up again, he thought. The sermon droned on. Jaysus, I didn't even know some of those sins existed.

Thomas's daydream was jolted by a thumping sound on the pulpit. He became alert and saw Pastor Wilson raise his arm with his long, bony fingers extended. Suddenly, the pastor's arm came down and his palm thumped against the surface, almost knocking the black book to the floor.

A sliver of light across the Pastor's black suit attracted Thomas's attention. He looked around—People were stirring in the pews and heads were turning to the rear. The Pastor stopped talking and stared at the door.

Thomas stood and turned. Ah-ha, the door opened. He was stunned by the figure of a massive man filling the open doorway. Thomas couldn't make out who it was. Legs were spread, arms were up against both sides of the doorframe. The man was wearing a large hat that almost reached the top of the door frame.

"Doc! Are you here? We need ya, right now!" The man in the doorway exclaimed.

Thomas wasn't the only person who stood. Everyone in the room did. The preacher stood back of the pulpit, his mouth agape.

Thomas watched as Doc Wells, on the other side of the room, was jolted from his snooze by the person next to him. The doctor stood and brushed his clothes with his hands. He struggled past three sets of knees, bracing himself, while sliding his hand along the top of the pew in front. Doc's round face, clear of whiskers except for a graying mustache, appeared serious as he made his way down the side aisle. He ran a hand through his disheveled hair as he reached the door.

Thomas saw him put his hat on and go with the man in the doorway. The door closed with a loud thud. McGregor...Mitchell McGregor—that's who was in the doorway, Thomas thought. I recognized the voice.

Preacher Wilson had been talking sin, and his mouth remained agape during the interruption. Never noticed that scar before, Thomas thought. He stared at the preacher's left cheek. The light coming from the open door had lit it up.

After the door closed, sporadic murmurs spread quickly until the entire congregation engaged in anxious conversation. Thomas looked at the preacher. The scar had disappeared, but his eyes appeared frantic. He's all done preachin' for today, Thomas thought. He was seriously concerned why Mitchell McGregor had come for the doctor.

Preacher Wilson signaled the organist and the din of voices trailed off as organ music filled the room. Using a voice as loud as he could muster, the preacher began a song. The door opened again, and people began to file out.

Thomas grabbed Genevieve's hand and they edged their way to the door. Her palm felt slippery from the dampness caused by her worry about Grady, he thought. Squeezing by the mayor, he and Genevieve dashed out onto the churchyard. Looking west, Thomas saw the column of Gray Riders that had just passed. Anxiously, he waited for his parents, knowing they would want to know why the doctor was called.

22

MARTIN KINGSLEY AND HENRY HASTINGS ENTERED the church to talk to Pastor Zack Wilson.

"No...cannot do what you request...not Christian," the preacher said, rubbing his fingers tightly against his cheeks.

"Preacher Wilson, Jordon Jackson died fighting for us, for Missoura. If Christianity cannot accept him, then ah don't wanna be a Christian," Henry said, his jaw set firmly.

Martin looked the preacher right in the eye. "Preacher, we've lost three of our youngins' so far, and there likely will be more lost before the Federal intrusion is ovah."

Martin's leathery skin reddened. "Either you have a service for Jordon Jackson or ah'll see to it that we get someone who will."

The preacher stuttered and stammered, pacing back and forth, his coat tails whipping in the wind. "Ah shall, but only under one condition."

"What's that?" asked Hastings.

"Ah don't lead the procession to the cemetery."

Martin Kingsley stared at the preacher, his eyes glaring. Noticing that the preacher was perspiring he said, "Come on, Hastings, let's take our leave before ah strike this man."

He gave the brim of his hat a full tug and led Hastings out the door.

———

TWO DAYS LATER, PEOPLE FILTERED INTO THE CHURCH. Thomas and his family sat in their usual pew. Ahead of them were the Kingsleys. The pew behind was occupied by the Haggards.

Thomas strained his neck to see who was coming in the door. As he hoped, it was Mr. McGregor, his daughter, Jennifer, and her younger brother, James. As they took a pew behind the Haggards, members of the Gray Riders entered. They filled up the last three pews on the other side.

Noticeably missing was the organist Pansy Gooden. Thomas heard the rustle of many feet coming from the door. He turned. The casket of Jordon Jackson was perched on the shoulders of six black men. They were moving slowly up the aisle. He felt tears build as all the Riders stood.

Following the casket and pallbearers, the tightly grouped members of the Jackson family walked with their heads bowed. Joshua extended his arm to insure adequate space remained between his people and the mourning family ahead. Next in line came the Mortons. Four of the girls clacked sticks to the cadence of the pallbearer's steps. When they reached the front, the clacking stopped.

The black people filed into the pews on the opposite side. After the last person was seated, it became so quiet that Thomas could hear himself breathing. Moments later, one of the young girls walked to the front of the casket. She closed her eyes and broke out in song. It was the most beautiful voice that Thomas had ever heard.

Preacher Wilson was missing that day. There was no sermon, only song. Thomas heard the beautiful voices range from deep base to high tenors. He was deeply moved by the sadness of the music. When it ended, all the black people stood and bowed their heads.

Humming sounds filled the room after the pallbearers had lifted the casket onto their shoulders and began the slow walk toward the door. After they exited, they continued upward toward the cemetery.

Thomas and the rest of the mourners followed. He was absolutely mesmerized by the magnificent voices that continued to chant as the coffin continued up the hill toward the white cross. There was no wagon. There was no preacher. The crowd stood in absolute silence as a gray uniformed bugler penetrated the air with a song that Thomas had never heard before. The Gray Riders stood off to one side as the coffin was lowered into the grave.

During the return walk down the hill, Thomas overheard Martin Kingsley look at Henry and say, "ah'm sendin' four good ridin' steeds over to the Jackson's tomorra'. Ah've got the feelin' that we're goin to need their help....Ah 'eard in Tarrytown the other day that the redlegs 're gonna find us soon. We all need to stick together."

Henry Hastings nodded.

———

THE WHITE WOODEN CROSS IN THE MIDDLE OF THE CEMETERY appeared larger with each step as Thomas and his sister walked up the hill. They were in a procession directly behind their parents.

A week had passed since the Gray Riders had returned. Doctor Muldoon had worked on Paul McGregor valiantly, but lost the fight to a fever that persisted and worsened with each passing day. His fever had reached one hundred and eight degrees the previous evening, and the doctor knew that it would be the last for young McGregor.

A group of mounted Riders gathered on the small hill short of the woods. Their steeds grazed while they silently sat bareheaded in their saddles.

Mitch McGregor walked next to his father, a few spaces behind the undertaker's wagon. Thomas noticed that the younger Scotsman had his hair combed. It was parted up the middle and swept over his ears. Thomas saddened even more when he noticed the tears streaming down Jennifer's face. She walked next to her straight-backed brother, James. The color of his hair appeared the same as Mitch's, but cut shorter, and always neater.

Undertaker Phillips looked straight ahead, his tall, stovepipe hat bobbing from the effects of the uneven terrain.

Thomas held his sister's hand during the preacher's prayers. After Pastor Wilson finished, they turned to go down the hill. Thomas noticed that someone had placed a small cross at the head of Jordon Jackson's grave.

After the burial on the hill, some of the attendees gathered on the boardwalk in front of the hotel. Thomas visited with some of his school friends.

He heard a loud, crisp voice say, "Peoples, ah want you ta listen to what ah have to say." Thomas stared at George Walker standing on a box, pulling on the brim of his tall, dark brown, deep-creased hat. "Ah want to apologize to Henry Hastings and his family for what ah said at Carr's funeral. What ah said, ah didn't mean, and ah was wrong. Ah can see now that the Gray Riders are protecting this town, our land, and farms. They are all Missouran's, just like we are. We need to stay together, to resist the forces that mean us harm."

Shouts and cheers erupted. Hands were elevated to grasp those of the speaker. Thomas watched as his father and George Walker embraced. He saw Grady shake Mr. Walker's hand. He also saw Grady hugging Helen Walker. That one lasted longer than the others, Thomas thought.

23

ORLY MCGREGOR DISMOUNTED. He left his horse to wander and slowly walked to his son Paul's gravesite. The new stone had been delivered from Harrisonville the past week. He stared at the markings. *Paul McGregor, 1844 – 1861, Missouri State Guard.* The slim oak pole that supported a small flag already showed some gray streaks. It was blue with an arc of two rows of small, white stars above an insignia supported by two bears.

He turned his attention to the adjoining stone. It read: *Pricilla McGregor, 1813 – 1854, Rest in Peace.* He looked up at the heavens with his large, blue eyes. It's been seven years, he thought. Some of her clothes were still neatly tucked away in a chest in his bedroom. Orly could not part with some of the physical remnants of the woman that he had loved so much.

The conflict between states, which had despairingly taken the life of his son, had taken a furlough because of winter. He looked at the frost-covered grass. Soon, there would be snow, he thought. Mitchell and the other Gray Riders were all at their homes, but they maintained vigilance. Rumors and news in Tarrytown had it that a group of jayhawkers were killing and plundering in communities not very far away.

Jennifer, his daughter, had just reached the age of nineteen. She would soon be wed to Justin Haggard, he hoped. Even though Ben Haggard continued to own slaves, he supported their release. Ah think he would support 'em if they decided to become free.

Orly was certain that the conflict would become active again when spring came. His third son, James, would be eighteen and most certainly would take Paul's place with the Riders. He was saddened, thinking of the possibility of losing two more sons to the war. His friend, George Walker, had already lost both his sons.

He thought about the schoolhouse and how he had helped carry Carr Walker to the wagon. Our war began on that day, he thought. Nothing was ever the same after the schoolhouse skirmish. He mounted his horse and raised his right arm—his way of saluting the departed.

As he rode down Tarrytown Road, he passed the place where the Sunnerlands were murdered. That was another black day in our history, he thought. It had nothing to do with the war, though. Orly believed that his son, Mitchell, was part of the group that had hung one of the Erlocks.

After he read the story in Tarrytown about John Sunnerland's musket found in the Erlock house, his doubts about who killed the Sunnerlands vanished. They didn't need any more proof than that, he thought. He worried that some of the Erlocks were still about. Should a' hung 'eɱ all, he said to himself.

Glancing to his right, he saw a herd of Angus inside the Kingsley fence, just beyond their buildings. Martin sure has a knack for building them fences, he thought. Must have taken a lot of trees.

His son, Abel, is a fine young man. Orly had heard in the Frontier Saloon that Abel was about to join up with the Riders. He thought Martin's not going to like that. He wants to stay totally neutral.

After passing by MacTurley's Woods, he saw the Hastings's farm. Splendid buildings, he thought. Henry is a good farmer. He's got one of the finest Hereford herds around these parts.

Orly was sure that Henry and Emma were proud because their son, Grady, had been promoted to corporal in the Missouri State Guard.

Crossing the bridge over Bear Creek, he rode on between the Sunnerland land to the south and Haggard's farm to the north. He noticed Mitchell, James and a couple of the hired hands herding some of the sheep. Hundred and eighty was the last count that he had heard. The wolves that came down from Bear Mountain had taken eight of the young stock during the summer. Need more and better sheep dogs, he thought.

JAMES MCGREGOR DUG HIS SPURS INTO HIS HORSE. He had been helping his older brother, Mitchell, round up sheep. Glancing down Tarrytown Road, he saw a rider—his father, he thought, so tall in the saddle. Ah wish that I would grow that tall—maybe ah will.

James was only eight years of age when his mother had passed away. He remembered the comforting arm of his sister, Jennifer. She had kept her warm arm around his head when the preacher prayed at his mother's gravesite.

"He'll be eighteen next year—old enough for the Riders," James had heard his father tell Mr. Hastings in Tarrytown last week. He remembered that the hairs on his arms rose with tingling pleasure when he heard his father say those words. Watching his brothers ride off with the Gray Riders gave him one of the most thrilling feelings that he had ever experienced.

Watching my brother's casket being lowered into the ground was the worst experience that I've ever had, he said to himself. Ah have to weigh my feelings, and make a decision. After working through his thoughts, he decided....It's because of Paul that ah want to join the Riders. Ah cannot allow his death to go without cause.

His thoughts came back to the sheep. The dog-gone ram he was attempting to steer homeward was stubborn. "Hey, Jimmy-boy, that ram too tough for ya?" he heard his brother yell. James gave the left rein a sudden tug, and the ram was forced away from the corner and joined the main flock where his brother and Clement had them under control.

At supper that night, all heads were bowed as Orly McGregor recited a prayer at the dinner table. He sat at the head. Mitchell and James sat on one side. Jennifer was on the other, next to a vacant chair. They all stared at the emptiness. Then Orly said, "Amen...May Almighty God bless Paul."

24

JUBAL HAGGARD LOOKED OUT THE WINDOW AT THE SNOW. It's expected in March, he thought. Visibility is sporadic at best. Jubal watched the whirls of snow the wind created. He was anxious to get to Tarrytown and the General Store. His reading materials were in low supply.

His brother, Justin, had returned from the barn. "Pa, the calfin' heifers are all inside, safe and sound."

"Good job, Justin. Ah'll go out and check 'em before supper," responded his father, Ben.

Jubal watched his mother, Anna, stoke the fire, her large, blackish eyes reflecting the flame. She hoisted a chunk of wood and dropped it onto the flames. He sat down on his favorite chair where he could see their roadway.

"Pa, there's a rider comin'," Jubal stood and said excitedly. Ben Haggard walked over to the window. "Wonder who that could be, Jubal, any idear?"

"No, Pa, dunno who that comin'."

They watched as the rider dismounted and hurried to the door. Ben walked over and opened it. "Cole, what brings ya out 'ere on such a stormy day?"

Cole Younger brushed some of the snow off. He removed his hat.

"Here, Cole, let me have that. Jubal, would ya dry this by the fire?"

"Mr. Haggard, the redlegs have been causing trouble west of 'ere the past two days. They put a torch to the Smith place....Burned the house and barn to de groun'."

Justin and Anna had joined Ben and Jubal by the door where Cole Younger was standing, his eyebrows dripping water from the melting snow.

"I 'ear that your place may be next, best get your guns ready. I'm goin to ride to Kingsley's and then over to the Hastings…warn them. Got about ten Riders comin over 'ere in about an hour. God, ah hope they git 'ere in time."

"Gotta be off. Ah'd appreciate my hat back," Cole said, his facial expression changing from a limited smile to a strained look of uneasiness.

Anna walked over to the hearth, picked up the hat, and shook off the droplets. "There you are, Cole and God be with you." Her olive-colored skin had paled, her large, blackish eyes showed concern.

Cole Younger pulled the hat down snuggly on his head and went out the door quickly. Jubal watched as he mounted and galloped eastward toward the Kingsley's.

———

SNOW CONTINUED TO FALL AS JUBAL ANXIOUSLY WATCHED out the window. He couldn't imagine that anyone would be out for any reason in this kind of weather.

"Here they come, just like Cole said," Jubal said, his stomach feeling the tension.

His father came over to the window and peered out. "Looks like it, son. Wonder why they stopped there?"

"Pa, one of 'em has a torch."

"That ain't the Riders! Justin, grab your musket! Anna, get ready to do the reloadin'."

Jubal saw his brother grab one of the muskets and go around to the back window, blowing out lamps on the way. Justin pushed up on the window and stuck the barrel out. Putting his hands over his ears, Jubal saw him aim. "Kaboom!" The man carrying the torch dropped off his horse, falling into the snow below.

"Jubal, take that musket and watch that other winder!" his father yelled.

Jubal opened it, as Justin had done in the kitchen. He saw three riders come by. They had revolvers and were about to open fire. Suddenly, in a maze of whirling white, two other riders appeared. They carried long batons. Before the invaders could react, the batons, whirling round and round, knocked them off their horses.

Jubal watched in amazement as one of the baton-wielding riders dismounted and clubbed at the three fallen invaders. Feelings of emotion overwhelmed him when he saw one of their faces—it was black. The Jacksons! Another rider approached—one of ours, Jubal thought—Grady Hastings. The Gray Riders had arrived in time.

Jubal yelled, "Grady is here, so is Elkanah Jackson and his brother!"

"Hold your fire, Justin, the Riders are 'ere. Can't tell who is who...best we wait," Ben said and took a deep breath.

"Ah see Mitch ova there, Pa!" Justin exclaimed.

Jubal could hear the terrifying neighing of horses and the popping sounds of gunshots. "Got 'em!" he heard one of the Riders yell.

"Look out, Cole!" another screamed.

Jubal saw Cole Younger jerk the reins on his horse and go sidesaddle. Another shot rang out, and Cole's attacker fell to the ground.

Only one of the invaders remained mounted. He was surrounded by five of the Riders. Jubal saw him put his hands up. He heard another shot. The redleg fell off his horse.

Minutes later, a knock on the door drew his father away from the front window. The door opened, and Mitchell McGregor, Grady Hastings, and Abel Kingsley entered. They shook off the snow. Mitchell showed his big smile, his large blue eyes glittering in the light. "Those redlegs won't be botherin' you any more, Mr. Haggard."

"Much obliged to ya and the others," Ben Haggard responded, stretching both arms over his head and clapping lightly. Perspiration covered his forehead and flowed gently into his shaggy, tilted eyebrows.

"If it's alright with you, Mr. Haggard, some of 'em are gonna bed down in the barn. They wanna hang roun' till mornin'. We gotta figure out what to do with them bodies, ah reckon."

"Help yourselves to the barn, Mitch," Ben said, his face displaying gratitude. He took a deep breath and added, "Get them winders closed, boys. Getting' cold in 'ere."

"Is it cold enough for ya out there, Grady?" Ben asked.

"All weather is good, really. You gotta' expect this, livin' in Missoura," Grady Hastings responded.

Ben clamped his lower front teeth into his upper lip and nodded.

Jubal heard a knock on the door an hour later. Mitch McGregor and Grady Hastings stood there with an armful of weapons. "You're to 'ave these, Mr. Haggard. We're going to spread the rest of 'em roun'."

Grady said, "ah would appreciate it if some of the Riders could settle into one of your barns, Mr. Haggard."

"Yup…sure can, Grady, ah already told Mitch. Justin, would ya clear some space in the main barn?"

"Sure will, Pa. Jubal, would ya come out and help?"

"What about the horses?" Jubal's father asked.

"Your Joshua's gonna get some of 'em. The others we're going to give to Elkanah and Baskhall. They helped out, ya know."

"Is that who was waving those clubs?"

"Sure was—They're goin' to have muskets next time."

25

HARSHEST WINTER IN YEARS, BEN HAGGARD
THOUGHT, as he rode toward Tarrytown Road. The snow had all
melted, and he appreciated the meadowlarks and their song. He
thought about the raid by the redlegs. He didn't feel a bit guilty about
burying all of them in one grave. It took his sons and five of the
neighbors an entire day to dig the hole—six feet deep 'twas, near the
railroad tracks to the north—no markings, no nuthin', he said to
himself.

Patches of white snow which were protected from the sun
interrupted the dull browns and grays of the landscape. After passing
the Sunnerland roadway, he observed the clusters of horse-high bushes
at the border of the Hastings land, near the road. They extended
northeastward down toward the creek.

He halted his horse on the bridge that spanned Bear Creek. Henry
Hastings's Herefords were grazing on the western side of the creek,
near the Sunnerland property line. Good lookin' herd, he thought—
came through the winta' just fine. Ben saw more remnants of winter's
snow all along the north tree line of MacTurley's Woods. High above,
he saw two hawks soaring, occasionally diving while hunting the
narrow grassland between the woods and the road.

He rode past the school, and smiled when he saw the children
playing in the schoolyard. The tall, black-dressed figure in their midst
surely has to be Master Styles, he thought. The other tall one is Henry's
boy, Thomas.

Ben rode down town. Dismounting at the hitching rail in front of
the General Store, he walked in.

"Howdy, Ben, 'eard ya had a ruckus out there," Seth said.

"Shuh did, the boys taught 'em a lesson. Those that came a burnin' won't try it again."

Seth laughed. "No, ah reckon not. Did ya hear the news from out east?"

"Naw...what's there to hear?"

"McClellan is movin' south into the Carolinas. Gonna be a big fight."

"Who's McClellan?" Ben asked.

"He's a big General. Lincoln picked 'em to be the main one—a West Pointer, 'e is."

"Genevieve, would ya take care of Mr. Haggard's list?" Seth asked.

"Well, hello, young lady. How's your family?"

"Mother and Father are well. Thomas is in school and you've seen Grady lately. He's fine, too. Sure gets called out a lot...one of the Gray Riders and all."

Ben watched with interest as Genevieve processed the purchase by moving small levers on what he thought was a strange looking machine.

"That'll be three dollars and forty cents," she said.

Fumbling among a cluster of coins in his palm, Ben lay some on the counter. "There you are, young lady. Hello to your parents, Miss Hastings."

"Thank ye, Mr. Haggard."

———

THOMAS FELT EXCITED. He had read that the Union army was moving south after being defeated so soundly at Manassas. When are they evah gonna learn? he thought. Lincoln—you woulda' thought he had more brains than that.

Schoolmaster Styles had been correcting papers. His narrow glasses were halfway down his nose. The test, taken by the seventh and eight grades, was on Missouri Civics. The room was quiet enough to hear the mutterings of the master. "Oll correct...oll correct...nay correct...."

The schoolmaster stood and stared at the students. Most of them looked up from their desks. The Master shook his head. "Thomas Hastings! Come forward, please."

Thomas rose from his desk. "Yes, sir," he said meekly.

Looking around with a painful look on his face, he slowly moved into the aisle and trudged forward to the desk.

"Master Hastings, you intrigue me. What's this mean, right there?" The schoolmaster pointed.

"That means that President Lincoln has it all wrong. He means to free the slave—that's good, but at the expense of enslaving us 'ere in Missoura."

"Thank ye, Mister Hastings, that will be enough."

When Thomas returned to his seat, Sarah Kingsley had the giggles.

"What's botherin' ye?" Thomas asked, sneering.

"Oll correct for me…nay correct for you," she answered, laughing.

26

*O*N NOVEMBER 28*TH*, 1861, during a meeting of the confederate congress of Missouri, the majority voted to secede from the Union. They became the twelfth state to do so.

Major General Henry Halleck, Union commander of the Federal Department of Missouri, sent General Curtis to drive the Missouri State Guard and their General Price from southwest Missouri. General Price was forced to retreat into Arkansas.

In Arkansas, Price teamed up with General McCullough to form the Army of the West, under General Earl Van Dorn. On March 7*th* and 8*th*, at the battle of Pea Ridge, General McCullough was killed. General Price resigned from the Missouri State Guard and joined the regular Confederate Army.

Later that spring on March 13*th*, General Halleck issued a proclamation outlawing guerillas. Any of them captured would be treated as a prisoner of war. This was a response to the guerilla *activities of William Clarke Quantrill, a well known southern sympathizer.*

One of western Missouri's young riders who joined Quantrill in January was Thomas Coleman Younger, son of Henry Younger of Harrisonville. Frank and Jesse James also joined the group.

Quantrill's band and sub-bands of western Missouri locals patrolled the farms to protect them against marauders, who roamed western Missouri performing evil and searching for spoils.

27

ABEL KINGSLEY, ONE OF THE NEWEST MEMBERS of the Gray Riders, had participated in the defense of the Haggard farm, which had been attacked by a gang of redlegs earlier in the month. His father, Ben, had changed his thinking after the attack. The Gray Riders had saved his farm and even perhaps the life of him and his family.

The Gray Riders lost some of their members to other bands during the early months of 1862. Some of them joined Quantrill and others the Bloody Anderson's group.

Abel and the remaining members of the Gray Riders mainly patrolled the Tarrytown area, protecting the towns and farms in that part of western Missouri. Most of the Gray Riders lived within ten miles of town.

Justin Haggard and Grady Hastings led a group of twelve Riders, patrolling eight miles northwest of Tarrytown. After that wanton attack by a group of jayhawkers, most efforts by the local farmers, including Martin Kingsley, to resist the work of the Gray Riders had ended.

Abel rode next to James McGregor, second from the rear, when the Riders reached the Tarrytown Road. Approaching his nineteenth birthday on April 15th, he anxiously thought about getting home and helping his father with the spring planting.

When the Riders came up to the McGregor property, Mitchell and James peeled away from the group and trotted their horses up their roadway. The group was down to six. Justin Haggard left the group next. Lafe and Jesse Sunnerland waved farewell as they headed toward their farm.

Abel saw Grady Hastings watching a pair of hawks drift and float over the Tarrytown Road as he stopped at his turnoff. "Thanks for comin', Abel. Ah'm real glad you joined the group."

"My pleasure...."

Abel and Elkanah Jackson rode on. Abel was about to say goodbye to Elkanah when he spotted four riders coming toward them on Tarrytown Road. "See them?" he asked Elkanah.

"Shah do. Wonder who they is?"

"Erlocks! Sure as shootin'," replied Abel sternly, tension building in his stomach.

"Reckon they're up to no good," responded Elkanah.

Those Erlocks scare the dickens out o' me, Abel thought, slightly raising both heels to ready the spurs. We'll ride to the Hastings's farm if they keep comin'.

The four horsemen turned sharply at the corner of MacTurley's Woods and headed south along the eastern edge of the Hastings's property.

"Elkanah, let's head home."

———

"PRIAM, LOOK...ELKANAH COMIN'...HE AH COMIN' HOME." Priam and Virgilia Jackson remained brokenhearted over the loss of their oldest son at the Battle of Lexington. But they had difficulty delaying their number three son, Baskhall, from joining up with the Gray Riders. He wanted to join so badly.

Elkanah Jackson rode his horse slowly along the eastern border of the Kingsley property. He pulled on the reins gently when he saw his mother and father standing on the porch. After waving, he applied spurs to his horse and galloped the rest of the way.

Elkanah dismounted in front of the porch. His father was smiling, but his mother was not. She still grieved from the loss of her eldest son. Elkanah hugged his father and turned toward his mother. She reached out her hands. He grabbed them and looked into her teary eyes.

28

JUSTIN HAGGARD AND HIS FATHER HAD GONE RIDING. They supervised the last of the spring planting on a morning in mid-May.

"Joshua does grand," Ben said.

Justin watched the family head lead a line of slaves who were dropping hemp seeds into a furrow that his eldest son had dug with a plow and two horses. He noticed the horses were being steered back toward the barn.

"Pa, ah plan on marrying Jennifer McGregor next month."

Ben Haggard turned his head, lips tightening, the sun reflecting off his leathery face. "Justin, the war…Why don't ya wait until after the war?"

Justin's silver-gray eyes opened to their widest. "This war is never going to end. Even if Lee and Lincoln settle, the redlegs and jayhawkers will never give up until either us or they are all dead."

"Have you approached Orly McGregor yet, son?"

"No, I haven't. Ah decided to talk to you first."

"Good, let's talk it over with your mother this evening."

"Pa, I'm twenty-one years old. Ah've fought in two battles for Missoura. Ah think ah've earned the right to have a wife," said Justin seriously.

"Yup….You sure have earned the right. Ah was just hopin' that you'd wait until the war was over," Ben added and scrunched his lower front teeth into his upper lip.

"This war could take a long time, Pa. It should've been over a long time ago. It could go on for years."

"We'll talk to your mother this evening, son. Ah'm off to see to the northern herd."

Justin watched in silence as his father dug a spur into his horse and rode northward without looking back.

———

THE CHURCH IN TARRYTOWN BUSTLED WITH PEOPLE. The last two pews on each side in the rear had some empty spaces. Pansy Gooden watched Pastor Wilson for a signal to begin the wedding march. Voices coming from just outside the door reached the ears of those inside.

Thomas Hastings sat with his parents in the fifth row, on the bride's side of the church. Grady sat with Jesse Sunnerland on the other side in the seventh row. Thomas saw the pastor signal, and the music began. He joined the others and stood, straining his neck to see who was coming up the aisle.

Minutes earlier, he saw the groom, Justin Haggard, and his best man, Mitchell McGregor, come in by the side door. Thomas thought Justin appeared extraordinarily nervous—his tall frame stiff as a board. The groom's hands fidgeted nervously, and his right shoulder dipped. Thomas saw him peek over his elevated left shoulder toward the door. The procession was about to begin. Thomas stared at Justin. There is one excited man, he thought.

Thomas smiled as he watched the groom dressed up in a black, wool frock coat and matching trousers. My, what a fancy vest, he thought. He had heard someone describe it as brocade. The cravat sure looks starched—probably hard as a board.

Everyone's attention was glued to the light-splashed center aisle as the front door opened. Genevieve Hastings, the maid of honor, emerged first. Her mother had patterned Genevieve's dress after a winter halter print she had found at the General Store. The beautiful pink gown was made of silk satin overlaid with pink lace flounces, and her sheer stole was the same color. The white gloves she wore were of kid material, and her fan of blue silk.

Most of the people in the church took their eyes off Genevieve and focused on the marvelous-looking woman in the back of the room—the bride. Thomas continued to watch his sister, Genevieve. Magnificent! he thought.

The music softened a bit, and the bride, wearing a wide smile, slowly made her way down the aisle. Thomas thought his sister looked real good, but the bride was not to be outdone. She wore a white dress—silk, Thomas thought. That's a strange looking netting on top her head. Orange and white flowers, attached to the netting, hung down her back.

Thomas's heart skipped a beat. Looking beyond his sister, he caught a glimpse of Sarah Kingsley. She was dressed all in blue except for a white collar. His focus on the wedding procession was temporarily lost as he felt his chest swell with emotion. Even as the bride accepted the arm of her husband-to-be and looked up at Pastor Wilson, Thomas continued to think about Sarah and the blue dress.

This is gonna take forever, Thomas thought, and yawned. Asking those two all those questions was enough. Why does he have to preach on the bad things that can happen in a marriage? This is supposed to be a happy event. Thomas felt a pang of anger.

The rustling sounds made by people shifting their positions on the pews increased, he noticed. Suddenly, a loud snoring sound interrupted the preacher. Thomas glared at the other side of the aisle. He strained his neck to see who it was.

Banker Douglas Herron sat up straight. His face became red as an apple, Thomas observed. Pastor Wilson stepped from behind the pulpit. "May I remind everyone that this place is the Lord's home?" He cleared his throat and returned behind the pulpit.

Good thing it wasn't Pa, Thomas said to himself. He would 'ave heard about this for weeks from my mother. Pa has fallen dead asleep more than once, Thomas thought, and smiled. His Pa would take the verbal assault from his wife for about a week.

Then he would stand up and say, "Those preachers go on and on about nothin'. How would you all like it if I stood here and preached to you for half an hour? Maybe that's what I should do…start giving a few sermons of my own. Ya all need it, God knows." Then his father would stomp out of the house. Thomas remembered how he, Grady and Genevieve laughed, but his mother didn't.

Thomas's mind continued to wander until he saw Justin kiss his new wife. That's a lot better, he thought. Justin looks a lot more relaxed. Again, there was a lot of shifting going on in the pews. A few more throats cleared, but everyone got quiet when the couple turned.

Justin's silver-gray eyes were beaming as he and his new wife led a procession down the aisle. Jennifer was smiling while grasping his arm. Their pace increased, and in moments they were out the door. Thomas strained to get another glimpse of Sarah as she followed her parents down the aisle. Thomas angered when an over-sized lady blocked his view of the Kingsleys.

Thomas's eyes blinked as he passed through the big door. The bright sun blasted everyone that exited the church. Two carriages waited in front of the door, and he watched the men of the bridal party assist their ladies to their carriages.

After the wedding party boarded both carriages, they headed for the Tarrytown Road. He watched with excitement as they turned toward the Haggard farm.

He saw Abel Kingsley assist his sister, Sarah, into a black carriage. Oh, how I wish that I could've done that, he thought.

Other carriages followed the Kingsleys, and Thomas was glad when his father finally got in line. They were on their way to the Haggards.

———

THOMAS HASTINGS AND HIS PARENTS arrived at the Haggard's farm amidst an exaggerated bustle of laughter and joyous activity. He saw several bottles passed around amongst the men, including his father. I wonder what that tastes like, he thought. It sure seems to make their eyes glow, and the words get louder and louder.

In the Haggard's farmyard, an extensive manicured lawn area served as a setting for several long tables. Clusters of oak trees provided shade for the mingling guests. Off to one side of the trees, still in the shade, three musicians tuned their instruments. Two of them are fiddles, Tom thought. He wasn't sure what the other one was. It was somethin' that he'd never seen before.

His stomach gurgled and yearned as he watched four servants carry out large baskets that smelled of food. They began sorting the contents on four long, large tables.

Well beyond the tables, standing and talking to a lady, he saw his brother. Now, what's he doin? Thomas asked himself. He saw Grady gently lift up the right hand of Helen Walker and kiss it. He looked at Helen's face and saw a glow that he hadn't noticed before. Her dark brown eyes sparked.

Uh-oh, there's Sarah. She stood between her parents. Once again his heart began to flutter. How pretty she looked in that blue dress. Magnificent! The hoop of her dress must be as wide as a wagon wheel, he thought. I hope she separates from her parents sometime this evening. Then I'll get a chance to talk to her—maybe even a dance.

"Hey! Thomas. Are ya daydreaming, or what?" Jubal Haggard chided as he sauntered by. "Oh, I see...the one in blue. You've got your eyes on her, huh?" added Jubal mockingly, his dark eyes dancing and glittering.

"Never you mind, Jube, mind to yar own affairs," answered Thomas firmly.

"Well, I'll be danged. The youngest Hastings is in love. Ha, ha. Supposin' you'll be marryin' next, huh, Thomas? Huh?"

Thomas gave Jubal a shove and moved away to where the musicians were about to begin the entertainment. Sarah had disappeared. Wonder where she went? I'll just hang around the music, and she'll show up sooner or later, he thought.

———

EMMA HASTINGS AND A GROUP OF OTHER LADIES sat in the shade near the house where they could watch all the activities. "I do declare, I've never seen a more beautiful bride," she said to Angie Walker, who was seated next to her.

"Oh, hear that music. I love those fiddles! Gonna be some dancin' tonight," Emma said gleefully, her hands clapping lightly.

"There'll be more than dancin'. Look at that handsome couple," Angie added gleefully.

"Ah, there comes my Henry. Looks like we'll be doin some eatin', and soon. Those tables look absolutely divine."

"Hello, Mrs. Walker. Glad that you and your family could make the weddin'," Henry Hastings said.

"Ah wouldn't 'ave missed this for anythin', Mr. Hastings. My, but you and yar boys look so handsome today."

"Why, thank ye, Angie Walker...."

"I love those hammertail frock coats and the wide-notched, shawl collars," Angie added.

Emma saw her husband's eyes narrow and a furrow form on his forehead. She knew that Henry was thinking of the two Walker boys, Carr and Will. She was glad that the bad feelings between him and George Walker had ended.

She realized how much Thomas missed Carr. They had been inseparable. Her mind drifted to the many times that Carr would ride over on his horse. She remembered the happiness she had felt while watching the two boys ride toward the creek to seek adventure and explore. Thomas doesn't ride much anymore, she thought. Hopefully, he will find another friend.

"Come on, Emma. Let's jin up with the others," Henry said to her, interrupting her thoughts.

———

THOMAS WATCHED THE DANCING and stood next to Jubal Haggard.

"Well, when ya gonna ask her, Thomas? No courage?" Jubal asked and poked him in the back.

"Ah don't know how ta do that buck dancing, Jube. Ah see you're not out there jiggin'. So, who's lacking courage, huh?" Thomas laughed.

He looked up and saw Jubal grimace. The music had stopped.

The lead fiddler stood up and announced that the next selection was to be a reel. My God, here she comes, Thomas thought, his heart pounding.

He stood there gaping as Sarah Kingsley and one of her friends approached.

"Well, Thomas Hastings, would you like to be my partner for the reel?" Sarah asked, her blue-streaked hazel eyes gleaming.

Thomas found himself speechless while staring at her full, red lips and the pretty freckles on her cheeks.

He felt Jubal's elbow poke his ribs. For what seemed an eternity, he stood there with his mouth partially open. "I would consider that a pleasure, Miss Kingsley." Thomas couldn't believe that he had said that. When he put out his arm and her soft hand succumbed to his grasp, he knew he was in heaven.

Sarah's long blonde hair splashed over her petite shoulders. Her dress was a blue silk satin overlaid with pink lace flounces.

The couples lined up across from each other, and the music began. At first, Thomas felt clumsy and self-conscious, but after the second time through the outstretched arms, his agility knew no boundaries.

Thomas's feelings were on an all-time high the rest of the evening. He had just completed his fourth dance with Sarah. Jubal had been occupied with Sarah's friend, Pritzy. From time to time, he would glance toward his parents who were sitting and watching. In a passing moment, he caught his mother's eye. The glow of happiness that he saw at that moment he would remember forever, he thought.

Thomas thought about asking Sarah for the sixth time. He started walking toward the group of young ladies that were gathered around one of the tables. Looking up at the sky, he saw a glow. What's that? he wondered. Looks like a fire.

Without thinking, he yelled as loudly as he could, "Fire! Fire!"

"It's the Sunnerland place!" he heard a man exclaim.

General panic followed in the next few minutes. Men scrambled to their horses and hurriedly hitched them to wagons. Within ten minutes, Thomas heard the snap of a whip, and two wagons headed toward the Sunnerland farm—his father driving one of them.

29

HENRY HASTINGS'S CARRIAGE HAD ARRIVED at the Sunnerland farm. His passenger was the big and tall Orly McGregor. George Walker's team had gotten there first. Martin Kingsley and George were standing by their carriage, their faces lit up by the glare of the fire. The Sunnerland barn was totally engulfed in flames.

"The horses...were there any in the barn?" Martin yelled.

Henry sniffed—the stench had penetrated his nasal area. "Martin, can you smell 'em? Somethin' in there really stinks. Gotta be some horses in there."

The sounds of other horses and carriages coming up the roadway drew their attention. Henry glanced back and saw Lafe and Jesse Sunnerland in the lead carriage, not sparing the whip.

Jesse leaped from the carriage and ran over to the men who were keeping their distance from the intense heat. "Jaysus, Prince was in there. My Prince!" he exclaimed, his dark eyes wide with anxiety.

"No, Jesse. Stay back. It's too late...much too late," said Henry, his words firm with authority.

"Whoever did this is gonna pay," Lafe said, his squeaky voice up a pitch.

"How many horses did you have in there?" George Walker asked, his long, narrow face dead serious.

"Four, only four...They were our best saddle horses—the best," answered Jesse. "Why would anyone do this?"

Ben Haggard had joined the group and said, "'twas them redlegs, sure as shootin'. They would've done the same to me 'en my family if Younger hadn't warned us."

"Not so sure, Ben. Them Erlocks could 'ave somethin' ta do with this. Remember that Lafe and Jesse hung one of their boys," Henry said.

After organizing a water bucket brigade, the men continued to splash the other buildings. Henry was pleased that they limited the flames to only the barn. The fire continued to lighten the sky and surroundings for the next few hours. After it lessened, and the other buildings were secured, some of the men began to leave.

"We need a meetin' 'en soon," Henry told Orly McGregor. "Ah sent Grady and some of the others to ride out to some of the other farms. Hopefully, this is the only one that gits burnt....Orly, there are dark days ahead of us."

Henry steered his pair back to the Haggard's farm. *The Gray Riders are the answer,* he thought. *We need a roun' the clock patrol.*

———

GRADY HAD RETURNED TO THE HAGGARD FARM and found Thomas wringing his hands and standing with a group of people. "Thomas, you stay here with Genevieve and your mother. Some of us are gathering the Riders together. Don't go anywhere with anyone until you hear back from Pa or me. Understand?"

Grady saw his brother nod. *Ah reckon he's glad that he's left with the women and all the young ladies,* Grady thought. *Ah saw how he was fixed on the Kingsley lass.*

"Come on, Mitch. Is the team ready?"

"That she is, lad. Let's go," Mitchell McGregor drawled, snapped the reins, and the carriage headed toward Tarrytown Road. Grady was pleased with the responsibility given him by his father and Ben Haggard. It was put upon him to organize the Gray Riders. The carriage reached the road and headed east. Grady was going home to round up his equipment and horse.

Grady had a sunken feeling as he passed by the Sunnerland land. The glow from the barn fire transmitted an eerie appearance to the dark sky. *What about all the other farms?* he asked himself. *Will they be goin' up in flames, too?*

"Can you get any more out of that pair, Mitch?" Grady asked.

"That's about all they can do right now," Mitch answered.

After arriving at the Hastings's farm, Grady got his horse saddled and all his equipment together. He could see that Mitch was having a hard time staying awake.

"Let's go, Mitch, back to your place."

As they passed by the Sunnerland road, Grady saw a carriage coming toward them from the fire. He halted. "You go on, Mitch. Ah want to see who this is."

He stayed on his horse and watched the carriage approach. He saw the solemn face of his father who was leaning forward handling the reins. Next to him, slightly bent over, was the burly-haired Orly McGregor.

"Nuthin' much more we can do over there for now, son. We're headed back to the Haggards to pick up our families. You do what you can with Mitch to check out the other farms. How were things at our place?"

"Just fine, Pa. Giddy-yap!"

Grady caught up with Mitch's carriage just past the Haggard road. He followed until the carriage pulled up by the stable at the McGregor's.

————

THE GRAY RIDERS SET UP CAMP next to a grove of trees near the Tarrytown Road and western border of the Haggard farm. Grady and Mitch succeeded in recruiting eight riders, and they successfully checked out all the farms in the area without incident.

"Grady, do ya think we should set up a sentry?" Mitch asked, his large, blue eyes widening.

"Naw, ah think not. Whoever did the burnin' is long gone. If anyone comes roun', we'll hear 'em."

Mitch nodded and wandered over to his saddle, which was abutted against the base of a tree. He yawned and noticed that his brother, James, was already asleep. *I sure miss Paul,* he thought. *More 'en anyone can imagine.*

Before retiring, he walked over to the horses. Half were grazing and the others were lying down. Looking up at the starry sky, he wondered if Paul was up there somewhere, looking down on him and his brother.

30

CONSTABLE FRANCIS MULDOON LEANED against the wall outside the door to his office. He scratched his right ear and greeted people as they entered his office. "Much obliged, Lance," he said to the man who had spent part of the morning setting up chairs in the meeting room.

The constable bent his right knee and pushed the heel of his shiny, black boot against the wall. "Howdy, George, glad ya could make it. Sorry about your loss," he said. "Yar son died fightin' for his country. No shame in that."

They shook hands and George Walker entered the meeting room. He nodded. His thick neck supported a firm, unshaven, square jaw.

The constable watched as Orly McGregor rode up and dismounted. Now, there is one big man, he said to himself. Two horse-lengths behind, his two sons, Mitchell and James, followed.

The trim front edges of the constable's black suede vest spread apart as he took a deep breath. He thought about Paul McGregor and the funeral—saddest one ah've ever been to. Who would've ever believed that ah could still cry?

"Howdy, Orly. Welcome, boys. Glad ya could all come."

The constable entered his office and closed the door. The hullabaloo of noisy conversations ceased when he raised his hand.

"Ah'm glad that ya all could come. Seems the townspeople are getting upset with some of the burnins' that have been occurin'."

The constable raised his hand above his head and slid off the desk. Putting his right fist on his waist and slowly rubbing the thumb and forefinger of his other hand along the sides of his chin, he cleared his throat and looked at Lafe Sunnerland. "Sorry about the loss of your barn and horses, Lafe," he said. "The reason ah called this meetin' is to prevent the likes of that happenin' agin'."

George Walker stood, and the room became dead still, except for an occasional squeak from someone shifting in a chair. All eyes were on George. He was holding his tall, dark hat in one of his hands.

After a deep sigh, he spo... "Once again, ah would like to apologize to Henry Hastings for accusing him of being responsible for my son's death. Ah've lost both of my sons now. It's a pain that will be with me for the rest of my life. Ah want you all to know that if ah had another son, he would join the Riders...the Gray Riders. It seems to me that neither north nor south is gonna protect our farms. We have to do it ourselves. Ah cannot give you another son, but I have plenty of available horses."

Constable Muldoon watched the stiff, lean farmer sit down. He was glad that Walker had joined up and abandoned his Union connections.

The talk at the meeting went on for another hour. Muldoon was pleased that the group had united.

———

"LOOK HERE, JESSE," LAFE SUNNERLAND SAID while poking around the barn ruins. "It looks like only one horse burned. What happened to the others? There should be four."

Jesse walked over and stared at the bones and blackened flesh remains. The sight caused his throat and stomach to retch. His thoughts were on his mare, Maggie. Was she the one that lay there? "Ah counted about six sets of tracks that left the barn and headed south."

"Let's go take another look," Lafe responded.

After saddling up, they slowly rode south of the barn following a maze of hoof tracks. After reaching a field beyond the horse pasture where the ground was softer, Jesse dismounted. He squatted and studied the tracks. "Lafe, look here...three sets didn't imprint as deeply as the others. They had no riders, ah reckon."

"Our horses! Did the bastards that burnt our barn steal three of our horses?"

Jesse remounted. "Come on, Lafe. Let's see where these tracks go."

"Hold on, Jesse. Why don't you ride over to the McGregor's and get Mitch and James? Ah'll fetch Grady Hastings and meet you back here."

"Good idea, Lafe. See you in about an hour," Jesse replied. He galloped his horse across a field to the McGregor's. Glancing at their buildings, he saw an occasional whiff of smoke coming from the barn.

———

LAFE AND GRADY RETURNED TO THE SITE of the tracks which they had been following. Jesse had not yet arrived with the McGregor boys.

Lafe looked across the fields toward the McGregor farm. "Grady, it may take Jesse some time to fetch Mitch and James. Ah'm gonna ride ahead and follow the tracks. Would you wait here for the other boys?"

"Yup, ah will, but don't take any unnecessary risks, Lafe," Grady responded.

Lafe spurred his horse and walked it up the slope toward Bear Mountain, following the hoof tracks. They head right over there, Lafe said to himself. Ah've never noticed that trail before. The opening is well disguised. Wonder if ah should wait for the boys, he thought.

Cautiously, he walked his horse onto the path. It narrowed, and Lafe continued walking his horse anxiously. He pulled on the reins and put his hand on the horse's mane. He listened. Flicking his wrist, his horse continued forward. He stopped the horse again when he noticed an opening in the timber, just ahead. Taking a deep breath, he looked around and listened. Dismounting, he led his horse to the edge of the clearing.

———

"WHERE'S LAFE?" ASKED JESSE when he returned with Mitch

and James.

"He went on ahead," Grady drawled.

Jesse frowned, his dark eyes glaring. He anxiously spurred his horse and began following the tracks. The other riders followed.

"They crossed over here," yelled Mitch McGregor who was following the narrow stream southward.

"Geez, they're headin' southeastward," Grady Hastings said after they crossed the creek.

"Wouldn't be them Erlocks, now would it?" asked Jesse. Ah wouldn't think they'd come near this place after we hung one of 'em."

"Ah wouldn't put it past them Erlocks. They're a bad lot. Who knows how many of our beef herd they've rustled," Grady added. "Look at this...them tracks lead straight east along our line."

After arriving at the beginning of MacTurley's Woods, Jesse raised his hand. The group stopped.

"What do ya think?" Mitch in his deep voice asked as he swept a heavy tuft of straw-colored hair from over his ear.

Jesse looked back at Grady. "If we find Maggie over there, we're gonna have to kill some of 'em...probably old Victor hisself."

Grady Hastings said, "No use goin' ova to old Muldoon. He wouldn't do anythin' about it anyhow. Besides we got nothin' on 'em unless we find Jesse's Maggie."

––––

GRADY HASTINGS WASN'T CONVINCED that the Erlocks did the burning and horse stealing. He rode a bit farther and noticed that the tracks veered south. "Hey, fellers, them tracks don't go to the Erlock's."

Jesse galloped over and dismounted. "You're right, Grady. Looks like the tracks lead toward the top over there." He pointed toward a break in the trees. "Where the devil is that brother of mine?"

Grady felt excited as Jesse led the group to the top of the mountain. Jesse signaled a stop and dismounted. He walked around the edge of a clearing near the summit. Jesse walked back to his horse.

Jesse looked back with his large, dark eyes and said, "They dismounted here and rested their horses. See the markings? The tracks head west, over there toward that trail."

Led by Jesse, the horsemen came to an area where the trees were sparse. He raised his arm and put a finger to his lips. The riders all dismounted. "Ah heard somethin'," Jesse whispered. "Did anyone else hear that, too?"

Grady turned his head and listened. Probably a deer, he thought. Suddenly, a louder noise perked his ears. "Geez, it sounds like branches breaking," he whispered and raised an arm.

"There's someone over there," Jesse said softly and pointed. "Let's leave our horses here and go on foot."

Silently, the group followed Jesse into a narrow path through the trees. Grady thought he heard a voice and stopped. The others did the same.

"Ya all wait here. Ah'm going to have a look," whispered Jesse.

Grady reached down to his holster and felt the revolver. Probing a strap, he unsnapped it and grasped the weapon with his fingers. He drew it out and checked the cylinders. To his satisfaction, they were all charged.

Grady watched as Jesse disappeared down a turn in the path. His green eyes locked on the large, blue ones of Mitch McGregor. "We better git back on our horses," Grady said.

After mounting, Mitch winked and lifted his revolver. "Ah'm ready to go."

They caught up with Jesse, who had also remounted, and all eyes were on the path as Jesse slowly moved up the narrow trail. Grady saw two bald eagles soaring and circling near the western edge of the woods. Then he heard another sound. "Ah wonder what the devil that sound was?" he asked.

No one answered.

The minutes dragged by and Jesse was getting uneasy. Grady watched him fidget in his saddle. Jesse looked back at the other riders and said softly, "ah don't like the looks of this. Lafe should've been up 'ere waitin' for us."

"We best move ahead quickly," responded Grady.

"Darn tootin'...let's ride," Mitch said. "Come on, James."

Grady felt the spreading branches tug at his hat as he followed Jesse on the narrow trail. "Geez, ah reckon that we've gone a quarter of a mile," he whispered.

Grady heard a shrieking sound coming from ahead and saw Jesse pull on the reins and turn his head. "Grady, go git the other boys. Ah'm gonna get closer," he whispered.

"They're right behind me," Grady said softly.

"Good boy," Jesse whispered to his horse as he inched it forward. Chills went down his spine when he peered into a clearing. Jaysus, that's Lafe with the rope around his neck...if that horse bolts, he's a dead man, he said to himself, his heart pumping furiously.

31

JESSE SUNNERLAND TOOK A DEEP BREATH. Reaching down to his sheath, he felt the handle of his blade. Grabbing his pistol, he used his left hand to hold the reins and the pistol together. He reached down with his right hand and grabbed the handle of the long knife, lifting it from its scabbard. Raising the knife, he looked back and saw that Grady held a Colt in one hand.

Jesse turned and nodded to Grady, his dark eyes wide with excitement. When Grady returned the nod, Jesse spiked both spurs into the horse's flanks, and pushed his body forward with all the power he had.

———

LAFE SUNNERLAND FELT CERTAIN HIS LIFE WAS OVER. He could feel blood trickling down the side of his neck—the coarse rope gradually tightening. Lafe thought about his father and mother and their brutal end. He wasn't sure, but the four men that were passing a bottle of whiskey around may have had something to do with their murders. He thought one of them was an Erlock.

"*Blam! Pop! Blam! Blam!*"

He was elated as he saw Jesse and the others attack, his abductors dying on the ground. Lafe knew that he had only one chance to survive. He lowered his head and whispered to his horse, pleading with it not to bolt. The rope burn that he felt on his neck was negligible compared to what it would feel like if the horse took off, he thought.

His nostrils sucked in a wave of arid gun powder smoke. Lafe saw his brother galloping toward him. He saw the glint of a large knife blade and held his breath. Moments later, he felt the rope tug at his neck as the piece above him fell to the ground.

"Get off the horse!" Lafe heard his brother yell. He felt the cold metal on his neck as Jesse sawed into the rope. The sound of Jesse's pistol shot strained his ears. His hands were tied behind his back and he felt Jesse sawing at the rope. The bindings were gone, and he was free.

The shooting had ceased. He heard yells and whoops as his saviors celebrated their destruction of his abductors.

Lafe spent the next two hours sitting with his back against a tree, watching his fellow Riders digging and burying the four dead men. His felt his neck. Mighty sore, he thought, but it's there, and ah'm alive.

He forced a smile as he watched Grady Hastings approach. "That about does it, Lafe. How's yar neck? Doggoned close call, ah'd say."

"Ah thought ah was a goner, for suh, Grady. You boys comin' out of them there trees was a sight to behold…never forget it," Lafe squeaked, grinning.

32

JENNIFER HAGGARD LOOKED OUT THE WINDOW of a Pullman car. She was sitting next to her husband, Justin. Her thoughts about the glorious honeymoon she had experienced with her husband in Kansas City occupied her mind. The love she shared with Justin was far greater than she had ever dreamed it could be.

Justin snored lightly in the seat next to her, occasionally jerking his head and repositioning. She was continually amazed at the new clothes he had purchased in the city. The brown, wool frock coat he wore was unbuttoned, exposing a neat, dark brown vest. She smiled as her thoughts drifted back to their room.

He had shown her his spare, detachable collar, which he had put on just before leaving the hotel. He wore his new, tan trousers slipped over his brown boots. To accommodate his long legs, Justin sat in an awkward position, she noticed.

Jennifer couldn't believe that their wedding day had actually arrived. It seemed to take years, she thought. If only my mother had been alive to ride to the church with me and father. He looked so handsome in his black top hat and boots. She experienced a new, exhilarating feeling that morning during the ride in the carriage to the church.

Going up the aisle, she almost fainted when seeing Justin standing near the preacher. Her father's arm kept her from falling. She could still feel the warmness of his first kiss after the words from the preacher, "I now pronounce you man and wife."

Their wedding day would have been perfect if it hadn't been for the Sunnerland barn, she thought. At least Justin wasn't involved.

She was so happy that they had arrived safely at Stillman Mills late that night. The recent violence that had occurred in western

Missouri the past few months worried her. The hotel was suitable and clean, but she was looking forward to Kansas City.

Early the next morning, they boarded the train for the big city. When she stepped into the red carpeted lobby of Vellman's Hotel on the next day, Jennifer was thrilled. She couldn't believe the exquisite dinner that had been served to them in their room.

Jennifer had hoped that the few days spent in Kansas City would never end. She realized Justin might be taken away from her after they returned home to the small house that her father-in-law had built for them. She took several short breaths and felt the tension in her stomach.

She was sad when they boarded the train in Kansas City for their trip back to Stillman Mills. Jennifer was enjoying the view of the countryside. Justin had fallen asleep while holding her hand.

Justin stirred and awoke in a short period of time. He turned and smiled while gently rubbing his eyes. "Where we at, beautiful?" he asked, smiling broadly.

"We passed through Independence a few minutes ago. I would wager that Stillman Mills is close to an hour away."

———

JUSTIN LOOKED AT HIS BRIDE AND GLOWED. She's the most beautiful person on earth, he thought. Ah'm looking forward to living with her in our new home. Coming home to her after spending all day with the herds will be like heaven.

He wondered if the war was going to force him to leave his bride at times. Except for some local incidences, the war seemed to be far away. One of the articles that he had read in the Kansas City newspaper fascinated him. A Confederate cavalry general is creating havoc with the federals in Virginia. Stuart was his name—Jeb Stuart. The article explained how Stuart's cavalry, over a thousand strong, sawed down telegraph poles and successfully attacked and burned down federal camps.

Gosh, if what ah read is true, the war will be over soon. He sat up straight in his seat. Leaning to his left, he kissed his wife's cheek.

Justin liked the warm feeling of her hand when she reached over to touch his.

"Ah wonder why the train is slowing," he said to his wife. "There's no town in this area."

"Look, Justin, over there." Jennifer pointed. "There's some riders."

"Holy Jaysus, those are Union's. See the blue?"

"Oh, Justin, I'm frightened."

"Ah, don't worry, they shouldn't bother us," he responded as the train continued to slow.

————

CAPTAIN GREGORY OF THE UNION CAVALRY watched confidently as the train screeched to a halt. His main interest was to check for rebel weapons that might be aboard. He also had been ordered to watch for the transportation of rebel troops. After ordering four men to board each car, he sat on his horse and waited. He counted seven cars.

The captain walked his horse slowly down the length of the train his men had entered. He scanned the countryside, anxiously watching for lookouts. His awareness that bushwhackers had been seen in the area on the previous day worried him.

Two of his men emerged from the fourth car. They dropped to the ground and waited for someone to bring their horses. The captain sank a spur into his horse and approached them. "Find anything, boys?" he asked.

"Naw, nothing in that one, sir," said one of the Bluecoats as he pointed.

Two cars down, he saw one of his boys push a gentleman off the ladder and onto the ground. Flicking his reins, his horse advanced to them. "Who's that?" the captain asked.

"It's one of the Reb's, Captain. He claims that he's not been in the fightin'."

"Hey there, Reb. Where are ya headin'?" asked the captain.

"Just goin' home with my wife. We're on our honeymoon."

"Ya want to take a look at 'er, cap. She's really a looker," responded one of the Bluecoats.

"Naw. Hey, look, Reb, I'm gonna let you go this time, but you keep your nose clean. Understand?"

"Yes, sir. Ah'm not armed and causing no trouble. Thank ye."

———

JENNIFER WORRIED DEEPLY. She had pleaded with the soldier to leave them alone. The Bluecoat spit on the floor and grabbed Justin's arm. "Ya come with me, Reb. We're gonna see the Captain."

"Don't worry, Jennifer. Ah'll be right back. The captain's a gentleman. Can't say that about this one," said Justin sharply.

The Bluecoat elbowed Justin on the side of the head "Don't get sassy with me, Reb. You come along peacefully, or we'll drag ya out."

Jennifer put her palm over her round mouth. She had anxiously watched as the two Bluecoats pushed her husband down the aisle.

"Don't worry, ma'am. He'll be back," a man said.

Jennifer looked across the aisle and saw a gray-haired gentleman who had spoken the kind words.

"Thank you, sir. I pray that you are right."

Jennifer rose from her seat and paced up and down the aisle, occasionally glancing out a window. She couldn't see what was going on, and was worried sick that Justin would not return.

33

BEN HAGGARD FELT THE HEAT FROM THE METAL ROOF as he walked up and down the railroad depot platform in Stillman Mills. He lifted his hat and toweled his brow with a bandana. Darn hot today, but not surprising....It is a July afternoon, he said to himself.

Walking to the far end of the platform, Ben's hazel eyes scanned the horizon to the west.

"Should've been here by now," said the dispatcher. "It's a good two hours late."

Ah should've resisted the idea more, Ben thought. This is no time to be travelin' on a train, especially with a woman. Justin wouldn't listen. He insisted that he and Jennifer would be fine. Ben remembered reading an article in the newspaper a couple of weeks ago about a train being stopped by Union cavalry. They took twelve Missourans off the train at gunpoint. Never did 'ear what happened to 'em.

"Hey! There she comes!" Ben heard a man yell from the other end of the platform.

Ben's stomach knotted as he anxiously strained to see down the long line of tracks. The dispatcher had come running out onto the platform. "Thar she is," he said and flipped out his pocket watch. "Two hours late," he added, and hustled back into the depot.

The thin column of smoke that was going straight up into the sky was like heaven to Ben. Ah best not git too confident, he thought. Anything could have happened. He glanced around the platform and noticed several people awaiting the east bound's arrival.

The dark form of the locomotive appeared larger and larger as it steamed toward town. He thought about Anna and her instense worry about their two sons. Justin had survived two battles thus far. She worried further that their son, Jubal, would join the Riders. He was only sixteen years of age.

Ben felt badly that he didn't visit his daughter and grandsons who lived in Stillman Mills. They're safe and sound, but my son and his daughter-in-law are not, he said to himself as he grabbed his upper lip with his lower front teeth.

The ugly grunting of the steam-powered locomotive was like music to his ears. Ben could feel the ground shake under the platform. After the brakes were applied, it began to slow. He anxiously watched the windows of the passenger cars, but could not see any of his family.

His nostrils got a whiff of wood burning as the huge engine rumbled by, and the wheels screeched before the train came to a complete stop.

Ben cautiously walked toward the rear cars, anticipating the passengers would disembark there. A man dressed in a railroad uniform stepped to the ground, and set a stool on the platform. That has to be the conductor, Ben thought. The trainman extended his arm and assisted the first passenger off. Others followed. Ben had stopped a short distance away. His heart was pounding, his eyes straining to see Justin and Jennifer.

The laughing and hugging of happy people spread throughout the platform. The conductor was watching the door, anticipating that more people were coming down. Then Ben saw her—the colorful dress—his daughter-in-law, Jennifer. A young man dressed in a brown coat assisted her. Does Justin have a brown coat? he asked himself....No, ah don't think that he does.

Ben's eyes saw him stand....It *was* Justin! His son had returned safely, and Ben felt elated.

———

JUBAL HAGGARD RODE HIS PAINT, PRINCE, down their roadway onto the Tarrytown Road. His mother refused to allow him to ride into town without an escort. Reversing his direction, he rode back toward the house. This was the sixth time that he had ridden out and looked eastward toward Tarrytown, hoping to see his brother's carriage on the road.

At last he saw a cloud of dust to the east. Reversing his direction, he nudged a spur into Prince's side and galloped out to the Tarrytown Road. "Hallelujah, it's them...They're comin'!" he yelled.

Disobeying his mother, he galloped toward the dust cloud.

———

THE CARRIAGE TRANSPORTING JUSTIN AND JENNIFER passed by the church in Tarrytown. Standing next to the entry door, Pastor Wilson waved. Justin's father, Ben, sat tall in the saddle, trotting his horse close behind the carriage. He waved at the pastor and felt great relief that Justin and his bride had returned safely from Kansas City.

Passing along MacTurley's Woods, he felt nervous because of what had happened to the Sunnerlands. Even though their murders had occurred the previous summer, Ben remained extra alert on this stretch of road, his hazel eyes scanning the edge of the timbers.

Ben patted the wooden stock of his musket, making sure it was in the scabbard and accessible. He knew the Colt in his holster was loaded. Justin always carried two revolvers, and Ben was sure they were in the carriage. Ben was glad when Justin put the horses to a fast trot. He doesn't trust this neck of the woods either, Ben thought.

After passing over Bear Creek and coming astride of the Sunnerland roadway, he spotted a rider coming from the west. That has to be Jubal, he thought. He couldn't contain himself and disobeyed his mother again. Seeing Jubal wave his hat high over his head caused Ben to smile.

34

MAYOR OWEN PRITCHARD STOOD on the boardwalk across the street from the Grand Hotel. He was looking east when George Walker stopped by to talk. "Anything happenin' out at Sunnerland's barn?" the mayor asked.

"Not yet, Owen, but the lumber should show up any day. That is, if the jayhawkers don't get to it first," George answered, his dark eyes narrowing and looking eastward.

"Ho...something comin' now...sure a big pile of dust out there toward Mills," said the mayor.

George Walker looked. "Yar right, Mayor, that could be the Sunnerland lumber comin', ah reckon so."

They stood and watched as the dust cloud got closer. "Looks like four pullin' the first wagon," the mayor said.

"Yup…and there's four more behind them. It looks like six wagons comin'. Ah betcha' they're full of lumber, too," George responded. "That means we can get started tomorra'," he added.

"Hey, there's someone else ridin' by them wagons. Betcha' it's Lance. He's due sometime today," Mayor Pritchard added.

"Good time to get across the street. Looks like a lot of others are doin' the same," George said and began crossing the street.

George stomped onto the boardwalk in front of the General Store. "Hey, Seth, looks like the mail is comin' in, ah reckon," he drawled.

"Yup, and we'll know if there's big news or not by how fast Lance comes down the home stretch."

A crowd had gathered, and they anxiously watched Lance walk his horse down the middle of the street. "Drat that Lance," one of the men said.

"The news must be big today," another replied.

"The more people waitin', the more he slows down," George Walker responded, sitting down on a bench, bringing his lips tightly together.

———

HENRY HASTINGS HAD BOTH REINS IN HIS HANDS. He sat on the buckboard bench next to Emma, who was holding a red and yellow bag on her lap. She had on that delightful gingham skirt which she usually wore on shopping days. The previous day, she had requested a ride into town for sewing supplies.

Thomas occupied a stool in the back. Henry glanced back when he heard him loudly remark, "Sure a lot of dust to the east. Wonder who that could be?"

"Probably the lumber wagons…ah reckon they're due any day now," Henry answered.

The barn needs to be completed before winter sets in, he thought. It's going to take more time because most of the youngins' will be on patrol with the Gray Riders. Thomas is growing fast. He'll be a big help. Both the Sunnerland boys may be gone.

As they passed by the church, he could see the first wagon. Sure a large gathering of people in front of the General Store. Mail must be comin', too, he thought.

Passing the store, he saw Emma exchange waves with slim-waisted Beth Kingsley, who was standing on the boardwalk. Her dress of pink and brown calico was mostly covered with an apron of dark brown canvass. "There must be .ne news," Emma said. "Lance is being swarmed."

Pulling up next to the livery, Henry looked back and saw that Thomas had jumped from the wagon and had joined the people surrounding Lance Milburn.

"There you are, Toby," Henry said after jumping off the wagon and handing him the reins. He promptly walked to the other side and assisted his wife down from the wagon.

"Emancipation! What's that?" he heard someone yell as they approached the General Store.

"That means slaves are illegal!" someone else shouted.

"What's that mean?"

"The coloreds are all free—in the Union, that is."

Henry was handed the front page of one of the newspapers. *President Lincoln has freed the slaves by signing the Proclamation of Emancipation on August 4, 1862.*

———

PRESIDENT ABRAHAM LINCOLN on September 22, 1862 announced that as of January 1, 1863, any state or persons within a state who held slaves would be considered in rebellion against the United States.

His proclamation, a follow-up to an act of congress, stated that all persons who had been held as slaves would forevermore be free on that day.

The executive government of the United States, including the military and naval authorities thereof, would recognize and maintain the freedom of said persons.

35

THE SOUNDS OF TIT-A-TAT...TIT-A-TAT...TIT-A-TAT...began shortly after sunrise at the home of Lafe and Jesse Sunnerland. Thomas Hastings heard those sounds over and over again. Elbows and arms flaying in the air were driving nails with hammers. His father, who was high up on the frame, yelled, "O'er here, Thomas! Ah need some more nails!"

Thomas had watched with awe the previous day when the crew had used eight horses to raise the framed ends and two sides. At a critical moment, Thomas feared the ropes were going to break. "Get back away from there!" his father yelled at him.

Today he counted seven men up on the frame of the roof. His stomach growled, reminding him that lunch should be coming soon. He looked toward Tarrytown Road, hoping to see the food wagon coming.

"O're here, Thomas," Orly McGregor drawled.

Using a ladder, Thomas trudged up the steps, securing his position with one hand and holding a bucket of nails with the other. Where is that food wagon? he wondered again.

"Riders comin'!" someone yelled from up above.

When Thomas was part way down the ladder, he looked toward the Tarrytown Road. Two horses kicked up dust and had just passed by the Haggard's roadway. He looked toward Tarrytown, hoping to see the food wagon approaching.

When he stepped onto the ground, he saw the riders turn onto the Sunnerland roadway. "Grady, the riders are comin' this way!" Thomas yelled.

"Bring me the ladder, Thomas...quick!"

Thomas's legs swaggered as he carried the long ladder to Grady's position and thumped it against the barn frame. After adjusting it, he heard Grady say, "Thomas, get me my holsters! They're over there by my coat."

Thomas waited anxiously for his brother to come down the ladder. He noticed the others up on the barn roof had stopped their work and were watching the riders. He handed Grady his pistol belt and watched him strap it on.

Grady moved to the edge of the building and watched the two riders. "There's somethin' familiar about 'em," he said.

Thomas yelped, *"It's Cole Younger!"*

Grady walked out to the roadway to greet the visitors. Justin Haggard had come down the ladder, and he caught up with Grady.

Thomas watched the second rider. That's Frank James, he said to himself, feeling elated. Lafe Sunnerland and Mitch McGregor had joined Grady and Justin.

The two visitors remained on their horses. Thomas noticed Cole Younger point eastward a few times.

Thomas watched the men talk for a few minutes, then Cole Younger and Frank James turned their horses and rode off.

The food wagon turned off the Tarrytown Road onto Sunnerland's roadway. Finally, lunch was on its way! Thomas watched the riders move aside and wave as they met the food wagon.

———

"LONE JACK...WHERE'S THAT, GRADY?" Henry had asked.

"East of here about a day's ride," Grady responded while they sat around the dinner table.

Thomas's blue eyes widened while waiting for more response.

"Yeah, the Yankees were spotted headed in that direction a couple of days ago, according to Cole and Frank," added Grady, who forked down two more pieces of steak.

Thomas and his father anxiously waited for Grady to finish chewing, both leaning their stomachs against the edge of the table.

"There ain't much over there. What would the Yankees want with that town?" asked Henry.

"Ah think they're out to get us all! We're goin' up there to chase 'em off," exclaimed Grady. "There are about seven hundred of 'em, ah hear," he added. "Worse than that, some of 'em are Missourans."

"Missourans! What's goin' on? Why would our own people fight agin' us?" asked his father.

"Dunno, Father. It's all politics…that Lincoln and his righteous bunch."

"When are ya all plannin' on leavin', son?" Henry asked.

"We're gonna ride up there with some of Quantrill's men in a couple of days. Younger is goin' to let us know," answered Grady.

"We've got plenty of time to get that barn up. Are the two Sunnerlands goin' along?" asked Henry.

"Yup, as far as ah know they are."

"Ah'm takin' a ride into town tomarra'. The paper from Jefferson City should've come in today, ah reckon," Henry said. "Ah'm anxious to read what's goin' on about the war," he added.

36

THOMAS SAT ON THE BUCKBOARD SEAT next to his father. They had just passed the Haggard's roadway when he saw the hawk. It's Keeya, he thought…I'm sure it is. After watching the hawk drift and float for another minute, he had no doubt. The hawk swooped lower and came so close that Thomas could see its eyes. Is he tryin' to tell me somethin'? Thomas asked himself.

Glancing at the schoolhouse when they passed, he thought about the day that Carr Walker died in the schoolhouse. I will miss 'em when school starts up in the fall. I wonder if Ebenezer Styles is comin' back? I sure liked Miss Stoner a lot better, but then, she will never be back…mainly because Carr got killed.

"There sure are a lot of people hangin' roun' in front of Seth Miller's store," his father said, interrupting Thomas's thoughts. "I reckon there is some news."

Thomas saw a man push another in the chest. They must be arguin', he thought. It's probably about what Grady and Pa were talkin' about last night. He thought about his older brother who had gotten his gear together and rode off a couple of hours ago. Sure hope he gets back safely.

"Hello, Toby," his father said, handing the livery stableman the reins. "What's goin' on in front of the store?"

"It's the mayor...He's hell-bent on sidin' with the Missoura Seventh Cavalry. They're ridin' with Union's Major Foster, ah hear. They may be comin' this way. Gonna be a big fight."

Thomas grimaced as he thought about the possibility of another shootout in Tarrytown. People gettin' all shot up en kilt. He had gotten off the wagon and waited for his father who had gone into the livery with Toby.

Then he heard a yell coming from the direction of the store. "Hey, Pa, I'm headin' ovah to the store," Thomas said, pulling at the brim of his scratchy bowler.

"Good, son, ah'll be there shortly."

As Thomas got nearer, he heard intermittent jeers and cheers. A crowd of people had formed a circle. Within it were two men, each stripped to their waist. They cautiously circled each other and jabbed when they had a chance. Sitting on the ground was Banker Herron, who held a towel to his face.

"Mr. Walker, what's happenin'?" Thomas asked.

"Well, hello, Thomas. Seems that feller with the black trousers got arguin' with the banker. He hauled off and hit 'em with his fist...knocked him to the ground. That other feller, in the brown breeches, didn't like that one bit. Instead of pickin' on older people, why don't you try me?' he had said. Since then, they've been a dancin' around, neither gettin' much hittin' in."

Thomas felt a hand on his shoulder. He looked up and saw that his father had arrived. He better trim them whiskers or mother is gonna get on 'em, Thomas said to himself, smiling.

"Hello, George. Looks like we gotta war goin' on right here," Henry Hastings said, tugging on the brim of his black Stetson.

"Henry, the news ain't good. Read about it yourself in the newspaper. The war's breakin' out all over the state, and some of it's gettin' mighty close. It says there's a big union force movin' this way from yonder Lexington. Ah imagine Grady and some of our boys will do some fightin'. Ah hear some of Quantrill's men have been roun' here recruitin'."

"Yeah, George, you're right. As a matter of fact, Grady left earlier today. Cole Younger and Frank James came out to the Sunnerland place a couple of days ago."

"Henry, if ah had to do it all over again, ah would've never let Will jin up with them union people. Their leaders are a bunch of nuthins. Just because they went to college, they think they know it all. Will got kilt because one of their Captains led them the wrong direction."

"What were the two men fightin' about?" Henry asked.

"Our distinguished banker's got some leanin' for the Union, and said somethin' bad about the Gray Riders. The hot-headed black-trousers man got angry and hit 'em. The other feller just likes to fight. They're both over at the saloon drinkin' together right now."

Henry Hastings laughed.

Thomas felt moisture forming in his eyes thinking about Will Walker's funeral. He saddened even more remembering the embarrassing tongue lashing that his father had received from the same man he was now talking to. I'm sure glad my father and Mr. Walker are friends again.

———

HENRY PULLED THE LEFT REIN and the buckboard turned onto the Hastings's roadway. "Hey Pa, looks like we have visitors," Thomas said anxiously.

"Ah think ah know what that's gonna be all about," responded Henry.

"What, Pa? What?"

"Sammy has been wantin' to join Grady and the boys for some time. Gotta hunch it's for real this time."

"Hello, Samuel, what kin a do for ya today?"

"It's my boy here, Massa. Ah can't talk any sense into 'em. He been sayin', "If they don't let me jin up with the Gray Riders, ah's agonna' run away."

"Thomas, would ya take the team to the barn? Ah've gotta talk to that man."

"Yes, Pa," Thomas answered.

When Thomas returned to the house on foot, the Mortons had left, and he could see them walking back to their shacks. "What happened, Pa?" Thomas asked.

"Samuel promised replacin' Sammy with two of his kin, both young and strong. So, ah'm gonna let Sammy go…We'll see what Grady has to say. Maybe they don't want Sammy."

37

JUBAL HAGGARD SAT ON HIS SADDLE and gazed toward Bear Mountain. He felt moisture building in his small, dark penetrating eyes as he watched Jennifer and Justin embrace. Looking eastward, he saw the rising sun looking like a fireball, its lower half partially hidden by a spike of trees from MacTurley's Woods.

Jubal couldn't handle watching his brother say goodbye to Jennifer any longer, and he began walking his horse slowly down the roadway. By the time Jubal reached the Tarrytown Road, the sun had fully emerged. Looking back, he could see his brother's horse galloping toward him.

Ah've never seen anyone look more handsome than my brother does in that gray jacket, Jubal thought. He has stripes, too, just like Grady Hastings.

ANNA HAGGARD WATCHED OUT THE WINDOW. The sun emerged over the trees. Her large, blackish eyes saw her son, Jubal, walking his horse slowly toward the Tarrytown Road. I'm glad that I cannot see them saying goodbye to each other, she thought. They must be on the other side of the house. We said our goodbyes last night, and I couldn't bear another.

Her lips began moving again as she moved her fingers over the string of beads that she held in her left hand. She wasn't aware that anyone else was of the Roman faith in the Tarrytown area. She thought about her parents who lived in Italy. I know that my mother is praying for Justin, too.

Anna had granted permission to Jubal to ride with his brother until they reached Tarrytown. He was further allowed to spend time in town with his friend, Thomas Hastings. They would ride back home together, she had been assured.

Her finger stopped moving for a moment when she saw Justin in the saddle. He was galloping his horse to catch up with his brother, who had already reached the Tarrytown Road. So tall and handsome in that gray uniform he was, she thought. Moments later, he was gone. She could feel her heart tumbling into her stomach.

———

VIRGILIA JACKSON WORE A CHECKERED red and white apron. She stood in front of the kitchen stove, stirring the contents of a pot. The steam coming from the pot caused her to cough.

"Priam. ah don't wanna Elkanah to go. I've lost one son and that's enough."

"But, Mamma, ah have to. Ah'm part of the Gray Riders."

"Dun matter, son. The Riders are agin' freein' us. We's fightin' on the wrong side. President Lincoln is the right one," Virgilia replied firmly.

"Mamma, Lincoln didn't free us. Massa Kingsley did. We is on the right side. Ah need to revenge Jordon gettin' kilt."

"Priam! Talk some sense into this youngin'. Tell 'em he's wrong."

"Virgilia...I'm sorry...Elkanah is not wrong. He's fightin' for us and the Kingsleys. Abel is goin' along, too. Ah feel honored that the Hastings, McGregors, and Haggards want Elkanah to go with 'em. Ah'd go myself if ah wuz younger."

Virgilia set out four soup bowls on the table, saving the fifth one to bang down on the table in front of her husband.

Priam threw up his hands and said softly, "Virgilia, you need one for yerself."

"Ah'm not hungry. How can I think about eating when my son is goin' off to fight?"

Elkanah lowered his head, his kinky, long, black hair almost touching the soup bowl. "Mama, ah'll come back...ah promise...."

———

"TAKE IT SLOW, JUBE. Mitch should be along soon," said Justin after joining his brother on the Tarrytown Road.

Looking over his back, Jubal could see a rider coming. "That must be Mitch now," he said.

"Whoa!" said Justin.

"Hey, who ya got there?" drawled Mitch McGregor after he caught up. "Jube, are ya goin' with us on this one?"

"Naw, he's ridin' along as far as Tarrytown. Him and Thomas Hastings are going raise some ruckus together," Justin said.

"We better talk to Constable Muldoon and let 'em know what he's in for," Mitch said, laughing, his large, blue eyes sparkling.

After crossing Bear Creek, they found Lafe and Jesse Sunnerland waiting at the head of the Hastings's roadway.

"There come three riders from o're there," said Jubal as he pointed. "Must be Grady, and Thomas, and...."

"And who, Jube?"

"Dunno, Justin."

"Well, ah'll be danged....It's Sammy!"

Jubal felt the excitement as the Riders gathered together. Looking ahead, he could see two more riders. "Hey, Justin, who are they?" he asked.

"Why, that's Abel Kingsley...and looks like...yup, that's

Elkanah."

"Elkanah!" exclaimed Jubal.

"Yup, he's gonna jin us...."

———

THOMAS FELT THRILLED THAT HE AND JUBAL had been granted permission to ride into Tarrytown with their brothers. He had a couple of gold coins that gathered dust in his dresser drawer. School season approached and he intended to buy some supplies at the General Store.

He glanced at his brother frequently while the two rode up their roadway. Imagine, riding next to a real cavalry uniform, he thought. Jubal aligned with Thomas, and they rode next to each other in the rear position as the column moved past MacTurley's Woods and into Tarrytown.

When they arrived in town, he marveled at the large number of horses tied to hitching rails. A large group of men mingled amongst the horses, most of them clad in gray.

The two boys continued on to the livery while their brothers and others joined up with the other men. Thomas smiled when he heard several shrieks and yells coming from where the Riders had gathered.

"Come on, Jube. Let's jin the fun," Thomas said.

The two boys ran toward the General Store.

"Hey, here's a couple more....Get 'em a musket!" shouted one of the Riders.

"Good idear, but someone has to stay behind to protect our women," said Mitch McGregor laughingly.

"Heaven help us all," added Lafe Sunnerland. "We may as well ride to Washington and surrender to Abe."

Thomas watched and listened in awe to the high-spirited Gray Riders as they bantered and jostled each other.

His feelings became mixed as the Gray Riders mounted and the sergeant yelled, "Form a column of two!"

He stood stiffly next to Jubal and watched, leaning against the wall of the General Store as the Riders rode slowly out of town on the road toward Stillman Mills.

38

GRADY AND JUSTIN RODE abreast of each other, in fourth position, in a column of two that stretched a quarter-of-a-mile westward.

Justin asked, "Do ya know what the date is, Grady?"

"Yup...It's the 15th of August."

Grady thought about his talk with Cole Younger and Frank James at the Sunnerland farm, three days previous. He and Mitch had learned that there were Union forces headed south from Lexington and other places. Cole had asked the Gray Riders to join up with Quantrill, whose men were stationed about seven miles southwest of a town called Lone Jack. Both Cole Younger and Frank James were currently members of Quantrill's band.

"Strange name for a town—Lonejack," Mitch said, his straw colored hair sticking out in all directions.

Grady saw the sergeant raise an arm, signaling a halt. He gently pulled on his reins.

Justin said, "Whoa! Wonder why we're stoppin'? We just watered the horses a few miles back."

Grady glanced at his riding mate, his green eyes narrowing.

"Rider comin'," Justin added with a flare of excitement.

"Yeah, ah see 'em, and whoever it is...comin' hard," Grady said. "Yeah, imagine naming a town after a tree," Grady added, laughing.

While watching the rider approach, Grady looked forward to closing out the day and spending the night in his new tent. He thought about his mother and her rhetorical opposition to the war.

"It's sheer madness," she had said the night before at the dinner table. Her eyes were moist, and he watched a single tear emerge from the corner of her eye and roll down her cheek. Grady grasped his mother and held her close. He released her torso and grabbed her hands—the trembling stopped when he tightened his grip. Grady concerned himself about the deep wrinkles in her forehead.

The sound of galloping hooves approaching interrupted Grady's thoughts of his mother. The rider, wearing a wide, black Stetson, brought his horse to an abrupt halt next to the leader of the column. Sergeant York is getting an earful, Grady thought as he watched the rider gesture with his arm, pointing north, then turn in the saddle and point southeastward.

"Can you hear what he's sayin'?" asked Lafe Sunnerland, who rode directly behind Grady.

"No, but he's sure spittin' it out," Grady answered.

He saw Jesse Sunnerland's large, dark eyes narrow. The two brothers were riding side-by-side. Jesse's almost as tall as Justin, Grady thought. Jesse became a man on the day that he cut the rope that was about to hang his brother up on Bear Mountain. If the horse had bolted, Lafe would have been dead.

"Ho! Yaw!" the sergeant yelled, sending a tingling sensation up and down Grady's skin. The sergeant pointed forward and the column began to move eastward again.

———

ABEL KINGSLEY ROLLED A SPUR against the body of his horse. He watched the lead riders in the column disappear behind a grassy hill. Next to him was a young man whom he had met the previous day. "Ah'm Preston from out Independence way," the Rider abreast of him had said softly. "Where you from?"

"Near Tarrytown," answered Abel. "What made you jin up with us?"

"Gotta do what ah kin…dad-blamed redlegs burnt my neighbor's house down…kilt everyone."

Abel did not respond. He thought about the Sunnerlands and their barn fire. At least no one got hurt.

Abel liked Preston. They appeared to be the same age. For the past ten miles, Preston had been talking about the woman friend he had left behind. Wish ah had a woman, Abel thought. Ah'll work on that when ah get back. He thought about Jessica Walker with the long, blond hair and the sparkling, blue eyes. She's beautiful...need to do somethin' about that when ah git back home. Martha Miller is a good looker, too. Her father Toby is a little strange, though. None matter, he thought, and glanced back westward toward the setting sun.

Abel felt the tension in his stomach heat up as the sun disappeared behind the hills to the west. Rubbing his chin with his fingers, he could feel whiskers developing. Suddenly, Abel felt a lot older than eighteen.

———

GRADY'S BACK HURT HIM. He had strained it working on Sunnerland's barn. Riding his horse most of the day since sunrise didn't help any, he thought. That tree in the distance reminded him of that barn. It towered over everything around.

Because it was getting late in the day, Grady thought that they would spend the night in the timber ahead, where the single tree towered.

Grady felt pleased when the sergeant turned the column slightly and headed toward the tall tree. Minutes later, Sergeant York raised his hand to signal a halt. The sergeant said, "There's a creek down there in the middle of that timber, and that's where we're gonna set up camp."

When the column got close to the timber, the sergeant turned his horse toward the creek bottom and waved. The column followed him down. "All right, boys, spread out, and find a place for your tents. Don't forget to water your horses first, though."

Grady removed his pack from behind the saddle and unfastened the cinch. Laying the saddle down on the ground, he led his horse down to the water.

Afterward, he set the horse out to graze with the other horses and began setting up his new tent.

"What ya got there, Hastings, a dog tent?" Justin asked, his head bobbing with laughter. "Your toes are goin' to be stickin' out at the end," he added.

"Never you mind. It's what they're usin' in Virginia. Ah reckon it's easier to set up and take down," Grady said and smiled.

———

THE DISTANT SOUND OF A HARMONICA saddened Justin. He hoped that his wife would temporarily move into the main house while he was gone. They had discussed the possibility, but Jennifer wished to remain where she was. She would have someone to talk to all the time, he thought. Jubal would watch over her as he had promised.

Justin heard the sound of approaching horses. Looking southward, he saw five riders approaching. One of them carried a blue flag. Justin stood with Grady, who also watched the riders approach. Grady recognized one of the riders as Sergeant York.

"Boys...Good Evening...This here's Captain Larkin. He's got a few things to say...gather roun'."

"Are you Hastings?" the captain asked.

"Yes, sir. What can ah do for ya?"

"Tomorra' mornin', four hours before first light, we're riding to a town called Lone Jack. There's a nest of Yankees there, and we need to drive 'em off. Ah'm part of Colonel Cockrell's unit.

"We're jinin' up with Colonel Thompson and Colonel Hays. Soon after that, Quantrill will catch up with us. Our plan is to surprise the Bluecoats and drive 'em out of Jackson County.

"Ah want all of the Gray Riders to jin us. What do ya all say?"

"Sir, if ah can speak for the Riders, we'll be ready," replied Grady.

Justin slowly nodded his head. He saw a large bonfire raging farther up the creek. He thought about Jennifer, and he wished that she was nestled close to the fire in his parents' house. He felt certain that his father would give up his rocking chair for the evening and offer it to Jennifer.

"Ah'm goin' over there by the fire," Justin said to Grady after the Captain and his aides had left.

"Jin' you in a short minute," Grady responded.

39

LIEUTENANT WILLIAM FARNSWORTH OF THE SEVENTH Missouri Cavalry was among a contingency of eight hundred Federal troops, under the command of General Foster. He had been promoted to lieutenant recently after agreeing to join the Federal forces. At the beginning of the conflict, he and other men from Missouri had been fighting for the confederacy. They were captured at the first battle of Independence. Switching sides initiated a wave of guilt feelings, but the choice was a solid alternative to rotting in a stockade.

The Captain of his unit had said there were more or less four thousand rebels in and around the area of a town called Lone Jack. When Farnsworth's men neared the town, they found a handful of skirmishers who they engaged and drove off.

As the cavalry approached the town on the evening of August 15th, a band of rebels who were camped on the high ground in the town were fired upon. After driving them off, General Foster's men returned to the town. They set up their tents and built campfires on a stretch of high ground, near the center of town where a lone, tall, spreading, blackjack oak tree stood.

The lieutenant and his men settled in for the night. He wished that he could visit his sister near Tarrytown, but doubted it would happen. William hadn't spoken to her since she had lost her son, Will, at The Battle of Wilson's Creek. According to Angie's letter, Will had died in Grady Hastings's arms. Farnsworth had heard rumors that a large Confederate force might be near, and he wondered if one of them would be Hastings.

William remembered his sister telling him about the group of local young men who were headed by Hastings. They fought in the battle of Lexington. They called them the Gray Riders in the Tarrytown area. Two of them were killed while pushing the hemp bales from the river almost to the top of the ridge.

———

JUSTIN HAGGARD HAD AWAKENED DURING THE NIGHT. After freeing his left shoulder from under his body, he stretched his arm to regain feeling. Peeking beyond the flap of the tent, he felt relieved to see darkness in the east and not the beginning of daylight.

He closed his eyes and visualized Jennifer curled up under the covers, asleep in their bed. No, he thought. She would be in the big house. Jennifer would be in Jubal's bed, and his younger brother would be tossing about in a makeshift bed in the drawing room.

He thought about the fear he had seen in Jennifer's eyes when their train was stopped and boarded by Yankees on their return trip from Kansas City. Ah thought I was a dead man when they dragged me outside and pushed me down on the ground. By some miracle they spared me and allowed me back on the train. Ah can still feel the warmth of Jennifer's hand, and her snuggle after returning to my seat.

A deep sadness flooded his brain. The thought of never seeing his new bride again caused him to flip his body around onto his stomach. Damn those abolitionists…damn Lincoln. They should tend to their own affairs and not interfere with ours here in Missouri.

———

THE EASTERN SKY APPEARED HAZY ON THE MORNING of August 16 in 1862. Grady Hastings had awakened early. He felt pleased with his new tent. It was made with white duck material, a new product gotten from a raid on a train that was transporting Union supplies. Feeling dry and comfortable, he lay on his back and thought about the upcoming day. The Yankees are camped on a hill. Ah wonder how we're goin' to go after 'em? From what I heard last evening, we're gonna do a massive assault. Quantrill's boys should be near by now, too. We can sure use all the help we can get.

The sound of footsteps and hand slaps against neighboring tents tightened his stomach muscles. The time is drawing near, he thought. Closing his eyes, he patiently awaited for the sound of his tent to be slapped.

"Aye, fancy 'tis," the gruff voice said as Grady heard the slap.

Hastily and methodically, Grady arranged his gear and took down his tent. He noticed that Justin had made slow progress and stood by his upright tent. He's dreaming about his new bride, and ah don't blame him one bit, Grady thought. Ah wish that Justin had not come on this trip. But there was no stoppin' 'em. He insisted on going with us.

A short distance away, several fires grew in size. He could smell the bacon and coffee. "Come on, Justin, let's get over there. Ah'm starved."

Grady sat on the ground next to Justin and relished his first cup of coffee, even though it looked ugly black. "Hey, Justin, git yar knife handy. This coffee needs cuttin'."

When Justin laughed, Grady gladdened, and thought it helped his morale. He saw Lafe Sunnerland devour a palm full of bacon, and his tongue extrude from his mouth and lick his blond whiskers. No one eats more than Lafe Sunnerland, Grady said to himself, smiling.

Grady slung the pack over his shoulder and picked up his saddle. He advanced toward a timbered area where the horses grazed within a makeshift corral. After arriving, he looked back down the gentle slope. In the darkness, the men who approached appeared to have enlarged heads—saddles carried on their shoulders. Elkanah Jackson and Sammy Morton arrived first.

Grady thought about his father and how he had debated whether to allow Sammy to join the Gray Riders. Ah'm glad that's he's here with us. There's probably no one has more physical strength in this camp, except perhaps Elkanah. If push comes to shove up there in Lone Jack, those two could make a difference.

Minutes later, all the Gray Riders were mounted. They waited until Captain Larkin, one of Colonel Cockrell's officers, arrived. He directed them to form a column of two and follow.

———

ABEL KINGSLEY FELT TIRED. He hadn't slept well the previous night. When he heard the slap on his tent, he awakened from an extraordinarily deep sleep. I'll never wake up, he thought. What am ah doing here anyhow, in this God-forsaken place? He thought about his comfortable bed at home. If ah was there now, ah'd be peeking out the window waiting for the beautiful sunrise.

My father is up by now, anxiously waiting for a steaming breakfast, he thought. Mother is the best cook in this world. Abel visualized the pan with the sizzling bacon, which would be next to a thick fixing of brown-charred dumplings.

His sister Sarah's blue streaked, hazel eyes would be sparkling, reflecting the spurting flames in the large rock-based fireplace. Still dressed in her night clothes, she would help her mother clean the table.

Abel closed his eyes and saw his Father put on his jacket and adjust his hat before placing it on his head. Routinely, Martin joined his foreman to inspect the Angus herd, which would be scattered all over the land. His father would lead the ride and examine all the animals. My God, that man loves his herd of black cattle, Abel said to himself.

Mother allowed Sarah to sleep some of the mornings, at least until her father had returned from the early ride. That sure didn't happen to me. Ah had to be out doing chores by the time father returned, or there would be hell to pay.

Abel could still feel his father's cold, strong fingers, which he had grasped during the farewell. Mother clung to him as if she was never going to let go. Abel remembered the deep feeling in the pit of his stomach when he had turned to look back after trotting out to the Tarrytown Road. His father and mother were standing on the porch watching. Martin's arm was around Beth's shoulder. Sarah stood off by herself, waving with both hands.

Ah wonder what my mother is gonna think of my new whiskers? he thought while rubbing the skin areas next to his chin.

The sound of boots trudging by his tent jerked Abel's mind into reality. He crawled out of his tent and quickly took it down.

"Thought you were gonna sleep in this mornin', Abel," his newly found friend, Preston, said.

"Not much sleep for me last night. Did ya hear that confounded owl hootin' all night long?"

"Ah slept like a boulder," Preston responded.

After rolling the tent up into his pack, Abel picked it up and slung his saddle onto his shoulder. Looking east, he could see a red streak on the horizon. They hurried to catch up with the others, who were plodding up the slope toward the horses.

40

THE MORNING SUN hid partially behind a large hill, Grady observed as the column turned slightly toward the south. Into a shallow valley they rode. He saw an arm go up to signal a stop. A rider from the front trotted toward the rear saying, "Dismount … dismount…prepare to proceed on foot…dismount."

"On foot!" Justin exclaimed. "Ah don't like the sound of this."

"We did it at Lexington, and it worked. Remember?" Grady responded.

"Ah'd much rather be on my steed, regardless," Justin responded.

"Ah hope they know what they is doin'," Mitch McGregor said, his saddle squeaking as he rocked front to back. Mitch's gray roan fidgeted, and he worked the reins to stay directly behind Grady.

Sergeant York, with a musket under his arm, approached on foot. "Men, we're goin' on foot yonder there." He pointed. Hear that wagon coming? It's full of muskets. They all need loadin'. Don't forget to have yar Colts ready to shoot. You're gonna need them, too."

Grady asked, "How many men we got all together, Sergeant?"

"Ah would say about three thousand, countin' what Thompson and Hays have," the sergeant answered.

When the wagon pulled up, each man grabbed a musket and began the process of tapping in a load. There was a lot of murmuring and grumbling.

"Boys, don't be angry with me. Ah don't make the rules. The colonel thinks that we can surprise 'em at their breakfast by goin' on foot."

After the men had their muskets loaded, the sergeant led the Riders around a small hill, and stopped them at the edge of a field, which was laden with tall grasses and weeds. "Spread out in a line, but ah want only three strides between each one of ya."

Grady took a step into the tall grass and saw the red rim of the sun edging up over a grassy ridge to the east.

"When we get to the yonder rise, you'll need to crouch to remain unseen," added the sergeant.

When the line neared the rise in the field, Grady heard sounds coming from beyond—a few neighs, clatters of metal canteens and plates, some laughter, and an occasional cough. His heartbeat increased to a torrid pace while thinking about what was beyond the rise.

The sergeant whispered, "Stay low…Keep your heads down….No talkin'…do ya hear me?"

Grady looked at Justin and saw intense sadness in his face. Farther along, Abel Kingsley reminded him of a cat ready to spring at its prey. Four arm-lengths away to his right, Mitch's face appeared somber. His blue eyes appeared bigger than Grady had ever seen them before. Some of his long, blond hair protruded straight back from under his hat. Looks like a dog's tail, Grady thought, smiling.

Just beyond Abel, Elkanah and Sammy crouched side by side. The musket in Elkanah's brawny arm looks like a child's toy, Grady thought. Earlier, he had noticed that they each had an unusually long sheath attached to their belts. Wonder where they got the blades that go into them leathers?

When they got within a few paces short of the rise, the sergeant signaled a halt. He crouched and cautiously crept to the summit. Grady watched anxiously when the sergeant raised his head to look beyond the rise. The sun's rays lit up the top of his hat like a candle. Grady glanced from side-to-side, making sure everyone held fast. He noticed Mitch was lecturing his brother, James.

The McGregor brothers had a loss to avenge, Grady thought. *How can ah ever forget that desperate wagon ride from the hemp bales to the field hospital after Paul was wounded?*

All eyes were glued on Sergeant York as he crept back down the slope. "Boys, when ah give the signal, all of ya advance. After we get over the ridge, we all need to stay low until ah give the word to stand and aim. The Yankees are having breakfast, and they haven't spotted us yet."

———

GRADY'S BACK HAD BEEN HURTING from staying low in the tall grass since they had left their horses. *Pounding nails while hanging from the rafters of Sunnerland's barn didn't help matters either*, he said to himself. *That's where my back problems started.* Grady was anxious to straighten up and run. The sergeant was apparently waiting for a command from down the line. Grady got on his knees and rotated his torso to relieve his back and shoulders.

"Now," the sergeant muttered hoarsely.

Grady tightened the grasp on his musket and quickly got to his feet. Noticing that Mitch was already moving forward, he took three long steps towards the rise. Beyond Mitch, standing and looking as thin as a piece of straw was his brother, James. *Ah don't think young James should be here*, Grady thought. *They've already lost one.* Losing Paul seemed to be harder on James than anyone else.

Moving cautiously, Grady reached the top and caught the sun's rays right in his eyes. He lowered his left arm and felt for each Colt. He remembered loading each with six shots as he felt them stuck inside his belt. According to the sergeant, the Bluecoats in Missouri didn't have revolvers.

Blinking rapidly, he took two steps past the rise, all the while remaining low and partially hidden in the tall weeds and grasses. Stopping for a moment, he saw thin columns of smoke rising from the campfires ahead. His heart leaped into his throat when he saw many blue-clad men milling about.

"Take it slow, lads," he heard his sergeant whisper.

My God, we're so close....Ah cannot believe that we haven't been detected, Grady said to himself.

"Halt. Prepare to fire," he heard the sergeant say.

Looking to his right, he saw Lafe and Jesse Sunnerland on their knees with muskets at ready position. Lafe massaged his neck by twisting and turning his head. It's still sore from the rope burns, Grady thought. Nothing scares that man after coming so close to death up on Bear Mountain.

Getting down on one knee, Grady brought his musket to eye level and pointed it. The end of the barrel wavered too much, he thought. Ah've got to steady it....Aim at a blue uniform.

Grady's forefinger gently and anxiously rubbed the trigger. He could hear his own breathing—the moments of waiting felt excruciating. He fixed his sights on the generously rounded stomach of a blue uniformed man. Does he have a mother waiting for him? Grady asked himself. Banish the thought—this is war. They invaded our land.

"Crack!" The first shot was fired.

Grady steadied his body and pulled the trigger. The field exploded from the loud barking sounds of gunfire coming from up and down the line. The man behind him fired as Grady knelt to reload. His eardrums felt the pain, but in less than a minute he stood and fired again.

The intensity of the booming noises from thousands of muskets is far greater than either Wilson's Creek or Lexington, he said to himself. Grady's need to cough thwarted his attempt to take aim. Puffs of white smoke hung over the ground like a heavy fog on a cool morning in October.

The men behind him were standing and ready to fire. Grady ducked and gasped for clean air to breathe. After the screaming balls passed over his head, he glanced at the ground ahead. Bluecoats scurried in all directions. Some of them lay on the ground, trying to crawl.

His lungs cleared, and he steadied and pulled the trigger. The

Bluecoat in his line of fire fell. While going back down on his knees, he looked along the staggered firing line on both sides. There must be at least a thousand of us, he thought.

Another wave of ear-splitting blasts from behind him added to the arid smell in the air. Grady aimed at a group of Bluecoats who were clustered behind a large tree. "Crack!" Two of them fell. While tapping powder into his barrel, he wished his hands were free to place over his ears.

Before he dropped the ball into his barrel, he heard a swishing sound. Glancing up, he saw several men move ahead and stop to aim.

Down the line, he heard his sergeant yell, "Move ahead! Move!"

A herd of panicky horses, approaching from the south, galloped across the line of fire. Many of them fell. Grady watched as Bluecoats took advantage of the newly found breastworks, and they dropped behind. He saw heads bobbing behind the carcasses.

The men in the line in front of him dropped down to reload. Grady leaped ahead and leveled his musket. He heard a ball scream past his ear.

After firing and hitting nothing, he heard the yell of an officer, who was standing well beyond Mitch and James. "Advance!"

The officer's saber pointed toward the enemy, but he just stood there and didn't move. Ah've never seen that man before, Grady thought. Do ah wanna run across that clearing and face the firing line from behind that hedge? He looked up and down the line. He saw the determined face of Lafe Sunnerland.

Laying his musket down, he removed both Colts from his belt. "Come on, boys!" Grady yelled.

Running toward the fallen horses, he fired as he advanced. Grady felt his hat being blown off his head. Not having time to feel the top of his head, he dove behind the first horse. He heard the thud of a ball hitting the carcass. Thick flakes of smoke masked his view of the grounds ahead.

"That was close," Grady heard Mitch drawl while plopping down alongside him.

"They're runnin!" he heard James yell.

"Hold it, Brother James. Stay right here. We don't know what's behind that hedge," Mitch said anxiously.

"Where are Abel and the other boys?" Grady asked.

"They're off to the left a bit. Cannonball split us up," Mitch drawled.

41

ABEL COUGHED FROM THE BLUISH SMOKE that had come from a cannonball which had exploded between him and Grady. Even though temporarily blinded, he kept advancing.

When his vision returned, he saw a tall building with three levels of windows. Probably a hotel, he thought. Puffs of smoke, reminding him of giant cotton balls, floated in front of some of the windows. The screams of musket balls sent him running.

Another cannonball exploded near Abel, diverting his advance and sending him in another direction. He saw a body hurtling through the air and drop crudely into the tall weeds. Confused, he thought that he was running away from the cannon, but the Bluecoats appeared closer than ever.

He was close enough to one of the cannons to see the fire flash erupting from the barrel. "Ka-boom!" The whistling sound that passed overhead caused Abel to drop flat into the weeds. A ball that had landed and exploded just behind him created heat that engulfed his head. Fragments of metal and soil landed on his back. He shivered and placed his hands over the back of his head. The crack of musket fire amidst the screams and yells of men filled the air.

During a lull in the commotion, he heard someone yell, "Advance! Advance! Ya! Ya! Ya!"

Discarding his feelings of fear, he suddenly found himself running toward the town. Looking right and left, he felt good as he saw others moving forward. There are hundreds of us. We're gonna win! His musket was ready to fire, his bayonet fixed. He touched the holster attached to his belt. All the cylinders in his .41 Colt were capped and ready.

Abel became exuberant when he saw Bluecoats leaving their positions and retreating to the cornfield behind the hedge on the eastern edge of town.

"Look at 'em run!" he heard Lafe Sunnerland yell in his high-pitched voice.

A musket ball grazed the top of Lafe's right ear and sent him to the ground.

"Ya all right?" asked Abel, stopping next to him.

"Jaysus, that was close," responded Lafe as he ran his fingers over his forehead. "Ah'm sure glad that I'm not as tall as Justin."

Abel felt naked as he emerged from the tall weeds and entered an open area of the town. He made a run toward the two vacated artillery pieces. Arriving out of breath, he was joined by Lafe and Jesse Sunnerland.

"Abel, you look mean as hell," yelled Lafe, who attempted to turn the wheels of one of the cannons.

"Ah think ah kilt myself a Yankee!" Abel yelled.

"Which one?" asked Jesse. "There are plenty of 'em lying about."

"Oe'r there," said Abel, pointing.

"Go get his boots!" Lafe said, his voice shrieking.

Abel laid down his musket and dashed over to his victim. He stripped the dead soldier of his musket and pulled off his boots. "Crack!" Abel saw pieces of soil fly by. He grabbed his bounty and dashed back behind the artillery pieces.

"Ah'll be danged....They're comin' back!" Lafe yelled.

Abel saw a long line of Bluecoats jumping over the hedge and advancing. The line doubled, then tripled. He felt his stomach twisting as he prepared to fire. Pulling the trigger, he saw one of the Bluecoats go down.

"Back...back to the field!" Abel heard Grady yell from further down the line.

Rather than attempting to reload his musket, he got up and ran. Abel experienced a burning sensation after his right shoulder was nicked by a ball. Gasping for air, he dropped into the tall grass. Looking up, he could see fire through some of the windows of the three story building.

———

GRADY HAD JUDGED THAT HIS GROUP could not withstand the Bluecoat charge. After leading them back into the weedy field, he turned to look. The Bluecoats stopped at the artillery pieces and did not chase, allowing him and the others to cease their retreat and take a stand in the field. "Stay low, men, stay low...turn and be ready to fire when ah stop," Grady commanded.

He stopped and got down on his knees. Looking around, he made sure that the others were doing the same. "Jesse! Far enough! We'll take a stand here!" Grady yelled.

"Hey! They're back at the cannons!" Mitch yelled, his blue eyes glaring over the tall weeds.

"Stay low!" repeated Grady. For the first time, he noticed the three story building was in flames. No longer did musket fire come from the windows.

After catching his breath, he looked right and left, feeling glad that everyone up and down the line had also retreated and were regrouping in the field. He saw the sergeant trotting over toward him.

Grady put his head down and felt the top of his head. He remembered that his hat had gotten shot off. Bringing his fingers down, he was relieved when he didn't see any blood.

"Hastings, we're gonna charge again. They don't have that much stamina up there. We're goin' to drive 'em off for good this time."

What? Again? Grady questioned. When is this goin' to end? Where are the others? Quantrill should be near. We can't do it alone.

Checking his musket and pistol, Grady readied for another advance. He looked at Mitch who was crouched in the tall grass to his immediate right, "Mitch, we're goin' after 'em again. Git ready."

Sifting through the tall grass, he moved up and down his line, advising all to prepare for another charge. I wish we had our horses, he thought. We could run those Yankees clear out of Missoura.

Looking southward, he saw a rider coming his way, galloping full tilt. The rider stopped momentarily. "Ah got ammo...need some?"

Geez, that's Cole Younger. That means Quantrill is near, Grady said to himself. Feelings of elation and admiration filled his mind as he watched the rider gallop toward the next group, pulling up momentarily and extending a splint basket heaped with ammunition. When Younger reached the end of the line, he turned his horse and galloped back, clods of dirt flying through the air. Shouts of support followed the courageous rider as he galloped by.

———

"CHARGE!" THE YELL SENT A SURGE OF ADRENALINE through Abel's body. He looked to his right and saw Grady standing and waving frantically. He was yelling, "Hee-ya! Hee-ya! Forward! Forward! Let's go!"

My body feels as light as a feather, Abel said to himself. Ah'm blowin' with the wind. He ran as hard as he could until he had difficulty breathing. That big building has flames up on the roof. It's gonna burn down for good, he thought.

Looking around, he suddenly found himself alone. Some distance behind him, he could see the others also advancing. They'll catch up, he thought. He ran again, toward the town as fast as he could. Stopping short of the edge of the field, he crouched and looked back.

Four Bluecoats had moved between him and Grady's line. Where'd they come from? he asked himself, alarmed. Elevating his body slightly, he leveled his rifle at a Bluecoat.

"Zing! Zing!" Abel heard two consecutive balls screech past his head before he had a chance to fire. Dropping to the ground, he heard someone yell, "Stay down, Abel! Ah'm comin'!"

Abel peaked over the tops of the weeds. He saw Justin running his way. Two of the Bluecoats turned. They leveled their rifles—"Crack! Crack!" Abel saw Justin reel, his musket flying out of his hands. Justin fell into a cluster of tall weeds.

"My God...my God...he's hit...Justin's hit," Abel muttered.

His feelings of remorse were short-lived when he saw that the four Bluecoats had their muskets aimed at him.

Crack! Crack! Two of them fired and missed. Abel dove behind a patch of taller weeds. Crack!—another shot. He heard the ball whistle overhead. Crack! Abel felt a sting in his left shoulder.

Using his right hand, he lifted his revolver from its holster. He tried to take aim at one of the Bluecoats, but his hand trembled too much. He pulled the trigger and nothing happened. Panicking, he looked up and saw that all four Bluecoats had reloaded again.

Abel saw a flash of metal coming from behind the Bluecoats. With his mouth agape, he saw someone running toward the Bluecoats. Wildly waving long sabers in the air, Elkanah Jackson and Sammy Morton attacked them before they could react. One of them turned, and abandoned his attempt to aim at Abel. Instead, he took a stand with his bayonet. Elkanah swung and knocked the musket from his hands.

The first Bluecoat had fallen, and Sammy engaged two of the others. Both of them succumbed to the frantic Sammy and his long, swift, moving blade. The fourth Bluecoat had dropped his musket and ran toward Lone Jack.

Abel saw Grady Hastings pull up and take aim. Crack! He missed the Bluecoat.

Abel heard a wave of yells coming from the town. He looked past the dead horses and saw a huge wave of Bluecoats emerging from behind the hedge again. They were advancing rapidly. "Fall back!" someone yelled.

Without reloading his musket, Abel ran westward as fast as his legs could carry him. He caught up with the others, his lungs hurting severely. Moments later, he could move no further. Falling to the ground, he puffed and panted, attempting to regain his breath.

Glancing up over the grass, he was relieved that the Bluecoat advance had been thwarted. "Abel, are you all right?" he heard Lafe Sunnerland ask, his voice panting.

"Ah'm good...but...but, what about Justin?"

42

THE SUN WAS PARTWAY THROUGH THE SKY, still short of its noon position. "They're leavin!" Grady yelled. His fists, each grasping a Colt, held high up above his shoulders. His wide-eyed emerald green eyes were gleaming. "They're movin' out. We've won!"

"Let's go after 'em!" Grady heard Jesse exclaim.

"Naw…ah don't have any energy left, Jess. Ah'm thirsty, hungry, and simply worn out. Ah need to rest, and right now," Grady responded.

The Gray Riders showed the aftereffects of a battle. Most were lying down, their shirts and trousers torn to shreds. Others hunched onto one knee, reloading their muskets, not trusting the retreat. Some stood and stared at the retreating Bluecoats.

Lafe Sunnerland moved about counting the survivors, his face showing deep concern. "Justin…where's Justin?"

———

ABEL'S HEART LEAPED INTO HIS THROAT. He suddenly remembered Justin going down. Taking a deep breath, he looked at Grady. "Ah saw him fall….Justin was hit o'er there where the four Bluecoats were." He pointed.

"Show me, Abel…where!" Grady exclaimed.

Abel left his musket lying in the grass and ran toward the area where he had seen Justin fall. Catching up with him, Elkanah Jackson asked, "Where he fall, Abel?"

"Right over there next to that brownish cluster of tall weeds."

His sunken, hazel eyes looked down and searched the ground

around the weeds. Abel had feelings of desperation. Where could've
he gone? he asked himself. He took off his hat, exposing disheveled,
dark hair that was parted in the middle and hanging below the ears.

His thin face cringed as he looked up at Elkanah.

"Dunno, Abel," Elkanah said. "Maybe Grady know."

Grady had caught up with Abel and Elkanah. "Who ya lookin'
fer?"

"Justin…ah saw 'em go down right about 'ere," yelled Abel, his
voice sounding desperate.

"Blood…there's some over 'ere, down in that bent grass," Elkanah
said, looking at Grady.

"Jaysus!" Grady exclaimed. "That's one of Justin's revolvers
layin' there. I know it…seen it many times."

Abel stared at the Colt, and placed his right palm over his forehead.
"My fault!" he cried. "Justin came over to save me, because ah got
too far ahead."

"It wasn't your fault, Abel," Grady said, his Colts back in his
belt. He took a deep breath, his green eyes narrowing. "It wasn't
your fault. There's not a man in all of Missoura who could've shown
us more bravery than you did on this day, Abel."

———

SERGEANT YORK APPROACHED THE RIDERS. "Boys, you
did one hell of a job. Drove dem Yankees clear out. Your horses are
comin' back to ya. Stay right here. Everybody rest."

"What happened to Quantrill?" asked Grady. "When ah saw Cole
Younger, ah thought Quantrill had arrived."

"He went off to Independence with about fifty of his men to
retrieve gunpowder…many barrels ah heard…left behind by Colonel
Thompson's men. We need it. Cole Younger did that on his own…no
one could have shown more courage than that."

Abel was feeling remorse. He anxiously looked toward the town,
hoping to see Justin Haggard. Minutes later, he heard the sound of
horse's hooves. Guided by several riders, the steeds that they
dismounted and left beyond the big hill were being brought forward.

After mounting, Abel followed Grady and the others into Lone Jack. Bile erupted from his stomach—some of it filling his mouth. The blood and body parts scattered on the ground were more than he could bear.

Abel dismounted and walked his horse around the bloody grounds of the battlefield. He felt relief after not recognizing Justin as one of the bodies that he had seen lying in the dirt. For each of the fallen soldiers, there seems to be at least one dead horse, Abel thought. He looked back and saw Grady turning some of the heads of the fallen. Standing next to Grady's horse, his neck down, and nibbling on the grass, was Justin's horse.

"Jaysus, where could've he gone?" Abel muttered. Could've Justin been taken prisoner? he asked himself. Feelings of remorse overwhelmed him as he thought about what had happened. If ah'd paid more attention, Justin would still be with us.

Abel gasped. His newly found friend, Preston, lay on the ground— half his head shot away. Bringing his hands up to cover his face, Abel began to sob.

He felt the big arm of Mitch McGregor wrap around his shoulder. "What's the matter, Abel?"

"It's my friend, Preston. He rode next to me the past two days. He's been shot...dead."

Mitch tightened his arm and said, "Abel, that's part of war. He's one of many lyin' roun' on this ground, who 'ave died for our rats."

After retrieving Preston's belongings, Abel packed them into his saddlebag. "Mitch, ah gotta bury this man. He rode alongside me all the way from Tarrytown." Abel's voice trailed to a whine. Wiping the tears from his eyes, Abel lifted Preston off the ground and hoisted him onto his shoulder.

43

GRADY AND MITCH RODE ABREAST, leading the Gray Riders in columns of two back toward Tarrytown. Sergeant York had remained with Colonel Cockrell's men. Grady had told the sergeant that the Riders needed to return home. Their farms and town were in grave danger because of the marauding jayhawkers. Sergeant York agreed with Grady, and he expressed gratitude for their participation in Lone Jack.

Grady did a head count of thirty-four, and his thoughts soured when thinking of Justin. We did lose only two, but why did Justin have to be one of them? he asked himself, sadly.

"God speed," the Sergeant had said.

Grady thought about Jennifer Haggard and how she would handle the news about Justin missing. He dreaded the thought of being the bearer, but realized that it was his responsibility. She'll be devastated. Ah'm glad that she's not alone.

Later that evening in camp, after nightfall, he lay awake in his duck tent, even though his mind and body felt tired beyond belief. He thought about Paul McGregor and Jordon Jackson who had both died in the battle of the Hemp Bales. Actually, Paul didn't die there, but he did later. The frantic ride on the wagon to get his brother to the hospital saved him for a few days.

When sunrise came, Grady heard Mitch McGregor's slap across the top of his tent.

———

ANNA HAGGARD SAT ON A ROCKER next to the front window. Her mind focused on the agony of war. Her daughter-in-law was in the house preparing dinner. Ah don't know what that girl will do if anything happens to Justin, she thought. She's already lost a brother.

She listened to the creaking of the rocker—back and forth, over and over again. Waves of drowsiness overtook her brain and she fell asleep. Her long, black hair hanging to her shoulders tickled a section of her neck, causing her to wake up.

The Riders had been gone for five days. No one in Tarrytown or anywhere else had received any word. She had watched her husband ride up their roadway every day since Justin had left. Ben showed her a bounce of courage each time he mounted. "He'll come back....You'll see," he would say before leaving.

Each day when he returned, the bounce was missing. His demeanor showed sadness and depression, she thought. Tomorrow he will go again—and the next day.

I cannot bear to see Jennifer walking out to the roadway each time Ben turns his horse onto the Tarrytown Road. She walks up the road a bit and just stands there—then turns and slowly walks back to her house, her chin lowered. It's so sad, Anna thought.

I haven't seen Jubal smile since he returned with Thomas Hastings on the day that the Riders left, she said to herself. We only want to make a living and live in peace. Why...oh why, are we tormented so much? Jesus, Mary Joseph, please give us some answers.

Anna thought about getting off the rocker and fetching a cup of tea when she saw movement on the Tarrytown Road. The creaking stopped as she sat still and watched. Four horses turned onto their roadway.

She stood and her mouth gaped open. Is it Justin? He's come home, she said to herself with eager anticipation. Watching a few moments longer, she noticed that there were only three riders...one of the saddles didn't have a rider. Anna held her breath. She felt her heart rate increase. Something is wrong, she sensed, her face wrinkling with anticipated grief.

Her head began to swim, and she became dizzy. Sitting back down on the rocker, she steadied herself and clasped her hands tightly. Without being aware of leaving the rocker, she stood, and slowly her legs begin to move forward. She walked through the door and onto the porch.

Should I fetch Jennifer? Anna asked herself. She felt tormented, remembering that Jennifer had gone up to the loft for a rest. Turning, her heart skipped a beat as she saw Jennifer in the window.

The horses and riders were getting closer. Strange how they are moving so slow, Anna thought. She heard the front door open and turned to see Jennifer standing in the doorway.

"What is it? Who's coming?" Jennifer asked, her voice trembling. "Is it...is it Justin?"

Anna didn't answer, but continued to watch the approaching riders. Suddenly her knees buckled and she almost fell, bracing herself on the window frame. Her olive-colored facial skin paled. It's Grady Hastings and I know why he's here, she said to herself, anguished.

"Anna, Anna, are you alright?" Jennifer asked and rushed to her side.

"It's Justin...Justin...I'm afraid."

Jennifer wrapped an arm around her mother-in-law's waist. "The Lord is with us. Let us go and meet our visitors."

———

"MISSING—JUSTIN IS MISSING!" Ben Haggard exclaimed after rushing over from the barn. His eyes narrowed, barely showing their dark, gleaming stare.

Grady lowered his head, his feelings a mixture of sorrow and pity. He looked up to see Ben move over to his wife and Jennifer who were leaning on each other.

Grady lowered his head again and stared at the ground, holding onto the reins of his horse as Abel and Elkanah sat hunched in their saddles. Glancing up, he saw that Jennifer had collapsed and Mrs. Haggard helped her to a bench.

"Sorry, sir. Ah dreaded bringing the news," Grady said to Ben after he had separated from the two women.

Jennifer regained her composure. Her head turned toward Grady. "Missing—is he a prisoner? Did you see him get taken?" she asked, thin creases forming next to her blue eyes.

Grady looked up and readied to answer. He hesitated when he saw Jubal come running up from behind the house.

Jubal ran to his mother. "What's happened? Is it Justin?"

"Jubal, your brother was wounded at Lone Jack, and then he disappeared...likely taken prisoner," Grady said, his voice harsh.

Jubal's short, deep breaths turned into uncontrollable sobs. Grady stepped over to the younger man and they embraced.

"Maybe he escaped, Grady. No way that they could hold onto Justin," Jubal said, his voice trembling.

Elkanah and Abel remained in their saddles, tears filling their eyes.

Grady spoke again. "Abel saw Justin go down in the tall weeds. No one saw him after that. We searched that area thoroughly on horseback after the battle."

"How about his pistols...did you find them? Was there any blood?" Jubal asked, his words flowing rapidly. "Well, was there?"

"Jube, we did see some blood, but there was blood everywhere. Yes, ah did find one of his Colts, the one with the ivory handle. It's in Justin's saddlebag."

"Any of the other Riders hurt?" Ben asked, sinking his lower front teeth into his upper lip.

"Yes, a young friend of Abel's from Independence by the name of Preston was killed. Abel had his shoulder grazed by a ball. Everyone else is good."

Anna's face had been buried in her husband's chest. She looked up. "Grady Hastings, we appreciate you coming over and sharing the news, also for bringing Justin's horse and belongings. Please leave us now...to our grief."

"Yes, Ma'am...ya know we're all as sorry as could be."

"Of course, Grady...of course," Anna responded, her voice trailing off to a whisper.

Grady mounted his horse. He saluted, and rode off at a slow pace behind Abel and Elkanah. He didn't look back until they reached the Tarrytown Road. Breathing deeply, Grady looked up and down the road, seeing no one. He glanced back at the Haggard place and saw them entering the house.

"Let's go home, boys," he said.

———

THE TOWNSHIP OF VAN BUREN IN JACKSON COUNTY of
*western Missouri made history on August 16, 1862. The small town
of Lone Jack hosted one of the bloodiest battles of the Civil War.*

*Federal forces in Lexington under Major Emery Foster moved
toward Lone Jack with the intention of interrupting a recruiting
expedition by Confederate Colonel Jeremiah Cockrell. They had
additional incentive because of a stinging defeat in the Battle of
Lexington the previous week.*

*Blistering heat didn't slow down Major Foster as he encountered
skirmishes on the outskirts of town on the evening of August 15. His
forces occupied Lone Jack that night and placed two cannons on
Main Street, the new addition in the southern part of town.*

*The day before the battle, Colonel Cockrell was joined by forces
led by Colonels John Coffee and Charles Tracy. They had successfully
recruited a number of locals to join their forces. A decision was made
to attack the federal forces in Lone Jack at dawn.*

*In the dark early morning hours on the 16th, the Confederates
dismounted and approached on foot, west of the town, across an
overgrown field. A Confederate recruit stumbled in the field
accidentally discharged his weapon.*

*Vicious hand to hand combat resulted across a 60 foot wide street
under a merciless sun. The fierce fighting raged for five hours while
the two cannon on Main Street exchanged hands five times.*

*The number of dead numbered close to 300. Also, over 100 horses
were slain. The fallen men were buried in two parallel trenches near
the old Black Jack oak tree—one trench for the blue and another one
for the gray. Major Foster suffered a fatal wound during the heat of
the battle and died soon after.*

*Even though the Confederates had possession of the field when
the battle ended, claims of victory by either side remain in dispute.*

Information about the battle was provided by *www.mprarchives*
on the Internet, and *The Story of Lone Jack* by Romulus L. Travis.

44

THOMAS HASTINGS SAT ON THE BUCKBOARD seat next to this father. Thomas had gotten a pair of new black boots recently and they were neatly tucked into his light gray duck trousers. They were heading to Tarrytown for supplies. As they passed along MacTurley's Woods, he noticed the leaves were changing colors. Yellows, reds, and oranges mixed in with the greens.

Passing by the schoolhouse, he saw a one horse carriage parked—probably Mr. Styles, Thomas thought. He's gettin' ready for me and the others.

I'm sure gonna miss Jube, Thomas said to himself. He's too old for school, and with Justin gone, he's gonna be doin' more things on the farm. Dunno if he's old enough to ride with Grady and Mitch yet.

"Keeya! Keeya!" Screams coming from the direction of the timber drew Thomas's blue eyes to the sky. "There he is," he whispered.

"There's who?" his father asked.

"Keeya, my hawk. See him soaring over there?"

"So that's your hawk. I always thought it was mine."

Thomas laughed and said, "Pa, you don't have as much imagination as I do...not nearly enough to claim a hawk."

Henry Hastings laughed, his wide-bottomed sideburns shaping to his cheeks.

Thomas missed his brother, who was away a lot patrolling regularly with the Gray Riders. Grady did spend about every seventh day at home, sometimes arriving and leaving in the wee hours of the morning. Grady told him stories about chasing redlegs out of Jackson County during his most recent visit.

They pulled up in front of the General Store. Tying the reins to a hitching rail, Henry Hastings entered the store, but not before his son bounded through the door first.

"Well there, young man. Are ya anxious for school to start?" asked Seth Miller.

"Yup, sure am. I wanna know more about what's goin' on out east," answered Thomas.

"Have you 'eard about Antietam?" Seth asked Henry and Thomas.

"Antietam...what's that?" Thomas responded.

"It's a town in Virginia...big battle there a couple of weeks ago. Ah 'eard we run those Yankees clear out. Lots kilt...more them than us," Seth said.

After sacks and crates of supplies were loaded onto the wagon, Henry flicked the reins and the horses moved forward. The black horses don't need much direction, Thomas thought. Pa doesn't even need those reins. In moments, the horses trotted up the middle of Tarrytown Road.

"What do ya think happened to Justin?" Thomas asked his father.

"Wish we knew, son....It doesn't look good. Ah 'ear that most of the prisoners die, sooner or later....He's in God's hands now."

Thomas's mind imagined a wall built with wooden posts sunk into the ground. The wall extended for as far as he could see. Justin was standing inside, and planning an escape. He would put together a rope of hemp and leather. On a dark, moonless night, he and others would scale the wall to freedom.

45

LAFE SUNNERLAND SAID, "NOW, THAT'S A REAL TENT. No more freezin' to death at night."

Nights in Missouri become chilly in November. The Gray Riders, who had camped for the night along a ridge a few miles southwest of Tarrytown, numbered thirty-two. They had picked that spot because of the grand view and nearness to an escape route, which led high into the timbers of Bear Mountain.

"Yup, but we need a couple more of them," added Mitch McGregor. "We're gonna to have to draw straws to see who spends the night in the big one tonight."

Lafe pointed eastward. "Look. There're some riders comin'. See that cloud of dust? We may be leavin' fast."

"Ah hope it's Grady and Abel," Mitch responded. "More fightin' doesn't appeal to me anymore today."

"They're not Bluecoats," said Lafe after setting down his eye glass.

"Nope, it's Grady and Abel. Wonder what the news is?" Mitch asked, his facial hair in total chaos.

"Good. Ah'm glad we don't have to wake the others. I think they're snoozin'," said Lafe. "Last ah looked, Elkanah was sawin' a big one," he added.

"We'll soon find out, Lafe....They're comin' hard. Hey, they've got someone with 'em."

"That one looks like a Bluecoat—cap and all," said Lafe as they watched the riders plod up the hill.

Abel waved from the saddle as he dug both spurs into his horse to get to the top of the hill. Grady rode behind their prisoner, who followed Abel's lead.

After reaching the encampment, Grady dismounted and said, "Boys, this 'ere is Private Jeffries. We picked him up on that ridge o'er there." Grady pointed to the northwest.

"He claims to have been scoutin' for two cavalry companies that are headin' this way. We've got to move out of 'ere—and fast," Grady said. "They'll be 'ere in about an hour," Grady added.

"Ya wouldn't be lyin' to us, mister?" Grady sharply asked his prisoner.

"No, Sir. It's God's fact. Two companies, about one hundred fifty men."

After the Riders packed the tents and supplies, Jesse Sunnerland asked. "Why run? Why don't we take a stand there, in the timber?"

"They're too many of 'em, Jesse," responded Abel. "Way too many...our thirty-two wouldn't stand much of a chance."

"Ah, we can take on three times our size," retorted Jesse. "We got the revolvers."

"Some of the Yankees have six-shot revolvers now, too. They're not Colts, but just as good—Remingtons," answered Grady. "Besides, ah don't like us to be in a position to git attacked. Ah'd much rather do the attackin'. If we had another thirty men, ah think we could take 'em."

LIEUTENANT FARNSWORTH COMMANDED two companies of the Missouri 7th Cavalry in early November. He followed orders to patrol south of Independence all the way to Lee's Summit. Low, dark gray clouds slowly drifted by at dawn. After breaking camp the companies advanced southward, following a creek bottom. Farnsworth had ordered four scouts to ride the eastern ridge, and four others to picket westward.

The Lieutenant watched the eastern slopes anxiously, expecting to see his scouts approaching with news. He couldn't see the sun because of heavy cloud cover, but his stomach told him it was getting close to the noon hour. Scanning the valley ahead, he looked for good ground to make a noon stop. He chose a stand of timber, near the railroad tracks that connected Independence with Jefferson City.

Farnsworth ordered eight of his men to ride out and spell the scouts, who were riding the ridges. He was sitting on a stump and finishing his beef jerky when three of the four scouts on the eastern ridge returned. "Where's Jeffries?" the Lieutenant asked.

"Dunno, Sir. He was a mite ahead of me when he disappeared. There didn't appear to be any hostilities…no gun fire. He's out ahead o're there somewhere," one of the scouts said, pointing.

"Very well. You men have something to eat. We'll be heading out in half an hour."

"Yes, sir," the lead scout said, saluted, and returned to his comrades.

GRADY HASTINGS LED THE GRAY RIDERS toward the southeast for the rest of that day, all the time keeping an eye on his Bluecoat prisoner. He felt more secure when the dark blue tops of Bear Mountain became visible.

"Do ya think they're followin' our tracks?" Mitch asked.

"Not takin' any chances. That's why we stayed in the creek for a mile or so," Grady answered.

"Yup…figured as much," Mitch replied. "How far do ya plan on goin'? Shuh looks like snow."

"See ova there…that dip in the mountain? If we can make it by dark, we'll be safe enough."

"What are we gonna do with Jeffries?"

"Ah need to talk to 'em for a spell, and then we'll let 'em go, but only if he promises that he'll ride for home."

"Grady, ah think he's from Missoura. Seems to me ah 'eard him say that, back there a spell. Maybe a change of clothes and he can ride with us."

"I'll see what he has to say later tonight, in camp. Yeah, we could use another man."

———

"WHERE'RE YA FROM, JEFFRIES?" asked Grady of his prisoner.

"Same area as Farnsworth," he replied.

"Who's Farnsworth?" asked Mitch.

He's our company commander. We both come from up north…north of Independence, east of St. Joseph."

"What are ya doin' in the Union cavalry?" Lafe Sunnerland asked angrily.

"We had no choice. It was either jin up with them or get shot," replied the prisoner.

"What if ah said, jin up with us or get shot? What would ya do?" Grady asked.

"Got any extra gray clothing?" the prisoner asked.

"Gotta first name?" asked Jesse.

"Yup, surely do. My name is Robert."

"Was Farnsworth at Lone Jack?" asked Grady.

"Sure was. Ah was with 'em, too. We were the first ones there, the night before the big fight. General pushed us pretty hard that evening."

"What general was that?"

"General Foster, we came all the way from Lexington."

"We were in that weedy field to the west of town. We snuck up on you guys pretty good," added Grady, smiling.

"Yeah, ah can't believe we didn't have any pickets out that a way. Guess we thought everyone got chased away the night before."

"Did you take any prisoners when you rode north?" Mitch asked, his large, blue eyes squinting.

"Sure did...must have been a dozen of 'em."

"Do you remember seein' a real tall one? Tall and slim he was," added Grady.

"Come to think of it, there was this one fella. He was a head taller than the others. They were all pretty shaggy, you know. The tall one was limpin' real bad. Felt sorry for 'em. Ah think he eventually fell down and someone put him in a wagon."

"Thanks, Jeffries," said Grady. "When we git back home, we'll get you some new duds," he added.

For the first time since he was captured, Robert Jeffries smiled from ear to ear.

"This is very good ground, Abel. Let's go talk to the rest of the boys. We're going to set up camp here, then tomorrow, you and ah are goin' home for a spell."

46

ABEL THOUGHT ABOUT HIS MOTHER, BETH, and how she would be so happy to see him riding up their roadway. His father would be busy tending the black herd along with Burt and the other hands. Sarah would be all smiles. Abel thought about her protruding, front teeth and the thick, red lips that created a friendly circle. I think that mother of mine has the finest smile that ah 'ave e'er seen, he thought.

After dinner, snow began to fall, sending up puffs of steam from the dinner fire. Abel had finished chewing a chunk of dried beef. Fatigue set in and he wandered to his tent. Sleep came quickly.

Abel crawled out of his tent and looked around. The first light of dawn exposed low hanging, dark clouds that had dropped a massive blanket of snow on the ground. Tree branches were hanging so low that some of them had broken. The tents were all partially caved in. Slipping his fingers into a glove, he brushed some of the snow off his tent.

Looking at a form next to Grady's tent, he smiled, seeing only a part of Jeffries's hat. He was lying under a tarp, which was totally obliterated by the snow. Using his arm, Abel swept it across one side of Grady's tent.

"Any sign of anythin' movin' down there?" Grady asked Abel from within the confines of his tent.

"Nothin', except for a couple of deer browsin' in the field down below," Abel replied, pointing. "No way that the Bluecoats could sneak up on us up 'ere, huh, Grady?"

"Naw, likely not, but ah peeked out my tent a good dozen times anyhow," Grady responded. "I figured that Mitch was watchin', too. He usually does."

Abel stomped over to the place where they had made a fire the previous evening. He kicked away some of the snow from around the ring of rocks. Using his gloves, he scooped out some of the snowy ashes.

"We'll fetch some wood," Elkanah said as he and Sammy stomped toward a fallen tree. Minutes later, Abel had a fire going. Mitch brought over a bag of dried beef. "Ah got some bread in my bag," Abel said.

Half an hour later, they all gathered around the morning fire. James picked up the steaming coffee pot and moved from man to man, filling cups as he went, his back remaining stiff and straight.

"This snow changes the whole war," Jesse said. "Who wants to be out there fightin' with all that snow on the ground?"

"Ah agree with you, Jesse, but I'd rather not fight in any kind of weather," James replied, coughing.

Returning back into his tent, Abel began taking it down.

"What ya doin', Abel?" Mitch asked.

Grady walked over and said, "Mitch, I'm takin' Abel with me. We're goin' home for a couple of days. When we get back, it'll be your turn. You can take Lafe and Jesse with ya."

———

GRADY AND ABEL MOUNTED THEIR HORSES and made their way down the slope, shortly after the noon hour. The snow had ceased falling. Their eyes constantly scanned the white fields below for signs of the Union cavalry. "What do ya think, Abel? About eight inches of snow, huh?"

"Yup, that's about right. Looks like the Bluecoats have gone. No sign anywhere," answered Abel.

"Let's hope they didn't go on to Tarrytown. We should be able to find out at the McGregor's," said Grady.

The two riders angled northeast toward the McGregor property. An hour and ten miles further, they reached the split-rail fence. Following it northward, they rode toward the Tarrytown road.

After reaching the road, they stopped their horses and dismounted. "Doesn't look like many have been by here," Grady said.

"Nope. Hey, they're some tracks in Haggard's field," said Abel.

"Could be the cattle," responded Grady.

They followed the road until they arrived at the McGregor roadway. "Let's go see Orly and find out if there's been anything going on," said Grady as he put his horse to a trot.

As they approached, Grady could see the McGregor hands busy feeding the cattle down by the barn. Orly waved as they approached.

"Howdy, Mr. McGregor...looks like a fine day," said Grady.

"Not for us and the cattle with all that snow, Hastings. Where're you two headed?"

"Abel and ah are gonna spend some time at home for a couple of days. There's been some Union cavalry activity west a few miles. Nothin' around here, though," Grady answered.

Orly licked his lower lip with the tip of his tongue. "Say hello to your parents, boys," he drawled in his Scottish brogue.

————

GRADY AND ABEL ANXIOUSLY SCANNED the Tarrytown Road in both directions from the McGregor roadway, hoping not to see any strange riders.

"Hey! Grady. What's happened to the Haggard buildings?" asked Abel anxiously.

Grady stopped his horse. He could plainly see the McGregor buildings, which they had just left. Straining his eyes, he looked northeastward. "Jaysus, something's happened to the house. It looks different...no roof," he said.

"He-Yaw! He-Yaw!" Grady yelled and dragged a spur against his horse's flank. They galloped down the Tarrytown Road, anxiously heading for the Haggard's roadway. After turning, Grady reined his horse. "Abel, there's something weird about those buildings. Something has changed. The roofs are gone."

Getting closer, Grady stopped and exclaimed, "Smoke, Abel! The buildings been burnt....The insides have caved in. Jaysus Almighty!"

They galloped their horses, braking to a stop next to the house. White plumes of smoke rose from the rubble and disappeared into the low hanging clouds. The charred remains of the internal walls of the house appeared naked in a sea of snow. "Look! There's someone down o'er there!" Abel exclaimed.

Trudging through the snow on foot, they came upon Jubal Haggard on his knees, leaning over a bulk in the snow. "Jubal! Jubal! What happened?" asked Grady frantically.

Jubal didn't say a word. He didn't look up. Abel and Grady crouched down next to the bulk.

"Holy Jaysus, Abel. That's Jennifer. She's been kilt."

Grady put his arm around Jubal's shoulder. "Who was it, Jube, the jayhawkers?"

Jubal straightened his back, and Grady looked into his eyes. They were glued to his sister-in-law lying in the snow. Grady had witnessed much grief during the past year, but none of it resembled the look of desperation on Jubal's face.

Grady attempted to pull him away. Jubal growled and grabbed onto Jennifer.

"Grady, look over there. There's someone else!" Abel ran toward a second bulk, also covered with snow. "It's Mr. Haggard, Grady. Jaysus, he's dead, too!"

———

GRADY LEFT JUBAL AND JOINED ABEL, who used his hand to brush the snow off Ben Haggard's body. "Abel, where's Anna?" Grady asked frantically.

Abel looked up with a fearful look in his deep hazel eyes. "Oh, God, Grady! Ah hope they didn't git her, too."

They trudged to the other side of the house. Stopping, Grady said, "Over there, Abel. Ah'm afraid to go look."

As they hurried toward the third bulk in the snow, Grady thought about the day when he and Will Walker had found the Sunnerlands on the Tarrytown Road. He felt a similar chill as they moved quickly toward the mound in the snow. His heart began to beat faster, anticipating what they were going to find.

Brushing the snow off the person's face, he cringed. "It's her....It's Anna. They're gonna pay for this...as long as ah'm alive. Ah'll kill the bastards when we find 'em," Grady said solemnly. "Mark my words, Ben, Anna and Jennifer....They're gonna pay....We'll drive those bloody jayhawkers out of Missoura."

"What are we gonna do with Jube?" asked Abel, his voice filled with uncertainty.

"Abel, ride like hell for my father's place. Get him to get a wagon out here. Then ride to Tarrytown and notify the constable. Have him come along, too...bring someone with 'em. We need lots of help."

"Ah'm on my way," answered Abel as he dashed toward his horse.

Grady trudged back around the house where Jubal remained with the body of Jennifer. He grabbed Jubal's shoulders firmly. "Jube, you're freezin' to death. Get on my horse with me. Ah'll take you to my home. It's warm there."

Grady got his horse. He then had to forcefully drag Jubal away from the body. Grady coaxed him to mount and sit down behind his saddle. Grady then mounted and nudged his horse back onto the roadway. He made sure that Jubal was hanging on, then he set his horse into a gallop. Half an hour later, he arrived at his father's house.

———

GRADY DISMOUNTED AND HELPED JUBAL down off the horse. He guided the destitute young man to the door where they were met by his mother, Emma. She said softly, "Your father and Thomas are getting the team ready. Abel Kingsley told us the shocking news. He's already ridden for the constable. "Oh, Jubal, you poor boy," she said guiding him through the door.

Emma grabbed Jubal's hand and led him to a chair by the fireplace. Squaring up her chin, her face was laden with pity. "You're frozen, Jubal. We've got to thaw you out. Grady, would you get some of your extra clothes from the loft?"

She removed his hat and touched his thick, black hair. It was soaked and had small slivers of ice stuck to the clipped edges.

Grady stomped up the narrow steps, and then brought down dry clothes for Jubal. He headed outside to change horses. Inside, Emma helped Jubal out of his wet snow-covered clothing.

Walking back toward the house, Grady saw two wagons on the Tarrytown Road heading westward. He hoped it was someone headed for the Haggard place.

He then went back into the house to see to his mother and Jubal. Minutes later, Grady went back outside, mounted and rode out to meet the wagons. He arrived at the Tarrytown Road ahead of them. As they got closer, he recognized his father and the constable on one wagon.

Henry Hastings pulled on the reins, bringing his team to a stop.

"Grady, we're headin' over to Haggard's to pick up the remains. Are you comin' along?"

"Sure am, Pa. Who's in the other wagon?"

"Martin and Abel Kingsley."

"Pa, didn't you see anything last night? There must 'ave been flames to see."

"All ah could see last night was snow. If the Sunnerlands would've been home, they might have seen it. None of our hired men in the bunkhouse saw anything either. Nobody saw nuthin'."

"Giddy-yap!" yelled Henry Hastings.

47

THOMAS GLANCED OUT THE SCHOOLHOUSE WINDOW. That's pa's team, he said to himself. He watched clods of snow splatter against the front of the wagon as the two horses galloped onward. Why's he galloping the pair? Why is he in such a hurry? He's not due in to pick me and Genevieve up for a couple of hours, he thought.

"Master Thomas, please pay attention to your work," Mr. Styles said sharply.

"Sorry, Mr. Styles, but my father's team just galloped by. There could be an emergency," Thomas replied softly.

Ebenezer Styles rose from his desk. Thomas watched with tension as the Schoolmaster's long strides brought him next to his bench. "Thomas, you're behind on your reading. Whatever is going on out there does not affect you in here. Is that clear?"

"Yes, Mr. Styles."

"The blue clad militia was gathered in the field ahead. Their leaders were attempting to organize them into a line," Thomas read.

Thomas found it impossible to concentrate on the words. The excitement he felt at that moment compared to the time the Union cavalry was chased by the Gray Riders. Glancing up at Mr. Styles,

Thomas felt upset. The stubborn schoolmaster wasn't here when my friend Carr got shot, Thomas thought, frustrated.

"*General Cornwall rode up and down the front line of the Redcoats. They were about to advance against a large group of local militia gathered in the field ahead,*" he continued to read.

Looking up from the book, his eyes caught more movement on the road. My Lord! It's my pa again, he said to himself. This time there's someone else. It's the Constable. What? Another wagon? He watched as the wagons disappeared beyond the corner of MacTurley's Woods.

Looking up, Thomas's eyes met those of the angered schoolmaster. Looking down, he continued to read: "*A bugle announced the charge. Four lines of Redcoats advanced.*" He slammed the book shut.

———

THOMAS BURST OUT OF THE SCHOOLHOUSE DOOR immediately upon hearing the clanging of the bell. He ran all the way to the General Store.

"Gen, what's goin' on? Why did Pa come into town early?" Thomas asked, gasping for air.

"Thomas, there's been a burnin' over at the Haggard's. That's all ah can tell you. Maude was across the street when Pa picked up Constable Muldoon. All they told Maude was that all the buildin's were burnt."

Seth Miller entered the room. "Hello there, Thomas. How's the schoolin' goin'?"

"Not so good today, Mr. Miller. I'm all anxious to know what's goin' on over at the Haggard's."

"You're gonna find out soon, ah reckon so. Here come a couple of wagons now," the store owner drawled.

Thomas dashed out the door and saw two wagons coming into town from the west. They were followed by two riders. He held his breath when the first wagon veered and pulled up in front of the undertaker's. It was Pa and the Constable. Thomas remained standing on the boardwalk in front of the store. He didn't have the stomach to approach the wagons. He watched with disdain as a group of men carried a sheet-covered body into the building—Someone got kilt.

Minutes later, the men returned and gently lifted a second body from the wagon. They staggered slightly from the weight, almost dropping the body to the planking.

Thomas went back inside the store and stood behind the window overlooking the street. Genevieve walked over to him. "What's goin' on, Thomas?" Genevieve asked with a worried look on her face.

Thomas turned. "The Haggard's. Pa and some others are carrying dead people from the wagon into the mortuary. I'm afraid one of them might be Jubal."

"Oh no, Thomas, not Jubal," Genevieve replied, placing both hands over her face.

————

GENEVIEVE RETURNED BEHIND THE COUNTER while Thomas continued to watch the activities outside. She anxiously awaited the end of the day. Her heart wasn't in her work after listening to Thomas. Glancing over at him, she felt sadness for her brother and how he feared for his friend Jubal.

"Genevieve, your father will be over to pick you up in a bit. I saw him crossing the road. Ah reckon ya can go home a little early," her boss said.

"Oh, thank you, Mr. Miller."

Henry Hastings came through the door. He stopped and stomped—shaking off chips of snow that were pasted to the bottom of his boots. He looked around the room and spotted Thomas over by the door.

Genevieve had just pushed the cash register drawer shut. She saw her father walk over to Thomas. Her heart felt as if it had stopped beating. She watched her father talking seriously to her brother.

Suddenly, Thomas threw his hands up in the air. He ran over to the counter. "Jube's alive! He's at our house!"

"What about his parents and his sister-in-law, Jennifer?" Genevieve asked, her face expressing fear.

Thomas put his head down. Tears filled his eyes.

"Oh, no. All of 'em?" she asked, her voice trailing off.

Genevieve put her forehead in her hands and sobbed. Thomas did not look up.

———

GENEVIEVE HUDDLED NEXT TO THOMAS on the bench seat of the wagon. She couldn't stop shaking, thinking about the Haggards. Thomas pulled a gray blanket over their shoulders. Their father remained in the General Store talking to some of the men.

Genevieve looked into her father's eyes when he came out and climbed into the wagon. She saw sadness and defeat.

Her father spoke slowly. "We're all tryin' so hard to mind our own business, here in Tarrytown. This is our reward...senseless killings."

Genevieve grabbed Thomas's hand and began to cry.

She feared meeting up with Jubal when they got home. Justin's gone....His parents are gone. "What am ah gonna say to Jubal, Pa?'

"Ah think the less you say the better, ah reckon so," their father responded.

"But, Pa, I've got to say somethin' to 'em. I'll give 'em a big hug at least. He needs our help," responded Genevieve.

Henry Hastings glanced at his daughter and didn't say anything. He flipped the reins and yelled, "Git-on-there!"

Their wagon had pulled even with MacTurley's Woods when Thomas exclaimed, "Two riders ahead, Pa!"

"Better hand me my musket, Thomas. Bring that holster up on the seat next to me, too."

"I'll get the pistol out, Pa," responded Thomas nervously.

Genevieve had been sitting next to her father and moved over slightly to allow space for the musket. She placed her mitten clad hand on the long barrel to hold it in place. Thomas removed the revolver from the holster. Holding it both hands, he aimed toward the road. "The riders have stopped coming," she said, somewhat relieved.

"Looks like they stopped at the Kingsley roadway," responded Thomas.

"Ah'm hopin' it's Grady and Abel," Henry said anxiously.

Genevieve saw one of the riders wave. She was certain that it was her brother. The other rider waved, too. "Pa, it's Abel and Grady. Thank the heavens."

She felt the wagon slowing as her father pulled gently on the reins.

"Hello, Abel. Hello, Grady. Ah'm sure glad it's you two!" yelled Henry loudly, feeling mountains of relief.

"Pa, Abel's ridin' home now. Ah'll follow you back to our place," said Grady.

———

THOMAS GOT OFF THE WAGON FIRST, and helped his sister down. He dreaded entering the house and being forced to look at Jubal. Hesitating before going in, he looked back and saw his father drive the wagon toward the barn. Genevieve jerked her arm away from Thomas's grasp. "Come on, Thomas. Let's do our duty," Genevieve said firmly.

As he entered the house behind his sister, he could hear the rustle of his mother's skirts. "Oh, you're home. I was so worried," Emma said.

In a darkened corner, lit only by splashes of light coming from the wood fire, Jubal's head was barely visible. The blanket wrapped around his body covered most of his face.

Thomas removed his boots and coat and watched anxiously as his sister edged over to the rocker. He saw her place a hand on Jubal's head.

Getting no response, she walked to the stone fireplace and rubbed her palms together. "What's for dinner, mother? Will Jubal eat with us?"

"Jubal ate some soup while you were away. I think he needs to be left alone...at least for now," she replied.

Suddenly, the door burst open. Henry and Grady entered, bringing with them a draft of cold air. Emma rushed to greet them, and accepted a hug from Grady and another from her husband.

"Come on over to the fire. Warm yourselves. Dinner will be ready in a few minutes," Emma said.

When the Hastings family bowed their heads at the dinner table, Thomas noticed that Jubal moved his head slightly. He hears us, Thomas said to himself, slightly encouraged.

––––

AFTER DINNER HAD ENDED, Emma and Genevieve cleaned off the table. Grady walked to the head of the stairs. Showing a deep strain on his face, he turned and said, "Ah'm beat 'en am goin' to bed."

Thomas sat on a chair by the fireplace reading a book which he had brought home from school. Genevieve worked on a quilt in her usual chair. Henry and Emma talked in low tones, sipping coffee at the dining table.

An hour later, everyone, except Jubal, had gone to bed. Jubal remained on the rocker. The big clock on the wall ticked away into the night.

Suddenly, a shrill scream interrupted the stillness of the night. "Ahhheee!"

Emma was the first to reach Jubal, who was standing and pointing toward the door.

"Jubal...Jubal, talk to me," she said placing an arm on his shoulder.

Thomas came down the stairway, taking two steps at a time. After landing on the floor with a thud, he paused, seeing, his mother embracing Jubal.

Emma took Jubal's right hand and held it with both of hers. She repeated, "Jubal, please tell me what happened."

"Jennifer...she was shot. My mother was shot....Ah saw it all. They did it—the jayhawkers. They set fire to our house, forcing us into the snow. Then, they shot my father. I hid....I saw it all!"

Thomas remained standing by the stairway. His father had come out of the bedroom, and watched from the doorway. Genevieve knelt next to the railing up in the loft.

"Jubal is back," Emma said and clasped her hands together in prayer.

———

THOMAS SHIVERED IN THE COLD AIR. He left the house, carrying a bag which contained some of his belongings. His father and mother had announced at breakfast that Genevieve, his mother and he were going to take up temporary residence at the Grand Hotel in Tarrytown.

Thomas wasn't certain what that meant, but he readily obeyed and packed his things. His father had said that no one was safe alone on the farm any longer, after what had happened at the Haggards.

Grady and Henry discussed what it would take to fix up the Haggard bunkhouse to provide winter lodging for the Gray Riders. "It ain't burned too bad," Grady told his father.

"The storage area in the back could be converted to a couple dozen bunks, ah reckon. There's plenty of feed and water for our horses. We could patrol the Tarrytown Road and surroundings the rest of the winter."

"There's enough good lumber left in the barn to fix the roof. Ah think you have a great idea," Henry said.

"When is mother coming to the hotel?" Genevieve asked her father after they had gotten seated in the wagon.

"Ah'll bring her in this afternoon, ah reckon. She needs more time to get her things together," Henry answered.

"What's gonna happen to Jubal?" Thomas asked.

"Not for sure, but ah've got a hunch that he's gonna join the Riders," answered Henry.

His father nudged the horses with the reins, and the wagon began moving up the roadway. Thomas looked back and felt secure, seeing Grady following on horseback.

48

LIEUTENANT FARNSWORTH AND HIS TWO COMPANIES of cavalry were returning from Lee's Summit. They had encountered only two groups of rebels who had opened fire and then fled into the hills. One of his privates had been struck in the arm with a rifle ball. After treatment of the wound, the private had no difficulty riding.

"What's that ahead of us, Lieutenant?" asked a sergeant.

"The Tarrytown Road...goes east to Jefferson City," answered Farnsworth.

How far east do ya plan on ridin'?" the sergeant asked.

"Stillman Mills, and then we're turnin' north toward Lexington."

"Are you expectin' any hostility along the way?"

"Yup...there's a bunch of them Quantrill riders hangin' around here. They may put up a fight."

An hour later they crossed a creek. "That's Tarrytown ahead," said the sergeant.

"There's a livery at the other end of town. We'll use it to water and feed the horses," responded the lieutenant.

"What's goin' on o're there, near that church?" the sergeant asked.

———

BEFORE GRADY TOOK HIS SEAT AT THE END OF THE PEW next to Mitch, he looked down the line. Lafe Sunnerland and his brother, Jesse, sat next to Mitch. Beyond them sat James McGregor. Grady's heart gladdened when seeing Elkanah Jackson and Sammy Morton. My boys are all here, he thought.

Grady watched the funeral ceremony, with a deeply saddened heart. His dark brown hair was combed straight-back, and his face showed his feelings. Losing Justin was enough, he thought. Now, it's the whole family, except Jubal. At least he was spared.

During the sermon Grady thought about Justin and all the times they had ridden into battle side by side. First there was Wilson's Creek where they chased the Bluecoats back to Springfield. At Lexington, they had charged up the hill together. Grady smiled, thinking about the huge hemp bale that he and Justin had pushed clear up the hill. The strategy worked and we drove the Bluecoats away from the ridge, and forced 'em to surrender, he remembered.

Pastor Wilson finished with the eulogy. The pallbearers were gathering around the coffins.

Grady tapped Mitch on the arm. "Let's head outside right now."

"Wait, who's that?" Mitch asked.

"Dunno, but she's gonna sing," Grady answered. Grady's heart melted as he listened to Elisha Jordon sing the beautiful song, *Amazing Grace.*

The Riders, deeply touched, quietly slipped out of the pew and passed through the huge door. Grady sucked in some fresh air and stretched his body.

Jesse was staring westward and said, "Someone comin'."

"What do ya see, Jess?" asked Grady recovering from his huge yawn.

"Riders comin', not sure, but it may be cavalry."

"Cavalry, you mean the blue kind?"

"That's exactly what ah mean," responded Jesse firmly.

Feelings of panic radiated through Grady's body. He looked around and realized that they were short-handed. They either had to run for it, or stay with the funeral.

The three coffins were about to be placed onto a wagon. "Let's help, boys." Grady said, moving toward the wagon.

"Geez, Grady. Are we just gonna stand here and watch 'em go by?" Mitch asked frantically.

"We better do exactly that. Do ya see how many there are?" responded Grady after scanning the road westward, trying to see the end of the column. It appeared to stretch as far as he could see.

LED BY THE PASTOR, THE WAGON carrying the three caskets began crossing the road. Grady joined his family for the walk up the hill. The other Riders melted into the procession, slowly making their way toward the cemetery. The officer, leading the Union cavalry, raised an arm and the entire column came to a halt short of the procession.

Feelings of passion spread through Grady's body when the officer removed his wide-brimmed, black hat and signaled the rider next to him. Grady saw the second Bluecoat's hat go down. Turning in the saddle, the rider next to the officer signaled to those in back of him. Like dominoes, all the Bluecoats in the entire column removed their hats.

As the long funeral procession stretched all the way from the church to the large cross in the middle of the cemetery, the Union cavalry did not move. After the last of the mourners had passed and a trailing dog crossed the road, Grady heard an officer yell, "For...ward!"

Grady kept glancing back at the long column as it slowly moved eastward. When his family had reached the cemetery, he moved over to stand next to Mitch. The pastor had begun to read from the black book. As the words melted into the hillside, they watched the rear end of the cavalry column disappear around the corner of the hotel building.

Abel joined them and remarked, "That officer who took off his hat first was at Lone Jack."

"How da ya know that?" Mitch asked.

"Ah saw 'em. He was mounted not far away when Justin got shot."

"What's Elkanah up ta?" Mitch asked anxiously as he watched him walk partway down the slope by himself and stop.

"Ah reckon he's in some sort of a daze," responded Grady. "Let's find out."

Grady and Mitch walked over to Elkanah, who was still standing and staring off in the distance.

"Elkanah, what 'cha doin'?" Mitch asked.

"Ah's watchin' the road where a great man has jest passed by."

49

SNOW CRUNCHING UNDER HIS FEET, Thomas walked from the hotel toward his school. He had said goodbye to Genevieve and Emma in the hotel lobby. His mother had had that usual look of concern in her face. I sure miss Grady and my father, he said to himself.

Thomas's father had come into town on the previous day and reported that Jubal had joined the Gray Riders. He had moved out to the Haggard bunkhouse.

"Jubal's a different person," his father had said. "He practices shooting every single day. His riding skills are something to behold. I pity the first jayhawker that mixes with that young man."

"Wait for me, Thomas," a girl's voice called from the boardwalk behind him.

He turned and saw Sarah Kingsley running toward him. Feelings of delight brought a warm smile to his face. Thomas watched snow chunks kick up from her boots as she approached. The strands of her long, blonde hair bounced off her shoulders.

"Sarah, you look pretty this morning," said Thomas, his voice crackling.

"Why thank you, Thomas," she replied, gasping for air after she stopped running.

"What do you think Mr. Styles has in store for us today, Sarah?"

She laughed. "Nothing that you and I can't handle, huh, Thomas…unless he…."

"Unless, he what?" Thomas asked, stopping to face her.

"Unless…unless he brings out Shakespeare again," Sarah laughed, her freckled cheeks bubbling.

"Heaven help us if he does that," responded Thomas as they continued to walk.

They moved from the boardwalk onto the Tarrytown Road, continued past the church, and turned toward the school yard. Reaching the school, they walked up the steps together. Thomas held the door open for Sarah, her gingham skirt swishing as she passed under his arm. Much to his dismay, two other students snuck in under his arm, preventing him from escorting Sarah to her seat.

After all the students were seated, Mr. Styles stood in front of the class. "Has anyone ever heard of Fredericksburg?"

Thomas was the only one who had raised his hand.

"Yes, Master Hastings."

"It's a town in the state of Virginia."

"Very good, Thomas. Do you know what happened there?"

"No, I do not, Mr. Styles."

"A major Civil War battle took place there a few days ago. Do you know what part of Virginia it is located in?"

"Yes. It is on the Rappahannock River, about halfway between Washington, D.C. and Richmond."

"Astounding, Thomas. Can you tell us any more about its location?"

"Ah, yes. The Potomac River is not far to the east. Westward are the Appalachian Mountains."

"Approximately how far is it from Fredericksburg to the Potomac, Thomas?"

"Two days ride, sir."

"How far is it from Fredericksburg to the Appalachian Mountains, Thomas?"

"Not sure of that one, Sir, probably several days' ride."

"Yes, correct. Of further interest, beyond the city, towards the mountains, is an elevated ground, called Marye's Heights. Along the peak of these heights is a stone wall. General Burnside, Union Commander, unwisely sent his forces against a Confederate stronghold that was concentrated behind the wall. Our brave forces won a major victory at Fredericksburg."

The schoolmaster moved to the front of his desk. He lifted up his oversized hands and began to clap. The rest of the class joined in, some standing and cheering.

———

THE WINTER PASSED SLOWLY FOR THOMAS and his friends, who were residing at the hotel in Tarrytown. He longed for spring and to return to his home. His father visited often. Thomas gladdened when hearing that some of Jubal's pain had lessened, and his mind begin to heal.

The Gray Riders were holed up in the bunkhouse at the Haggard's farm.

His walks to school with Sarah were a strong, warm highlight. "Look, Sarah, a robin," said Thomas as he watched the new arrival hop around on the edge of the road.

Sarah didn't answer. It became apparent to Thomas that she, too, was lonesome for her home. They walked quietly past the church and stepped onto the boardwalk near the hotel.

"Look, Thomas. A single rider is approaching from Stillman Mills. It's not Lance. Mail is already in today."

Thomas's eyes scanned the Tarrytown Road past the livery. The horse's gait appeared labored. The rider's hat seemed to move with the horse's head, as if they were one.

Sarah and Thomas reached the front door of the hotel. "I'm going in, Thomas," Sarah said, brushing a thick strand of blonde hair from her face.

Thomas's curiosity and interest were drawn to the horse and rider as they passed the livery. He remained on the boardwalk and continued to watch. The rider's chest is pressed against the mane as if he's asleep, Thomas thought. He had overheard some of the men at the Frontier Saloon talking about deserters. Most of them would skirt the town.

As the rider came abreast, Thomas stared. There was something about the shape of him that continued to attract Thomas's curiosity. It appeared as if the rider's upper body was long and thin. The rider made no attempt to change gait or pull over to a hitching rail.

Suddenly, Thomas's heart jumped into his throat. "Justin!" And then he called to anyone who could hear. "It's Justin Haggard....He's alive....He's come home."

50

JUSTIN HAGGARD HAD FELT THE BALL TEAR INTO HIS KNEE and then his hands lost possession of his musket. As he went down, he glanced and saw the long barrel fly through the air and land several feet away. He feared for Abel, who was surrounded by four Bluecoats. His attempts to rise to see above the weeds failed. Justin heard the loud noises of shots fired very near, and he feared the worst. Without his musket, and unable to find either one of his two revolvers, he began to crawl.

Feeling the stinging feeling in his knee, he reached back. His head began to shake when he withdrew his hand and saw the wet blood. Ah've got to get back behind our line, he thought desperately.

Attempting to crawl, he discovered that one of his legs couldn't move without extreme pain. Using both hands and one leg, he advanced slowly. The noise of battle appeared to fade farther and farther into the distance as time went by. He used all the strength in his strong, lean body to continue to crawl. Becoming exhausted, he fell into a deep sleep.

Justin awakened when two people picked him up by the shoulders. They began to drag his body. He felt excruciating pain and exclaimed, "Hey! My knee!"

Opening his eyes, he could see that his aggravators were two Bluecoats. "So you're awake, Reb. You're goin' for a ride on that wagon o'er there."

Damnit, ah musta' crawled in the wrong direction, Justin said disgustingly to himself.

After being shoved onto the wagon with a bunch of other

prisoners, the pain lessened. He lowered one of his hands down to his knee and felt the bulk. It's swollen to twice its normal size and hot as hell, he thought. At least the bleeding has stopped.

Raising his body onto an elbow, he looked around and saw scores of Bluecoats and horses. They're organizing into a column, Justin thought. Wonder where they're taking us?

His body felt jolted when the wagon driver flicked the reins, and the two horses plodded toward the column. His knee, feeling every single bump from the wheels rolling over rough ground, began to throb.

Closing his eyes, he dreamed of Jennifer and home. He thought about their bedroom and how she had decorated it to perfection.

The wagon stopped. "All right, Rebs. I've got somethin' for ya all to chew on—water, too."

Lifting the dipper to his lips, Justin felt instant relief in the parched tissues of his mouth. His teeth hurt as he attempted to chew the jerky. Slowly, he chipped off small pieces and swallowed them. Food and water allowed Justin to ignore his swollen knee for a time. Reality and pain returned when the wagon jerked into motion.

Justin closed his eyes and attempted to create a world of fantasy, but the jostling of the wagon gave him no respite from his pain. It seemed as if they had traveled for hours. He opened his eyes and looked at the man next to him. "Where do ya think we're goin'?" Justin asked.

"Lexington, ah 'eard one of the Yankees say."

Justin thought about Paul Sunnerland lying in a wagon on his way to a decrepit hospital tent. That was at Lexington, too. Ah can't die from a ball in the knee. Paul's wound was higher up, he thought to himself.

———

JUSTIN'S MIND WANDERED IN AND OUT of consciousness when the wagon finally came to a stop. The moans and groans that had come from the wagon the entire distance suddenly ceased. Justin's mind went blank, a feeling of immense relief.

He awakened from the clunking sound that came from the tongue of the hitch when it dropped to the ground. Justin heard the plodding of hooves and the jingle of the harnesses as the two horses were being driven away.

Wonder how many of the boys are still alive? he thought. No one seems to be moving. Overcoming stiffness and soreness, he successfully sat up.

Looking through red-streaked eyes, Justin scanned his surroundings. Hundreds of tents dotted an expansive area of clearings and trees. A massive number of horses were feeding on bales of hay a short distance away from the tents.

Hearing footsteps, he faced two Bluecoats who had approached the wagon from the rear. "All right, Rebs, you can all get out now."

Justin slid off the back edge of the wagon box. He felt waves of dizziness resulting in the inability to move. One of the Bluecoats gave him a shove and he fell to the ground. Attempting to rise, he realized that his entire right leg had no feeling.

Two other Bluecoats came walking by. "Hey, there, Reb, bet you could use a stick," one of them said, observing Justin's knee.

Justin nodded, his eyes pleading.

"You stay right here, and I'll round up a couple," the Bluecoat said.

Justin got up on his good knee and swung his arms and shoulders from side to side. Within minutes, the Bluecoat returned with two crude saplings. Justin watched with passion as his captor brought out a large knife and began to shape the pieces. "There you are, Reb. Hope that helps," the Bluecoat said as he laid the pieces by one of Justin's arms.

"Let me hep ya," a fellow prisoner said.

Placing a sapling into each of Justin's hands, the prisoner grabbed him under the shoulders and helped him to his feet. Once standing, Justin felt dizzy. He realized that he had not attempted to stand since being shot. He took a strained first step, then another. "Thank you. Where ya from?" he asked his fellow prisoner.

"Harrisonville...ah'm Jud."

"Ah'm from Tarrytown. My name is Justin."

———

THE PRISONERS WERE DIRECTED TO A GRASSY AREA not far from the wagon. They helped each other gather whatever possessions they had to increase their comfort during the night. Justin thought his situation improved since riding in the wagon. Even though he didn't have a saddle for a pillow, or a blanket for cover, he slept well. The next morning's dawn brought about the fear of spending another day in the wagon.

A pair of Bluecoats brought over a pan full of beef cuts and some hardtack. One of the prisoners whispered, "Water."

"We'll get you some, Reb," one of the Bluecoats answered.

A few minutes later, the two Bluecoats returned with four canteens. The feeling of water going down his parched throat was like going to heaven, Justin thought.

"Men, it's time to get back on the wagon," a guard said roughly.

Justin managed to walk to the wagon on his own, pleasing himself immensely. He was able to get into the wagon by himself by sitting on the back edge first. Laying down the crude crutches next to his body, he felt tension waiting for the wagon to begin moving.

Justin and his fellow prisoners spent only part of another day in the bumpy wagon. Late in the afternoon, he could feel the wagon going downhill. He peeked over the edge and saw the big river. The wagon headed down a roadway that led to a pier. Black smoke erupted from a dirty looking smoke stack, which was part of a boat anchored to a crude dock of planking.

"Where do ya suppose we're goin' now?" he asked Jud.

"They're puttin' us on that boat for a cruise to Jefferson City. Then, we're goin' by train to a place called Butler in Illinois."

"What's at Butler?" Justin asked.

"A Federal prison, ah 'ear," Jud responded.

Justin happily said goodbye to the wagon, even though the boarding of the boat was tedious. He trudged behind the other prisoners to a flat area of the deck near the back of the boat. Justin lay down, cringing from the smell of the oil-stained planking. Thinking about his geography learning in school, Justin's mind gladdened with the fact that Jefferson City was not far away.

He propped himself up against a railing and saw the grassy slope that he and Grady Hastings had pushed hemp bales upward during the battle of Lexington. He felt comforted knowing that they had won that day. The Bluecoats had been driven away from the high ground.

The deep, sad sound of a fog horn interrupted his thoughts. Justin could hear the engines sputter and groan, while the boat backed away from the pier. The view of the heights above the river is spectacular, Justin thought as the boat slowly made its way up the river.

The boat moved smoothly through the water, allowing the prisoners some comfort compared to the wagon ride. Feeling his wounded knee, Justin thought the swelling had gotten worse.

"Look at those big birds up there," one of the prisoners said.

Justin opened an eye and saw two bald eagles soaring high above the tree line. He opened his other eye and watched the shoreline for a few minutes. Ah'm gonna survive this, he said to himself.

———

AT JEFFERSON CITY, THE BOAT PULLED ALONGSIDE a pier and stopped. The walk up the long, wooden stairway was excruciating for Justin, but he finally got to the top. His newly found friend, Jud, stayed with him all the way. Once again they were herded onto a wagon.

"They're takin' us to the railroad station," Jud said.

"Those are cattle cars," Justin said when the wagon stopped.

While Justin attempted to traverse a set of tracks he felt a prod in his back. One of his captors used the stock of a musket to push him along.

After they got into the railroad car, the remains of hemp bales in the box allowed them to insulate the roughness of the train ride. "Lift up a bit, Justin. Ah've got another wad of hemp for ya," Jud said.

"Thank ye, Jud."

In spite of the jostling of the railroad car, Justin fell asleep. When he awoke, he could no longer see through the opening allowed by the large, open sliding door—it was dark outside. On and on the train clattered into the night. By morning, it had crossed the Illinois state line and continued on to Butler.

Five days after embarking on the big river at Lexington, the prisoners reached the Butler Prison. "Come on, Justin, lean on me," said Jud as the long walk to the prison gate began. When they finally entered the prison confines, they were the last two to register at a table manned by two Bluecoats. After Jud had a tag tied to his shirt, one of the Bluecoats got up and walked around to look at Justin's leg.

"Hey, Reb, looks like you need the hospital. You sit right over there and someone will come by to pick you up."

"Ah'm fine," replied Justin.

"Reb, you do as ah say. You understand?"

"Yes, sir," Justin replied. He trudged over to the compound wall and sat down.

———

BY THE TIME A WAGON HAD COME FOR THE WOUNDED, Justin had fallen asleep. Rudely awakened, he resented the pushes by sneering Bluecoats toward the wagon. After getting on, he dreaded the thought of what might occur next.

Justin could see the tent up ahead. At least it wasn't very far away, he thought. Two Bluecoats helped him walk from the wagon to the tent. A short distance away, severed limbs were piled high. Justin felt ill from the stench.

Upon entering, Justin felt the prods on his back directing him to join a gathering of other wounded soldiers. Laying his two crutches next to the canvas wall, he sat down and awaited his fate. His eyes looked up, and he saw a wavy ceiling. The sounds of groans and screams didn't effect him. He had heard so many the past few days that the sounds didn't aggravate him any longer.

Justin realized they were going to take his leg. He was terrified with the thought but knew what would happen if they didn't—he would never see Jennifer again. While thinking about his wife, Justin fell asleep.

The reality of his situation sliced through his mind as two men grabbed both his shoulders and began dragging him along the ground. He felt sickened by the appearance of their blood-stained aprons. The pain in his knee tightened every muscle in his body as they lifted him onto a table.

Justin felt something wet being sprinkled on his leg. The two men grabbed his arms and pinned them to the side of the table. He heard an awful grating sound. Then, he felt the pain....It was like nothing he had ever felt before in his life. Light changed to blackness.

When he awoke, Justin couldn't speak. His attempts to move his lips failed. His mouth felt parched and he feebly attempted to beg for water. Moments later, a Bluecoat appeared with a pail. The soldier tried to pour water down Justin's throat. Most of it splashed onto his cheeks, but the moisture that did enter his mouth gave him new life.

He was surprised that the pain from having his leg removed was less than what the swollen knee had been. While in the wagon on the way back to the prison, he thought about the growing pile of limbs. Mine is up there, too, by now, he thought.

When the wagon stopped, he looked around. Instead of prison walls, he saw a railroad station with a train parked on the tracks. "Reb, we're sending you back to Jefferson City."

Justin stared at his captor, and ran the tip of his tongue across his upper lip. As he moved it against the hairs above, he felt consoled that his mustache had thickened.

"We know you can't ever fight again, so we're lettin' you go."

Justin felt his eyes water. He was goin' home. He would see Jennifer again. "Thank ye so much," he said to his captor.

"You get into that train and ah don't ever want to see you again," the Bluecoat officer said.

51

THOMAS RACED OUT ONTO THE ROAD. "Justin...is that you?" he asked frantically.

The horse continued to walk. "Justin, ah'm Thomas. Thomas Hastings."

The horse stopped, and Justin turned to look. Thomas saw sunken eyes surrounded by black circles. The face looked deathly paled and thin and covered with stained, scraggly hair.

Justin didn't speak. He turned his head and nudged his horse to go on.

"No...no...stay here, Justin. Come into the hotel with me!" Thomas exclaimed.

The horse continued to walk westward. Thomas ran across the street into the constable's office.

"Mr. Muldoon, Justin is back....Somethin's wrong. He don't act right!" Thomas cried.

"Who, son? Who don't act right?"

"Justin Haggard!" Thomas exclaimed loudly, anger flashing across his face.

"Well, ah'll be danged," the constable responded, his face splattered with delight.

"You don't understand. He's headin' out to the farm. We've got to stop 'em!" Thomas exclaimed.

The constable grabbed a hat and coat off a hook. He hurriedly put them on. "You're right, son. We can't let him go out there...."

Thomas dashed outside and saw that Justin had moved past the mortuary. "The leg, Constable...it's missing....The stirrup is empty. He's lost a leg."

"Ah'll see if ah can get some help," the Constable said. He

lumbered across the road to the saloon. Moments later, he came out. "No use, son. We're gonna have to let 'em go. He can find his way home, and Jubal is over there."

Thomas ran to the livery. "Toby! Toby!"

"What's the panic, Thomas?"

"Is Doctor Well's rig in here?"

"Why, yes 'tis."

"Harness it up. Git it ready. I'm takin' the doc out to Haggard's place."

"Haggard's place? It's done burnt down, I 'ear. What do ya think you're doin', Thomas?"

"Never mind, Toby. Git that darn carriage hitched up or I'll apply this fist to your teeth!" Thomas answered angrily, clenching his fingers.

"All right...all right," Toby responded.

———

THOMAS PUT THE WHIP TO THE DOCTOR'S HORSE. He galloped it to the Smith Building. Leaping out of the carriage and tying the horse to a rail, he raced to the door. Attempting to turn the door handle, he realized it was locked. He began banging on the door.

When it opened, he screamed frantically, "Doc, you've got to come! Justin Haggard just rode through town. He's on his way home. He's sick as a mule."

"Just a mighty minute, ah'll get my coat and bag," the doctor replied anxiously.

Thomas untied the horse and got back into the carriage. Anxiously watching the door, he said, "Come on, doc....Time's a wastin'," he murmured.

At last the doctor came out of his office and stepped into the carriage. "Heah-yah!" yelled Thomas and the horse began a fast trot westward. When the carriage got past the church, Thomas used a whip and the horse broke into a gallop.

"Easy, Thomas...Snickers is not accustomed to that type of

treatment."

Thomas slowed the horse back down to a trot when they got past MacTurley's Woods. "You're gonna have to let 'em walk a spell," the doctor said.

Thomas looked down the roadway leading to his home. He thought about his father, alone with the hands tending to the herds. Finally, they got across the creek, and he could see the Sunnerland house.

"There he is!" Thomas exclaimed anxiously. Justin's horse moved slowly, but it was almost at the Haggard's roadway. Thomas snapped a rein, sending the horse into a trot.

"You're gonna kill my horse, Thomas," the doctor said firmly.

"We gotta catch up with Justin. No tellin' what he'll do if he finds the houses burnt and everyone gone," said Thomas, his voice clattering with anxiety. The doctor hung onto the rail as Thomas turned the carriage sharply onto the Haggard's roadway.

Moments later, he passed Justin's horse. Pulling on the reins, he stopped the carriage and leaped free. Thomas put up both arms in an attempt to halt them. Thomas grabbed the reins, and Justin made an unsuccessful attempt to get them back.

"Justin...stay right there....Hang on. I'm leadin' ya home," Thomas said pleadingly.

Holding the reins securely in his hands, he got into the back of the carriage. "Doc, take it in. Go all the way to the bunkhouse. Please do as I say."

52

ABEL, LAFE AND JESSE SAT AROUND the big table playing cribbage. Grady stood by the window looking out. "Carriage comin'," he said. "Looks like a rider, too."

Lafe looked up at him and said, "Probably Lincoln hisself."

Abel grinned and said, "Shuh enough, Lafe. Tall Abe's comin' to surrender."

Jesse asked, "Just one rider, Grady?"

"Yup, just one rider and looks like...."

"Looks like who?"

"His horse is tied to the back of the carriage...strange."

Jubal had been napping on a bunk when he heard Grady talking about a rider. Getting up quickly, he joined Grady at the window.

Jubal and Grady watched as the carriage got closer and closer. Suddenly, Jubal raced to the door. He jerked it open and ran outside. Grady watched as Jubal ran toward the carriage. "Well, ah'll be....It couldn't be...."

Lafe joined Grady at the window. "Jaysus almighty...it's Justin. He's come back," he said, his voice squeaking more than usual.

Jesse pushed his chair away from the table and dashed through the door, followed by Grady and Lafe. They ran past the remains of Justin and Jennifer's house. Stopping at the beginning of the roadway, they saw Jubal reach the rider and go for the reins.

"Hey, that's Thomas back there, in the carriage," said Grady.

Grady, Lafe, and Abel ran toward the lone horse. They sided up next to Justin and supported him while Jubal led the horse to the bunkhouse door.

Jubal and the others gently slid Justin off the saddle. "Gotta get him inside—and fast!" Jubal said anxiously, his small, dark, penetrating eyes focused on his brother.

Quickly, they carried Justin into the house.

"Heat up some water!" Grady yelled when they got into the bunkhouse.

After they got his cold clothing off, James came over with a bucket of boiling water. Doctor Wells had removed his coat and jacket. He directed all those present to soak rags in the hot water. Under his supervision, they soaked Justin's limbs.

After drying the patient, Doctor Wells had Justin covered with warm blankets. "Dunno what else we could do for 'em right now, boys. Thanks for all ya help."

Jubal walked away from the bunk and said, "Thank God the doc is here." He walked over to Thomas and hugged him. "Thank ye, Thomas."

The doctor remained by the bed, holding Justin's wrist by his fingers. "Got any brandy here?" he asked after leaving the bed.

"Sure have, Doc....Want some?" James asked.

"Sure do," the doctor said and walked over to the table. He took a seat and added, "He's dehydrated, weak, and full of fever. You need to force in water, keep him cool. He won't be eatin' anything for a day or so."

"He's asleep now," said Jubal. "How does the leg look, doc?"

"It's healed up surprisingly well. That's not gonna be the problem. We gotta get rid of that fever....Hopefully, tomorrow it'll be improved. If you boys hadn't gotten 'em in here for another few hours, he'd surely have been dead."

Jubal added, "Gotta give Thomas credit for that, Doc."

The doctor sipped his brandy and said, "Thomas, would you drive me back to town?"

"Doctor Wells, ah'd consider that a privilege," responded Thomas, holding his chin high.

———

AFTER THE DOCTOR LEFT, Jubal sat on a chair next to the bunk where his brother was lying. "You're gonna make it, Justin. Ah did," Jubal said softly, laying his head down on the blanket next to his brother's shoulder.

The atmosphere in the bunkhouse changed. There wasn't any card playing or whooping it up. The boys sat around the table and talked in low tones, occasionally glancing at Justin's bunk.

Grady got up during the middle of the night, and after returning from outside, noticed that Jubal slept on the floor next to his brother's bunk.

"Jube, you need to go to your bunk. It's cold on that floor. We don't need another sick person."

Grady placed his palm on Justin's head. Still awful warm, he said to himself—too warm.

When Grady got up the next morning, he saw Jubal attempting to feed Justin broth with a spoon. Suddenly, Justin became delirious. He loudly stammered, "Jennifer...Jube..." over and over again. Finally, his voice trailed off and he fell asleep.

"Ah think that's good, Jubal," Grady said.

Mid-morning, Thomas and the doctor arrived in the carriage. Jubal anxiously went outside to greet the doctor. "He's still alive, Doc. Breathing seems good...still hot."

During the next six days, Thomas and the doctor rode out to the bunkhouse daily. Each time, the doctor would shake his head before leaving.

"Doesn't look good, huh, Doc?" Grady asked.

The doctor didn't say anything. He just put on his coat and headed for the door.

On the seventh day, the doctor turned to face his onlookers. He beamed and said, "Justin is gonna make it."

Cheers broke out. Thomas and Jubal danced around the wooden table.

53

WHEN CHRISTMAS CAME TO WESTERN MISSOURI IN 1862, it brought a lull in the fighting. On the eve of the holiday, a convoy of wagons and horsemen left Tarrytown and headed for the Haggard farm.

Grady and Jesse had improvised a good shelter for their horses using the remains from the burnt barn. They had been working out in the corral tending to the horses. Grady felt proud that they could comfortably house thirty horses. "Listen, Jess, do ya hear somethin'?"

Jesse set down his hay fork and listened. "Yes...the sound of bells. Someone's comin'."

They left the shelter and walked into the clearing where they could see the roadway. "Jess, there's a whole bunch of carriages comin'...some wagons and riders, too," said Grady.

"Well, ah'll be...it's Christmas. We've got company—lots of company."

Grady and Jesse walked out to the roadway to watch the visitors arrive.

The first carriage pulled up. "Hey boys, would ya like some cheer?" they heard Martin Kingsley say as he grabbed a bottle from his coat pocket. His smiling wife, Beth, sat next to him. Bundled up in a heavy blanket on the back seat, his daughter, Sarah, smiled from ear-to-ear, her thick, red lips stretched.

"Let the ladies off, Martin, and pull up your carriage over there by the barn...well, what's left of it," said Grady. "Oh, and don't forget to bring that bottle."

Martin Kingsley burst out laughing.

George Walker's carriage arrived next. His wife, Angie, sat next to him. Helen and Jessica, his two daughters, perched on the rear seat.

"Merry Christmas, Abel. Ah've got a present for ya," said George, and in a rare moment, smiled. He handed Abel a jug and added. "Careful, don't drop it."

Abel smiled. He pulled out the cork and brought the mouth of the jug to his thin lips. His Adam's apple bounced with each swallow. Lowering the jug, he wiped his lips with his other hand, plopped the cork back in, and handed the jug back to George.

"Good evening, ladies," Grady said, his heart melting from Helen's warm smile.

Henry and Emma Hastings pulled up in the third carriage. "Greetings, Grady, you too, Abel. Would ya help the ladies down, boys?"

Grady assisted his mother down from the carriage while Abel extended his hand to Genevieve.

"Hey, Thomas, Sarah's here, ya know," Grady chided his brother, who had gotten off his horse and was already halfway to the house.

———

WAR TOOK A BACKSEAT ON THAT COLD DECEMBER
EVENING. There was plenty of food and whiskey. Toby Miller
brought a banjo. Belle Streeter from Mamma's Kitchen strummed a
Christmas song on her guitar, as Lady Constance from the Frontier
Saloon sang. As the whiskey flowed, the music became louder.

For the second time since returning, Justin Haggard wore a smile.
He attempted to leave his bunk, but dizziness forced him to remain.
When Shol Clarity, the barber, did a solo jig, moving crisply to the
beat of Toby Miller's banjo, Justin clapped his hands along with others,
keeping time to the music.

The barber had ridden to the Haggard farm a day earlier and
shaved Justin's face. He had trimmed the ever-thickening mustache,
and saw the man smile for the first time. "His smile is for real," Shol
had said.

Thomas watched with delight when Lance Milburn joined in the
jig. The clapping got louder and louder. The distraction gave him an
opportunity to work his way next to Sarah Kingsley.

"Thomas, ah hear you're a hero. Getting the doctor to Justin so
quickly and all that," Sarah said.

"'Twas nothin', Sarah, anyone else would've done the same."

"Ah come on, Thomas, don't be so modest," he heard Jesse
Sunnerland say.

Thomas felt embarrassed when he saw his father move onto the
dance floor and roll up his sleeves. Moments later, he danced with
his wife. I've never seen that before, Thomas said to himself.

George Walker guided his resisting wife to the floor and begin
clapping and shouting. "Everybody dance!" he yelled, high-steppin'
around the floor.

Tall, large-framed Orly McGregor grabbed Lady Constance off
her chair and escorted her to the middle of the floor. Toby Miller
took advantage of the opportunity to play an Irish jig on his banjo.
Stiff-backed Orly is no longer stiff, Thomas thought. He's as loose
as the fiddle.

When a tan colored jug was passed around, it made its way into
Thomas's hands. "Go ahead, have a swig," he heard Grady say.
Thomas tilted the jug and imitated what he had seen the other boys

do. When the liquid reached his stomach, he coughed and grabbed his mouth. Quickly, Thomas passed the jug to his brother.

Moments later, he felt his body warm. Magnificent, what a feeling, he thought. Glancing over at Sarah, he felt that she looked prettier than ever. He firmly walked over to her and put out his trembling hand.

Guiding her out onto the floor, he wasn't sure what to do next. Suddenly, he felt his legs moving.

54

THE NEW YEAR OF 1863 BROUGHT WITH it a cold, snowy January and February. The Gray Riders patrolled very little during those two months. Other than tending to their horses, they spent most of their time next to a fire in the bunkhouse. By mid-March, most of the snow had melted and the Gray Riders patrolled daily.

Jubal smiled as he watched Justin mount his horse. He does as well as any of us, he thought. They had devised a side-saddle scabbard to secure his two crutches. Justin whittled two saplings down to near perfection to help himself walk.

"It's the last day of March today," Jubal had said.

After mounting, they followed the other six riders up the roadway onto the Tarrytown Road. Jubal had noticed that only two Union cavalry columns had come by the entire month of March. Both of them came from the direction of Tarrytown and moved westward without paying any attention to the Haggard farmstead.

Jubal saw Grady signal and lead the column of eight across a field that bordered a rocky ravine. They pulled up next to a grove of ash. Riding up from the bottom of the ravine, a group of horsemen whom Jubal had seen previously approached. The leader raised an arm in greeting as Grady did the same.

"Howdy, Hastings," said the leader.

"Who's that?" Jubal asked.

"Looks like Cole Younger," Justin answered.

Justin lightly touched his horse's flank with a spur, and his horse moved forward. "Howdy, Mr. Younger," he said.

"Well, if it ain't Haggard....Ah 'eard you were shot up and taken prisoner at Lone Jack. Glad to see that ya escaped," said Younger.

"They let me go....Didn't think ah was a threat anymore, with my leg gone and all," Justin answered.

Cole laughed. "Little minds make small decisions."

"Quantrill is lookin' for riders for a raid on a Kansas town. Would any of ye be interested?" Cole asked.

"What's over in Kansas?" Justin asked.

"Town by the name of Lawrence...it's full of abolitionists and the like. I 'ere that it's got warehouses full of plunder that the jayhawkers and redlegs have taken from us. Quantrill wants to pull off a surprise attack. He wants revenge and to get back some of the plunder."

Jubal had been listening intently. He nudged his horse forward. "Ah'll go with 'em, Mr. Younger."

Cole laughed. "Yar' a little young, but we'll take anyone we can git."

"When is this gonna happen?" asked Justin.

"Not sure of exactly when, but he's waitin' until some of the Union pull out. Perhaps about mid-August," answered Younger.

"Hell, if you're goin', Jube, so am I," Justin answered. "Ah got nothin' to lose. They burned my farm, and kilt my wife and parents."

———

SCHOOL HAD ENDED FOR THE DAY on an April afternoon. Thomas became impatient waiting for Sarah to finish her paper, and struck out on his own because he was extraordinarily hungry. Taking a shortcut, he walked briskly through the tall grass and onto the Tarrytown Road.

He saw Lance Milburn approaching on horseback from the livery. In spite of his hunger, Thomas bypassed the hotel and made for the

General Store where Lance would bring the mail.

Constable Muldoon came waddling across the road from his office. "Thomas, how's the learnin' goin'?"

"Good, but I wish that I was ridin' with Grady and the Gray Riders," Thomas answered.

"You'll probably git yar chance, young feller. Gotta keep some of ya roun' town to protect the rest of us," Constable Muldoon said, winking.

Entering the General Store, Thomas overheard men talking about a place called Vicksburg. "First one, we've lost. Can't mean that much," one of the men said.

"Lincoln's got himself a new general—Grant, they call 'em," another said.

————

SARAH KINGSLEY FELT LONESOME FOR HER HOME. She and her mother had been sharing a hotel room for the past few months. She gladdened when her father came to visit. He had been spending most of his time supervising their hired hands and maintaining the Angus herd.

The bright spot in her summer thus far had been her visits with Thomas Hastings. They would spend hours sitting on a bench and watching the world go by. One day, a huge column of Union cavalry came through town. They were lined up four abreast and followed by wagons and large weapons mounted on wheels. Artillery is what they were called, according to Seth Miller.

She felt amused, but Thomas wasn't, when one of the young cavalry riders smiled and waved at her. Sarah noticed Thomas appeared tense and squirmy while the cavalry lumbered through town. She thought about the Haggard's funeral and the cavalry that showed up that day. Everyone in Tarrytown still talked about the Union officer who had taken off his hat out of respect.

Yesterday, she was disheartened because Thomas had told her he had permission from his father to join the Gray Riders. She thought about her brother, Abel, and how he had changed since he had joined.

He wasn't the docile not wanting to get involved person that she knew a couple of years ago. She prayed for his safety, but she didn't like his new, hostile attitude.

Sarah enjoyed the General Store and looking at all the clothes. Genevieve Hastings had been working there most every day since everyone had moved to the hotel. An otherwise boring day improved dramatically by spending time with her. Often, they talked about boys and giggled. Sarah saddened when Genevieve told her about her feelings for Will Walker before he got killed in the battle of Wilson's Creek.

Sarah sat on the bench alone one late morning in July. She already felt the heat, which was normal for this time of the year. The mail from Stillman Mills was overdue. There were several people milling about, waiting for Lance to appear. Then she heard a yelp. "There he comes!"

His horse appears to moving slower than usual, she thought. That usually means the Confederacy has lost another battle. Earlier in the year, he had galloped into town to announce the victory at Chancellorsville. Three weeks later, he had walked his horse into town with the sad news that their hero, General Stonewall Jackson, had died.

A larger crowd than usual gathered in front of the General Store. The usual dirt and dust did not shake loose from Lance Milburn's clothing when he dismounted. Seth Miller appeared, and helped Lance remove the two huge saddle bags from behind the saddle.

"Gettysburg? Where's that?" she heard a man exclaim.

"Pennsylvania."

"What the sam blazes was Lee doin' way o'er there?"

"Lee got beat bad, it says here," Sarah heard someone else say.

55

JUSTIN HAGGARD FELT THE HEAT. It was past the noon hour on a hot, muggy, mid-August day. He rode next to Grady at the head of the Gray Riders column. They headed northwest to rendezvous with a group of Quantrill's men.

Two riders intercepted them while en route. They passed on the word that a column of Union cavalry had camped just around the bend beyond a grove of trees, which they could see from where they stood.

"We better split off now," Justin told Grady. "Jube and ah'll ride north and get around 'em."

Justin knew that Grady and the others didn't like the idea of him and Jubal joining up with Quantrill's riders for a raid into Kansas. "Grady, it's somethin' that Jube and ah 'ave to do. Those jayhawkers didn't show my family any mercy when ah was away. Someone has to pay."

Justin walked his horse alongside the entire single column, slapping hands with the other riders as he passed by. When he got to the end, he watched as Jubal did the same.

Justin returned to the head of the column, his silver-gray eyes beaming with confidence and said, "We'll be back before ya know it, Grady."

Grady and the other Riders watched as Justin and Jubal rode away. After riding a short distance, the two Haggard boys halted.

Justin took off his hat and circled it over his head three times. "He-yaw!" he yelled and galloped northward. Jubal saluted, and he also galloped off.

As they approached a grove of trees which they were about to circumvent, Justin looked back. Deep feelings of loneliness overcame him when he saw Grady and the others heading back toward Tarrytown.

Justin felt much like he did each day while a prisoner in Illinois. At that time, he had hope of returning to Jennifer. Now there wasn't any hope. His wife and her parents were gone. The jayhawkers had killed them. Looking into Jubal's small, dark eyes, Justin's feelings of loneliness turned into rage—he saw his mother in those beady blacks. They had a mission.

A couple of hours before dark, they found the Quantrill band they had been seeking. There must be close to fifty men, Justin thought. A man by the name of Clement led the band. Justin's bones ached and he needed sleep.

"We're ridin' through the night, boys," Clement had said. "We need to get to the Grand River by mornin'. Quantrill is gonna be there waitin' for us."

"Here, let me tie you boys onto your saddles. You may fall asleep....It's a long way," said one of Clement's sidekicks.

Justin thought he was going to die on that all night ride. The column rode on...and on...and on. At least only one of my legs can be hurting, Justin laughingly told himself.

———

JUBAL LOOKED OVER AT THIS BROTHER. My God, he's dead asleep on his horse, he said to himself. The leader of the column signaled a halt. Two riders galloped along the entire length. One of them said, "It's gettin' close to dawn. We're campin' over there in that timber. You all will be able to get some sleep."

"Right there, Jube," Justin said as they rode their horses into a thick grove of trees.

We're well equipped, Jubal thought. Grady borrowed me his new tent, and we've got extra blankets if the night chills.

Justin and Jubal dismounted, removed their saddles, and freed their horses to browse at will. "Plenty of grassy open areas in these woods," they heard someone say.

Justin opened a saddle bag and shared a cache of food with his brother. It had been prepared by the ladies at the hotel in Tarrytown. After eating and drinking their fill, the two brothers fell into a deep sleep.

Jubal awakened to the sounds of men talking in low tones and moving about. His stomach told him that the noon hour had passed. Pressed by the prodding of Quantrill's officers, they were ready for departure in an hour.

Fitting into the four columns of over four hundred men, Jubal rode next to his brother. Leaving the woods, they headed westward toward the Kansas border.

They rode in silence for the next couple of hours. Then Jubal asked, "Did ya hear that, Justin?"

"No...what did ya hear?"

"Someone up ahead said that we're in Kansas. Have you ever been in Kansas before?"

"No, can't say that ah 'ave," answered Justin.

The column turned toward the northwest. When sunset came, Jubal was hoping they would camp for the night. Instead, they rode on...and on...and on.

Long after dark, they were halted. Horses were allowed to graze and feed. Jubal sat down on the ground next to his brother. "What have we gotten ourselves into, Justin?" he asked.

"Been wondering the same thing myself, but ah keep thinkin' about Jennifer. Gonna get some revenge," responded Justin firmly.

The next stop to feed and rest the horses occurred four hours later. Jubal felt exhausted. Two men came around and again offered to tie him and Justin into their saddles so they wouldn't fall off. As the night progressed and the column rode on, Jubal gladdened that he had agreed to the tie-down. Glancing at Justin, he saw his brother bent forward against the mane, much like he had looked when he had returned from captivity.

———

DAYLIGHT CAME AND THE COLUMN PLODDED ON. Jubal anxiously waited for a signal to halt. Surely, we're gonna rest like we did yesterday, he thought.

Glancing at Justin, he noticed that his brother sat tall in the saddle, just like he had before losing a leg. Those silver-gray eyes…they look cold and calculating, Jubal said to himself. My brother is on a deadly mission. I'm glad he's on my side. The space between them and the four horses ahead had widened, forcing them to pick up the gait.

At last the column halted. Jubal, once again, thought they were going to rest for the day. He saw several riders break away from the front of the column and move along the line. They appeared to be untying those that had agreed to the ropes. Jubal raised his arms and allowed one of the riders to remove the rope around his waist. "Are we gonna stop for the day?" Jubal asked the man.

"Ready your revolvers….We're goin' into Lawrence to shoot up the place, and damn soon."

Jubal's resolve diminished until he thought about his parents and Jennifer. Looking over at Justin, he saw his brother spinning the cylinders of his three revolvers. Jubal did the same with his two Colts.

"What's the calendar say today? Do ya know?" Jubal asked another of the riders.

"August 21…Lawrence will pay today."

Suddenly, Jubal could hear yelling up ahead. He saw the front part of the main column spread into clusters of arm-swinging riders. The riders had spread out and were galloping toward a line of trees, behind which a church spire pointed at the sky.

The column totally disintegrated, drawing Jubal and Justin into a massive attack on the town. Galloping horses and screaming riders spread like wildfire through the streets. Jubal saw a horse's hooves throw up clods of sod as it traversed between two houses and jumped a wooden fence.

Shrilling yells and screams came from all around him. Jubal could see people running in the street. Gunfire erupted and he saw two of the citizens fall to the ground. "Kill…kill!" he heard men yelling up ahead. He and Justin followed the horses in front of them. They had turned onto a side street where more shots were fired.

Two men came out of a building holding white handkerchiefs

above their heads. Both of them fell from a barrage of pistol shots.

Jubal had two loaded Colt revolvers stuck in his belt. Grabbing the reins with his left hand, he grasped a colt with the fingers of his other. Pulling back the hammer, he pointed the gun toward an upper window and pulled the trigger. Looking around, he didn't see Justin. They had separated.

The group he was with were circling their horses and firing their pistols into the sky. A man appeared on the steps of a house. Three shots rang out, and the man fell. Jubal's heart began to race. He thought about his father, mother, and Jennifer falling in their farmyard. Jubal experienced feelings of guilt as he watched the man attempt to crawl back into the house while the hole in his chest spurt blood.

He followed the riders up the block and saw a man running from the back of a house, attempting to hide behind a hedge. Two of the riders raced toward the man. Jubal saw one of them empty his revolver and grab another.

Jubal was worried about Justin. He had had enough of this group and trotted his horse onto another street. Seeing no one, he began his search for his brother.

Turning a street corner, Jubal came upon a man who had fallen. He must be a business man, Jubal thought, because of his vest and waistcoat. The man stood up and Jubal pointed his pistol at the man's chest.

"Please, sir. I have a wife and two boys," the man pleaded.

"My parents and sister-in-law were murdered…murdered by the likes of your friends," Jubal said, his voice rising to a shrill pitch.

The man got down on his knees and clasped his hands. Jubal raised the pistol and pulled back the hammer. "Go…hide…git," Jubal said, his voice trailing off, moisture filling his beady eyes. He looked around and felt glad that no one had seen what he had just done.

The man got up and ran behind the closest house. Jubal just sat there on his saddle holding his pistol. He pointed it skyward and fired.

Sporadic gunshots could be heard coming from various areas. Turning onto another street, he saw the bodies of many men lying on the ground. Women and children were screaming and rushing to the sides of their fallen families. This ain't for me, he said to himself, anxious to find his brother.

———

ADVANCING TOWARD A CLUSTER OF RIDERS AHEAD, Jubal saw his brother, sitting on his horse with a revolver in both hands. Jubal saw the horse's eyes—full of terror from all the noise and smoke. Placing the revolvers back in his belt, Jubal rode toward him.

"Jube, how many of 'em did you git?" Justin asked.

"None, Justin…just couldn't do it. How about you? Did you get your revenge?"

"Ah couldn't do it either, Jube. These ain't the people that murdered Jennifer. This whole raid makes me sick."

"Why are ya wavin' those revolvers?" Jubal asked.

"So ah don't get shot."

"Is there some way we could git out of 'ere and head for home?" Jubal asked, his voice sounding rough and husky.

"Too risky right now, Jube….Let's stay together and wait for a chance."

By mid-morning, Jubal noticed the shooting had lessened considerably. He watched with disdain as members of the band raided building after building, robbing the inhabitants of their jewelry and money. In a whim, someone would pull a trigger and another citizen would fall.

———

"EVERYONE GIT!" JUBAL HEARD SOMEONE YELL from the other end of the street.

"Come on, Justin, let's ride," Jubal said, very happy to be leaving Lawrence.

They galloped their horses to the southeastern outskirts of Lawrence. Jubal could see that many of Quantrill's men were leaving the town.

"Justin, let's follow that bunch over there. They're movin' out of town fast."

When they caught up to the riders ahead, Jubal looked back. "Justin, looks like everyone is leavin'."

One of Quantrill's lieutenant's rode up, "Boys, let's stay organized....Column of two will do....We gotta move out fast. Our boys up on Oread Mountain have spotted Yankee cavalry."

The brothers squeezed their horses into the column, and the lieutenant hurriedly signaled a start. Setting his horse to a fast trot, the lieutenant led the column away from town. Jubal's serious need for sleep was put on hold. As they moved along, he looked over his shoulder, fearing that he would see Union cavalry.

The column moved along at a brisk pace, stopping only once to rest and feed the horses. Jubal watched the sun setting in the west and wondered what his friends in Tarrytown were doing. Ah reckon they're a lot more comfortable than Justin and ah are.

When dusk came, the lieutenant led the column to a stand of timber and signaled a halt. After dismounting, they fed and watered the horses. The lieutenant's aide rode up and down the column. "We'll rest here until the rest of 'em catch up."

Jubal spread out on the ground and fell asleep. Minutes later, he was awakened by the sound of many horses and riders. Opening an eye, he saw Quantrill ride by, waving his arms and yelling to his lieutenants. Jubal didn't like what he had heard. They would move on quickly, because Quantrill was expecting to be pursued.

When darkness came, the long column of over four hundred men kept moving. Except for stopping at times to feed and water the horses, they rode through the night.

———

ONE OF THE INDIVIDUALS WHO QUANTRILL WANTED TO PUNISH was a man by the name of Jim Lane. He was absent during the raid, but quickly organized a pursuit force after Quantrill's band had left town.

The day after the raid, word had reached General Ewing's

headquarters in Kansas City, and also a garrison in Little Santa Fe, just across the border in Missouri, where Union Captain Coleman was stationed. The Captain mustered his men together and a column of cavalry moved out immediately.

Because General Ewing was absent, the officer in command, Major Plumb, quickly organized riders and also began to pursue Quantrill. He converged southeast of Lawrence with Coleman and along with Lane's group, which came from Lawrence, eventually caught up with the fleeing band of raiders.

Along the way, the pursuer's added a Union cavalry contingency under the command of Lieutenant Leland, who they found at the public square in the town of Olathe.

Because they were outnumbered and ill equipped, the pursuers couldn't do much more than harass Quantrill's force. Their attempt at defeating Quantrill during the retreat was futile. They did have success in slowing Quantrill's raiders while his band was fording the East Ottowa Creek. Other than simple skirmishes, the pursuers could not stop the raiders from reaching the Missouri border. The next day, Quantrill's band was approaching the town of Paola. Bull Creek, just west of town, stopped their advance. After getting word that additional Union forces were gathering over the hill, just east of town, Quantrill led his raiders north, up a valley, and into a large stand of timber.

———

JUBAL FELT DEAD TIRED. They had ridden through the night again. When daylight came, he saw familiar landmarks. Hey, we're at the headwaters of the Grand River. This is where we came in, he said to himself.

It was a sunny morning, and Jubal yearned for a quiet spot by a stream where he could sleep. He had just dismounted when Quantrill himself came riding by telling everyone, "They're crossing the border west of 'ere in masses, and there's another bunch over that rise to the east. We must git out of 'ear immediately."

The band galloped northeastward for a period of time. Then some of them began to disperse into woods and ravines. Justin pulled the reins tight, stopping his horse abruptly. Jubal galloped by, but then turned and reined in next to his brother. "Jube, ah think we should leave the band and head for home."

Jubal nodded and followed Justin, who had found a path through the woods which led them eastward. They rode hard for an hour before stopping. "This should be far enough, Jube. Let's unsaddle and get some rest."

———

SHRILL SCREAMS FROM THE THROAT OF A BLUE JAY woke Justin from a deep sleep. For the first time since arriving home from Illinois, his mind felt clear. The days he spent lying under heavy covers in the bunkhouse were at best vague. His thoughts were pleasant, thinking about the beautiful Christmas party his friends and neighbors had put on. Round and round they danced.

Spending the past six days on a horse was something he could have done without. There're good people and bad people out there, he said to himself. How can one tell who's who in a frantic raid like the one he and Jubal had just experienced?

Justin's silver-gray eyes looked up at the trees and saw sun rays filtering through the branches. Hearing footsteps, he grabbed his crutches and stood. Justin smiled when Jubal showed up with their horses. "Hey, Jube, you're right on top of things. Way to go. The horses look better than we do."

"Good morning, brother. Ah hope that you slept well."

"Yup, sure did," answered Justin.

"I took the horses down by the creek, and they got a well deserved drink," Jube said.

"Let's get our things together and head for home, Jube."

56

JUSTIN AND JUBAL AVOIDED MAIN ROADS as they rode eastward toward Tarrytown. They traveled near out-of-the-way stands of brush and trees. Union cavalry was one thing, but their main fear was the jayhawkers. Occasionally, they would dip into ravines and watch for riders.

"Should be home in about an hour, Justin," Jubal had said. "It'll be good to see the boys again."

His eyes scanned the plains ahead and the ridges above. "There are some riders over on that ridge," Jubal said, pointing.

Justin turned to look at the ridge. "Yup, ah see 'em. They're watchin' us."

Jubal exclaimed, "Jaysus, Justin, they're comin' down!"

Justin flicked his reins, directing his horse toward a ravine. He turned again to look. "Hey, Jube! It's the Riders! That's Grady on the lead horse."

Jubal took off his hat and raised it high over his head. "*Wow-wee!*" he yelled.

Justin experienced feelings of elation. For the first time since leaving for Lone Jack, he felt normal, and some of his best friends approached on the slope ahead.

Grady leaped off his horse with Mitch, Abel, Elkanah, Sammy, Lafe, and Jesse close behind. He took off his glove and grasped Justin's hand. "We were worried about you boys! Welcome back!"

"Hey, Jube! Did you kill yourself any jayhawkers?" Mitch asked.

"Shuh did," Jubal answered, wincing.

Backslapping and handshaking went on for half an hour.

"What do ya boys say we head back for the bunkhouse?" Grady asked excitedly.

———

THAT EVENING AT THE BUNKHOUSE THEY CELEBRATED with steaks and a jug of whiskey. Jubal talked about the details of their ride to Lawrence, and what had happened there.

"So, how many jayhawkers did you bag, Jube?" asked Abel, his thin face populated with fresh, short, brown whiskers.

"Boys, ah just couldn't kill anyone. All those people in the street were ordinary citizens. They weren't the ones that came out here...."

Grady put a hand on his shoulder. "Ya did the right thing, Jube. Ya don't want nonsense killin' on your conscience. I wadda done the same."

"What's that poster say?" asked Justin. He pointed at a poster on a bench by the window.

Grady walked over, picked it up, and threw it on the table. "It seems as if this general wants all of us to leave the county within fifteen days. No exceptions."

The poster was titled, *Order No. 11*.

"What if we decide to stay?" Justin asked, smirking.

"They hang ya....If they can catch ya, of course."

"Hang woman and children? Naw, they couldn't do that."

"It's not up to us, Justin. We'll hide out in the ravines and woods. It's up to my father, Abel's father, Mitch's father, Orly McGregor, George Walker, and the others."

"We'll take care of ourselves," Grady added.

"For how long?"

"Dunno...probably until the general or someone else rescinds the order," answered Grady.

Justin had feelings of remorse. He strongly suspected that the general's Order No. 11 was a result of what had happened in Lawrence.

———

HENRY HASTINGS PACED AROUND THE ROOM of the hotel room. His wife was sitting on a rocker, working it slowly back and forth, back and forth.

"What does this all mean, Henry?" Emma asked.

"According to the order, everyone who lives more than one mile from either Harrisonville or Pleasant Hill has to vacate their homes within fifteen days," Henry said disgustingly.

"What about our houses, barns, and our cattle?" Emma asked, alarmed.

"We can take with us what we can haul in a wagon, but that's about all," Henry replied.

"What about Thomas?" she asked.

"He'll come along with us, ah reckon so."

"I can hear his footsteps coming up the stairs, Henry. He's not gonna like what you're gonna tell 'em," she warned her husband.

"Makes no matter. I have to do what's right."

The door opened and Thomas, out of breath, entered. "Guess what? Justin and Jubal are back from Lawrence...."

"Thomas, that's real good....Are they in good health?"

"Better than ever, Pa. Now, what is it you need to talk to me about?"

"Thomas, your mother and ah've been talkin'."

"Yes?"

"As you know, we don't have any choice except to leave Tarrytown, leave our farm...."

"Yup, ah will miss you all....We'll keep an eye out on the farm, all the farms."

"Thomas, ah want you to go along with us. Your mother and sister will need all the help they can get. You're young and strong. You can move much faster than ah can."

Thomas's chin dropped.

His mother added, "Son, you can join up with the Riders when you get back."

"But, I told Jubal...."

"Jubal has to be with the Riders. He has no kin left," Henry responded.

LIEUTENANT FARNSWORTH OF THE UNION CAVALRY thought about his dilemma.

Beth Kingsley is my sister. I'm gonna do what I can to get her and her friends out of this county to a safe place. *Sarah is my niece.* I'll not allow them to be harmed.

He had visited the constable a week ago. The law officer, who had aged considerably during the past year, was surprised that a Yankee cavalry officer would volunteer to escort them out of the county.

Better yet, he had a place for them to go—a land near Independence where his family lived. There were some deserted cabins that they could fix up.

The constable had promised he would see to it that everyone would be ready to leave. Today is the day, the lieutenant said to himself.

As his column approached the livery stable, he saw scores of wagons and conveyances scattered on the Main Street in Tarrytown. The lieutenant was pleased.

He signaled the column to a halt at the livery and rode on ahead with his aide. Pulling up in front of the constable's office, he dismounted.

"Anyone seen the constable?" the Lieutenant asked.

"Yup...he's in his office."

"Stay with the horses," he ordered his aide.

———

THOMAS LOADED THE LAST CONTAINER of their possessions onto the wagon. He watched his father check over the harness which was strapped around his two magnificent blacks that were hitched to the wagon. Looking across the street, Thomas saw two cavalry men dismount in front of the constable's office.

"Wonder what they're doin' here?" he asked his father.

"Ah 'eard they are gonna escort us all the way to Independence."

Thomas felt elated. He didn't wish to leave his home, but with Sarah in the wagon just ahead, and the presence of the Union cavalry. Nothing bad can happen to us now, he thought.

He experienced feelings of pride when his father asked him to take charge of the gray, which would be pulling the carriage. His mother already sat on the back seat. Genevieve would sit on the seat next to him.

Thomas knew at that moment that he would always remember seeing the two-column Union cavalry plodding up the middle of Main Street. After the rear of the column had passed by, Martin Kingsley flicked his reins, and their wagon pulled in behind the slow-moving Bluecoats. Kingsley had attached their carriage to the rear of the wagon. Thomas saw his father nod, signaling him to move into line. He nudged the gray, and he drew the carriage directly behind the Kingsleys.

Thomas passed by the church, then the school and cemetery. While passing next to MacTurley's Woods, he scanned the sky for Keeya. His hawk was absent. Looking back, he saw horses and wagons as far as his eyes could see.

Thomas didn't dare look at the Hastings's home when they passed the roadway. He was afraid that if he looked, he would cry. The Sunnerland barn looked tall and straight, still shining from the first coat of paint. The depressing remains of the Haggard's buildings loomed ahead. Thomas's feelings were buoyed, thinking about the bunkhouse that was hidden from view—the secret home of the Gray Riders.

Two miles past the McGregor land, his eyes gazed at a ridge that extended downward from the heights of Bear Mountain. He guessed at what his eyes would see on that ridge. "Look, Genevieve."

Seven riders sat stiff on their mounts and watched the caravan pass. Thomas saw seven hats go up in the air. Genevieve said, "Look, Thomas, Lieutenant Farnsworth is riding this way."

The lieutenant halted his horse and looked up at the ridge. Thomas felt extraordinarily warm inside when the lieutenant raised an arm and gave the riders up on the ridge a stiff salute.

57

GRADY HASTINGS LOWERED HIS ARM, and replaced his gray hat on his head. "Did ya see that, Justin?" he asked. "Was that a salute?"

"Ah reckon 'twas. That's the same cavalry officer who stopped his column to wait for the funeral procession. Remember?" Justin responded.

"Yup, ah sure do. I thought that we were as good as dead on that day."

"Helen Walker told me that she had an uncle in the Union cavalry in Missouri. Ah wonder if that's the feller who saluted. Makes sense, doesn't it? That would make him Mrs. Walker's brother," Grady added.

"Well, ah'll be hog-tied," Abel Kingsley responded, shaking his head.

Grady sat on his saddle in silence until the last of the wagons were out of sight. He experienced feelings of loneliness while thinking about his brother, Thomas, and the rest of his family. I miss Helen, too, he said to himself.

"Justin, tomorra' we need to git all the boys together and fetch whatever supplies we can find on our farms and in Tarrytown. Ah know that Pa left us a wagon."

"Why don't we just hang around the bunkhouse like we did before?"

"Justin, your bunkhouse is a great place, but we could be at a disadvantage. Things have changed. There will be regular Union patrols. We need to find a place in the mountain and build a shelter for this comin' winta'."

———

ABEL KINGSLEY'S FEELINGS hit bottom while watching the exodus on the Tarrytown Road. He saw his sister, Sarah, standing in the wagon and waving. Abel did feel good about the Jackson family. They chose to remain at their home, and Abel was confident they wouldn't be molested by the redlegs, jayhawkers, or Union forces and could remain neutral.

The fate of their Angus herd bothered him. Priam will take care of as many as he can, but the invading army will surely confiscate as many cows as they can find. He felt good about their horses. All of them are either with my father or up in Bear Mountain with us, he said to himself.

The exodus of the families from the area had swelled the ranks of the Gray Riders. We have forty-four riders, Abel said to himself. We also have an extra horse for each man.

Later in the day, Abel looked forward to scavenging for supplies in the farms and Tarrytown. Seth Miller had provided a key for the back door. He had saved several barrels of gun powder and six cases of caps and balls. We'll have enough ammunition to take us into next year, he thought.

"Hey, Abel, whatcha' thinkin' about?" Mitch McGregor asked, scratching the thick hair in front of his ear.

"Ah'm lookin' forward to goin' through my house one last time. We best do it soon," Abel responded, his light brown hair parted in the middle, extending over his ears.

"Ah know what you mean, Abel. James and I have cleaned out our house. We'll go with ya and some of the others into Tarrytown today," Mitch responded.

Grady Hastings walked over, a cup of coffee in his hand. "Ah'll be ready in an hour. How about you boys?"

"Ah'm ready right now," Abel responded.

———

GRADY ORGANIZED THE GRAY RIDERS into three groups to supply their camp with food and tools. He assigned one to search the farms on the north side of the Tarrytown Road. The second group would work the south side of the road, and a third band the town.

He remembered a water hole he had discovered in his younger years while exploring the mountain. They established their camp near it, and Grady felt they would have adequate water for themselves and their horses.

The backbreaking work of building a long, narrow cabin had been completed by the end of September. Seth Miller left behind several saws for them to use. The new bunkhouse had over forty beds. The crude shelter for the horses and cows out back will do nicely, Grady thought.

After the bunk house had been completed and supplied, he, along with Mitch, Justin, Jubal, Abel, Lafe, and Jesse spent many hours planning strategy. They all agreed that the redlegs, jayhawkers and Union forces would not attack them in the mountain.

We hold the high ground, Grady said to himself confidently. Now, it's time to focus on patrolling our lands.

58

THE SECOND DAY OF OCTOBER DAWNED CLEAR. Grady stepped outside, stretched, and yawned. He thought they were lucky to have two experienced cooks in their group. The smell of freshly fried bacon tempted his stomach.

He knew that it wouldn't be long until the jayhawkers, redlegs, or Union army would invade their farms and plunder. Thus far, all the patrols had returned without engaging in even the slightest skirmish.

Mitch and Lafe, along with other Riders, patrolled the southern area. Mitch planned to lead them as far as the railroad tracks.

After breakfast, Grady rode with Justin, Jubal, Abel, and others across the McGregor property. They crossed the Sunnerland and the Hastings's land and rode into Tarrytown. Each group carried four lever-action Springfield rifles that Seth Miller had saved for them. The store owner had hidden them in a crate underneath the floor.

Grady was amazed that the new rifles didn't need to use powder and caps. The bullets were different than balls, but they worked. Seth had said that Mrs. Walker had had something to do with his getting the rifles. Apparently, her brother, a Union Lieutenant, had sneaked the rifles from a Union supply boat at Lexington.

As his riders cut across the corner of the McGregor property, Grady looked back and saw Jubal and Abel. He counted twenty-two riders, four of them had carbines. Everyone else carried at least two Colts and a long saber, housed in a leather scabbard.

Pausing on the road, Grady and his riders remained keenly alert, scanning the area for marauding jayhawkers or Erlocks. Grady was relieved when they rode to the Sunnerland buildings and found there wasn't any evidence of damage to the buildings. He marveled at the beauty of the new barn.

After crossing Bear Creek, they rode to the crest of a hill which overlooked the Hastings's farm. Grady felt a rock hit the bottom of his stomach when he saw riders in the farmyard. A dark plume of smoke rose from the barn, and several dismounted men were milling about.

Raising his hand, he turned and looked at Abel, "Pass the word...ready pistols and carbines. We'll spread out and attack with sabers drawn."

Grady anxiously watched as the Riders formed a battle line. When the Riders were in ready position, he drew his saber. Pointing it forward, he screamed, *"Charge! Drive 'em out!"*

THE UNPREPARED INVADERS WERE NO MATCH for an angry Grady and his band, who rode into them and attacked with a fury.

Grady boiled inside, as he sliced his saber through the air, searching for a target. His first encounter happened against a man holding a torch. Grady's swung his saber powerfully, severing the man's hand, the torch splattering to the ground. He slid off his horse and sent the invader's soul to his maker.

Remounting, he galloped to join Mitch, who had taken on two of the marauders with his saber. Grady pulled a Colt from his belt and fired two shots. They dropped to the ground.

"Thank ya, Grady," Mitch responded and returned his saber into its scabbard.

Mitch mounted and they galloped to the other side of the barn. Abel yelled, "Look! Two of 'em are tryin' to git away!"

Grady, Mitch, and Abel galloped toward the creek in pursuit. The Riders closed the gap rapidly. When one of them turned, Grady saw fear in the marauder's eyes. His feelings were alternating between anger and passion. Grady looked back and saw his father's barn burning. Feelings of anger surged as he pulled a Colt from his belt. The fire from his gun and that of Mitch's and Abel's dropped the two invaders to the ground.

Returning to the burning barn, they dug a wide, shallow grave and buried the bodies. While riding back to their bunk house, Grady thought about the loss of the barn and how his father would feel.

59

GRADY STOOD HATLESS, OUTSIDE NEAR THEIR BUNK HOUSE. His cup of coffee steamed in the cool air, and his emerald green eyes were watching two horsemen galloping toward him, riding across the McGregor land.

The riders have to be two of our scouts, he said to himself. He expected them, but not until later in the day. Feelings of excitement rose in his stomach as the horses continued to gallop. Grady suspected that the news would mean action.

The horse's mouths jacked open as the riders jerked the reins. Their bodies steamed, and their nostrils snorted for air. Tully said excitedly, "Grady, there's a mess of Bluecoats comin' up the road from Stillman Mills."

"Any idear how many?" Grady asked, dumping the remaining coffee on the ground.

"Probably about a hunnert," Tully responded. "Mebee more."

"You two need rest, and yar horses need waterin'. Ah'll round up the boys."

The Riders in the bunkhouse had already been preparing when Grady rushed inside.

"Boys, saddle up! We're all goin' on this one!" Grady yelled, hurrying to his bunk. He buckled on his gun belt and pulled his hat on tight.

———

GRADY AND JUSTIN LED THE COLUMN OF TWO across the southern border of the Sunnerland property. Grady counted forty-two after the Riders had mounted.

They rode cross-country toward the northwest. Minutes later, they crossed the small rivulet that drained Bear Mountain into Bear Creek.

When they passed the Morton's home on the Hastings's land, Samuel and Tullaby were standing by their house, waving. Whoops and cheers erupted from the Riders. Further along, near MacTurley's Woods, Grady saw Sammy Morton carrying a musket. Sammy must be huntin', Grady thought as he waved.

As he led the column parallel to MacTurley's Woods, riding toward the Tarrytown road, he couldn't bear to look at the charred remains of his father's barn.

Suddenly, Justin exclaimed loudly, "Riders comin' on the road from the west!"

Grady signaled a halt and grabbed his glass from the saddle bag. After scanning the road westward, he said, "Four of 'em. They've crossed the creek and are still comin'.' "

"Do ya see any blue?" Justin asked.

"Naw, ah don't," Grady responded and continued to glass the horsemen on the road. Suddenly, he took his hat off and waved it wildly in the air.

"It's our kinfolk, boys," Grady said, putting his glass away.

Grady signaled and galloped toward the road, followed by the rest of the column. He stopped on the road and waved as Henry Hastings, Orly McGregor, George Walker, and Martin Kingsley rode up.

"What ya doin' here, Pa? Yar supposed to be carin' for Ma, Gen, and Thomas," Grady said.

"We've come to fight for our land, our property—right, boys?" Henry responded, a long, dark cigar protruding from his mouth.

The Riders responded with backslaps, shouts, and wide smiles.

"Form in with us, men," Grady said anxiously, remembering the threat ahead.

Grady laid a spur to his horse and hurriedly led the column along MacTurley's Woods.

After they had ridden past the timber, Grady slowed his horse. Then he said, "Justin, don't seem like the Bluecoats have reached Tarrytown yet."

They fast-trotted the horses, hoping to reach the town before the Union cavalry did. As they passed by the school, Grady thought about his brother. He'll be back there someday.

Halting at the eastern edge of Tarrytown, just beyond the livery, Grady signaled the Riders to spread out and form a battle line. It extended well beyond the livery to the north, and southward as far as the General Store.

"There they come," Abel said softly.

"Justin, the flag," Grady said, his voice quivering.

Justin unbundled it and placed the shaft into a holder attached to his saddle. The knitted flag, with a silver saber and single gray star embedded in a sea of blue, furled in the breeze.

Grady raised his saber high. He looked northward. He then cupped a hand over his mouth and yelled, *"Sabers!"*

He looked southward and again yelled, "*Sabers!*"

Pointing at the oncoming Bluecoats, he glanced at the Riders up and down the line. The sabers were up—eyes were gleaming—jaws were firm. Grady saw Orly McGregor holding his saber higher than anyone else. A cigar protruded from his father's mouth.

Forty-six shiny blades sparkled in the sunlight. The Bluecoat's column remained intact, and they continued to move forward. Grady realized that the Riders could be outnumbered by at least two to one, but he wasn't concerned. We will win this fight, he said to himself.

Closer and closer the Bluecoat column came. Grady noticed their pace had slowed. His heart pounded, and he cleared his throat.

Grady looked at the flag high above Justin's head. He felt inspired by his facial expression. Feelings of passion and justice overcame fear and doubt.

He looked into Justin's eyes again and screamed, "*Charge!*"

———

JUBAL HAGGARD GLANCED TO HIS RIGHT. He saw his brother holding the flag. Jubal anxiously waited for the command. He thought about his sister, father, and mother—all murdered. After hearing Grady's scream, he pointed his saber at the Bluecoats, and his horse thundered forward. "*Hey-yah!*" he yelled over and over again.

Justin Haggard glanced to his left and saw Jubal's hand tightly grasping his saber. He looked down at his empty stirrup. When he heard Grady's scream, his mind was filled with feelings of vengeance as he dug a spur into his horse's flank.

Elkanah Jackson's thoughts were about his brother, Jordon, and the deep sadness that his parents, Priam and Virgilia, had experienced. "*For Jordon!*" Elkanah yelled after hearing Grady's scream. He dug both spurs into his horse, wildly waving his saber as his horse galloped forward.

Lafe Sunnerland visualized the dreadful scene of his parents lying dead on the Tarrytown Road. The Erlocks took the life of my parents and now those Bluecoats up ahead are gonna pay, he said to himself.

He saw Justin raise the flag. When he heard Grady scream, he felt tears swelling in his eyes as his horse galloped forward toward the enemy.

Jesse Sunnerland glanced at his brother, Lafe. Their eyes locked on each other for a moment. He felt elated when he heard, *"Charge!"*

Mitch McGregor looked at his brother, James, and caught his eye for a moment. His emotions surged when he saw the flag go up over Justin's head. He heard Grady's scream, and dug in his spurs.

James McGregor thought about his brother, Paul, lyin' up there in the ground by the white cross. His heart leaped into his throat when he saw the blue flag go up over Justin's head. James heard Grady scream. Excitement swelled his insides when hearing the sound of forty-six sets of hooves pounding the ground.

Abel Kingsley watched Grady's face closely. He wanted to be the first one to break toward the enemy. He looked to his right and saw his father, his saber held high. Abel glanced at Justin. Today, we ride together. He saw Grady's head turn. Abel dug in the spurs just as Grady's mouth began to open.

Grady Hastings saw Abel's horse sprint ahead. He had feelings of pride as he heard his fellow Gray Riders yelling as they galloped toward the Bluecoats.

———

GRADY EXPERIENCED THE CLASHING SOUNDS of metal on metal—sounds of pistol shots filling the air—the smell of gun powder—the screams of men falling.

Seeing two of his fellow Riders go down didn't deter him from blasting away with his Colt and wildly swinging his saber.

The Bluecoats held their ground, and Grady realized that the Gray Riders were badly outnumbered. His enthusiasm began to wane as the Bluecoats appeared to be getting the best of the fight. He cringed as he saw Orly McGregor take down two Bluecoats with one sweeping stroke of his saber.

Grady saw a Rider go down. He thought to himself, we cannot give up now, and we must win this fight. Suddenly, he heard distant yells. Looking northward, he saw a long line of galloping horses. Grady saw the black flag.

"*Quantrill!*" Grady exclaimed, his confidence surging.

————

THE MASSIVE FLANKING ATTACK by at least a hundred Quantrill riders drove the Bluecoats from the field. Minutes later, the Gray Riders' battle for Tarrytown had ended. Some of them, still mounted, laid their heads on their horse's manes, exhausted. Others had dismounted and were tending to those who had been wounded.

Grady watched the rear of Quantrill's band as they pursued the remaining Bluecoats into the foothills of Bear Mountain. He looked around and counted thirty-eight. Putting his head down, he realized that six of the boys were lost. Three of 'em were brothers from west of Bear Mountain. He wasn't sure who the other three victims were.

He saw Mitch...Abel...Lafe. Grady felt relieved to see Justin walking his horse over. Jubal Haggard stood next to James McGregor. Grady saw tall Orly McGregor talking to his father, Henry, the long, slim cigar still in his mouth. Martin Kingsley and George Walker appeared unhurt.

Grady saw two riders approaching from the direction of the chase. He recognized Cole Younger, who reined up.

"Good work, boys. Ya won the fight."

"Thank ye, Cole," Grady said. "You fellers showed up in the nick of time."

————

AFTER THE GRAY RIDERS RESTED, they dragged the bodies into rows along the road. "We'll come back and bury 'em tomorra'," Mitch McGregor said, his voice squeaking. "The digger's got a pair of scoops back of his place."

Two of the boys rode into Tarrytown and came back with a team and wagon. The Riders loaded the scattered equipment into the wagon: saddles, pistols, muskets, sabers, boots, and belts.

When the work ended, they mounted and formed behind Grady and Justin. They rode past the livery and onto Main Street.

His eyes wandered up and down the empty boardwalks. He thought about the past when the town had been filled with mingling people—laughter and music flowing from the saloon.

Right now, the town is a graveyard of buildings, he said to himself. They'll all be back. We'll survive all of this.

Grady looked at the school as he rode by. He closed his green eyes and visualized his brother, Thomas, carrying an armload of books.

———

PASSING BY THE CORNER OF MACTURLEY'S WOODS, Grady led the column across the Hastings's land. They crossed Bear Creek, and he flicked his reins to guide his horse to the heights beyond. After reaching the summit of a hill, he looked back and saw the end of the column snaking across his father's land.

After the battle of Tarrytown, the Riders celebrated at their bunkhouse at Bear Mountain. The sounds of back slaps, shouts, and handshakes filled the air. Smells of whiskey and cigars were overpowering.

After the excitement abated, Justin Haggard stood, balancing on his one leg. He raised a glass and said, "George Walker...Martin Kingsley...Orly McGregor...Henry Hastings—welcome home."

———

HENRY HASTINGS WATCHED GEORGE WALKER down a shot of whiskey and lower his chin.

"Hey, George, are ya alright?" Henry asked.

"Ah've been thinkin' about Will and Carr. They gave up their lives in this God awful turmoil our country is havin'."

"George, ah feel for ya. Them two boys of yar ain't the reason for any of it. Burnin' down our buildings is one thing, but senseless takin' of lives is somethin' else," Henry responded.

"It's kill or be kilt," George said as he brushed his fingers across both eyes.

Henry brought a long, dark cigar to his mouth and bit the tip off. Lighting it, he got up and strolled to the door. "Ah'm goin' for a walk, George. Wanna come?"

"Naw, ah think ah'll retire for the evening. My mind is heavy with sorrow," George responded.

Henry watched as his friend staggered slightly while walking toward the other end of the building. Stepping outside, he closed the door gently. Looking up, Henry gazed at a sky full of stars. Someday this conflict will end, and all of us and our families will return to our homes...God willing.

END

EPILOGUE

After the hostilities in Missouri ended, the Tarrytown folks returned to their homes and businesses. All the farm houses were burned to the ground except the Walker's, Hastings's and Kingsley's.

Most of the buildings in Tarrytown were ransacked to the bone, nothing left except a broken, wooden rocker in the hotel lobby. Even Shol Clarity's barber chair was stolen.

Constable Muldoon had died at Independence and his office was taken over by a Federal Marshall.

Toby Miller got the Livery up and running in a week. The church and school were untouched.

There wasn't a single item left on the shelves of the General Store. In the bank, the room-high safe door was open, and papers were strewn all over the floor.

The day after returning, Douglas Herron, the bank owner, was seen placing a shovel into his wagon. Shol Clarity watched the banker steer his horse toward a mountain trail. Was he going to look for buried money, perhaps?

Henry and Emma Hastings bought a small house in Independence. They decided not to return to the Tarrytown area to live. Their daughter, Genevieve, did the same. Grady and his bride, Helen, built a new house on a rise of land close to Bear Creek.

Justin Haggard turned their bunkhouse into his permanent home. Jubal rebuilt the main house, readying it for his bride-to-be, Jessica Walker.

Abel Kingsley tripled the size of the Angus herd. He formed a partnership with Elkanah Jackson.

Mitch McGregor rebuilt the farm buildings, including a special small retirement house for his father. James left the farm and enrolled in a college in Kansas City. Each time that he visited his family, James rode to the cemetery in Tarrytown. He always placed a rose on Jennifer's grave.

Lafe and Jesse Sunnerland sold their land. Lafe became a stagecoach driver, and Jesse joined the Pony Express.

Lieutenant Farnsworth was promoted to Captain in the Union cavalry. He later transferred to an eastern region, and was present at Appomattox when Lee surrendered to Grant.

The Union and Confederate men who fell during the Battle of Tarrytown were buried under two large, dirt mounds, a short distance east of town. A black wooden cross marked the center of each site.

Thomas watched several wagonloads of lumber making their way through town. The wagons were headed to the McGregor's where Thomas would someday help Mitch and James build a new barn.

He was dressed in his new, hammertail, frock coat. Brushing a smudge of dust off his black trousers, he stepped up into the Hastings's carriage.

Flicking the reins, he directed his horse toward the Kingsley's roadway. He had reserved a table in the refurbished hotel and was taking Sarah out to dinner.

—Ten Years Later—

"Are you comin' north with us, Thomas?" Bob Younger asked.

"No, I'm afraid not. The farm needs my attention. Besides, I can't leave Sarah alone. She's with child."

"I understand. Good luck."

"Where are ya headin'?" Thomas asked.

"Up north...Jesse and Frank want to settle a score with a scoundrel who Frank met during the war...now a banker in Minnesota—a place called Northfield."

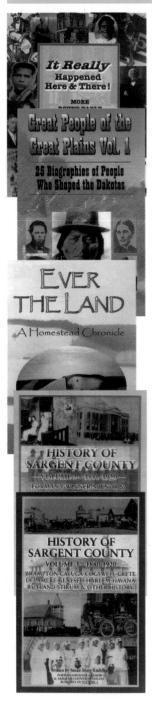

NEW RELEASES

It Really Happened Here & There
This takes off where Ethelyn Pearson's "It Really Happened Here!" left off... More entertaining stories and true accounts: The Mystery of the Headless Hermit, Herman Haunts Sauk Centre, Hunting Trip Gone Wrong, The Swinging of Thomas Brown, Moltan Hell Created Creeping Molasses Disaster, Preachers Do Too!, Skinned Alive, Run Into A Blizzard or Burn!, Life and Death of Ol' Mother Feather Legs, How the Dakotans Fought Off Rustlers, and much more!!!! Written by Ethelyn Pearson - Author of *It Really Happened Here!*
(136 pages) $24.95 each in an 8-1/2 x 11" paperback.

Great People of the Great Plains Vol. 1
25 Biographies of People Who Shaped the Dakotas
This is the second book for Keith Norman and the first in this series. Keith has always had an interest in the history of the region. His radio show 'Great Stories of the Great Plains' is heard on great radio stations all across both Dakotas. While the biographies within this book are a bit too long to fit the time constraints of a radio show, listeners will find the events and people portrayed familiar. For more information on the radio show and a list of his current affiliates check out Norman's website at www.tumbleweednetwork.com.
Written by Keith Norman - Author of *Great Stories of the Great Plains - Tales of the Dakotas* (124 pgs.)
$14.95 each in a 6x9" paperback.

Ever The Land
A Homestead Chronicle
This historical chronicle (non-fiction) traces the life of young Pehr through his youth in the 1800's, marriage, parenthood and tenant farming in Sweden; then his emigration to America and homesteading in Minnesota. Multifarious simple joys and woes, and one deep constant sorrow accompany Pehr to his grave in 1914.
Written by: The late Ruben L. Parson (336 pgs.)
$16.96 each in a 6x9" paperback.

History of Sargent County - Volume 2 - 1880-1920
(Forman, Gwinner, Milnor & Sargent County Veterans)
Over 220 photos and seven chapters containing: Forman, Gwinner and Milnor, North Dakota history with surveyed maps from 1909. Plus Early History of Sargent County, World War I Veterans, Civil War Veterans and Sargent County Fair History.
Written by: Susan Mary Kudelka - Author of *Early History of Sargent County - Volume 1* (224 pgs.)
$16.95 each in a 6x9" paperback.

History of Sargent County - Volume 3 - 1880-1920
(Brampton, Cayuga, Cogswell, Crete, DeLamere, Geneseo, Harlem, Havana, Rutland, Stirum & Other History)
Over 280 photos and fifteen chapters containing: Brampton, Cayuga, Cogswell, Crete, DeLamere, Geneseo, Harlem, Havana, Rutland and Stirum, North Dakota histories with surveyed maps from 1909. Plus history on Sargent County in WWI, Sargent County Newspapers, E. Hamilton Lee and bonus photo section.
Written by: Susan Mary Kudelka - Author of *Early History of Sargent County - Volume 1* (220 pgs.)
$16.95 each in a 6x9" paperback.

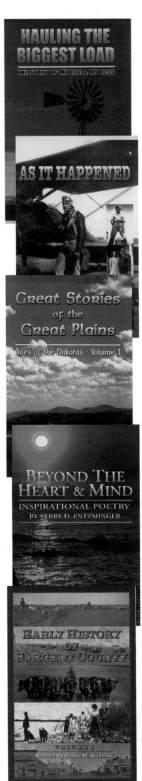

Hauling the Biggest Load - *The Story of My Life & My Loss*
This is an unusual story because of the many changes that have happened since the author's birth in 1926. In May 2002, he lost his son, John, in a car accident. None of those other experiences seemed important anymore... Richard needed something to try and take his mind off that tragedy. "I thought I had hauled some big loads in my life but I never had to have a load as big as this one."
Written by: Richard Hamann (144 pages)
$14.95 each in 6x9" paperback.

As It Happened
Over 40 photos and several chapters containing Allen Saunders' early years, tales of riding the rails, his Navy career, marriage, Army instruction, flying over "The Hump", and his return back to North Dakota.
Written by Allen E. Saunders. (74 pgs)
$12.95 each in a 6x9" paperback.

Great Stories of the Great Plains - *Tales of the Dakotas - Vol. 1*
The radio show "Great Stories of the Great Plains" is heard on great radio stations all across both Dakotas. Norman has taken some of the stories from broadcasts, added some details, and even added some complete new tales to bring together this book of North and South Dakota history.
Written by Keith Norman. (134 pgs.)
$14.95 each in a 6x9" paperback.

Beyond the Heart & Mind
Inspirational Poetry by Terry D. Entzminger
Beyond the Heart & Mind is the first in a series of inspirational poetry collections of Entzminger. Read and cherish over 100 original poems and true-to-the-heart verses printed in full color in the following sections: Words of Encouragement, On the Wings of Prayer, God Made You Very Special, Feelings From Within, The True Meaning of Love, and Daily Joys. (120 pgs.)
$12.95 each in a 6x9" paperback.

Early History of Sargent County - *Volume 1*
Over seventy photos and thirty-five chapters containing the early history of Sargent County, North Dakota: Glacial Movement in Sargent County, Native Americans in Sargent County, Weather, Memories of the Summer of 1883, Fight for the County Seat, Townships, Surveyed Maps from 1882 and much more.
Written by Susan M. Kudelka. (270 pgs.)
$16.95 each in a 6x9" paperback.

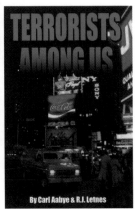

Terrorists Among Us
This piece of fiction was written to "expose a weakness" in present policies and conflicts in the masses of rules which seem to put emphasis on business, money, and power interests at the expense of the people's security, safety and happiness. Shouldn't we and our leaders strive for some security for our people?
Written by Carl Aabye & R.J. Letnes. (178 pgs.)
$15.95 each in a 6x9" paperback.

THE HASTINGS SERIES

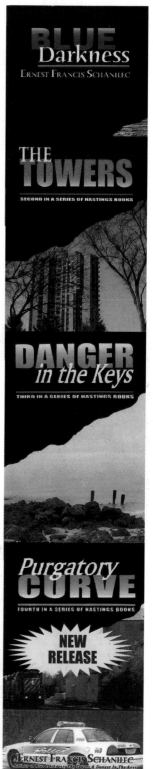

Blue Darkness *(First in a Series of Hastings Books)*
This tale of warm relationships and chilling murders takes place in the lake country of central Minnesota. Normal activities in the small town of New Dresen are disrupted when local resident, ex-CIA agent Maynard Cushing, is murdered. His killer, Robert Ranforth also an ex-CIA agent, had been living anonymously in the community for several years. to the anonymous ex-agent. Stalked and attached at his country home, he employs tools and people to mount a defense and help solve crimes. Written by Ernest Francis Schanilec (author of The Towers). (276 pgs.) $16.95 each in a 6x9" paperback.

The Towers *(Second in a Series of Hastings Books)*
Tom Hastings has moved from the lake country of central Minnesota to Minneapolis. His move was precipitated by the trauma associated with the murder of one of his neighbors. After renting an apartment on the 20th floor of a high-rise apartment building known as The Towers, he's met new friends and retained his relationship with a close friend, Julie, from St. Paul. Hastings is a resident of the high-rise for less than a year when a young lady is found murdered next to a railroad track, a couple of blocks from The Towers. The murderer shares the same elevators, lower-level garage and other areas in the high-rise as does Hastings. The building manager and other residents, along with Hastings are caught up in dramatic events that build to a crisis while the local police are baffled. Who is the killer? Written by Ernest Francis Schanilec. (268 pgs.) $16.95 each in a 6x9" paperback.

Danger In The Keys *(Third in a Series of Hastings Books)*
Tom Hastings is looking forward to a month's vacation in Florida. While driving through Tennessee, he witnesses an automobile leaving the road and plunging down a steep slope. He stops and assists another man in finding the car. The driver, a young woman, survives the accident. Tom is totally unaware that the young woman was being chased because she had chanced coming into possession of a valuable gem, which had been heisted from a Saudi Arabian prince in a New York hotel room. After arriving in Key Marie Island in Florida, Tom checks in and begins enjoying the surf and the beach. He meets many interesting people, however, some of them are on the island because of the Guni gem, and they will stop at nothing in order to gain possession. Desperate people and their greedy ambitions interrupt Tom's goal of a peaceful vacation. Written by Ernest Francis Schanilec (210 pgs.) $16.95 each in a 6x9" paperback.

Purgatory Curve *(Fourth in a Series of Hastings Books)*
A loud horn penetrated the silence on a September morning in New Dresden, Minnesota. Tom Hastings stepped onto Main Street sidewalk after emerging from the corner Hardware Store. He heard a freight train coming and watched in horror as it crushed a pickup truck that was stalled on the railroad tracks. Moments before the crash, he saw someone jump from the cab. An elderly farmer's body was later recovered from the mangled vehicle. Tom was interviewed by the sheriff the next day and was upset that his story about what he saw wasn't believed. The tragic death of the farmer was surrounded with controversy and mysterious people, including a nephew who taunted Tom after the accident. Or, was it an accident?   Written by Ernest Francis Schanilec (210 pgs.) $16.95 each in a 6x9" paperback.

March on the Dakota's - *The Sibley Expedition of 1863*

Following the military action of 1862, the U. S. government began collecting an army at various posts and temporary stockades of the state, in preparation for a move northwestward to the Dakota Territories in the early summer of 1863. The campaign was organized by General John Pope, with the intent to subdue the Sioux. Two expeditions were planned, one under General H. H. Sibley, organized in Minnesota, and the other under the Command of General Alfred Sully. Interesting facts, actual accounts taken from soldiers' journals, campsite listings, casualties and record of troops also included. Written by Susan Mary Kudelka. (134pgs.)
$14.95 each in a 6x9" paperback.

War Child - *Growing Up in Adolf Hitler's Germany*

Annelee Woodstrom was 20 years old when she immigrated to America in 1947. These kind people in America wanted to hear about Adolf Hitler. During her adolescence, constant propaganda and strictly enforced censorship influenced her thinking. As a young adult, the bombings and all the consequential suffering caused by World War II affected Annelee deeply. How could Annelee tell them that as a child, during 1935, she wanted nothing more than to be a member of Adolf Hitler's Jung Maidens' organization? Written by Annelee Woodstrom (252 pgs.)
$16.95 each in a 6x9" paperback.

The SOE on Enemy Soil - *Churchill's Elite Force*

British Prime Minister Winston Churchill's plan for liberating Europe from the Nazis during the darkest days of the Second World War was ambitious: provide a few men and women, most of them barely out of their teens, with training in subversion and hand-to-hand combat, load them down with the latest in sophisticated explosives, drop them by parachute into the occupied countries, then sit back and wait for them to "Set Europe Ablaze." No story has been told with more honesty and humor than Sergeant Fallick tells his tale of service. The training, the fear, the tragic failures, the clandestine romances, and the soldiers' high jinks are all here, warmly told from the point of view of "one bloke" who experienced it all and lived to tell about it. Written by R.A. Fallick. (282 pgs.) $16.95 each in a 6x9" paperback.

Grandmother Alice

Memoirs from the Home Front Before Civil War into 1930's

Alice Crain Hawkins could be called the 'Grandma Moses of Literature'. Her stories, published for the first time, were written while an invalid during the last years of her life. These journal entries from the late 1920's and early 30's gives us a fresh, novel and unique understanding of the lives of those who lived in the upper part of South Carolina during the state's growing years. Alice and her ancestors experiences are filled with understanding - they are provacative and profound. Written by Reese Hawkins (178 pgs.) $16.95 each in a 6x9" paperback.

Tales & Memories of Western North Dakota *Prairie Tales & True Stories of 20th Century Rural Life*

This manuscript has been inspired with Steve's antidotes, bits of wisdom and jokes (sometimes ethnic, to reflect the melting pot that was and is North Dakota; and from most unknown sources). A story about how to live life with humor, courage and grace along with personal hardships, tragedies and triumphs. Written by Steve Taylor. (174 pgs.) $14.95 each in a 6x9" paperback.

Phil Lempert's HEALTHY, WEALTHY, & WISE
The Shoppers Guide for Today's Supermarket
This is the must-have tool for getting the most for your money in every aisle. With this valuable advice you will never see (or shop) the supermarket the same way again. You will learn how to: save at least $1,000 a year on your groceries, guarantee satisfaction on every shopping trip, get the most out of coupons or rebates, avoid marketing gimmicks, create the ultimate shopping list, read and understand the new food labels, choose the best supermarkets for you and your family. Written by Phil Lempert. (198 pgs.)
$9.95 each in a 6x9" paperback.

Miracles of COURAGE
The Larry W. Marsh Story
This story is for anyone looking for simple formulas for overcoming insurmountable obstacles. At age 18, Larry lost both legs in a traffic accident and learned to walk again on untested prosthesis. No obstacle was too big for him - putting himself through college - to teaching a group of children that frustrated the whole educational system - to developing a nationally recognized educational program to help these children succeed. Written by Linda Marsh. (134 pgs.)
$12.95 each in a 6x9" paperback.

The Garlic Cure
Learn about natural breakthroughs to outwit: Allergies, Arthritis, Cancer, Candida Albicans, Colds, Flu and Sore Throat, Environmental and Body Toxins, Fatigue, High Cholesterol, High Blood Pressure and Homocysteine and Sinus Headaches. The most comprehensive, factual and brightly written health book on garlic of all times. INCLUDES: 139 GOURMET GARLIC RECIPES! Written by James F. Scheer, Lynn Allison and Charlie Fox. (240 pgs.)
$14.95 each in a 6x9" paperback.

I Took The Easy Way Out
Life Lessons on Hidden Handicaps
Twenty-five years ago, Tom Day was managing a growing business - holding his own on the golf course and tennis court. He was living in the fast lane. For the past 25 years, Tom has spent his days in a wheelchair with a spinal cord injury. Attendants serve his every need. What happened to Tom? We get an honest account of the choices Tom made in his life. It's a courageous story of reckoning, redemption and peace. Written by Thomas J. Day. (200 pgs.)
$19.95 each in a 6x9" paperback.

9/11 and Meditation - *America's Handbook*
All Americans have been deeply affected by the terrorist events of and following 9-11-01 in our country. David Thorson submits that meditation is a potentially powerful intervention to ameliorate the frightening effects of such divisive and devastating acts of terror. This book features a lifetime of harrowing life events amidst intense pychological and social polarization, calamity and chaos; overcome in part by practicing the age-old art of meditation. Written by David Thorson. (110 pgs.)
$9.95 each in a 4-1/8 x 7-1/4" paperback.

From Graystone to Tombstone
Memories of My Father Engolf Snortland 1908-1976
This haunting memoir will keep you riveted with true accounts of a brutal penitentiary to a manhunt in the unlikely little town of Tolna, North Dakota. At the same time the reader will emerge from the book with a towering respect for the author, a man who endured pain, grief and needless guilt -- but who learned the art of forgiving and writes in the spirit of hope. Written by Roger Snortland. (178 pgs.)
$16.95 each in a 6x9" paperback.

Blessed Are The Peacemakers *Civil War in the Ozarks*
A rousing tale that traces the heroic Rit Gatlin from his enlistment in the Confederate Army in Little Rock to his tragic loss of a leg in a Kentucky battle, to his return in the Ozarks. He becomes engaged in guerilla warfare with raiders who follow no flag but their own. Rit finds himself involved with a Cherokee warrior, slaves and romance in a land ravaged by war. Written by Joe W. Smith (444 pgs.)
$19.95 each in a 6 x 9 paperback

Pycnogenol®
Pycnogenol® for Superior Health presents exciting new evidence about nature's most powerful antioxidant. Pycnogenol® improves your total health, reduces risk of many diseases, safeguards your arteries, veins and entire circulation system. It protects your skin - giving it a healthier, smoother younger glow. Pycnogenol® also boosts your immune system. Read about it's many other beneficial effects. Written by Richard A. Passwater, Ph.D. (122 pgs.)
$5.95 each in a 4-1/8 x 6-7/8" paperback.

Remembering Louis L'Amour
Reese Hawkins was a close friend of Louis L'Amour, one of the fastest selling writers of all time. Now Hawkins shares this friendship with L'Amour's legion of fans. Sit with Reese in L'Amour's study where characters were born and stories came to life. Travel with Louis and Reese in the 16 photo pages in this memoir. Learn about L'Amour's lifelong quest for knowledge and his philosophy of life. Written by Reese Hawkins and his daughter Meredith Hawkins Wallin. (178 pgs.)
$16.95 each in a 5-1/2x8" paperback.

Outward Anxiety - Inner Calm
Steve Crociata is known to many as the Optician to the Stars. He was diagnosed with a baffling form of cancer. The author has processed experiences in ways which uniquely benefit today's readers. We learn valuable lessons on how to cope with distress, how to marvel at God, and how to win at the game of life. Written by Steve Crociata (334 pgs.)
$19.95 each in a 6 x 9 paperback

For Your Love
Janelle, a spoiled socialite, has beauty and breeding to attract any mate she desires. She falls for Jared, an accomplished man who has had many lovers, but no real love. Their hesitant romance follows Jared and Janelle across the ocean to exciting and wild locations. Join in a romance and adventure set in the mid-1800's in America's grand and proud Southland.
Written by Gunta Stegura. (358 pgs.)
$16.95 each in a 6x9" paperback.

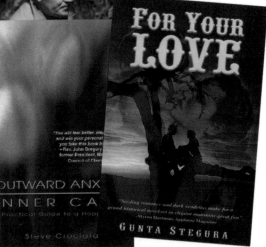

Bonanza Belle

In 1908, Carrie Amundson left her home to become employed on a bonanza farm. Carrie married and moved to town. One tragedy after the other befell her and altered her life considerably and she found herself back on the farm where her family lived the toiled during the Great Depression. Carrie was witness to many life-changing events happenings. She changed from a carefree girl to a woman of great depth and stamina.

Written by Elaine Ulness Swenson. (344 pgs.)

$15.95 each in a 6x8-1/4" paperback.

Home Front

Read the continuing story of Carrie Amundson, whose life in North Dakota began in *Bonanza Belle*. This is the story of her family, faced with the challenges, sacrifices and hardships of World War II. Everything changed after the Pearl Harbor attack, and ordinary folk all across America, on the home front, pitched in to help in the war effort. Even years after the war's end, the effects of it are still evident in many of the men and women who were called to serve their country.

Written by Elaine Ulness Swenson. (304 pgs.)

$15.95 each in a 6x8-1/4" paperback.

First The Dream

This story spans ninety years of Anna's life - from Norway to America - to finding love and losing love. She and her family experience two world wars, flu epidemics, the Great Depression, droughts and other quirks of Mother Nature and the Vietnam War. A secret that Anna has kept is fully revealed at the end of her life. Written by Elaine Ulness Swenson. (326 pgs.)

$15.95 each in a 6x8-1/4" paperback

Pay Dirt

An absorbing story reveals how a man with the courage to follow his dream found both gold and unexpected adventure and adversity in Interior Alaska, while learning that human nature can be the most unpredictable of all.

Written by Otis Hahn & Alice Vollmar. (168 pgs.)

$15.95 each in a 6x9" paperback.

Spirits of Canyon Creek *Sequel to "Pay Dirt"*

Hahn has a rich stash of true stories about his gold mining experiences. This is a continued successful collaboration of battles on floodwaters, facing bears and the discovery of gold in the Yukon. Written by Otis Hahn & Alice Vollmar. (138 pgs.)

$15.95 each in a 6x9" paperback.

Seasons With Our Lord

Original seasonal and special event poems written from the heart. Feel the mood with the tranquil color photos facing each poem. A great coffee table book or gift idea. Written by Cheryl Lebahn Hegvik. (68 pgs.)

$24.95 each in a 11x8-1/2 paperback.

Damsel in a Dress

Escape into a world of reflection and after thought with this second printing of Larson's first poetry book. It is her intention to connect people with feelings and touch the souls of people who have experienced similiar times. Lynne emphasizes the belief that everything happens for a reason. After all, with every event in life come lessons...we grow from hardships. It gives us character and it made her who she is. Written by Lynne D. Richard Larson (author of Eat, Drink & Remarry) (86 pgs.)
$12.95 each in a 5x8" paperback.

Eat, Drink & Remarry

The poetry in this book is taken from different experiences in Lynne's life and from different geographical and different emotional places. Every poem is an inspiration from someone or a direct event from their life...or from hers. Every victory and every mistake - young or old. They slowly shape and mold you into the unique person you are. Celebrate them as rough times that you were strong enough to endure. Written by Lynne D. Richard Larson (86 pgs.) $12.95 each in a 5x8" paperback.

Country-fied

Stories with a sense of humor and love for country and small town people who, like the author, grew up country-fied . . . Country-fied people grow up with a unique awareness of their dependence on the land. They live their lives with dignity, hard work, determination and the ability to laugh at themselves. Written by Elaine Babcock. (184 pgs.)
$14.95 each in a 6x9" paperback.

Charlie's Gold and Other Frontier Tales

Kamron's first collection of short stories gives you adventure tales about men and women of the west, made up of cowboys, Indians, and settlers. Written by Kent Kamron.
(174 pgs.) $15.95 each in a 6x9" paperback.

A Time For Justice

This second collection of Kamron's short stories takes off where the first volume left off, satisfying the reader's hunger for more tales of the wide prairie. Written by Kent Kamron. (182 pgs.)
$16.95 each in a 6x9" paperback.

It Really Happened Here!

Relive the days of farm-to-farm salesmen and hucksters, of ghost ships and locust plagues when you read Ethelyn Pearson's collection of strange but true tales. It captures the spirit of our ancestors in short, easy to read, colorful accounts that will have you yearning for more. Written by Ethelyn Pearson. (168 pgs.) $24.95 each in an 8-1/2x11" paperback.

The Silk Robe

- Dedicated to Shari Lynn Hunt, a wonderful woman who passed away from cancer. Mom lived her life with unfailing faith, an open loving heart and a giving spirit. She is remembered for her compassion and gentle strength. Written by Shaunna Privratsky.
$6.95 each in a 4-1/4x5-1/2" booklet. *Complimentary notecard and envelope included.*

(Add $3.95 shipping & handling for first book, add $2.00 for each additional book ordered.)